FALLING FOR THE BALDASSERI PRINCE

REBECCA WINTERS

A PROPOSAL IN PROVENCE

DONNA ALWARD

MILLS & BOON

First Published in Great Britain 2022
by Mills & Boon, an imprint of HarperCollins*Publishers* Ltd,
1 London Bridge Street, London, SE1 9GF

www.harpercollins.co.uk

HarperCollins*Publishers*
1st Floor, Watermarque Building,
Ringsend Road, Dublin 4, Ireland

Falling for the Baldasseri Prince © 2022 Rebecca Winters

A Proposal in Provence © 2022 Donna Alward

ISBN: 978-0-263-30209-7

01/22

MIX
Paper from
responsible sources
FSC™ C007454

FALLING FOR THE BALDASSERI PRINCE

REBECCA WINTERS

MILLS & BOON

To my wonderful parents,
who gave me a beautiful life and helped me
believe miracles happen more often than we know.

Their faith, goodness and love have made
this experience on earth magical for me.

I'll never be able to thank them enough.

CHAPTER ONE

Bern, Switzerland, early July

"Well, sis. Have you made a decision yet?"

Francesca Visconti pored over the information on the computer in her bedroom. She'd been living at home with her parents since her graduation last week from the University of Milan in Italy to become a veterinarian. "After careful consideration, there's an opening for a vet in France and one in Germany. Both sound promising."

"But?"

"There's another opening in Switzerland. Every professor of mine has talked about the head of that clinic. Dr. Daniel Zoller, the owner, is legendary. To get a position with him would be a dream come true. It's located near a biosphere reserve in the most breathtaking country on earth. I've been looking at the videos. The place is fabulous!"

"Why do I get the feeling there's a problem?"

"There are two actually."

"Start with the first one."

"One of the qualifications is that I would have to speak Romansh."

"Why?"

She smiled at Rolf who stood next to her. "Because the clinic is located in eastern Switzerland where Romansh is only spoken by a small percentage of the population."

"It must be tiny. You speak four other languages. That ought to be enough."

"But not the one that will get me this coveted position."

"How many qualified people applying will know that language?"

She blinked. "I have no idea."

"If I were you, I'd apply for it anyway because you've got more outstanding credentials than anyone I know."

Francesca looked up at him. "My fan club. What would I do without you?"

"If I recall, you were the one who encouraged me to go to graduate school in Paris. My French was horrible, but you helped me. Now I'm close to graduating and it's all because of you."

"I didn't do that much, but thank you."

"You're welcome. Now tell me the other problem."

"It's beyond serious."

He sat on the corner of her desk. "I'm listening."

"You and I grew up hearing about the battle between the House of Baldasseri in Switzerland and the House of Visconti in Italy. Three hundred years of fighting went on over the massive timber rights in eastern Switzerland they both claimed."

"Yup. And when the Baldasseri family prevailed, the Visconti family never got over it. The feud carried down over the years. Papa said life in their household was a living nightmare."

She nodded. "He's always said his brother Stefano was the personification of their dictatorial father and grandfather. Once they were dead, he was determined to claim those timber rights for their family."

"He's out of control. Dad said that when Stefano became head of the family, he was such a tyrant, he wouldn't even allow Papa to marry Mamma because she was a commoner. Dad married her anyway and Stefano turned it into a scandal that fed the media news and drove our father away."

"It's a horrible story," Francesca murmured. "Papa gave up his title for her and left Italy."

"Thank heaven."

"Agreed, but guess what? It looks like Stefano, in all his fury, has found a way at last to get his hands on those timber holdings."

"How?"

"Did you watch the news last night?"

"No. I was out with Gina."

"Well, at the end of the month, our estranged cousin Princess Valentina Visconti, our uncle Stefano's only child, is marrying Prince Baldasseri of Scuol."

"You're kidding! How did he manage that?"

"Who knows, and now I have a real problem. Take a look at this map of eastern Switzerland." She enlarged it for him. "The veterinarian clinic where I'd give anything to work is here in Zernez. The Baldasseri Palace is there in Scuol. The two towns are a twenty-minute drive apart.

"Do I dare apply for the position of veterinarian when my last name is Visconti, and Valentina Vis-

conti is my cousin? What if word gets around that a
Visconti is working at the clinic? I wouldn't want to
do anything that would create more trouble for Papa
here in Switzerland. Not after Stefano drove him out
of Italy with his cruelty."

Her brother stood up for a better look. It took a second before he said, "Why don't you make up a new
name?"

"Rolf…"

"Impress the clinic owner by introducing yourself
with a Romansh surname. Look up a bunch and let's
pick your favorite." He grinned.

Her brother could be a rascal, but he had a brilliant
mind. Following up on his suggestion, she produced a
list of Romansh names. "Do you like Andrin?"

He shook his head.

"Here's Gori."

"No way." They kept studying them until Rolf said,
"How about Linard? It's German Swiss for Leonhard
and Lienhard."

"Linard…" she said the name several times. "I like
it."

"That's a keeper." They both chuckled.

"Of course, I'd have to tell Dr. Zoller everything
first. And if a miracle happened and I got the job, I
would have to find a place to live in Zernez."

"Let's look at some rentals right now."

She researched available housing. "Oh, Rolf. Look
at all these darling Swiss chalets. It's like wonderland."

He nodded. "The prices are reasonable too."

"I really like this apartment. It's adorable with all
those window boxes full of flowers."

"Better investigate the inside first."

She studied the information on the home page. "It says two bedrooms." To her delight the interior looked exactly like what she wanted. "It'll be available in a week. If I lived there, you and Gina could come and stay with me sometimes."

"You can count on it."

She turned to him. "I'm getting ahead of myself, Rolf."

"Have you filled out all the paperwork and application for that clinic?"

"Yes, but I've been afraid to send it."

"Don't forget our father's favorite slogan. 'What we fear doing most is usually what we most need to do.'"

She jumped up and gave him a hug. "I'm so glad you're home this weekend. I'm going to send it in right now and see what happens."

Three days later Francesca received a response asking her to come for the initial interview to discuss the scope and expectations of the position. "At least I wasn't denied an interview right off," she told Rolf on the phone. He'd gone back to Paris.

"What name did you use?"

"Visconti. I had to since all my work and transcripts have my name on them."

"I get it. Just remember. This is only the beginning, Francesca. When is the interview?"

"Tomorrow at one o'clock. I'm going to take the train and rent a car after I get there."

"Sounds exciting. Call me tomorrow after you've met the paragon."

"You know I will."

At four in the afternoon of the next day, Francesca felt like she was floating on a cloud. She got in the rental car, deciding to drive back to Bern. She needed to process all that had happened. Hunger drove her to stop at a drive-through for a meal. While she ate, she phoned her brother.

"Rolf Visconti?"

"Francesca?" he cried.

"This is Dr. Linard who has promised to learn Romansh as fast as possible."

"I knew it! You got the position!"

"It's all so wonderful, *he's* so wonderful, I don't know where to begin. When I explained about Papa and the Visconti family, Dr. Zoller said he'd arrange for a government regulator to give me a waiver to use a different name at the clinic. Can you believe it?"

"I can, and I think you're too excited to talk coherently."

"I am." Tears poured down her cheeks. "I'll never be able to thank you enough for pushing me into sending in my papers. The clinic is incredible, and my position includes occasionally working with a biologist at the nearby bioreserve. This is a once in a lifetime opportunity for me and I'm so grateful."

"No one has studied harder or deserves it more."

"Thanks, dear brother. While I'm still here, I'm going to drive to that apartment and see if it's still available. Depending on the outcome, I'll put down a first month's rent."

"How soon does he want you?"

"As soon as possible."

"Whoa. Are you ready to plunge in?"

"You can't imagine how excited I am to get started on my career."

"Well, I couldn't be happier. Mamma and Papa will be over the moon for you."

"I know. I need to call them now. Love you. Talk to you soon."

Scuol, Switzerland, July 28th

"Hey, buddy."

The dog lifted his head from the blanket, making a welcoming sound. But he didn't jump off the end of the bed and run to Vincenzo like he used to do.

With a heavy heart Vincenzo walked over to him and wrapped his arms around him. "You feel horrible, don't you? You're not alone," he murmured. "Forgive me for leaving you on your own for part of this Thursday. I had an official duty to perform and couldn't take you with me. We'll go visit Daniel first thing in the morning. He'll know how to help you."

The vet *had* to do something. Vincenzo knew that his dog, an unfailing source of love and devotion over the last seven years, was on his last leg. But he couldn't imagine losing him, not yet.

His dog watched him while he got ready for bed. As he was throwing on a robe, his cell phone rang. Vincenzo assumed it was either his mother or his younger sister Bella. He loved and missed her. She was away on vacation with her best friend Princess Constanza in Lausanne, Switzerland. But she loved their dogs too and worried about Karl. Vincenzo was anxious to talk to her, but when he went to click on, he saw the caller ID.

A call from Prince Rinieri Baldasseri of San Vitano, the second cousin he loved, came as a surprise.

He worried that something else could be wrong with him since his tragedy and clicked on. "Rini?"

Instead of hearing him speak Romansh, Rini broke out in fluent Italian and didn't stop. Vincenzo was fluent in both as well as German and English. His cousin sounded so incredibly happy, he sank down on the side of the bed in shock.

After Rini had first gone missing presumed dead and then lost his memory in an earthquake last month only speaking Romansh, it was nothing short of a miracle to hear him sound and act like the old Rini.

"Hold on, Rini. Run all this by me again. Slower this time. Explain to me what's happened since we last spoke."

"My world has changed! Luna asked me to take her to Venice. When the fireworks went off, I'd been asleep and thought I was back in the mine when the earthquake hit the area. I jumped out of bed, needing to save the other miners. But before I could climb out the window, Luna grabbed me and held me back.

"She told me the booming sounds I heard were coming from the yearly fireworks show. After I could process everything, I suddenly realized I was with her. I also saw we were in the same hotel room we'd used during our honeymoon. Everything came back to me."

Beyond elated, Vincenzo got to his feet. "I'm overjoyed for you, Rini. I hear your euphoria and can't tell you how happy this makes me."

"I'm hoping to make you even happier. You don't have to act in my place any longer. I know how much you hated the whole idea of having to be King one day. So, *I'll* go on being the Crown Prince as if the amnesia had never happened. You're off the hook for something you never wanted in the first place."

"Thank heaven." Vincenzo closed his eyes for a moment over this news that had turned his life around once more in the most astounding way.

"*You*, my friend, can now get back to your life and your coming marriage. I spoke to the grandparents last night. They'll be forever grateful to you for stepping in when you did."

Vincenzo could scarcely contain his excitement. "I'll be on my knees to your wife for suggesting you go to Venice. Fireworks of all things. Who would have dreamed…?"

"None of us. And guess what else? We're going to have a baby!"

That meant the line of succession would go on with Rini's children. How wonderful for them. "You can't ask for more than that, you lucky dude. We'll talk again soon."

"Luna and I want you to bring your fiancée and come to dinner at the palazzo. I'll call soon to set a time."

"Sounds terrific." The two cousins had been close friends since childhood. "Welcome back, Rini. I've missed you."

"Ditto."

They both hung up. Vincenzo walked over to the dog in a daze and gave him another hug. Would that there might be one more miracle to transform his life. The engagement to Valentina Visconti had been his parents' horrendous idea from the start.

Vincenzo had never met Valentina and had only seen pictures of her in the news. Upon a first meeting a year ago, he knew he could never love her. The last thing he wanted to do was marry her. Vincenzo couldn't bear the thought of it, but it had been his father Marcello's dying wish.

Vincenzo's mother wanted the marriage at all costs too because Valentina came with the last name of the most powerful family in Italy. Of all the eligible princesses, his mother felt Valentina to be the grand prize, a fact she never let Vincenzo forget.

Marcello had been the second son of Alfredo Baldasseri, King Leonardo's brother, and had always felt a failure, never getting recognition, never measuring up. But in this one area where he could please the whole Baldasseri family and his wife, Marcello had exacted a deathbed promise from Vincenzo to marry Valentina.

The guilt had weighed heavily on Vincenzo to be the good son, something he couldn't ignore. Now that his father had passed away, his mother was determined he would follow through. She was close to irrational about it.

He knew in his gut Valentina didn't want to marry him either. When he'd said as much to her in the beginning, she'd played dumb and wouldn't admit anything. But he knew she was hiding something. At that point he realized she didn't dare fight her powerful father Stefano Visconti and Vincenzo knew why. Through him, Stefano was using his daughter to get at the Baldasseri timber fortune, a treasure the Visconti family coveted. His hold on Valentina was as binding as the vow Vincenzo's parents had forced out of him.

If only he could find a legitimate way to prevent the farce of the coming marriage…

Zernez, Switzerland, July 29th

Friday morning Daniel Zoller's eyes lit up when Francesca let herself in the back door of the veterinary clinic a few minutes before eight-thirty. The owner and head veterinarian of the Zoller Veterinary Clinic let out a sigh of relief. "Good. You're early. I have a patient in one of the examining rooms already. Dr. Peri is in another one. The bad news is, I found out our receptionist might be late coming in."

"Don't worry. I'll run the waiting room until Haida gets here."

"Bless you. I don't understand how we were so lucky you applied for the opening here. You've only been with us two weeks, and already I don't know what we'd do without you."

The warmth of the genius vet made him everyone's favorite whether they were a coworker or patient. She smiled. "I love being here and working with the legend. Thank you, Daniel."

As she'd learned earlier, the job required fluent Italian, English, German and a passable ability to speak Romansh. She'd thought the last would disqualify her, but Rolf hadn't let her be discouraged by her fears. Her brother had forced her to believe in herself.

Daniel had been so impressed with her credentials, he'd hired her anyway with the understanding she'd learn Romansh. Having vowed to learn the language of the people in the area, she'd been studying it on her off hours and practiced it everywhere she went.

The middle-aged doctor disappeared through a door that led to the main hall with examining rooms on either side. Twenty-four-year-old Francesca walked over to a closet and put on a fresh uniform. She fastened the knee-length light blue outfit with short sleeves and headed down the same hall to the front of the building.

After becoming a fully certified doctor of veterinarian medicine from the University of Milan, Italy, Dr. Francesca Giordano Visconti had investigated career opportunities. The one that had appealed most had been the opening here in Zernez. The village itself was a Tyrolean fantasy. To be working in the mountains where she could ski in winter and hike in summer thrilled her heart.

Francesca had found a great apartment and couldn't be more excited to do the work. She'd dreamed of being a vet since she was a little girl with a succession of dogs she'd treated like babies. Her parents had indulged her because she'd always loved animals and had been an outstanding student.

Excellent marks in academics had gotten her through high school early and she'd pushed ahead, graduating first in her class at the university. To her joy, that achievement had won Dr. Zoller's approbation.

Francesca couldn't be happier as she entered the reception room and sat down at Haida's desk. A list of scheduled appointments for the day would keep the clinic busy.

While she waited for the ten o'clock patient to arrive for a weekly checkup, she got on the computer to study a new list of Romansh vocabulary words. She heard voices as lab technicians and animal care workers had shown up to get busy. When the buzz of the front door sounded, Francesca lifted her head, then let out a quiet gasp.

It couldn't be—but it was.

Prince Vincenzo Baldasseri!

The Crown Prince of the Baldasseri royal family of San Vitano, a country on the Swiss/Italian border, had just entered the clinic. He'd come in with a medium-sized male Bernese Mountain Dog on a leash.

As she'd told Rolf, she'd known that the Prince's immediate family, including his beautiful sister Princess Bella, lived in the Baldasseri Palace in nearby Scuol, Switzerland, a village where the royals had been born and raised. He ran the timber business for the Baldasseri monarchy.

Still, Francesca couldn't believe what she was seeing. Over the last five years she'd watched various clips of him on the news. She'd also studied more videos on the nearby Biosphere Reserve since applying for the position here. The Prince had been featured in several of them where he explained his family's interest in preserving it for the future.

She'd thought the tall, dark, brown-haired royal had to be the most gorgeous man she'd ever seen in her life. In fact, she'd played the video several times, which was totally unlike her.

Though Francesca had dated here and there, she'd had no serious relationships. That would come later. School had been her priority. The idea of meeting and falling in love with a man as breathtaking as Prince Vincenzo would be pure fantasy.

Since he was engaged to her cousin, she was more than ever thankful she'd thought up a different last name and could use it. Estranged from the Visconti family before Francesca and Rolf had been born, her parents had moved to Bern, Switzerland. Her father had started a packaging business there that flourished.

She and Rolf were total strangers to the other members of the Visconti family.

When she'd been hired for this vet position, she'd told her father she would be using a different last name. That way she could avoid notoriety as a Visconti while she worked in Switzerland near the Baldasseri royal family in Scuol. She'd been way ahead of her father's wishes on that score.

"*Buongiorno*," she called to the Prince.

He approached the desk with a look of worry on those hard-boned features that made him so handsome. "I haven't seen you here before." His deep male voice resonated to her insides.

"No. I'm new."

After studying her with an intensity that reached inside her, he said, "I don't have an appointment, but I need to see Daniel about my dog. Is he here?"

Everyone wanted Daniel. "He's in with another patient." She glanced at the wonderful dog with the tricolored coat who stayed near his master. He was the male version of her adorable Mitzi, another Bernese Mountain Dog she'd loved before leaving for medical school. "May I help you?"

"Thank you, but Karl is used to Daniel. How long do you think he'll be?"

"I have no idea. Maybe if you'd explain the problem to me?"

He checked his watch. No doubt he was in a hurry. "Karl has heart disease that causes him to cough and faint. But today I've brought him in because he now has a lump below his right eye. Is Dr. Peri here?"

"I'm sorry. He's with another patient. But I can try to help you. I'm Dr. Linard."

"*You're* a vet?"

Others had reacted the same way. She knew she looked young and obviously didn't have Daniel's experience. Heat swept into her cheeks. "I've only been here two weeks."

"Congratulations. You must have replaced Dr. Zenger. Daniel wouldn't pick anyone to work here who isn't the best."

"Thank you but give me ten years and then tell me that again." An unexpected smile broke out on his face. The man's looks and charisma melted her to the floor. "Until Daniel can see you, why don't you bring Karl in the examining room and we'll take a look."

He nodded and they followed her down the hall to one of the rooms. She put her stethoscope around her neck, and checked him out. Karl indeed had a heart condition and wouldn't survive much longer. She leaned over to examine the dog's darling face. Memories of Mitzi assailed her. The Prince held on to him. She touched the lump and moved it around.

"That's very fleshy and could be an abscess." She looked up into the Prince's vivid blue eyes fringed with dark lashes staring at her intently. "Was he kicked or hit by something?"

"Not that I know of. It's been there for a while. I thought it would go away, but today I realized it has grown bigger."

"Hmm. How old is he?"

"About seven years now."

"Has the fainting grown worse?"

"It's been happening more and more after he exercises."

"I see." This breed had a life span of six to seven

years. Francesca knew all about it. Her dog had died at six years while she'd been away at the university. She moved the lump again. "I don't feel a bone in it, so tell you what. In case it's an infection, I'm going to give him an antibiotic."

Francesca walked over to the corner where she kept her microscope and supplies. After filling the syringe, she returned to give him a shot. "Good boy. You handled that like a man." She bent down to ruffle his head and tickle him. To her surprise the dog licked her face the way Mitzi used to do.

The Prince chuckled. "He likes you. I haven't seen him do that to anyone but me."

"He knows I like him too." She stood up. "Take him home over the weekend and bring him back midweek. If it's worse, I'll open it up and take a look to see what's going on. But today we'll give him a break. We don't want Karl to be in pain, do we? Not when he's struggling with a bad heart." She patted him. This time he licked her hand. "You're a sweetheart."

"He feels the same about you," came the deep voice again. "When I bring him back, he won't have any problem letting you handle him."

His comments touched her. "We can hope," she teased with a smile.

"Tell Daniel I came by."

"I will. May I have your name?" As if she didn't know.

"Vince. He'll know who I am and bill me," he murmured and turned to leave with his dog.

Vince… So the Prince shortened his name.

"*A revair*, Karl."

The Prince paused at the door. "You speak Romansh too?"

"I'm trying to learn it as fast as I can. In case your dog understands it, I hope he'll forgive me if my pronunciation needs more improvement."

Their eyes met. "I understand it too. You said it perfectly." His gaze swept over her. "Daniel knew what he was doing when he hired you, Dr. Linard."

With that compliment, he and Karl left the room. As they walked toward the reception area, Francesca took in his casually dressed six-foot-three, rock-hard physique. Talk about an unforgettable man. As for Karl, the black-and-white dog with the rust markings couldn't be more adorable, bringing back memories of her own dog. How sad his life was coming to an end.

CHAPTER TWO

TWENTY-EIGHT-YEAR-OLD Prince Vincenzo Rodicchio Baldasseri walked out to his black Mercedes and lifted Karl into the rear seat. His dog looked back at the clinic through the window.

"You liked her, didn't you, buddy? Incredibly, so did I," he muttered to himself.

With the soft gold of her hair in a longish pixie-like style and those velvety brown eyes, she reminded him of an ornament of an enchanting fairy you saw hanging on a Christmas tree. There was a becoming flush on her cheeks. She was all fresh and sparkling. No ring on her finger. Her smile and knockout figure the uniform couldn't disguise had lit up his universe.

Lucky Karl had licked those enticing lips. That was the moment Vincenzo had needed to leave the room. He'd enjoyed his share of girlfriends before the engagement he'd been forced into by his parents' emotional blackmail. There'd been a few strong attractions, but nothing fatal. Yet even his sick dog had succumbed to Dr. Linard's spell.

She was a vet! Daniel, the best in Switzerland, had hired her. He chuckled that she'd said goodbye to Karl in Romansh. What other surprises were in store when he saw her again? He found he couldn't wait for the next appointment. But that's where his thoughts had to stop. The promise to his parents had turned his life into a living hell. It meant honoring it in every sense of the word.

The arranged engagement had been a union both royal families pushed hard for. On the surface Valentina acted willing enough, but deep down he knew she was only obeying her father's edicts. Thoughts of the coming wedding meant they would have to go through the rest of their lives in a marriage lacking the most important ingredient in order to make it work.

Bella had been sick for him. His childhood friend Luca Torriani groaned for him too. The three of them had been inseparable until the end of high school; then everything changed. These days he and Luca didn't often see each other though they stayed in touch. His friend had always known Vincenzo's deepest feelings about wishing he weren't being forced to marry a royal.

While he was lost in thought, his cell phone rang, startling him. He clicked on. "Mamma?"

"Finally. Why didn't you answer earlier?"

"I had to take Karl to the vet. How's Grandfather?"

"He's well enough. We heard from your great-uncle Leonardo in Asteria last night. You need to come home and explain to us what's really going on. What he told us makes little sense."

Of course! The two old brothers had already been on the phone. King Leonardo would have told Vincenzo's grandfather that Rini had recovered his memory and would end up being King one day instead of Vincenzo. They had to have discussed what his mother would consider to be a catastrophe in the Baldasseri family where Vincenzo was concerned.

Little did they know the astounding news had over-joyed him, relieving him of the enormous burden he'd been carrying since the earthquake. The news that Rini was back better than ever would not only upset his mother, it had to have devastated Stefano. Vincenzo would phone Valentina to discuss it, but he needed to see about Karl first.

"I'll be there as soon as I can." He hung up and called his assistant Fadri. "Something urgent has come up. I won't be in the office today. Ring me if there's an emergency."

"Of course, Your Highness."

They hung up. Vincenzo turned on the engine and left the clinic's parking lot.

The half an hour drive back to Scuol took him past the three-hundred-year-old Baldasseri Timber Company. Full summer with all its color had come to the Engadin. He'd grown up in a timber family, learning every aspect of it. Timber had helped support the Baldasseri family both in Switzerland and in the country of San Vitano for three centuries. In the past, many a war had been fought over it, particularly with the Visconti family.

Vincenzo had headed the business since his father had passed away from a bad bout of flu a little less than a year ago. Being engaged had made it impossible for Vincenzo to live a bachelor existence any longer; therefore, he'd poured himself into the timber business to expand where he could and bring in more money to support his favorite causes.

Until his father's death, Vincenzo had been living in a town house in Scuol. Since then, he'd moved back in the palace to help with his grandfather who had to be on dialysis for his kidneys.

Soon he pulled into the courtyard and carried Karl up the staircase to the apartment of his grandparents, Prince Alfredo and Princess Talia Baldasseri. His mother was also there.

Both women sat by Alfredo's bed waiting for Vincenzo. The old man with thinning gray hair lifted his hand and waved it in greeting, but Vincenzo knew he felt miserable most of the time. His heart went out to him. He kissed the hand that had waved to him, then he brushed kisses on the cheeks of his grandmother and mother.

"Thank you for coming so quickly, son. We've had the most confusing news. It couldn't possibly be true."

Vincenzo put Karl down and pulled up a chair close to them. "I'm afraid it is and I know all about it. Rini phoned me yesterday and we talked for a long time."

His sixty-three-year-old redheaded mother, Princess Maria Rodicchio Baldasseri, sat back in the chair as if in shock. "How can you be so composed after hearing such news? Why didn't you let us know the instant you hung up?"

"One question at a time, Mamma."

"Is it really a fact that your cousin no longer has amnesia?" his grandmother asked.

"Completely true, and I can't tell you how happy that makes me. Rini is back to normal. You should hear the joy in his voice. He and Luna are in ecstasy, especially since they're expecting a baby."

"Another heir?" his mother cried in despair.

"Mamma—it's all the greatest news anyone could have!"

Her body trembled in anger. "Is it the best news that

you're *not* going to be the Crown Prince after all? It isn't right! Leonardo designated you to take over for him. He should behave like a true king and allow his word to stand."

"But Rini has regained his memory. It's *his* right!" His gaze met his mother's and he saw the bitter disappointment in those blue eyes he'd inherited. "Rini is ready to do his duties again. He was always the perfect choice and the whole country is thrilled he didn't die in the earthquake."

"But, Vincenzo—"

"No buts, Mamma. An announcement will be made on the ten o'clock news tonight that he no longer has amnesia, that he'll go on assuming his duty as Crown Prince. Let's be grateful for the miracle that has happened to him. I know I am. Though I filled in for a brief time, it wasn't what I wanted to do. If I'm being truthful, I never wanted it," he murmured.

The thought of my coming marriage is anathema to me.

"How dare you say such a thing!" she cried. Her aspirations for him had always been over-the-top.

Vincenzo got to his feet. "I dare because I was never in line. One day Rini will make a great king. You know he will. He spent time here on vacations with our family. No one could replace him, certainly not me. Rini is the one to take over the kingdom when the time comes. That's his destiny, not mine."

Her skin grew mottled. "Your father would have been the perfect one to be King one day. If that flu hadn't taken my Marcello—" She couldn't finish her thought and broke down. He knew his mother still grieved for him. Nothing had been the same with his father gone.

"But Papa was never in line and Rini's father is dead. So is Rini's elder brother Paolo, who would have been named Crown Prince if he hadn't been killed at a young age. That left Rini and he's back to his old self. Face it, Mamma, none of it was meant to be for me. I was the last resort after the King thought Rini couldn't function, but no longer. With a baby on the way, the succession will be ensured."

"It isn't fair," she said in a withering tone. "I can't bear it."

"You've talked to Valentina?" his grandfather asked the important question.

"I'll call her in a little while."

His grandmother looked stunned, but said nothing. His mother buried her face in her hands. "This is going to come as the most terrible news imaginable to Valentina and the Visconti family."

Yes, Vincenzo mused. Valentina and her parents had expressed their joy that he'd been installed as the Crown Prince. To think that one day soon their son-in-law would become King of San Vitano; moreover, the Visconti family would hold valuable shares of timber stock they'd never been able to get their hands on. Those were huge considerations anticipated by that family.

But all that had changed now. His marriage would take place here in Scuol instead of the country of San Vitano. Without the incentive of Valentina being Queen one day, this latest news had to be a severe disappointment to her. But Vincenzo knew the real reason for the marriage. Stefano wanted to get his hands on the timber business. Valentina was the sacrificial lamb to accomplish it.

"I wish Bella were back from vacation," his mother moaned. "She's going to be terribly upset too."

No. Bella knew the truth of Vincenzo's feelings and would be thrilled he no longer had to perform that duty. She'd told him more than once that he should never have promised their father he'd marry Valentina. She'd thought it cruel of their mother to force their father to elicit that promise from him.

"If you'll excuse me, I'll go to my study and call Valentina. We need to talk before it's announced on TV and the newspapers. I'll check in with you again later."

The dog followed him out of the room and down the hall. Vincenzo didn't look forward to his conversation with Valentina who'd been caught up in the knowledge that one day she would be Queen. The day after Rini's reported death, Vincenzo had been informed that he was now the Crown Prince. When Rini was later found alive but having lost his memory, Vincenzo had had no option but to retain the title. Knowing that Leonardo's life was coming to an end, it appeared that becoming Queen was all Valentina could think about.

Her interest seemed to have grown into an obsession. That was because for reasons of her own, she hadn't wanted their arranged marriage. He imagined she thought that being Queen might compensate for what was missing between them. That's what came from not being in love. Who knew what her reaction would be when he got her on the phone?

Six o'clock in the evening rolled around at the vet clinic. Francesca splinted the dachshund's leg. She would love a dog, but it didn't pay to be in a rush when she'd barely settled here. Another few weeks and she'd find a darling dog to love and take care of. Her landlord had agreed she could have a pet. Of course, it would have to come to work with her, which meant she needed to discuss it with Daniel.

After the patient left, Francesca removed her uniform and put it in the laundry bin at the back of the clinic. Just then Daniel walked in. "How did it go today?"

"I had a surprise visitor named Karl."

He chuckled. "Vince's dog."

"Yes. He brought him in because Karl has a fleshy mass under his right eye. I could have opened him up, but instead I gave him an antibiotic and suggested he come back if it didn't get better."

The older vet nodded. "I'd have done the same thing. He's slowed down so much he's not going to be around soon. No point hurting him unnecessarily. His death will be a blow to Vince."

"The deaths of my dogs almost killed me."

"You lead with your heart. That's one of the reasons I hired you."

She admired this man so much. "Good night, Daniel. See you tomorrow."

On that note Francesca walked outside to her yellow Volkswagen and headed for her apartment in an eight plex. She lived on the second floor with a window box full of daisies outside her front room. En route she stopped to buy some groceries. She wanted something simple to fix and eat, like a ham omelet and toast.

After washing up, she cooked her meal and sat down on the couch to phone her parents. She owed them a call, but had been too busy until now. Her brother Rolf was finishing up his studies in Paris. Her parents had become empty nesters. They talked for a long time before hanging up, then she turned on the TV.

When the ten o'clock news came on, she found herself staring at a clip of Prince Rinieri Baldasseri. After meeting Prince Vincenzo this morning, what a coincidence to see his relative on the screen! The Baldasseri men were sinfully gorgeous.

A miracle has happened in San Vitano. Prince Rinieri Baldasseri, who lost his memory in an earthquake at the Baldasseri Gold Mine, has recovered it completely. To the joy of his grandparents, the King and Queen of San Vitano, today he has been proclaimed the Crown Prince once again. Congratulations to him and his wife, Princess Luna, who are expecting their first baby.

The Prince's second cousin Prince Vincenzo Baldasseri has been serving in that position and is also to be congratulated. No longer Crown Prince, he can attend to his duties full time as head of Baldasseri Royal Timber Enterprises in Scuol while he prepares for his nuptials to Princess Valentina Visconti of Milano, Italy.

Francesca turned off the TV, trying to imagine what it would have been like to have amnesia, then suddenly remember everything. Incredible. She got up and walked to the kitchen for a drink of water.

The news meant that Prince Vincenzo was no longer the Crown Prince. How did he feel about that? No doubt he'd have more time to prepare for his wedding.

As Francesca got ready for bed, she knew that if or when *she* ever got married, she planned to spend as much time with her husband as possible. Being the wife of a king would make it difficult to spend enough time together to suit her.

She considered it a plus for Valentina who was engaged to one fabulous man with a very sick dog.

Francesca's own parents had always been in love and enjoyed a close, wonderful marriage. She would never settle for anything less.

July turned to August. On Tuesday morning Francesca got busy vaccinating Mrs. Corsin's three healthy Bernese Mountain Dogs. The twelve-week-old pups were Francesca's favorite breed and too adorable for words, especially the one male she ended up cuddling. He licked her several times. His sweetness reminded her of Karl.

"What's the name of this one?" she asked the owner.

"Artur."

"Artur…" She spoke to him. "I could take you home with me." He was so cute.

"Do you have a pet, Dr. Linard?"

She put him in the crate. "Not since I moved here about three weeks ago, but it won't be long before I get one."

"I have a tentative buyer, but it might fall through. Would you be interested? Artur seems to have taken to you."

That did it. Francesca didn't hesitate. "I would love a call. I'll give you my number." When that was done she heard a knock on the door. Haida poked her head in. "Sorry to disturb."

"I'm just leaving." Mrs. Corsin gathered the crate with her puppies and left the room.

Haidi smiled at Francesca. "You have a patient wait-ing without an appointment."

"I'll be right out."

Her brows arched. "It's an *important* patient, if you get my meaning," she murmured with a glimmer in her eye before she hurried down the hall. Haidi was only a few years older than Francesca and a lot of fun.

The word *important* could only mean one thing. Francesca's heart ticked over in reaction, surprising her. She washed her hands and headed toward the front desk. The Prince sat in one of the chairs, studying something on his phone. Karl lay at his feet. When the dog's brown eyes saw Francesca, he made a sound and slowly got up.

"That's a wonderful greeting, Karl." She hunkered down to ruffle his fur and received another lick. "How are you feeling?"

"Not so well," his master responded and stood up. Once again the deep voice curled through her body, stirring her senses. Her gaze flicked to the Prince dressed in a tan crew-neck shirt and jeans that molded to his long, powerful legs. His dark wavy hair and hot blue eyes took her breath.

"I'm sorry to hear that." She patted the dog and got to her feet. "Come on. Let's go take a good look at you."

Karl followed on leash. When they reached the ex-amination room, she lifted the dog's head and took another look at the fleshy mass. "You poor darling. I'm afraid there isn't improvement, so I'm going to open it up and see what I find." She eyed the Prince. "If you'll put him on the table and steady him, we'll get this over."

She noticed the play of muscle across the Prince's broad shoulders as he handled his dog with gentleness and care. You could tell a lot about a person's character by the way he treated his pet.

Francesca deadened the mass and felt around. "There's no bone or object in there. It appears to be sheer infection." She finished up the procedure and gave his dog another injection. Then she took Karl's vital signs.

"What's the verdict?" he murmured.

She lifted her head and their gazes locked. "I have to be honest, Your Highness. He—"

"Daniel *told* you who I was?" he interrupted.

"No. I've seen you on TV several times and on the videos featuring you discussing conservation efforts at the biosphere. Dr. Zoller suggested I watch the latest ones. I was going to say that Karl is in a bad way."

He studied her features for a moment, causing her chest to flutter. She wondered what he'd been thinking. "I know I should have put him down, but I can't bring myself to do it yet."

She heard his pain. "Since I've been through the experience with my own dogs growing up, I know what an agonizing decision that is. Take my advice and think about it a little longer, but not too long. You'll know when the time is right and you can't bear to watch him suffer any longer. Then phone the clinic. Whoever is on call will come."

He swallowed hard. "I want his passing to be peaceful, so I'll ask for you. I wasn't wrong the other day. He likes you." Everything he said was getting to her which was absurd. She'd met attractive men before;

however, the engaged Prince was off limits in every conceivable way.

"Your dog is precious." Francesca fought to keep her voice steady and kissed his head. "See you soon, Karl."

The dog made a whimpering sound before his master picked him up. "Thank you, Dr. Linard. You have a special way."

She watched him carry his dog toward the front of the clinic. His hard-muscled silhouette with the dog in his arms was a sight she'd never forget.

The Prince remained in her thoughts all day. When your beloved pet wouldn't be on this earth much longer, the heart hung heavy. She knew what it felt like. Between memories of Mitzi and now Karl, she'd told Mrs. Corsin she'd buy Artur if he were available.

While Francesca fixed herself a salad for dinner, she took a call from the brother she adored. "Rolf— What's new? Are the Parisian girls more exciting than Gina?"

"No way." He laughed. "Right now I'm working on my French and will tell you more *once* I can string a conversation together."

"I know what you mean. Romansh isn't the easiest language to learn."

"You were always a whiz at everything. I bet you're fluent already."

"Don't I wish. So what's new?"

"That's why I'm calling you. When I was home Sunday to see Gina, I heard the folks talking about some problem to do with the other side of the family that involved Valentina. They didn't realize I'd over-heard them talking. Do you know anything about it?"

"Yes. It was on the news. Prince Vincenzo is no longer the Crown Prince of San Vitano."

"Yeah. The amnesia that Prince Rinieri suffered and recovered from is all the talk everywhere."

"Stefano is undoubtedly upset because Valentina won't be the Queen after all. That side of the family cares too much about titles. It's why Papa broke with them in the first place and has rejected all claims to his."

"Smart man, our father."

"I couldn't agree more, Rolf. Do you want to know a secret?"

"I'm all ears."

"You have to keep this to yourself. Swear you won't tell anyone?"

"I promise."

In the next breath she told him about Karl. "He's this wonderful Bernese Mountain Dog. Guess who he belongs to?" Then she told him.

Her brother whistled. "So *you're* the Prince's vet?"

"Daniel is his vet, but he had another patient so I took care of his dog. Amazing, huh. But the folks don't know, and I'll never tell them. It's a good thing I was prepared with a new name. A Romansh one at that, thanks to you."

"Funny how you were worried about this."

"I'm thankful the Prince doesn't have a clue I'm a Visconti or that I'm Valentina's cousin. He never will. So how is Gina?"

"We miss each other."

"I can only imagine."

"Hey—I've got to go. Do me a favor, Francesca. If you hear anything more from Mom and Dad about what's going on, call me. I can't help but be curious."

"That works both ways," came her honest response. "Ace those engineering tests, bro. Talk to you soon."

Francesca hung up and watched TV before getting ready for bed. After all these years she was amazed the subject of Valentina and her fiancé had come up at the same time Francesca had been treating his dog. The strange coincidence made it difficult for her to fall asleep. She especially couldn't put the picture of the Prince out of her mind. It alarmed her that he remained there through the rest of her work week.

CHAPTER THREE

BECAUSE OF BAD TRAFFIC on Friday after leaving Milano to see Valentina, Vincenzo arrived late in Scuol for a meeting with his personal solicitor and high-powered attorney Marko Fetzer. He hurried inside his private office at the Baldasseri Timber Company.

"Marko? Forgive me for not being on time."

"No problem, Your Highness. I haven't been waiting long. You said it was urgent."

"Extremely." He sat down in his leather swivel chair and eyed him. "This is about the papers you've been arranging for the transfer of a hefty percentage of Baldasseri timber stock to the Visconti account."

He nodded. "Everything is ready."

"I can always count on you. But there's been a change in plans. I want you to shred them."

The other man leaned forward in surprise. "Is that because you have something else in mind?"

"No. The news I have to tell you isn't meant for another soul's ears yet."

"You have my word."

"I know that. The fact is, my engagement has been permanently called off."

The miracle he'd been praying for had happened.

Valentina had accused Vincenzo of neglecting her over the last year, of not even pretending to be in love. He knew it was a ruse to cover what was really going on with her. Now that he wouldn't be King, there was no point to their bogus engagement and she had returned the ring he'd given her.

Vincenzo realized she too had been working on a way to get out of the sick alliance their parents had concocted. Hallelujah! The wedding wouldn't be happening! He was *free*! Stefano must be in a complete frenzy, but it was no concern of Vincenzo's.

Silence followed before Marko said, "I'm so sorry, Your Highness."

"Don't be. These things happen. I have no doubt it'll be announced on the news at some point."

If Marko only knew the joyous state of Vincenzo's mind. He got to his feet. "Thank you for having taken the time to prepare the transfer. You're so good at what you do, expect another bonus for your service."

Now that their meeting was finished, Marko smiled and stood up. They shook hands before he left the office.

Vincenzo followed him out, anxious to get home to Karl. He'd left him in his mother's care. His dog's welfare and Dr. Linard's loving care were all he could think about as he drove to the palace and raced up the stairs to his own suite. Released from the ghastly vow he'd made to his father, Vincenzo could live again and intended to!

"Hey, buddy." He hunkered down to pet Karl who lay in his dog bed. He licked Vincenzo and moaned, letting him know he was glad he was back.

"I came as soon as I could." He kissed his head.

The sound of footsteps caused him to turn his head. "Mamma."

"Oh, good—you're back! Why didn't you come to Alfredo's bedroom? Your grandparents and I have been waiting hours to hear from you."

"I had to see Karl before doing anything else." And stop at the office for a vital private business transaction that would send Stefano into a new uproar. The timber stock was still out of his reach and always would be. "Has he eaten anything?"

"No, but he drinks every so often."

The condition of his dog had deteriorated since the last visit to Dr. Linard. "Thank you for watching over him. I'll carry him and we'll all talk."

With care he picked Karl up and walked through the palace to the suite where his grandfather was the most comfortable. Vincenzo sat down on the love seat with Karl next to him and ruffled his fur.

His grandmother flicked him a glance. "At last."

"Tell us everything, darling," his mother implored him.

Vincenzo's next words would bring the house down, but they had to be said.

"Valentina has called off the wedding."

"What did you say?" His mother jumped to her feet. "That's impossible."

"You heard me, Mamma."

"I don't believe it!" She looked shell-shocked, but his grandmother said nothing. Vincenzo didn't understand her silence. That was strange.

"I do," Alfredo spoke up at once. "From the time the suggestion of a betrothal between Valentina and Vincenzo was proposed, they knew he was second in line for the throne. When Rinieri was injured and couldn't carry on as Crown Prince, that put my grandson at the forefront. They expected Vincenzo to become King."

Vincenzo thanked his grandfather silently. That was as good an excuse as any the older man could think of for her getting out of an engagement neither of them wanted.

"He still should be," his mother cried.

"No," Alfredo muttered. "Now that Rinieri is miraculously better and expecting an heir, Vincenzo is no longer a candidate. I'm afraid the disappointment was too much for them and Valentina."

Letting out a cry of pain, his mother left the bedroom. His grandmother followed. Vincenzo walked over to the bed and grasped his grandfather's hand. "You're right, Nonno."

Thank heaven the old man was a realist, even if he didn't know what was going on in Valentina's head. The problem was Vincenzo's mother. She'd grown way too attached to Valentina and was obsessed by her dreams for the two of them. Now the visions of the wedding and all it would signify in the years to come had gone up in smoke. Bella, on the other hand, would be thrilled for him. She believed in true love, period.

Dimmed gray eyes focused on him. "How are you handling this?"

"I'm fine, Nonno. I've already met with Marko and taken care of things."

"You were wise not to have the financial transaction take place until the day of the wedding. If I'm not wrong, you're much more worried about Karl than the woman you almost married."

"Nobody fools you," he murmured. Vincenzo patted

his arm and stood up. "I need to have Karl put down, but I'm dreading it."

"Daniel will take care of it."

Yes, but Vincenzo didn't want the owner of the clinic to perform that service. Someone else had been on his mind for the last week giving him restless nights. He no longer had to feel any guilt about that. "What can I do for you before I see to Karl? Shall I ask Mother and Nonna to come back?"

"No. We need to give them time. Elsa will be bringing my dinner in a few minutes."

Elsa wasn't only a wonderful caregiver, she'd become his grandfather's friend. "I'll be in later to say good-night."

He walked over to the love seat. "Come on, buddy. Let's go back to my room and I'll ring for dinner. Afterward I'll let you sleep with me. How does that sound?"

An hour later he finished some business calls and phoned Luca with his news. His friend was overjoyed for him and agreed something serious and secret had to be going on with Valentina for her to break off the engagement with that neglect excuse. After they hung up, he was eating his dinner when his mother came in the suite. "We need to talk, Vincenzo."

"Please sit down. I know the news of our broken engagement has come as a blow to you."

"But not *you*?"

He walked over to the couch and put his arm around Karl. "If you want to know the truth—and I believe you'd prefer honesty between us—I'd like the kind of marriage you had with Papa."

"We were happy." His mother sank down in a chair. Her marriage to his father had been special.

"I never felt Valentina and I were right for each other, but for Papa's sake and yours I was willing to try and make it work. Now I don't have to."

"I knew you weren't enthusiastic, but I'd hoped you and Valentina would grow closer. She has to be devastated."

"Valentina wanted to be Queen, Mamma." Might as well use his grandfather's words. "In time her parents will find her another prince who will elevate her to the status she wants." He had no idea what Valentina really wanted.

His mother sat forward. "What we have to do now is arrange for a betrothal between you and Princess Constanza. You need to be settled with a wife, and I like her. If your father were still here, he'd insist on it." His mother had become much more overbearing since his father's death.

Vincenzo shook his head. "No more of that, Mamma. Rini met the love of his life and married her even though she was a commoner. He had the right idea. I'm no longer looking for a princess. When I meet the right woman and fall in love, I'll marry her."

"You can't mean that! I forbid it."

He burst into laughter. "Mamma—look what has happened. You and Papa tried your best for me by finding Princess Valentina, but it didn't work. I honored your wishes. Now I would like you to honor mine and accept how I feel."

"But Constanza has been crazy about you since she and Bella became best friends years ago. She's lovely and an heiress who would bring Lorchat Robotics Corporation with her."

"I like Constanza, but I'm not in love with her and never could be. It's out of the question. When the right nonroyal woman comes along for me, I plan to marry her."

She got to her feet. "Wait until your grandparents hear about this."

"You can talk to them, but no one will change my mind."

"Vincenzo? You're not thinking clearly right now," she said in an authoritative voice. "I'm going to leave you and we'll talk again tomorrow."

He walked her to the door and kissed her cheek. "You need a good night's sleep, Mamma. Thank you for taking such good care of Karl today. That meant more to me than anything."

"He's been a remarkable dog. It pains me that he's gotten so old. But I'm more pained to think that you won't be marrying Valentina. I know you liked her. Don't forget that she's been in love with you for a whole year. Since you refuse to consider Constanza, I'd like to believe there's still hope for you and Valentina. This isn't over yet. Wait and see. Good night."

He shut the door behind her. His poor mother. She refused to see the truth and wasn't about to give up on her dream. No doubt she would try to think up an added incentive to win over Valentina and her family, but Vincenzo had news for her. Without the timber fortune, nothing else could make up for it with Stefano. Fortunately, Bella would be coming home from her trip soon. He needed an ally.

His gaze flicked to the loving dog who lay there without moving. It was time…

Daniel had worked out a schedule. Each vet would work at the clinic one Saturday a month, half day for emergencies. Francesca was just finishing up her Saturday duty before leaving at two when the last call came in at the desk. She picked up. "Zoller Veterinary Clinic—"

"Dr. Linard?"

Her pulse raced. She knew that deep voice. "Your Highness? How's Karl?"

"I think you already know." His mournful tone said it all.

"Why don't you bring him to the clinic. We're closing in a few minutes, but I'll stay and we'll take care of him."

"Thank you. I'm on my way."

Francesca clicked off, steeling herself not to give in to the sadness. She went to the examining room to prepare the IV that would relax Karl and put him to permanent sleep.

When everything was ready, she walked through the clinic and opened the front door. A glorious August day greeted her. She leaned against the framework with her arms folded across her waist. The Prince's image had been on her mind since the first day he'd come in the clinic with Karl. This would be his last visit. She should be glad because her attraction to him was too strong and pure insanity.

Francesca started to turn away when she saw his black Mercedes approach. As she watched his tall, fit body get out and carry a limp Karl toward her, sadness crept through her. Pain lines defined the Prince's unforgettable male features.

"*Bun di*, Karl," she murmured good morning in Romansh and kissed the top of his head. He lifted it a trifle, but not enough to lick her. "Follow me." She walked ahead of them until they reached the designated room.

Vincenzo laid him on the table. He leaned over. "You're with friends, Karl." His dog moaned as if he understood completely.

Her gaze collided with the Prince's mournful eyes. "If you'll steady him, I'll administer the dose in his back leg. It'll relax him and send him into sleep."

"This is it," he whispered. His grief reached inside her.

"Yes, and the best way. Merciful. When you two are in heaven together one day, he'll thank you."

"You believe that?" he whispered.

"I'm planning on being reunited with all my pets. My latest dog, Mitzi, had to be put down while I was away at medical school. I plan to see her again one day."

Tears had filled those incredibly blue eyes. He looked down. "It's okay, buddy."

The dog didn't stir as Francesca inserted the IV. She stared at Karl. "You're going to have the most wonderful dreams. You'll be running and chasing everything in sight. You'll be joined with other dogs who will be there to play with you. Your life is just beginning, darling Karl."

Within a minute and a half, he was gone. She knew the Prince needed time alone with him, so she left the room and went out to the desk to wait.

He appeared ten minutes later, his eyes still moist. She looked up at him from the computer.

"Karl passed without any trauma. That's because he knew he was in the hands of an angel," he told her.

"Thank you, but you gave him the constant love in his life. Do you want an urn with his ashes delivered to the palace?"

"No. I have pictures and videos to remember him."

"My sentiments exactly."

After a pause, "Dr. Linard, when will you be off work?"

Her pulse sped up for no good reason. Why did he want to know that? "In fifteen minutes." She needed to take care of Karl.

"Do you have plans for the rest of the day?"

She blinked. "Only to go home and get some house-work done."

"If I come by then, would you be willing to take a drive with me to Karl's favorite spot where he loved to chase around?"

The invitation thrilled her to the core of her being, but it was out of the question. "Surely your fiancée, Princess Valentina, will want to go with you." Francesca would never consider it.

"I'm afraid not. Our engagement has been called off permanently."

Permanently? She reeled. *He wasn't marrying her cousin? What was going on?*

The news surprised her for several reasons she didn't dare examine. "I'm so sorry, Your Highness."

He shook his dark head. "It was an arranged en-gagement that didn't work out."

What? She had so many questions, but couldn't ask one. "Still, this must be a painful day for you."

"Learning about *your* dog, only you could understand my feelings at the moment." His emotions stirred hers. "Will you come with me?"

She could hardly breathe, let alone refuse what her heart wanted. "I'd love to. I bet Karl will be there wondering what took you so long."

A compelling smile broke out on his handsome face. "Imagine his joy when you show up with me."

CHAPTER FOUR

FIFTEEN MINUTES LATER Dr. Linard left the clinic and walked to Vincenzo's car carrying her purse. The sun gilded her hair. Without her uniform, her feminine curves looked fabulous in jeans and a short-sleeved print blouse. She had to be five foot five. Her beauty electrified him.

He got out. "Why don't I follow you to your home, and we'll go from there."

"Luckily I live here in Zernez."

"Perfect. Don't mind my security people trailing us. They go where I go."

She smiled and walked over to a yellow Volkswagen. He loved her choice of car and enjoyed trailing her to the apartment complex with flower boxes where she lived.

"I'll run in and be right out."

"No hurry," he called to her. He noticed she lived on the second floor. When she returned, he opened the front passenger door for her and they were off. Her flowery fragrance wafted past him.

"Where are we going?"

"To the mountains outside Scuol about ten minutes from here."

"What made them so special for Karl?"

"He liked to find ground-nesting birds and bark at them. His favorites were several families of skylarks and corncrakes hiding in the grass."

She smiled. "I never did hear him bark."

"He loved scaring them."

Francesca's laughter infected him. "I can only imagine how much you're going to miss him. He had the sweetest disposition."

"I never had a dog like him."

"You're lucky he was able to live with you to the very end. I told you about Mitzi. She was a Bernese Mountain Dog like Karl. I was away at school and didn't get to say goodbye to her."

He took in her profile. "I'm sorry about that. Our pets mean a lot."

"You're right about that."

"Where did you study?"

"In Milano."

All the time she was in school there, his former fiancée lived in the same city. But it was no good to think about the "what-ifs."

Vincenzo took a turnoff and the car climbed to a higher elevation. He parked at a vista overlooking the familiar alpine scenery and turned off the engine.

"What a beautiful sight!" She turned to him. "This is heaven. Can you see Karl yet?" Her warm brown-eyes twinkled. The sad day was turning out to be something else.

"Why don't we try to find him?" he teased.

"You're on."

They both got out and followed a path that led to

some trees. "Karl would sit here and wait until he heard the low buzz-like call of the corncrakes."

Her eyes wandered over him. "Will I know it if I hear it?"

This playful woman was getting to him. "Let's find out." They both sat on a log where Karl would sit at his feet.

Different kinds of birdsong filled the air while they listened. After five minutes the funny buzz sounds rent the air. She jumped up with the joy of a child. "I heard it!"

Nothing got past her. He stood up. "You certainly did. Maybe Karl is spooking them for you."

"Oh, I hope so!"

They stood there together smiling into each other's eyes and waited. Pretty soon they heard more on-and-off buzzes. A couple of the little birds scuttled through the grass. "Karl's after them, all right."

She looked up at him, her face glowing. "Thank you for bringing me here. The second I heard your voice on the phone earlier, I knew the reason. But being here where you said Karl loves to play has relieved much of my sadness."

His eyes darkened. "Mine too."

"From now on I'll think of him up on this mountain having the time of his life. I love the mountains too."

He didn't want this day to be over. "How would you like to get a bite to eat on our way back?"

"That sounds good. I skipped lunch because of the shorter day."

"I couldn't eat anything today, but now I find I'm hungry."

"Understood."

Vincenzo drove them to Zernez, asking her more about her work with Daniel. He stopped at a drive-through for ham-and-cheese croissants, which they both enjoyed.

Much as he'd wanted to take her to a restaurant, he didn't want to create publicity until the news of his broken engagement had circulated and died down. For now, this kind of excursion would have to do. Despite saying goodbye to Karl, he couldn't remember the last time he'd been this relaxed and happy. She'd made all the difference.

Once he'd driven her to the apartment complex, he shut off the engine and turned to her. "I want to thank you for helping me get through this day."

"To be honest, it helped me too," came her unexpected response without looking at him. "I find I'm attached to all my patients, especially ones that look like my last dog. Karl headed the list. Daniel says I need to toughen up, but I have a feeling there's no cure for it."

Every word out of her mouth enchanted him. He had to see her again. "Since you told me Daniel asked you to watch some videos on the Biosphere Reserve, I thought you might be interested in meeting the biologist who used to work with Dr. Zenger. The conservation board is meeting Tuesday evening at the information center here in Zernez. The chief ranger of the park will be speaking."

"I would absolutely love it!" she exclaimed without hesitation. "I was envious when Daniel told me Dr. Zenger helped take care of some of the animals up there. What time does this meeting start and I'll drive over."

"Seven o'clock. The information center consists of

three buildings. The meeting will take place in the Planta-Wildenberg castle. I'll look for you there."

"Thank you so much for giving me the opportunity, and for the dinner." She started to get out of the car.

"It was my pleasure. See you there."

He waited until he could see she was safely inside her apartment, then he left for home with a new excitement. Only three more days before he saw her again.

When Tuesday arrived, it dragged on. After talking to a couple of plant managers who had complicated problems, Vincenzo took off for Zernez later than he'd intended. Dr. Linard had arrived ahead of him. She was surrounded by mostly male members of the board in the small conference room. Gian Mattlis, the head biologist, was talking animatedly with her. No surprise there. She looked fabulous in a peach-colored two-piece suit with short sleeves.

"Your Highness," one of the reserve authorities greeted him. "We've been getting acquainted with Dr. Zenger's replacement at the Zoller clinic. Dr. Linard is a very welcome addition."

The grin on the chief ranger's face revealed his interest too. "I'm going to take her up where I can guarantee she'll see some ibex and chamois."

Vincenzo's gaze flew to those chocolate orbs of hers. "That ought to be a great adventure, Dr. Linard."

Her gentle smile connected. "I'll look forward to it."

The president of the board called the meeting to order. "Now that His Highness is here, we can get started."

Vincenzo walked over to her. In high heels she stood a little taller. The perfect size for him. "Shall we take a seat?" He found two on the first row for them.

After a reading of the minutes of the last meeting, it was the ranger's turn to talk. "We need to be concerned about the laws that have been applied in the reserve. Are they doing the job?

"To review what we know about the ibex, if you kill the wrong animal, you pay a fine and get nothing. Heaven forbid if you shoot the animal and leave it wounded, which is where Dr. Linard comes in. Naturally you lose your license.

"At present, the reserve here in Graubünden is only allowing locals to hunt the ibex for a very short window in time." He read some statistics. "We don't want them to make the endangered species list. Before you leave this meeting, please write your suggestions about the rules and put them in the box here on the desk."

The ranger played the most recent video they'd made about the biosphere. Vincenzo noticed Dr. Linard appeared enchanted as they watched the flourishing wildlife in the upper elevations. He preferred taking in her reactions and counted the minutes until it ended and they could leave to be alone.

"Are you hungry? I left straight from work, and now I'm starving. After I follow you home, let's get something at the drive-through."

"You're reading my mind."

Her answer meant she wasn't ready to say goodnight yet. He picked her up in front of her apartment and they decided to go for meat pies. From there he drove her to a nearby park and turned off the engine so they could eat.

"Um… This is delicious, Your Highness."

"I agree."

She glanced at him. "I noticed you didn't write any suggestions in the box."

"That's because the board already knows my feelings," he explained.

"Which are?"

"I'd rather there was no hunting at all in the reserve. I'd love to leave it as pristine as the day it was created."

Her eyes played over his features. "You really mean that, don't you?"

"Yes. There's a time and a place to hunt, but centuries ago wise stewards wanted to create the place we now know as the Biosphere Reserve. A place untouched by man."

"That's a thrilling concept and gives me gooseflesh just thinking about it. The idea of those beautiful animals being wounded kills me."

"I felt the same way the first time I hiked there. My friend Luca and I found a baby ibex in serious trouble. It lay against its mother who'd been shot and was dying. We took it to the vet and it recovered, but that incident did it for me."

"I admire you more than you know for doing all you can to preserve nature this way."

"I'm afraid I face a lot of opposition. Trophy hunting is lucrative."

"Many bad things are, but you're still willing to do something about it. I feel honored that you made it possible for me to be there tonight. Just so you know, your fight is mine."

Where had this adorable woman come from? He started the car and took her back to her apartment. "Don't be surprised if the chief ranger gets in touch with you to take that hike and other things. He didn't look that happy when you left the room."

"I saw his wedding ring, so if he calls, I'll let him know I would never spend time alone with a married man."

With whom *did* she spend time? "Tell me—is there someone important in your life?"

She looked away. "Not yet."

How could that be? "Are you enjoying your work?"

"Being a vet is all I could ever want, but I'm not doing so well learning Romansh."

Vincenzo smiled. "Karl understood you."

"He was a genius. It's harder than I thought."

"That's because nobody speaks the standard form except possibly some news announcers. I think you've already figured out it's a conglomeration of dialects. I've sorted through dozens of them and they each have their own grammar."

"Can you speak every dialect?"

"I'm not Karl. I suggest you try to pick up one. At least then when you speak it, you won't sound phony."

"Have I been sounding phony?"

One brow lifted. "The truth?"

"Oh, no—" Color rushed into her cheeks. "What must Daniel think?"

Vincenzo burst into laughter. He couldn't help it. She ended up laughing with him. He loved it that she didn't take herself seriously. "You know exactly what he thinks or he wouldn't have hired you. Between you and me, he knows it's impossible to master. The fact that you promised to try had to have delighted him."

"You always make me feel good. Thanks for everything this evening, Your Highness. Good night."

She got out of the car before he could come around. Soon she reached the second floor and waved to him. There was no woman in the world with a personality as charming as hers. That's when it hit him.

He wanted to be with her all the time.

Around noon Sunday, Mrs. Corsin called Francesca to tell her one of the puppies was available if she still wanted it.

Francesca said she'd love to buy it. Mrs. Corsin planned to bring the puppy to the clinic on Thursday when she was in town for another appointment. A new dog would keep Francesca busy so she wouldn't think about Prince Vincenzo anymore.

Being with him at the information center and their talk afterward hadn't been a good idea. During the time they'd been together, she'd forgotten he was a prince. They'd laughed and shared some special moments in such a natural way, she hadn't wanted the evening to end.

Later in the day her mother phoned, giving her news she'd already heard from the Prince. So much for putting him out of her mind. "Your father has been told through certain sources that there'll be no marriage between the Visconti and Baldasseri families. Word is that Stefano is in a fury."

Francesca took a deep breath. The Prince had told her the called-off engagement had been arranged. That personal information wasn't public knowledge. This wasn't a conversation she should have with anyone, not even her mother. "I'm sure both families are upset, Mom."

"Your dad is certain the plans were called off because Prince Vincenzo is no longer the Crown Prince."

"Probably." It was time to change the subject. "How are you two?"

"Missing you. How's work?"

"I love it, and guess what. I'm buying a dog."

"That doesn't surprise me. What breed?"

"It's a male Bernese Mountain Dog, twelve weeks old and adorable. Three puppies were born. I inoculated them and fell in love with one that snuggled against me and licked me."

Laughter came from her mom. "Your dad will be delighted to hear it. We wondered how long you could last without one."

"Not long apparently. After he has settled in, I'll take pictures of him on my phone and send them to you."

"Do you have a name for him already?"

"Yes, it's the one the owner gave him. Artur."

"How cute!"

"He's named after her favorite pianist, Arthur Rubinstein."

"*Arturrr...* I love it."

"It's perfect, and now I've got to buy some stuff before the store closes so I'm ready by Thursday when I bring him home."

"He'll be the happiest pup on earth living with the sweetest girl in the world."

"I love you, Mom. Give Dad a hug from me."

Late Monday afternoon Daniel asked Francesca to come to his office before she left. As she stepped inside still in her uniform, it stunned her to see Prince

Vincenzo sitting there in a gray suit and tie. He got to his feet, possessing a male virility she couldn't ignore.

His intense blue eyes focused on her. "Dr. Linard?"

"Your Highness."

"I'd hoped to catch you before you went home. Please, sit down."

Francesca sank into the other chair, far too excited over their visitor to do anything else and angry about his effect on her.

"I was telling Daniel that you were a hit at the last board meeting. I've had several calls from the members about you. They feel that with your background as a vet, you would be a great spokesperson for our cause."

"That's very kind, but I'm a novice barely out of veterinary school."

He shook his dark head. "According to Gian Mattlis, your philosophy about preservation of the species impressed him so much, he's hoping you'd be willing to narrate part of our next video for the reserve. He'd like to do it next month. Since it will have to be filmed on a weekday, I wanted Daniel's permission before approaching you."

"Which you have." Dr. Zoller smiled at her.

Francesca stirred uncomfortably in the chair. "I'm honored by your confidence in me, Your Highness, but I couldn't do something like that, let alone in front of a camera. It's not me."

The Prince's gaze fused with hers. "What happened to, 'your fight is mine'?" Guilt smote her. "Will you at least let me give you a small tour to see the reserve before you decide you can't do it?"

"Of course, she will," Daniel answered for her.

"I was thinking tomorrow if that's at all possible."

Daniel nodded. "It will be no problem for her to be gone for the day."

Francesca's boss knew why she didn't want to get involved, so why wasn't he helping her get out of this? "If you're sure, Daniel."

"Preserving the integrity of the reserve is of paramount importance. As your employer, I'm pleased for you to be included."

"It would please *me* no end, Dr. Linard." Those electric blue eyes mesmerized her.

"Very well. I'm honored that you'd take me on a little tour."

The Prince got to his feet with a look of satisfaction. "I'm due at the palace now. Plan for me to come to the clinic at eight thirty in the morning for you."

"I'll be ready."

After he left the office, Dr. Zoller cocked his head. "You've been bestowed a personal compliment by the Prince himself."

"I realize that, but I would have preferred not to get involved."

"We both know you wanted to turn him down because you're a Visconti, but maybe it will never be necessary. Remember, he's no longer engaged to your cousin. His association with that name has been dissolved and I've never seen him happier in my life. There will be other women. Give it a little more time before you decide you have to reveal your secret to him."

Daniel did have a point, but Francesca had the feeling he knew a lot he wasn't telling. The two men had been friends for years. She got to her feet. "This isn't the best time for me. I'm just getting started on my career and I'm buying a dog. It's more than enough."

His hands parted. "If you really feel that way, I can contact him today and tell him you aren't interested after all. Naturally it's your decision."

"No. Please don't do that. I said I would. See you in the morning, Daniel."

CHAPTER FIVE

FRANCESCA LEFT THE clinic and drove home. The thought of a whole day with the Prince out in nature filled her with an exhilaration she didn't know how to contain. What to wear?

She spent a restless night waiting for morning to come. After some deliberation she dressed in jeans and a new khaki shirt with roll tab sleeves and a collar.

When she reached the clinic, she saw a van with the Biosphere Reserve logo parked in the lot. As she parked and got out of her car, she saw this tall, hunky male walking toward her in jeans and a dark green pullover. Good grief. With that dark hair and those cobalt eyes, no better-looking man had ever been born.

"*Bun di*, Dr. Linard," he said in Romansh. "Right on time. I'm glad because it's a beautiful day and we've a lot to see. Have you eaten breakfast?"

"I did, and presume you did too. Thank you."

"Do you have to go inside the clinic first?"

He was almost rocking on the heels of his hiking boots, exactly the way her brother did when he was eager to escape to somewhere. "I'm ready to leave now, Your Highness."

"Then let's be off. I've brought treats, water and a picnic, so we shouldn't be in want of anything."

Francesca knew this man had thought of everything. He was what every man should be, let alone a prince.

They walked over to the passenger side of the van and he helped her in. His hand accidentally brushed against her leg. It sent darts of sensation through her. Oh, boy. Already aware of him, his touch threw her into a new, deeper kind of trouble.

"We'll drive to the right side of the Inn River and continue driving to the three-thousand-meter level to take in the view. Italy isn't far away from there."

She eyed him. "I have a confession to make. In medical school, my professors sang Dr. Zoller's praises. Their remarks made me want to see if I could work there with him after graduation. Until I looked at a map, little did I know this biosphere reserve was located so close to the clinic. Since I've always loved the mountains, the proximity turned out to be a dream come true."

"I can understand your delight," he said. "The reserve is a magnet for nature lovers. Most of them are hikers who have to stay on the marked trails—however, some of the trails are off-limits in high summer, but we can drive to places I want you to see."

"This is a privilege I would never have expected, Your Highness."

He grinned. "Stick with me and see the wonders of the world."

She needed to stop staring at his handsome face or she'd have a heart attack. "You grew up surrounded by mountains."

"Yes. They've been the playground for my sister

Bella and me. When we were young, our mother didn't like us spending so much time away from the palace. We did it anyway in order to hike and try to catch fish with nets."

"How funny!"

He smiled. "It was fun too. In our teens we managed to sneak away after dark and camp out some nights until our parents found out."

"Uh-oh."

"Uh-oh is right. At that point everything was brought to a halt."

"You mean you had to grow up."

Their eyes met and she saw a sadness enter his that hadn't been there before.

"Afraid so."

"Now you have your duties."

Like Francesca's father, who had walked away from his to marry her mother. But she couldn't talk about that with the Prince.

Francesca looked out the window. She decided to stop worrying about everything and simply enjoy this trip. Having been invited by the Prince of the Engadin gave her a coveted entrée here. Being with him made her world feel magical.

"What about you, Dr. Linard? Do you have siblings who got into trouble with you?"

She laughed. "My brother Rolf made up for half a dozen adventurous brothers and sisters. He's a rascal, but I adore him."

"How old is he?"

"A year younger than I am. Right now he's finishing his engineering studies in Paris. When we were young, our parents took us to Chamonix, France, every winter where we skied to our hearts' content. Those mountains became our favorite place. You probably love to ski."

"Whenever I get the chance—however, there was a time when I worried I wouldn't be able to do much of it."

"Why was that?"

"My great-uncle Leonardo designated me to be the Crown Prince after my cousin Prince Rinieri came out of that earthquake with amnesia."

"What a terrible experience that must have been for him."

"It was a nightmarish time for him and for me. It meant responsibilities I didn't want to take on, *and* I had to cut down on my skiing." She laughed. "Luckily he recovered his memory."

"I don't blame you for how you felt. I can't imagine anything worse than being a king. It makes me shudder just to think about it."

"Do you really feel that way?"

"Absolutely. You don't have free agency when you're born into a royal family, but now I'm being rude to you. I'm sorry. I had no right to say that." Her father's struggle to become his own person would always live with her.

"Please don't apologize, Dr. Linard. I enjoy your frank speaking. It's more refreshing than you know. No wonder Daniel thinks the world of you. In case you didn't know, he's happy you applied."

"It's mutual, believe me. Do you know I almost missed the experience of meeting and working with him?"

"Why?"

"When I was searching for the right veterinarian opening six weeks ago, you can bet I looked for a good one in Chamonix."

"But nothing could compare with working for Daniel," he interjected.

"He's known everywhere, and I've discovered he's a remarkable doctor."

"Amen to that."

Over the next little while they passed grasslands, meadows, forests, all the elements of nature that caused people to flock to Switzerland's grandeur. Visitors were out en masse. He handed her a pair of binoculars. "If you'll look over on that crest, you may see some sights people spend thousands of dollars hoping to glimpse."

The Prince was loving this. So was Francesca, more than she would have ever dreamed possible.

She kept scanning the top of the crest and soon she saw movement. "Oh—there's a tan chamois! Your binoculars are so powerful, I can tell it has dark legs and two horns. It looks like a goat, only bigger."

He nodded. "More like an antelope?"

"Yes. It's beautiful! How wonderful we have creatures like this. I love it that you and your family have fought to preserve places where we can see them outside of a zoo."

"I suppose a zoo has its place, but there's nothing like the great outdoors."

They kept climbing higher.

All of a sudden, she cried, "There are two red deer and further on an ibex!"

His deep chuckle sent delicious chills through her body. "You've hit the jackpot today. Many are the times when you don't catch sight of an animal. Today they've come out for you."

The things he said...

He pulled the van to the side of the road and parked. "I'll get us something to eat and drink." Quick as a shot he got out and opened another door to grab some items. Once in front again, he handed her a water bottle and some Cailler Swiss chocolate.

"How did you know this is my favorite?"

His brows lifted. "Isn't it everyone's?"

They both laughed before she handed him the binoculars. "Your turn." She started eating several squares of chocolate. Heaven.

"Another Ibex has appeared. It must be its mate. They're having a great day just like we are."

Francesca averted her eyes. Every moment, every word with him was making this outing unforgettable.

"I'm going to drive higher. Who knows what we'll find?"

After putting the binoculars around his neck, they headed out again. She didn't spot any hikers at this point. "We won't see brown bears, right?"

"No."

"That's too bad. I love to watch them."

"They've been extinct since 1904, but some time ago a young bear did migrate here. It was a male and no population will develop without a female. I presume we'll see more from time to time."

"How do you feel about allowing them here?"

"They would be good for tourism though there is pressure against it in some sectors. I welcome them as long as we put appropriate safety measures like fencing in place. Brown bears are pretty shy."

"They're part of the whole animal world up here," she added. "I like the idea very much."

He sent her a sideward glance. "You see? You'd be perfect to help us do the next video, but I won't say another word about it. That will have to come from you."

Clever man to bring her here. Who could refuse this Prince who charmed her down to her toenails?

When they came to the edge of a forested area, he pulled off the road once again. "Time for lunch. We'll sit on the fallen tree over there and enjoy the eastern view of the Piz Pisoc."

Pockets of snow filled its mountainous crags. "What can I bring?"

His eyes glowed a burning blue. "Yourself."

Heat radiated through her. They both got out and he pulled a cooler from the back. She followed his fit body over the grass. A few yards into the forest and they reached the fallen tree. He lowered the cooler and opened the lid. Two plates had already been prepared with food and he handed her one which she uncovered.

"This didn't come from the deli in town. It's a feast."

A chuckle escaped his throat. "My favorite cook at the palace made this meal for us."

"How am I so lucky?"

"Because you're with me." She loved his teasing. "I did stop at the deli for soda. I hope you like Pepita."

"I drink it quite often." She leaned down and reached for one that was chilling on ice. They ate in companionable silence for a few minutes, but she still felt terrible for what she'd said to him.

"Your Highness? Please forgive me for being so outspoken to you a minute ago. I can't believe I did that. No one has ever been kinder or more wonderful to me."

His eyes glinted. "Are you saying you're sorry enough to help with the video we'll be working on next month?"

"After what I did, I'm putty in your hands. Oh, dear—" She felt herself blush. "That's the wrong thing to say too. I'm so embarrassed."

A deep laugh poured out of him, disturbing some white-bellied alpine swifts clinging to the side of a nearby tree.

They finished eating and he packed everything up to take back to the van. "If you're ready, I'll drive us to a spot where we might see an old married couple I'd like you to meet."

Her eyes widened. "What are you talking about?"

"You'll see," he murmured. "At least I hope they'll show up."

He had her intrigued as they climbed to the summit where he slowed down. "Look to the right." She did his bidding. "What do you see?"

"No people."

"I'm talking about the old married couple. Look again." He handed her the binoculars.

She put them to her eyes. It took her a minute to cover everything. "All I see are two birds with large wingspans cruising around."

"Not just any birds, Dr. Linard. They're golden eagles, hunting for marmots. I've hiked close to their eyrie many times. Their marriage has lasted longer than those of some humans."

Francesca shook her head in amazement. "How wonderful! What a fantastic sight! I wouldn't have missed it." She turned toward him. "Thank you so much for bringing me here. I'll always treasure this day."

His compelling smile illuminated her insides. "It's been my pleasure and I'm sorry we have to head back to the clinic."

So am I...so am I.

They turned around and talked about the forthcoming video while they made the breathtaking descent. The last thing she wanted to do was leave this land of enchantment that included a man she couldn't believe existed, a man who... Her thoughts had to stop right there.

He handed her some more chocolate and her bottle of water, always looking out for her. She was desperate to find any faults in him. So far she hadn't found one. Her only problem was that she'd been born a Visconti, the natural enemy of a Baldasseri.

At quarter to five in the evening they pulled into the clinic parking area. The Prince drove the van over to her car and helped her get out. "When arrangements are made, I'll be in touch with you about filming the video next month. Now I'm due back at the palace."

"Of course." Emptiness filled her to realize it would be a whole month before she talked to him again. "Today's tour made me appreciate the great value of the biosphere. It thrills me to be a tiny part of something so important." She opened her car door. *"Buna sera,* Your Highness."

Vincenzo went into work early the next two days, anxious to get busy making up for being gone the day before. Over lunch on Thursday he took a call from his mother. Bella would be home from vacation today. At dinner his mother planned to discuss what he was going to do to fix the situation with Valentina. His poor deluded mother. He told her they'd talk later.

At four thirty he left for the vet clinic. By the time he arrived there, it would be the end of Francesca's working day. She was constantly on his mind. He'd never been so entertained in his life, nor as attracted, and couldn't wait a second longer to see her. Thoughts of her finally being willing to help make the video had brightened his mood.

The receptionist smiled up at him. "Prince Vincenzo?"

"I know I don't have an appointment, but I need to see Dr. Linard. Is she available?" Her car was still in the parking area.

"She's with a client, but I'll walk back and tell her you're here."

"Thank you."

As he stood there, a woman carrying an empty crate came through. She stared at him for a moment. It happened wherever he went. Vincenzo would never know the meaning of anonymity. He greeted her before she left the clinic.

The receptionist came back. "Dr. Linard will be with you in a moment." She walked to the front door and let herself out.

Five minutes later he heard footsteps. "Your Highness?"

He turned in the direction of Francesca's voice and feasted his eyes on her beauty. When their gazes met, those fabulous brown eyes looked worried. Why? "I'm glad I caught you before you left for the day," he murmured.

"I was about to go home." She sounded a trifle breathless. "I'm afraid Daniel is away until tomorrow."

"I came to see *you* about the script for the video."

She blinked. "The script?"

He cocked his head. "I was hoping you would put down some of your thoughts and we could go over them while we grab a bite to eat."

"You mean this evening?"

He sensed she was nervous. "Do you still have another patient?"

"Yes," she responded too quickly, averting her eyes.

What was going on with her? "Do you mind if I wait?"

"I might be a while."

"That's no problem for me, Doctor. My mother says I'm the bane of her existence." He heard a slight chuckle. "How can I convince you that I won't bite?"

She let out a troubled sigh. "It's not that. I'm afraid that if you knew about my patient, it might make you sad."

"In what way?"

"I can see it's useless arguing with you. Come with me."

Relieved she wasn't fighting him anymore, he followed her down the hall to the examining room she used. No one was there, but he spied a crate on the floor with a dog inside. It whined and she spoke to it.

"I told you I'd be right back. We're going home."

Vincenzo hunkered down for a good look. A playful Bernese Mountain Dog, probably three months old, was in the last stages of puppyhood. The male reminded him so much of Karl at the same age, his heart felt a pang. Now he thought he understood Francesca's comment and was touched by her concern for his feelings.

He flicked her a glance. "Your new dog is made in Karl's image."

She nodded. "I knew it would remind you of him. Maybe too much. I couldn't resist this one the other day when he and his siblings came in for their shots. I'm crazy about the breed."

"That makes two of us. What's his name?"

"Artur."

"Well, Artur. What a lucky little tyke to have Dr. Linard for *your* owner."

"I hope he'll feel that way. I need to get him home."

"Let me help with any paraphernalia."

"You don't have to, but I guess I can't stop you."

"I'm glad you understand that, since it's clear my former dog and yours had a lot to do with this acquisition. I feel partway responsible." Nothing could have excited him more.

"Karl was special."

Amen.

"What do you need carried to your car?"

"That satchel on the chair. We'll leave through the back door."

When they reached the rear of the clinic, she removed her uniform and put it in the laundry bin. Vincenzo opened the self-locking door while she carried the crate. He would have done it for her, but knew the dog needed to trust her first. With the satchel in hand, he walked to the car and put it on the backseat next to Artur. The dog began whining.

He shut the door and went over to his car. They drove in tandem and within a few minutes reached her apartment complex. He carried her bags and the satchel up the stairs and into her living room. Her apartment felt cozy and comfortable.

"I'll take him outside and be right back." After putting a collar around the dog's neck and attaching a leash, she carried him out and down the stairs. The house training would go on and on. Vincenzo knew all about it.

Once back inside, she undid the leash and let the dog run around to explore while she set out water and food for him in the kitchen. More memories of early days with Karl filtered through his mind.

"What are you going to do with him during the days when you work?"

She followed the puppy around. His eyes followed her gorgeous figure. "Daniel said I could keep him with the other pets in the clinic's boarding kennel. They have their own backyard for a place to play. I think he'll love it. Of course, I'll have to take him out every few hours, but we'll be together."

"He'll be in doggie heaven knowing you're there too." Vincenzo unpacked the satchel and sacks. She'd been to a pet store and had bought a doggie bed and some fun toys.

He reached for the pack of jungle plush pals and a rope to chew on. After getting on the floor, he rustled the rope around until her dog got excited and pounced on it. "Karl used to love to do this." For the next ten minutes the two of them laughed at Artur's antics as a tug-of-war ensued.

She got up from the floor. "I bought frozen pizza. Would you like some after I warm it up, Your Highness?"

"Sounds good." He continued to play with the dog

while she fixed them a meal and called him over to the small dining room table. Artur whined for their food, but they knew better than to feed him.

"Sorry, buddy. Karl was a beggar too."

She laughed. "They all are, but I have a jerky dog treat for him." She unfastened a wrapper and made him reach for it. Her happy laugh and appealing personality were like an elixir to Vincenzo who never wanted to leave. But he was due at the palace at eight and they'd finished eating. He knew she had work to do with her new pet and got up from the table.

Artur ran over to him. Vincenzo gave him a quick rubdown. "Thank you for the pizza and salad, Dr. Linard. Now I must get going, but be warned—tomorrow evening after work, *I'll* be bringing our dinner to repay you. Maybe we can work on some of your thoughts to put in the video." His eyes found hers. "Have fun tonight. I envy both of you."

CHAPTER SIX

BOTH OF US?

Waves of heat swept through Francesca as she watched her dog follow him to the door. She locked up and had a full evening before going to bed. Artur lay in his new doggie bed in a corner of her bedroom. Like a child, he didn't want to go to sleep until she'd talked to him for a long time. Francesca couldn't sleep either. Not while her mind remembered every moment of the evening with the Prince.

To her amazement, she'd felt so comfortable with him she forgot he was Prince Vincenzo Baldasseri. He had sat on the floor laughing and playing with the dog. Everything had seemed to come naturally to him. The man was so easy to be around, and there couldn't be another one on earth as attractive.

Francesca had found that out after their day of touring the biosphere where she'd discovered hidden depths to him. She'd had the time of her life. At this point it was more than a crush and it frightened her.

Prince Vincenzo wasn't a man you would ever let go. Her cousin had to be madly in love with him. Francesca could only imagine Valentina was in the depths of despair right now. Before long she expected to hear that his wedding to Valentina was back on.

She also needed to remember that his arranged engagement to her cousin had been broken recently. No doubt he was feeling the void in some way. Francesca had helped him with Karl and it was natural for him to be friendly with her. But not for one minute did she dare believe this bond between them would last.

If her cousin knew he'd spent this evening eating pizza with Francesca, a blood relative... The thought put the fear in her. Tomorrow evening she'd let him know once and for all that she couldn't be with him again except to do that one video. That was it!

After getting in bed later, she phoned her brother. "Rolf? I'm so glad you picked up!"

"Hey—what's wrong?"

She lay back against the pillow. "A lot has happened. Last week I had to put down Prince Vincenzo's dog. Karl was the sweetest thing and died peacefully."

"Your first patient and you had to put him to sleep," he commiserated. "I can only imagine how hard that was on you."

Rolf understood. In the next breath she told him about the conservation board meeting for the Biosphere Reserve and her trip there with the Prince. "He's asked me to help narrate the next video."

"Somehow that doesn't surprise me."

His comment caused her to sit up. "Why on earth would you say that?"

"I may be your brother, but I have eyes. You're even more beautiful than our cousin. Over the years my friends have commented on it. I'm not at all surprised the Prince is interested in you. But unlike them, he's not intimidated by you."

She trembled. "What are you saying?"

"The Prince is after you, Francesca. You're brilliant as well as gorgeous. That's hard on a lot of guys. When are you making this film?"

Her hand tightened on her cell. "Next month, but it's not a good idea."

"Why?"

"You *know* why." Heat swarmed into her cheeks. "I'm a Visconti and so was his fiancée."

"So? Didn't you just tell me that Dr. Zoller said it's over and the Prince has never been happier? If he'd loved her heart and soul, he wouldn't have broken with her. I can promise you that."

She clung to her cell while his logic sank in. "Even so, our cousin isn't just anyone. She's family, even though they don't recognize us. To spend any more time with the Prince she almost married would be... well, it would be—"

"Outrageous? Ludicrous?" he broke in with a laugh. "Come on. We're all humans first. Prince Vincenzo wants to get to know Dr. Linard, the vet. Admit you want it too! He has no idea that you're a Visconti in hiding. So go on being Dr. Linard and see where it leads."

"Rolf—don't joke about this."

"I know what's bothering you. You've finally met the man who turns you on."

"Rolf!" she snapped.

More laughter rolled out of him. "I knew it. Gina thinks he's a stud too, but I forgive her for that. I'm glad you called. This is the greatest news and I'll be waiting to hear the next episode of Dr. Linard's secret life in Scuol. It would make a great sequel to *All Creatures Great and Small*. Love you."

They disconnected.

After Francesca had been up part of the night with her dog, Friday morning came too soon. She took care of him and they left for the clinic. She had to hope Artur would learn to like the kennel. He whined his head off when she left him in the yard with the other dogs. But each time she appeared throughout the day to see to his needs, he'd settled down a little more.

Her working day involved two surgeries and the usual vaccinations and setting of limbs. She faced the end of the day with alternate feelings of excitement and dread over what was coming. They drove back to the apartment. Francesca had been going nonstop and felt it as she took care of her dog.

Every minute she listened for the Prince's approach. Until he arrived, she took advantage of the time to snap pictures of Artur with her phone to send to the family.

While she filled his water dish, he started to bark. He hadn't done much of that yet. Someone had come to the door and knocked. Artur dashed toward it. Her heart almost palpitated out of her chest as she followed him.

Upon opening it, she came close to fainting. Vivid blue eyes beneath dark brows and wavy dark hair pierced hers. The Prince had come dressed in an open necked linen sport shirt and chinos, the epitome of an Adonis. He carried a sack of something that smelled delicious, but she couldn't think or concentrate.

The dog jumped around him making excited sounds. Artur smelled a friend as well as food. Francesca had to hold back her own excited feelings. "Come in, Your Highness."

He flashed her a smile, walked in and put the sack on the kitchen counter. Then he hunkered down to play with the dog. "I can see you're loving your new home, Artur. I brought you a present too." He pulled a canine party bone treat out of his pocket and unwrapped it. "These were Karl's favorites."

The dog grabbed it and ran off to chew on it.

Francesca stared down at him. "You're spoiling him."

He stood up. His eyes played over her features. "It's your fault." Those words and the way he said them made her legs go weak. "I hope you're hungry. I brought Chinese."

She swallowed hard. "You couldn't have picked anything I like more. If you want to freshen up, the bathroom is down the hall on the left."

"Thank you."

By the time he returned, she'd placed the food on the table. He'd also brought a bottle of wine which he poured into drinking glasses she'd provided.

"This is delicious," she said a few minutes later.

"I'm glad it tastes good to you." His eyes played over her. "What's your schedule tomorrow? I enjoyed our outing so much, I'd like to do it again. We'll take Artur to the mountains with us and discuss the script then."

She could hear Rolf's words. "He has no idea that you're a Visconti in hiding. So go on being Dr. Linard and see where it leads."

Francesca wanted to go with him so badly, she refused to listen to the warnings in her head. "If I come, you know we'll have a puppy with us and that means a lot of work."

He stared at her over his wineglass. "To be honest, I miss Karl and would love it more than you know." Francesca believed him. "I'll come by at eight thirty for you. Have a good night."

The second he left the apartment, Francesca sank down on the couch afraid over what she'd done. Should she have put the Prince off? What would happen if he found out who she *really* was? The dog sensed her distress and plopped himself in her lap. "Oh, Artur, have I made the biggest mistake of my life? What am I going to do?" When she finally put the dog down and went to bed, she sobbed into her pillow, tossing and turning all night.

Francesca's gorgeous image had been robbing Vincenzo of sleep. When Saturday morning came, he got up excited. Once showered and shaved, he pulled on a sport shirt and jeans. Before taking off, he wrote a message to be delivered to his mother that he had business this weekend. If an emergency cropped up, she should leave a message on his phone.

He drank his coffee and grabbed a roll to eat on his way out of the palace. Despite a warm August morning, he saw storm clouds gathering over the mountains in the distance. Nothing could dampen his spirits as he headed for Zernez.

After a stop at the deli, he drove to Francesca's apartment. She stood waiting at the bottom of the stairs with a bag and the crate next to her. He got out and helped her into his car. She looked beautiful dressed in jeans and soft pink pullover.

"It's your turn, Artur." After setting the crate in the backseat, he walked around and they took off. The dog barked when the thunder grew worse.

"Oh, dear," she murmured. "He's not used to it."

Vincenzo chuckled. "He's a mountain dog and will soon adapt. This weather couldn't be more perfect for him."

Like thieves stealing away in the night, they whizzed toward the mountains. He'd never known this kind of contentment. "Are you cold? Hot?"

"I'm perfect."

Yes, she is... "Tell me how your work is going overall."

"I love it. How lucky am I to do what I love for a living! What about your work?"

"When you're the only son of a prince, you're supposed to grow up doing what you're told to do. At first I wasn't that interested, but in time my views changed."

"How?"

"I saw the potential for expansion within the country and made new goals that would benefit the monarchy and some of my favorite causes. In that regard it turned out to be a good thing."

"The Biosphere Reserve is your case in point." She lowered her head, thinking of her father who'd done a great favor for her family. As a result of breaking with the Visconti side, her parents had allowed her and Rolf to lead their own lives.

"I'm afraid I wasn't as courageous in other areas." He made a turn that would lead them up the mountain to his chalet. "My father had dreams for me. Mother supported him in everything. The two houses of Baldasseri and Visconti decided to merge those dreams by arranging a marriage to Princess Valentina."

"How did *you* feel about that?" she asked in a quiet voice.

"I should explain something to you. From an early age I sensed my father, the younger brother, felt he was a disappointment to the Baldasseri family long before he married my mother. He suffered from terrible inferiority. I wanted to take away his pain because I loved him. The only way to do that was to be an obedient son. They raised me that I should enjoy dating, but never forget that when the time came, I would be marrying a princess."

"You obviously listened to them, which makes you a wonderful son."

"Not so wonderful, Francesca. After his death I realized how long I'd been lying to myself about what *I* wanted out of life."

A moan escaped her lips. "When did he die?"

"Soon after I was betrothed."

"I'm so sorry you lost him."

"It was hard. My mother is still grieving. They had a good marriage."

"So do my parents," Francesca admitted as a loud clap of thunder resounded, causing the dog to whimper.

Vincenzo reached back to knock on the crate. "We're almost there, buddy." The rain had started to splash down. He turned on the wipers.

"Your mother must be devastated that your marriage has been called off."

"I'm afraid so. One can only hope she will get over it. She cared for Valentina."

"What about your grandparents?"

"They don't say anything. Deep down I think Grandfather knows I'm not suffering over anything but the loss of Karl. I'm praying his kidneys hold out for a long time. I'll want his backing and my grandmother's when I decide to marry the woman I can't live without."

A noticeable pause ensued before she asked, "What about your sister?"

"Bella and I watch out for each other."

She nodded. "My brother and I are the same way."

"What are his plans?"

"He's in engineering right now and will marry his girlfriend, Gina, at Christmas. Is your sister betrothed?"

"No. She's taking her time. Mamma has ideas for her, but she's very particular. Between us she's searching for the perfect prince who we know doesn't exist."

Her laughter resounded. "I saw her picture on television while she was vacationing with Princess Constanza in Lausanne. What a beautiful girl! Actually, they both are. I imagine they're besieged by any number of suitable princes."

"But none that either of them wants," he quipped.

He slowed down as the road curved around. The one-story chalet appeared nestled in the trees. "We're here, Francesca. I'm sure Artur can't wait to be let out. I'll go first and unlock the door. After you run in, I'll bring the dog and the groceries."

Francesca sat there in shock that the Prince had confided such private things to her. His ability to open up to her touched her to the depth of her soul.

He'd said they were coming to his little ski hideaway, but it was surrounded by pines and turned out to be an elegant Swiss mountain home with a vaulted ceiling, stone fireplace, two bedrooms with en suite bathrooms, a loft, dining area and a kitchen with every amenity. Hardwood floors were covered with area rugs. Francesca could live here forever in this paradise and wanted to explore. But Artur needed to go outside.

She attached his leash and walked him under a tree for some protection from the rain. Before coming with the Prince, she'd made a bed in the crate so her dog had a place to sleep near her. When she took him back inside, he'd put the crate near the fireplace with the door open. He'd also put out food and water bowls in the kitchen. Her dog darted for them. Artur had to be as wildly happy as she was to be here.

"Why don't you use the guest bedroom there on the right to freshen up while I make us a fire." A stack of wood stood next to the grate hearth.

She smiled. "When you mentioned a hideaway, I imagined a cot in a one-room cabin with a leaky roof and an outhouse in back."

Deep rich male laughter poured out of him. "My mother wouldn't have allowed it. Nothing was too good for her son. She makes certain it stays clean."

"Well, you can tell her for me, I'm *glad*." His chuckles followed her as she went in the bedroom with her bag. Before using the bathroom, she walked over to the window. The cloudburst had passed over. By afternoon they'd be able to go for a walk. She felt like she'd arrived in heaven.

A fire blazed as she went back to the living room. She noticed that Artur was following him while he laid out a feast of pasta on the dining room table. "I can see my dog would rather live with you."

He lifted his dark head. "Then all I have to do is win *you* around and we'll all be happy."

Her breath caught at his remark. She wouldn't be here with him if she didn't want it far too much. "What can I do to help, Your Highness?"

A frown appeared. "The first thing I'd like you to do is call me Vincenzo."

Whoa.

"The 'Your Highness' business has gone on far too long."

She shivered in reaction.

"Why don't you get some wineglasses out of that cupboard and we'll eat. I don't know about you, but I'm famished."

"I am too."

In another minute they sat down at the table. He poured the wine. Everything about him appealed to her. When those brilliant blue eyes focused on her, she trembled inwardly from their fire. They began to eat.

"Deli food never tasted better," she commented in order to break the spell he'd cast on her.

"It beats my cooking," he quipped.

"And mine."

His gaze impaled her. "It has to be obvious to you by now that I want to get to know you better. I'm sorry if it feels like I've been hounding you. Forgive me. When you said you didn't feel right about doing the video, I should have accepted your decision as final and left you alone."

Francesca couldn't take this any longer. "I'm glad you didn't," she admitted in a shaky voice. "I really do want to participate in the project, but you're not just anyone. I've had a talk with my brother about you be-cause…because you're a prince."

"And?" His eyes smiled. He was irresistible.

"He told me I was making a mountain out of a mole-hill."

More laughter poured out of him. "I've been called many things, but never that."

"Rolf believes in going with the flow."

"He sounds like my kind of man. I'm glad you lis-tened to him, and your honesty disarms me. After I brought Karl into the clinic and met you, I talked with my sister where you're concerned."

She swallowed hard. "What advice did she have for *you*?"

"She didn't, because she knows that with my bro-ken engagement behind me, I will make my own deci-sions about the rest of my life from here on out. *You* are one of them, yet I don't even know your first name."

Uh-oh. "It's Francesca."

"*The free one* in Latin. Beautiful. With your frank personality, it suits you more than you know."

She was starting to feel ill.

"I find I can't stay away from you, Francesca. Does that frighten you?"

Couldn't he hear her heart racing? "Yes."

"What can I do to make you feel more comfort-able?"

Francesca looked away. "You can't."

He drank some wine, then put down his glass. "That's a word I don't recognize. I believe in my gut there *is* an us and I believe you know it too. Give me a specific I can live with, and I won't ever bother you again."

She drew in a quick breath. "If I tell you the reason, you're going to blame Daniel. I don't want to ruin your relationship with him. He thinks the world of you."

Vincenzo was totally intrigued. "And you. Otherwise he wouldn't have hired you or agreed for you to help with the video. What does Daniel have to do with your unwillingness to go out with me?"

"When I explain, I realize you're not going to want to have anything to do with me. But will you promise not to blame him?"

The depth of her anxiety spoke to him. "I swear it."

She clutched her hands beneath the table. "Since joining the clinic, I've gone by the name Dr. Linard. In truth, my birth name is… Francesca Giordano Visconti."

CHAPTER SEVEN

THE EARTH STOOD STILL for a second. "As in—"

"Princess Valentina Visconti," Francesca clarified for him.

Vincenzo's thoughts reeled. "How close a relationship?"

"Your former fiancée is my first cousin. Our Visconti fathers are estranged brothers."

The revelation stunned him. Both women were so different physically and emotionally, he would never have guessed that such a blood tie existed. He sucked in his breath. "Tell me more."

"My father, the former Prince Niccolo Visconti, fell in love with Greta Giordano, a commoner. Naturally it created a scandal because no Visconti had ever married a commoner before. Surely you know all about that history from Valentina. He made the decision to renounce his title and broke with the family. They moved to Bern where they married. He had business contacts there and started a packaging company."

He nodded. "When I first heard the story, I thought your father sounded like a man after my own heart."

"He's wonderful. In time, my brother Rolf and I were born and raised there. Neither of us has ever met the other side of the Visconti family. I've only seen pictures of Valentina on the news. There's been nothing between our families, but when I applied to Daniel's clinic which is in your territory, I had to be honest with him from the very start."

"I can see where this is heading. Go on. I want to hear everything."

She sat back in the chair. "During my interview, I had to explain the situation to him concerning the hostile history between the Baldasseri and Visconti families, and my relationship to Valentina. That's when he told me he was *your* vet."

Vincenzo smiled. "Quite a coincidence. We go back a long way and he knows a lot about my history."

"I couldn't believe he knew you so personally. I thought of course he'd turn me down for the position. Instead, he said he wanted to hire me. After he spoke to a government regulator, a waiver was signed so I could use any name I wanted. That way there would never be a connection. My brother and I came up with the Romansh name Linard. When you walked in the clinic with Karl the first time, my greatest fear was realized and I almost fainted."

"Meeting you turned out to be the greatest day of my life."

Her breath caught. "Don't say that—"

"Even if it's true?"

"But I've been living a lie. We can't see each other anymore, Vincenzo—" she cried. "You've just come out of an engagement to my cousin."

"A broken one that was arranged by both our families, not by *me* or Valentina."

Her head reared. "You're saying—"

"I'm saying exactly what you *know* I meant. Valentina and I were forced to meet only a few days before the engagement happened. Our families met at a regatta on Lake Garda where it was made official. Love had nothing to do with any of it.

"We were both guilted into making a commitment by our parents. We never slept together or came close. That was a commitment I made to my dying father. To Valentina's credit, she had the honesty to break it off while I've been trying to find a way for us to get out of it. Now we're both free and I've never been more relieved."

"Daniel told me how happy you were."

"He knows me very well. He also realizes that neither you or I could help that we've met each other, Francesca. You think I don't understand why you waited this long to tell me? I get it. Just remember that one day soon Valentina will be betrothed to someone else and none of this will matter anyway. In the meantime, it shouldn't stop us from enjoying a moment together here and there."

She shook her blond head. "It won't be here and there, Vincenzo, and you know it!" He watched the color flood into her cheeks. "I'm terrified to consider a relationship with you no matter how short-term."

"Why short-term?"

"Once word gets out about us and my true identity, it will bring grief to all the families, especially your mother. You said she cares for Valentina."

"That will fade with time, and we'll be discreet. Unless…" a dark brow lifted, "you've already had enough of my company."

"I wouldn't be here with you right now if that were the case."

"Grazie al cielo."

"Vincenzo, we need to use our heads." Staring straight into his eyes she said, "I don't want to see you after today."

"You're lying. I can tell by that nerve throbbing at the base of your tender throat."

She moaned. "Don't say anything else. You're not an ordinary man."

"But I am."

"No. You live in a different world, the same one my father left. You know I've enjoyed being with you to say goodbye to Karl. I feel honored that you would have allowed me to take care of him when I'm aware of your relationship with Daniel over the years. I'll make that video next month, but that's all there can be."

"I don't accept that. We feel an attraction that isn't going away."

"Even if you speak the truth, we can't act on it. Think about your mother."

He sat forward. "What's your greatest fear, Francesca?"

He heard her sharp intake of breath. "My father gave up one life to marry my mother and move away for good. I don't want my actions to create a new crisis for them. What's yours?"

Vincenzo finished off another helping of pasta and put his fork down. "That you're too concerned over my mother's attachment to Valentina to give us a chance."

"It's more than that. I'm her cousin. That fact alone will bring terrible pain to your mom."

"I've already accomplished that feat by not fighting for Valentina. I'll warn you now that I have no intention of this being our last day together, and I'm not talking about making the Biosphere Reserve video."

"But Vincenzo—" she blurted, "to go on seeing each other would be playing with fire."

"I'm more interested in the fire we feel when we're together," he countered. "It happened that first day. What we need is more time together, though no amount of trying to assuage our longing for each other will be enough for me."

Our longing? Vincenzo had just identified what was wrong with her. Francesca couldn't stay still and got up from the table. Artur followed her over to the fireplace. She hugged her arms to her chest and stared into the flames. Soon another pair of arms slid around her from behind.

Vincenzo pulled her against his tall, hard body and rubbed his cheek against hers. "I've been aching to do this since I discovered you at the clinic desk."

She'd been aching for it too. "Vincenzo," she moaned his name.

"Do you know at that moment my heart kicked against my chest? Who was this exquisite woman I wanted to take home with me? Lo and behold she turned out to be everything I ever wanted in a woman. What was more, she knew exactly what to do for my dog, enamoring him and me. I need to be closer to you, Francesca."

In the next instant he eased her around and his head descended. When his mouth covered hers, every sense sprang to life. The taste and feel of him thrilled her so much she found herself giving him kiss for hungry kiss.

Not until later would she realize how on fire she'd been for him and should have stopped what was happening. But she was in the moment right now and never wanted this ecstasy to end. Time passed as they clung, trying to get closer. Only Artur's barking could bring her out of her euphoria. She pulled away from Vincenzo in time to scoop up her dog.

"Did you feel ignored?" She kissed the top of his head and put him in his crate.

Vincenzo reached for her hand. "We're going to have to train him."

Her face felt hot as she looked up at him. His virile male beauty made her legs go weak. "My dog is smarter than I thought. He knew I was in trouble."

One corner of Vincenzo's compelling mouth lifted. "Your admission makes it easier for me to talk to you about us. Don't you dare say there is no us. At this juncture we both know better."

"I'd be a fool if I pretended otherwise." She moved to the couch and sat down. "But we need to be careful."

"So far I think we have been." He kissed her again and once more the world wheeled away to a place where only the two of them existed. By the time he relinquished her mouth and she came back to her senses, the sun had been out for a long time. She glanced down at the crate. "I'm afraid Artur gave up on us."

Their eyes met. "But you were right. He *is* a very intelligent dog. Let's find his leash and take him outside. We'll see if he looks for corncrakes the way Karl always did."

The three of them left the chalet and walked past the

pines to a high meadow filled with blue gentians and yellow buttercups. Thrusting mountain tops formed the backdrop. They took a long hike, stopping every few steps to kiss because they couldn't stay away from each other. Artur scrambled around enchanted, mirroring Francesca's mood.

"The problem now is, I want to keep you here with me, Francesca. But I don't want you to think I'm trying to take advantage of you—therefore, I'm going to drive you home."

"You're asking me to leave paradise."

"Didn't you know that's the reason why?" He kissed her fiercely. "Tomorrow's Sunday. I'll pick you up and we'll go on a picnic with Artur in the woods near the timber office. I know where you spend your working days. Now I want you to see where I spend mine. No one will be around but the night watchmen. That should be careful enough for you."

Vincenzo drove her back to her apartment. The only reason he could leave Francesca was because he'd be spending the day with her tomorrow. After saying good-night to the dog, he drove home. Intent on avoiding his mother who would ask too many questions, Vincenzo escaped to his suite in the other part of the palace.

Five minutes later he heard Bella's familiar knock on the door and he rushed to open it. "At last, you're home."

His beautiful, dark blond sister hugged him hard and they sat down together on the couch. "You don't need to say another word, brother dear. Mother is hopeless where you're concerned, but it's obvious that getting unengaged to Valentina has done wonders for you. There's a light in your eyes I've never seen before. So now I want the whole truth. What's really going on with you? I won't go away until you tell me."

Bella's return from vacation had been the medicine he'd needed and he unloaded on her. Those violet eyes of hers turned to a deeper tone as the revelation about Francesca's birth name and the story of her side of the Visconti family sank in.

He got up from the sofa and paced. "She's fighting me on this, Bella."

"Of course. That's because when word gets out, it'll create headlines across Europe. I can see them now, even though they won't be the truth—*Former Crown Prince Vincenzo Baldasseri of the royal family of San Vitano jilts Princess Valentina Visconti of Milano to take up with her estranged cousin Francesca Visconti, formerly of the House of Visconti.*"

Vincenzo grimaced. "The scenario is made for the media to plaster all over the world. Would you believe Francesca is worried about Mamma and her feelings for Valentina?"

"She sounds like a very nice person."

"Francesca is a lot more than that."

"She's right to be concerned. When our mother hears you've been seeing Valentina's cousin, she's going to explode."

"I'm not telling her yet. I need more time with Francesca first. Tomorrow I'm spending the day with her where we'll be alone."

"I can tell you've fallen hard, and there'll be no way she can resist you. I'm so happy for you. Considering she's a vet, her choice of dog tells you all you need to know about her feelings. Do you know when you showed me the photo of Artur on your phone, I thought I was looking at Karl. I miss him horribly."

"So do I," he murmured.

"You're going to have to find a creative way to convince her you're meant to be together."

"Thank heaven you understand. I want you to meet her and I'll arrange something. It'll have to be in private."

She got up from the couch. "Just let me know and I'll be there. Now I'll run to say good-night to the grandparents. Before I leave, I wondered if you've talked to Luca lately."

"Yes. He hasn't met anyone else yet."

A flushed Bella swept over to give him a kiss on the cheek. "Love you."

Early the next morning Vincenzo took off for Zernez. He stopped at a store for a picnic basket, then drove to the deli and filled it with food. Few clouds remained from yesterday's storm, increasing his joie de vivre.

When he pulled up to her apartment, she came hurrying down the stairs carrying the dog's crate and a bag. She wore a summery, short-sleeved print blouse and denims. The mold of her beautiful figure always took his breath.

He jumped out to put the dog and bag in the backseat. Before helping her in, he caught her to him and kissed her, unable to resist. Her flowery fragrance intoxicated him.

Artur made yapping sounds at being ignored, but they were both dying for each other. After Vincenzo started the engine, he reached back and slid a piece of jerky through the bars. "There you go, buddy."

Francesca smiled. "No wonder Karl loved you so much. I'm afraid maybe all this is a dream and I'm going to wake up to reality."

"We're both in the same dream, so if we wake up, we'll be together no matter where we are."

He drove them to the Baldasseri Timber Company outside Scuol. Located in the forest, the whole plant with its separate buildings could have taken up four city blocks. Beyond the structures lay a sea of trucks.

"Vincenzo—I had no idea of its massive size."

"This, along with the gold mine Rini heads, helps keep the Baldasseri family afloat. I thought you should see where I spend the bulk of my time."

He pulled up in front of the main entrance and turned off the engine. "Why don't I show you my office, then we'll drive to the area where Artur can get out and explore. We'll tie the dog's leash to this tree while we're inside."

"Perfect."

Several security men nodded to them as Vincenzo ushered her inside the foyer and led her down a hall past his assistant's office to his inner sanctum. The room contained one window behind his desk. There were a few chairs and a small table. What caught her gaze was the myriad of huge charts hanging on three immense walls and she let out a surprised gasp.

He slid his arms around her waist from behind. "This isn't like a normal office. I like to see what our business is doing. It's vital I keep my finger on all the areas where we plant and harvest trees. My working day consists of graphing the progress as the reports pour in. Each daily report reveals problems that need to be solved. This other chart displays my ideas for expansion. Little by little the business is growing."

"That's marvelous. I had no idea you were such a visual man. These charts are amazing! Another time and I want to study each one."

He turned her around, staring into her eyes. "I'm glad you said that because I want to take you somewhere totally private where I can study *you*."

Everything he said or did made her tremble with desire. "When did you start working here?"

"My father brought me here as a little boy. I learned all about the trees. He would test me. I had to name each kind and their best uses."

She grinned. "Let's see how good you are. What are they?"

His fantastic blue eyes ignited in challenge. "At four years of age I memorized them by their first letter in the alphabet—*A*, *B*, *F*, *L*, *M*, *O*, *P*, *S*."

She chuckled. "What do they stand for?"

"Ash, beech, fir, larch, maple, oak, pine and spruce. There are others, of course."

"Name one."

"The Swiss stone pine. Some call it the *Arolla*, known for its fragrance and ability to survive the winter."

"What tree is the most prolific?" she fired.

"The spruce, if we're talking the Engadin."

"It's apparent you were a brilliant student."

He kissed her mouth. "I knew after I met you that you're a woman with an exceptionally inquiring mind. It's just one of the reasons why I haven't been able to stay away from you."

Warmth spread through her body. She left his arms and walked over to one of the charts, astounded by the information. "So you work on these every day with your own set of hieroglyphs. Do I need a Rosetta stone to translate them?"

Vincenzo chuckled. "Probably something more complicated."

"That means your work would be difficult to decode. Can your assistant decipher them?"

"Most of the time."

"You're a genius! I'd like to learn."

"Come on, Dr. Linard. Let's leave the lab work for another time." He walked over and put his arm around her shoulders. "Artur must be wondering why we've abandoned him."

Together they left the building. The dog heard them coming and started yapping before they put him back inside the car. Francesca put her hand back on the cage. "I know you were worried, Artur, but we didn't leave you very long. Now we're going to have fun."

She turned to Vincenzo who drove them into the forest. "Did you bring Karl to work a lot?"

"From time to time. To solve his loneliness on weekdays, I got up for work at five and left at three. Once home, I spent hours with him and took him with me most weekends. What's so perfect with your situation is that you can keep Artur in the kennel and check on him throughout the day. It's the ideal setup for him."

"I'm really lucky in that regard."

They reached a small clearing where he parked the car. "While you take care of the dog, I'll do the rest."

She carried the crate and a bag of doggie treats to a

spot under the trees. After letting him out, she attached the long leash. "Come on, Artur. We'll go for a walk."

This glorious day in the mountains increased her feelings of joy to be out with the most wonderful man. How was it possible that she'd met anyone so perfect? Her ecstatic dog wanted to run everywhere and wore her out.

In the distance she watched Vincenzo spread a blanket near the crate. Next, he brought the picnic basket from the car. He thought of everything and always put her first.

Vincenzo grinned when Artur made a beeline for him. He'd emptied bottled water into a bowl for the dog. She fastened the leash to the trunk of a tree. He carried the water over to Artur. Her dog drank and drank.

Vincenzo chuckled. "I hope you've built up a similar appetite, Francesca. Judging by the weight of this basket, I bought more than we can consume in one sitting. It was too late last night to ask the cook to pack us a meal."

She sank down on the blanket. "I have no doubts that she's like everyone who knows you, and would do anything for you."

"Does that include *you*?"

"I agreed to do that video narration for fear I'd never see you again."

"I came close to cardiac arrest until you said yes." He pulled her next to him and began kissing her. Slowly at first, until their passion grew to a whole new level. She felt him let her go with reluctance. "I think we'd better eat," he whispered, "or I'm going to devour you instead."

"When my brother accused me of finally meeting the man who appealed to me, I couldn't deny it."

"I already like him." He reached out to trace the line of her brow. "My sister said virtually the same thing about you."

She sat up. "Our siblings know us well."

They reached in the basket for the food they wanted and began eating. Vincenzo tossed the dog a piece of ham.

Francesca eyed him playfully. "I can see why Karl was so devoted to you. Artur already worships the ground you walk on."

"Flattery will get you everywhere." Vincenzo finished his second helping of everything before centering his gaze on her. "I'm curious about something. It's clear that you're not involved with another man right now, but have you been in love before?

"I can't imagine that you haven't been besieged with men wanting a relationship with you. No man could meet you without wanting to hide you away all to himself. You saw what happened at the board meeting."

Francesca had been listening with her heart and smiled. "I had several boyfriends at the university, but no one special. I take it you're talking about real commitment."

His eyes searched hers. "I had girlfriends, but I couldn't get serious because I knew I was destined to marry a princess. What happened to Valentina and me shouldn't have happened to two people who should be free to choose for themselves."

"I agree," she said in a shaky voice.

"This last year was the unhappiest of my life. What made it worse was meeting Dr. Linard. Clear as the sun coming out, she epitomized the woman I never imagined could come into my life. She was the woman I should have been able to get to know. She touched my mind and my heart. I love the way she thinks, how she feels."

Vincenzo...

"The day Valentina broke the engagement, you could have no comprehension of the joy that brought me. All my thoughts had been centered on this other woman from the first moment we met. We've known from the beginning that something magical has happened to us. Tell me I'm wrong."

"You're not mistaken." He was saying all the thrilling things she couldn't have imagined would come out of him.

"Don't tell me it's too soon, Francesca. I don't want to live a lie while I keep planning on how to get to know you better without anyone finding out."

She averted her eyes. "Nothing could be worse than trying to hide it. We couldn't anyway." It was her heart's secret desire to be with him. "But—"

"But nothing." He reached out to cup her hot cheeks in his hands. "I have a suggestion that could take away some of your fear."

"What do you mean?"

"I'd like to meet your parents. They're the ones you don't want to hurt. I'd like to be open with them and ask their permission for me to spend time with you."

She shook her head. "I don't think they'd give it."

"Maybe not, but it would be worth a try to find out."

Before she could concentrate, his mouth sought hers again. This marvelous man wanted to see her enough that he would brave meeting her parents.

"Francesca? If they're agreeable, we could arrange to drive to Bern next weekend. It's only a three-hour drive if *I'm* at the wheel." She couldn't hide her smile. "I could meet them and we'd talk. What do you think?"

"I don't know if this will work, Vincenzo."

"Let's put it this way. If your parents are against my seeing you, we have to find out right away. Could you try to get your parents on the phone now? If all goes well for a visit next weekend, then we'll make plans."

He was right. She couldn't fault his thinking. Francesca couldn't say no to him. "All right."

Having made up her mind, she took the big step to phone them. Vincenzo took care of the dog while she pulled the cell from her pocket. "Mom?"

"Francesca, darling. I was just thinking about you. We love the pictures you sent of your dog. How's he adjusting to the kennel?"

"He likes being with the other dogs."

"What about your job? Are you happy?"

"You know I am. In fact, I'm happier than I've ever been. That's why I'm calling. I—I've met someone," she stammered. "It's a man who brought his sick dog into the clinic. We—"

A small cry of excitement came over the line, cutting her off. "Do you know how long your father and I have been waiting for that kind of news?"

"It's not *that* kind of news, Mom. I'm afraid it won't be what you want to hear."

"What do you mean?"

"We've only known each other for a short while. He

wants your permission to take me out in public. We could drive to Bern next Saturday if it's convenient."

"Since when do you need permission?"

She closed her eyes. "His name is Prince Vincenzo Baldasseri of Scuol."

The flat-out truth had to come as a huge shock. Her mother paused before venturing, "As in your cousin's former fiancé."

She swallowed hard. "Yes. Their trumped-up engagement was forced by their parents a year ago. It was never an affair of the heart for either of them. Now that it has been broken off, they both have been let out of prison. As you can imagine, he's more aware of the horrendous problems within the Visconti and Baldasseri families than anyone else alive, except you.

"In order for us to be seen together just to eat out at a restaurant, he realizes it could make the news and open up old wounds for you. But he refuses to hide in the shadows. I know he's right, even if it means we have to stop seeing each other. Because that's the kind of man he is, he won't go against your wishes. Neither will I."

More silence followed before her father joined in the conversation. "Francie?" It was the name he'd called her from childhood. "I've been listening to your conversation with your mom. I'm impressed by *this* Baldasseri. We'll be happy to meet him, but it will be better if we come to *your* apartment."

Message understood. His parents didn't need the attention. "You're right. Vincenzo is recognized everywhere."

"We'll come next Saturday and be there by lunch."

"I'll have it waiting for you. Artur will be ecstatic."

Her father chuckled. "I've loved all the names you've given your dogs, but this one kills me."

Tears filled her eyes over her parents' love and understanding. "Me too."

When she hung up, she turned to Vincenzo. "They're coming to my apartment next Saturday for lunch."

He folded her in his arms. "You have incredible parents." He kissed her hard. "With that call made, I have a plan for us. To make this real, I'm not going to try to be with you after work this next week. I'll go straight home from work each night and talk reason to my mother." Francesca's spirits sank. "But I want to see you every day for lunch."

Yes!

"When is your lunch break, Francesca?"

"There's no set time."

"Can you make one for us this next week?"

She nodded. "Let's say twelve thirty to one thirty."

He brushed his lips against hers. "I'm already wishing for tomorrow to come. Now I'd better get you home."

It was hard to leave. "We must drive your security men crazy driving all over the place."

"I try to keep them from being bored." He grasped her hand. "I'm relieved your parents are coming. All that's left is to gain their permission for us to be together, but I'm afraid we've put the proverbial cart before the horse."

"My father would laugh at that particular metaphor."

"I hope he's still laughing after we meet."

She prayed for that too. Her parents were marvelous,

reasonable people, but this situation was unlike any story you could think up in your wildest imagination.

Once they reached the apartment, he helped her up the stairs with the crate and gave her another kiss. "I'll see you tomorrow. Miss me."

He had no idea.

CHAPTER EIGHT

WHEN VINCENZO REACHED the palace, he parked his car in a hidden area around the rear near a private entrance only he used. Filled with an excitement he'd never known, he raced up the back stairway to his suite so he wouldn't be detected.

Bella came to his room right after and shut the door. She leaned against it, putting a finger to her lips. They stared at each other. In a low voice she said, "Princess Valentina arrived this afternoon by helicopter and has been waiting for you. I tried to warn you."

His dark head reared. "Before I left yesterday, I sent Mother a message that I had business and would be gone for the weekend. Are you saying that Valentina just showed up?"

"Mother invited her and she's staying the night because she doesn't want your engagement called off."

"But Valentina *did*. Something's not right, Bella."

"I agree. But you know Mamma. She's working on a plan that will get Valentina to change her mind and appease Stefano so the marriage goes forward. To make up for the fact that you're no longer the Crown Prince, she's going to give you and Valentina her royal

Sardinian inheritance from the sheep-farming industry. It should work."

"That inheritance still doesn't touch our timber assets and won't satisfy Stefano. Valentina won't buy it
either." In record time he packed a bag. "Does she have
any idea I'm here?"

"No."

"Did anyone see you just now?"

"I passed one of the maids in the hall."

"We can't worry about that now." Vincenzo shut the
lid. "I'm leaving and won't be back until after work
tomorrow." He rushed toward her and gave her a kiss
on the cheek. "You're an angel to run interference.
I'll fill you in later tonight. Expect a phone call after
you go to bed."

Before another second passed, he slipped out of the
palace and down the private stairway. Only his body-
guards trailing him would know where he was headed.
Their unquestioned loyalty would keep his secret safe.
He couldn't say as much for the staff.

Once he arrived at the chalet, he got ready for bed
and phoned Bella. After telling her about his plans
to meet Francesca's parents next weekend, his sister
sounded overjoyed. "You can count on me to help you
in any way I can." They hung up and he lay back down.
Next weekend couldn't come soon enough for him to
meet her parents. In the meantime, he'd be able to see
her throughout the week.

At twelve thirty on Monday, he watched Francesca
leave through the back door of the clinic and hurry
to his car. His pulse always raced when he laid eyes
on her.

Vincenzo reached across the seat to open the door

for her and drove them to the park where they had privacy. He kissed her soundly before they ate the deli food he'd picked up.

When they'd finished, he said, "Francesca? I have something to tell you. Though I'd rather hold back from saying anything because I don't want to ruin our lunch, this can't wait and has to be said. I would never keep anything from you."

She turned to him. "You sound so serious."

"I wish it weren't."

"You're starting to scare me."

"I don't mean to do that. Last night I returned to the palace to grab some sleep. I entered through a doorway rarely used so no one would see me. To my shock, Bella followed me into my bedroom. She'd tried to reach me by phone, but I didn't take any calls. She told me Valentina had flown to the palace by helicopter earlier in the day and was staying overnight."

"What?"

He nodded. "It seems my mother invited her so the three of us could talk about a reconciliation."

"That means Valentina wants you back."

"I don't think so since she's the one who called off our engagement. There's some mystery here I don't understand, but I'm going to get to the bottom of it."

"Your mother wants you to marry Valentina."

He shook his head. "There's more to it than that. I told Bella I wasn't staying and left the palace the same way I came in. Last night I returned to the chalet to sleep. When I talked to my sister at midnight, she said she didn't believe anyone knew I'd even been there. She texted me this morning after Valentina left in the helicopter to let me know the coast was clear."

"What are you going to do? Are your grandparents applying pressure too?"

"No, but they try to support my mother now that my father is no longer with us."

"Your poor mother wants you to be happy."

He grasped her hand. "I've never been happier in my life. One day soon she'll understand."

"I don't know, Vincenzo. She's lost your father and now all her dreams have been shattered."

"But they aren't *my* dreams." He leaned over to kiss her once more. "Let me finish. The simple truth is, I've fallen in love with you, deeply in love. You may say it's too soon for you to know what's in your heart. Maybe knowing how I feel, you would prefer that we don't see each other again. You can cancel the plans with your parents if that's your wish. But I'm well acquainted with my feelings and can't hold back what matters to me more than anything else in the world. I love you."

He waited until her brown eyes looked into his. She breathed deeply. "Do you think I would have spent time with you from the beginning if I didn't have feelings *I* can't deny? Your honesty has forced me to reveal what's in my soul. I love you too, Vincenzo, more than I ever thought possible. I'm so in love I'm almost sick over it."

"*Francesca*—you're the woman I'll adore forever." He pulled her against him and kissed the mouth he could never get enough of. "I know this is the wrong place to pour out my heart, but I can't help it. More than ever I need to meet your parents, to know if there's hope for a future. Speaking hypothetically, how would you feel about being married to a man who runs a timber company?"

She wrapped her arms around his neck. "You already know the answer to that. I loved every minute with you yesterday, and can't wait to learn more. The real question is, how would you feel about having a vet for a wife? I'm hardly the choice for a prince."

He smoothed the hair off her forehead. "The moment I met you, thoughts of Daniel helping me with Karl left my mind. You filled my every need and Karl loved you. I knew at once that no other woman could ever satisfy me while I lived on this earth."

"*Vincenzo*... It happened that way for me too," she confessed.

"The next question is, are you happy working for Daniel?"

"Totally."

"Then our only problem would be where we live."

Her heart pounded harder. "The palace is your home."

"Do you know I lived more than four years in a private dwelling in Scuol?"

"I can understand that."

He flashed her that compelling smile. "Naturally I paid visits home, but I liked my bachelor life with Karl, and only went back to the palace to live after my father died. My mother and grandparents needed me." He cocked his dark head. "Do you love your apartment?"

"Very much."

"I like it there too. It already feels like my home away from home. Were we to marry—I'm speaking hypothetically—how would you feel if I moved in there with you where you'd be close to your work?"

She bit her lip. "But Vincenzo, you're a—"

"Don't say it." He put a finger to her lips. "Forget I'm a prince."

"I do, most of the time."

"That's good. What's even better, your apartment is only a twelve-minute drive to my work. I've timed it." She chuckled. "On weekends we could stay at the chalet, or at the palace. Whatever we feel like."

"But your family will want you to live there with them all the time."

"You're wrong. They've had no future expectations about that. If Rini hadn't recovered his memory, Valentina and I would have been forced to live at the palace in San Vitano after the marriage. My great-uncle King Leonardo wanted me near him."

She shook her head. "So much has changed."

"Since meeting you, I feel reborn." He pulled her closer. "*Ti amo*, Francesca."

"*Ti amo*, Vincenzo. That much isn't hypothetical."

Their hunger knew no boundaries. No kiss was long enough or deep enough to satisfy them, but this couldn't go on. "I need to get you back to the clinic."

"I know." She eased out of his arms and sat over on her side of the car.

He started the engine and they left the park. Her admission of love had transformed his world. "Our talk has settled many questions that have made me happy beyond belief. My biggest worry is that your parents will decide they don't want me pursuing you. If that happens—"

"Don't think that way," she broke in. "They fought against the odds to find their happiness. I have to believe they'll grant us the same chance. My worry is that your mother won't be able to accept me."

"I'm working on it." He started the car and drove

them the short distance to the clinic. It was a wrench to have to leave her arms. An hour wasn't enough time.

When he parked, she turned to him. "Come to my apartment tomorrow at twelve thirty and we'll eat there. Tonight I'll fix our lunch and have it ready."

"Have I told you before that I love the way your mind works, *bellissima*? Much as I want to, I don't dare kiss you again."

She leaned over and kissed his lips gently. "Until tomorrow."

To his relief, the rest of his work week had never been busier. Their lunch dates kept him sane, but nothing stopped him from counting the hours to see her. Each night he called to let her know of his love and what was going on.

"Is there any more news about Valentina?"

"Only that my mother is worried about her. The breakup has caused her to be distraught."

"But that makes no sense."

"No, it doesn't. My mother is begging me to make things right. She's positive that if I get back with Valentina, she'll be herself again. Mamma is in denial. I don't know what it's going to take to make her see reason, but she'll have to in time."

"I don't know."

"I *do*." He and his mother had reached an impasse. Vincenzo was living for the meeting with Francesca's parents. Everything hinged on their approval. If it was given, life was going to go in a new direction no matter what.

At ten to ten on Saturday morning, Vincenzo knocked on Francesca's apartment door. He held the sack of groceries with the ingredients they'd decided on for this important meal. Adrenaline surged through his body as he anticipated what this day would mean for the two of them.

Artur kept barking. When she opened the door, he put down the sack and reached for her. "You look sensational and smell divine. I like your outfit," he murmured, eyeing the dark skinny denims and attractive hoodie.

The soft, pale green set off her coloring. Her brown eyes looked alive as they studied his blue pullover and cargo pants. The dog kept running around his feet, finally breaking the trance that held them both.

"Artur—" she called to him so Vincenzo could walk inside with the sack. He lowered it on the kitchen counter, then hunkered down to play with the dog. He'd missed him like crazy. The building attachment warmed his heart. But there was another attachment so strong, it propelled him to Francesca's side. She'd started emptying the sack.

He slid his arms around her and pulled her against him. "Good morning, Dr. Linard. Our daily lunch hours weren't nearly enough to satisfy me." In the next breath he covered her mouth with his own. Like flame to kindling they lost track of time pouring out their hungry need for each other. The taste of her, the way she felt in his arms filled his heart and drove every other thought from his mind.

"*Ti adoro*, Francesca," he cried against her lips.

"*Ti amo anch'io*," she answered. Her confession of love thrilled him in every fiber of his being. They clung until she had the presence of mind to ease out of his arms. "If I don't get started on this lunch, there won't be one."

They'd planned cheese fondue with French bread and Riesling wine. Vincenzo got busy helping her. While he set the table he said, "This is the most important meeting of the century. I want your parents' blessing more than anything I've ever wanted in my life."

She finished grating the cheese. "So do I. But what if they don't give it?"

"Do you honestly think they won't?"

"I—I don't know…" Her voice faltered. "This is one situation none of us could have imagined."

He put the wineglasses on the table. "In that case, how do you feel about a quick elopement? That would solve everything. We'd be total outcasts and start a new life where we're unknown. You could set up a vet practice and I would help you."

A smile broke out on her beautiful face. "I'd love it. But you're teasing of course."

This woman had been made for him. "I've never been more serious, Francesca."

"I know you are. That's why what you've said is so scary." Her comment coincided with the sound of footsteps outside the door, followed by a familiar knock. Artur barked.

Vincenzo's gaze flew to hers. "This is it."

"I'll let them in." She washed her hands and hurried over to let her parents inside.

As Vincenzo put bread and fondue forks on the table, he watched the loving affection the three of them had for each other. Francesca resembled both parents. She'd inherited her mother's attractive looks and her father's smile.

"Mom? Dad? I'd like you to meet Prince Vincenzo Baldasseri."

"Your Highness," they said in unison.

Vincenzo stepped forward to shake their hands. "Call me Vince."

"If you'll call me Niccolo."

Vincenzo had already been prepared to like him. The Visconti brothers shared a resemblance in their dark coloring and firm body builds. But Francesca's father had softer features and laugh lines not apparent in Stefano Visconti.

Francesca hugged her mother's waist. "Vincenzo, this is my mother, Greta."

"Signora Visconti. I've been waiting anxiously for this day."

"I'm Greta, and I've been eager to meet you too, Prince Vincenzo."

He was charmed by her. "Please let me be Vince to the two of you. Francesca is definitely your daughter. Among other lovely traits, she has your blond hair and warm brown eyes."

"They trapped me the first time we met," her father volunteered.

Yup. Vincenzo knew the feeling.

"You two have had a long drive," Francesca broke in. "Why don't you freshen up in the guest bedroom and bathroom down the hall while I put the dog in his crate. Otherwise, he won't leave us alone. Then we'll enjoy some fondue while we talk."

Francesca's parents were so wonderful and made Vincenzo feel so comfortable, she could have cried out for joy. The four of them ate fondue and drank their wine while she told them how Karl had brought her and Vincenzo together.

"After I put him down, we drove to the mountains where he used to play. I found myself wanting a dog just like him and fell in love with Artur. One thing led to another, and here we are." She darted Vincenzo a glance. "The dog is already attached to him."

Vincenzo sat back in the chair. "As the two of you are aware, I've become attached to your daughter. The bizarre coincidence that she's a Visconti couldn't have shocked me more. She was Dr. Linard to me."

Her mother nodded. "No one could question the innocent circumstances under which you met."

"The truth is, from the moment she greeted me, the instant attraction I felt for her was like nothing I've ever experienced in life and has only grown stronger. What made it so shocking was that I was still engaged to Valentina."

Her father shook his head. "When did your engagement come to an end?"

"A few days after I took Karl to the clinic. Later I received a call from my cousin Rinieri. He told me he'd recovered from his amnesia and was relieving me of the duty of Crown Prince. I'd never been so happy with the news that I wouldn't have to be King one day. A few days later Valentina broke our engagement. It has upset my mother."

"Of course. I've been through a traumatic experience in my own family," her father revealed. "When they couldn't be happy for me and Greta, we left Milano for good."

"Francesca told me." Vincenzo leaned forward. "I explained to her that my engagement to Valentina had been arranged by both families. The truth is, I was never in love with her. By the time I'd heard from Rini, I'd already met Francesca and understood what it meant to find that perfect someone you knew could fill your whole life. That's why I asked her if I could meet with you. I'd like your blessing to go on seeing her."

She felt her father's eyes on her. "Do you feel the same way?"

"Yes. It's why I called you."

"Even knowing all the repercussions that are going to happen?" This from her mother.

"Yes. But I'm afraid this could hurt the two of you, which is the last thing we want."

Her father reached for her mother's hand. "We've already been through our Gethsemane. Don't worry about us."

Vincenzo finished his wine. "I'm afraid there already is a problem that might influence how you feel about Francesca and me."

"Go on," her father prodded him.

"My sister told me that my mother invited Valentina to stay at the palace a week ago to try and get the two of us back together. I was away spending time with your daughter and didn't know anything about it.

"My mother wants to affect a reconciliation of which I want no part. I knew I had to meet with the two of you and let you know my intentions before I took Francesca to meet my mother and grandparents. The sooner they understand the situation, the better. Today, if it were possible, but that's asking a lot. Maybe too much."

A smile lit up her father's face and eyes. "Nonsense, Vince. I admire you for doing the honorable thing and putting Francesca first. You're wise to do this right away. You have our backing."

"Dad—" Francesca cried for joy.

Vincenzo got to his feet. "That means more to me than you will ever know."

Her mother grabbed Francesca's hand. "I couldn't be happier for both of you, and I have an idea. If you two want to leave for the palace now to state your case, your father and I will tend Artur and stay the night."

Francesca looked at Vincenzo whose indigo blue eyes blazed with light. His were asking if she wanted to accept her parents' offer. Their approval meant everything. "Vincenzo? If we go, you'll need to inform your mother that we're coming."

"I'll do it now."

"Use my bedroom. While you do that, I'll take out the dog."

"And *I* will do the dishes," her mother piped up.

Her father got up first. "I'll clear the table."

Out of the corner of her eye she saw Vincenzo shake her father's hand. But her parent had other ideas and gave him a hug. Nothing could have thrilled her more. She put the leash on the dog and took him out. "I promise you're going to love my parents, Artur."

A half hour later Francesca had changed to a light blue summer suit and they headed for Scuol. "You look fantastic." Vincenzo grasped her hand and never let it go during the short trip. "Meeting your parents has explained you as nothing else ever could. They're beyond remarkable."

"I'm glad you like them. They obviously approve of you."

"My prayers have been answered, but the meeting

with my family won't resemble what just happened with your parents."

"I'll be fine because I know my folks are behind us. Does your family know what this is all about?"

"No. I simply told my mother I needed to meet with the three of them right away and that I was bringing someone important with me."

"Any more word of Valentina?"

"No. According to Bella there have been phone calls."

"Dare I ask about that?"

"I didn't give Mamma a chance to talk, only that I would be home shortly."

After his mother thought she could reconcile her son and Valentina, she would go into shock when she met Francesca. So deep were her thoughts, she didn't realize they'd arrived at the palace until he'd parked his car in the rear and shut off the engine.

"Before we go in, I need this." He leaned over and kissed her with a thoroughness that left them both shaken.

"Just follow my lead." He got out of the car and walked around to help her. "We'll go up the back stairway to the drawing room on the second floor. My grandfather will be in his wheelchair."

He squeezed her waist as they walked past several guards and climbed the stairs of the elegant palace. When they reached the drawing room, he led her to his mother, then his grandparents where they were introduced to her. She didn't see his sister.

From his grandfather, who had lost most of his hair, she could tell from his long legs he was a tall man. Through the bone structure of his attractive features, Vincenzo got the fabulous looks of his Baldasseri genes. She also saw facial traits from his striking mother with her auburn hair. His grandmother was a lovely, older white-haired woman.

Vincenzo guided her to a love seat where they sat down. He clung to her hand. "Thank you for being willing to meet with me today because I have an announcement to make." All eyes focused on him with guarded anxiety.

"In the last month, a number of changes have happened in my life that have transformed me. First came the news that I'm no longer the Crown Prince of San Vitano. Following that came my broken engagement. Thirdly, and the most important one, I met the woman with whom I've fallen in love."

Gasps came out of the women. Francesca noticed his grandfather exhibited no reaction.

"I introduced her to you under her professional name Dr. Francesca Linard, a vet from the Zoller Veterinary Clinic in Zernez. She was the one who treated Karl and put him to sleep. What you don't know is that I soon learned her birth name is Francesca Giordano Visconti, daughter of Greta and Niccolo Visconti."

Vincenzo's mother got to her feet. *"Visconti?"*

Francesca's heart began to palpitate hard.

"That's right, Mamma. As I'm sure Valentina would have told you, there was a falling out in the Visconti household years ago. Prince Niccolo married a commoner and they moved to Bern, Switzerland. He rescinded his title and severed all ties with the royal House of Visconti. Later on, Francesca and her brother Rolf were born. She and Valentina are first cousins, but they've never met."

"You mean to tell me you're involved with Valentina's cousin? The woman you were engaged to for the last year?" His mother's shock and pain pierced Francesca's heart.

Vincenzo's blue eyes fell on Francesca. "For now and always."

Oh, Vincenzo... I love you so much.

"I haven't officially proposed yet, or given her a ring, Mamma. Only today did I meet her mother and father and ask their permission to get to know her better. Now that I have it, I've come to my family to ask for yours."

His grandfather shook his head. "You can't see her again, Vincenzo."

Francesca thought she'd been ready for his reaction, but it still hurt like a stab in the heart.

"I'm sorry you feel that way, Nonno, but my heart has dictated otherwise."

"There's another reason besides your heart that forbids it. This is a discussion you must have with your mother." He started to wheel himself out of the room. His wife got up and helped him. When they'd left the drawing room, his mother sat back down with her hands clasped.

"What other reason was Nonno talking about, Mamma?"

"It would be better if you and I were alone, my son."

Vincenzo squeezed the hand he'd been holding. "Francesca and I are together in everything."

His mother sat straighter. "Very well. Valentina flew to the palace a week ago and stayed overnight."

"Bella told me."

"Bella doesn't know everything."

"Then *you* tell me."

"Valentina is pregnant with your child. She just had it verified with her doctor. That's why she flew here, to tell you in person. More than ever it's imperative the two of you arrange to be married as soon as possible."

"I'm afraid it won't be possible. I was never in love with her and it's not my child. We never slept together."

Vincenzo had told her as much. The news had meant everything to Francesca. She held her breath waiting for his mother's response.

"Valentina wouldn't lie to me."

In the next instance Vincenzo got to his feet. "*I've* never lied to you. How far along is she?"

His mother lowered her head. "She said two months."

"Did she tell you all this in front of my grandparents?"

"Of course."

He shifted his weight. "Since I brought Francesca to the palace to meet my family, we'll discuss Valentina's dilemma later. Under the circumstances, I'll drive her back to Zernez. When I return later, I'll say good-night to you and the grandparents."

Francesca groaned to see his mother so devastated. She didn't know that her son had been telling the truth.

CHAPTER NINE

VINCENZO REACHED FOR Francesca's hand and ushered her out of the drawing room. They didn't speak going down the stairs and out the doors of the palace. Before he helped her in the car, he pulled her against him and rocked her in his arms. "I'm so sorry for what happened. This wasn't the way this day was supposed to end."

She threw her arms around his neck, aching over the unexpected news that had complicated his life and hers. "Don't worry about me. It's your mother's disappointment I'm feeling."

"Thank you for believing me, and being so sweet about my mother. Unfortunately Valentina couldn't have done anything to raise Mamma's hopes more than to tell her she was pregnant. If it's true, then this situation is proof that her arranged engagement didn't work. But if she isn't pregnant, then this is a ruse perpetrated by Stefano to get what he wants."

"Either way it's tragic, Vincenzo." She was heartsick.

He nodded. "Valentina pretended to be happy with our betrothal in front of the family, but this announcement is about to turn her life into a nightmare." He gave Francesca a swift kiss. "Come on. Let's get you home."

Back in the car, they headed for Zernez. "What are you going to do, Vincenzo?"

"I'm flying to Milano in the morning and confront Valentina. I don't know if she's pregnant or not. Before I met her, I heard she liked to party and had various boyfriends. Though she denied she was involved with anyone when we met, I didn't believe it. If she's pregnant, there is someone else of course."

"But not the man her family had picked out for her," Francesca murmured.

"She could be pregnant and two months along. But thanks to modern medicine, a DNA test can be done at nine weeks to prove paternity without injuring her or the baby. I'll go to her doctor with her and we'll soon learn the truth."

Francesca shivered. "What if she refuses?"

"In that case I'll go to her father and insist. The sooner she gets the test that proves I'm not responsible, the sooner she can sort out her life."

"Do you think her father will cooperate?"

"I doubt it. He's a very difficult man." Vincenzo turned his head to glance at her. "First I'll attempt to reason with Valentina."

"In her state, I don't know if that's possible."

"Maybe not," he said, making a turn near her apartment. "Why don't we discuss it with your parents? No one knows Valentina's father better than your own father. Perhaps he can shed some words of wisdom."

"My parents won't welcome this news."

"Would you rather I didn't tell them what happened?"

She shook her head. "The truth has to come out."

Vincenzo parked the car and turned, pulling her

against him. "Don't you know I'd give anything to spare you all this?"

"I feel the same way about you. We'll get through it."

"Yes, we will, my love." He kissed her with exquisite tenderness before they went up to the apartment. Before they reached the door, she could hear Artur barking.

"Now I know I'm home," she whispered against his lips before the door opened.

"Whoops." Her mother's small cry brought a smile to Francesca. "Come on in, you two."

They moved inside while the dog jumped up and down around them. Francesca picked him up and sat down on the couch, holding him on her lap.

Vincenzo planted himself next to her and put his arm around her shoulders.

Her mum and dad sat on the stools at the island in the kitchen drinking coffee. "Welcome back. You're home earlier than we expected, Francie."

"We had an unexpected evening, Dad."

"What happened?"

Vincenzo sat forward with his hands clasped between his knees. "After introducing Francesca to my grandparents and mother, she greeted us with news we hadn't anticipated." In the next breath he explained that Valentina had flown to the palace and told the family she was pregnant with Vincenzo's child. "Both families want the marriage to take place as soon as possible."

The stunned look on her parents' faces brought him to his feet. "I told them the baby wasn't mine. I'm flying to Milano Monday morning to confront

Valentina and her parents. My mother says she's two months along. Thanks to modern medicine, a test can be done. Then the truth of paternity will be known for all to see."

Francesca's mom slid off the stool. "I promise that her family will fight you before you can demand she get that test."

At this point Francesca got up from the couch and lowered the dog to the floor. "We're ready. Do you have any advice that could help?"

She watched her father walk over to Vincenzo with a gleam in his eyes. "Indeed, I do. I want you to inform the brother I haven't seen for years that you and my daughter are involved. Tell him *I* insist on the DNA test."

"Thank you, Niccolo. Good night, Greta." The two men shook hands. "I need to leave now. Francesca? Will you come out to the car with me?"

She followed him outside. He had no words and simply crushed her in his arms. "I'll phone you tomorrow. *Sogni d'oro.*"

She would need sweet dreams.

Monday morning the helicopter landed behind the Visconti palazzo. Vincenzo told the pilot to stay put. He wouldn't be here long.

Valentina, dressed in a pink suit and pearls, came running toward him with her dark hair flouncing about her shoulders. She was taller than Francesca. He could find nothing about her that reminded him of the woman he loved. She greeted him with a kiss on his cheek. "Thank you for coming so quickly."

He took an extra breath. "The second my family

gave me your news, you *knew* it would bring me as soon as I could make plans."

"It's so good to see you, Vincenzo. Won't you kiss me? Really kiss me." Her eyes beseeched him. Why? For whose benefit?

"We're no longer engaged, Valentina." He reached for her hand. "Come on. Let's go for a walk where we can talk in private. This will only take a few minutes since I have to fly back to my office ASAP."

She held back. "You can't leave! We have so much to plan. The family has arranged a special lunch for us in the small dining room upstairs. Vincenzo—" she protested in exasperation as he pulled her toward the rose garden to the east.

When he came to a bench, he put his hands on her shoulders and set her down. "I don't know whether it's your family or you who has decided that our former engagement is back on, but I'll let you know now. It will never happen."

"Even knowing I'm pregnant?"

"It's not my child, Valentina."

A look of terror filled her eyes. "No one else knows that."

Ah. She *was* pregnant!

That was all he'd needed to hear. He sat down next to her. "The truth will come out when you go to the doctor for a DNA test. Mother says you're two months along. In another few days you'll be able to have it done and name the father."

"I'll do no such thing." She jumped to her feet. "It's a dangerous procedure."

"Not true. In today's world it's safe for you and the baby."

"I absolutely refuse. You and I are going to get married." She'd dug in her heels, confirming his suspicions that her agenda had to do with her father.

Vincenzo got to his feet. "A year ago we entered into an arranged engagement. A few weeks ago, you called it off. Neither of us was in love. Proof of it is the baby you're carrying. I don't want to be unkind, but you need to marry the father of your child."

"I can't." He heard pain.

"That's between the two of you. He deserves to know you're expecting his baby. There's nothing else to discuss and I have to leave."

She cocked her head, gazing at him through narrowed lids. "I have no intention of getting that test. You and I *will* be married soon."

"Says your father? Afraid not, Valentina."

"Don't be too sure."

Vincenzo felt sorry for her, but he'd had enough. "Arrivederci, *Principessa*."

He wheeled around and walked in swift strides to the helicopter. Once strapped in the copilot's seat, he watched Valentina run toward the palazzo before she was out of sight. This morning's short visit was the last one he would ever make to the Visconti palazzo.

Once he reached the timber office, he phoned his mother and told her to expect him and Francesca that evening. Since his visit with Valentina, he had news. The three of them needed to talk.

At ten to three he was going over the latest reports at work when his assistant Fadri buzzed him. "You have a visitor, Your Highness. He doesn't have an appointment."

"Who is it?"

"Prince Stefano Visconti of Milano."

Vincenzo had wondered how long it would take Valentina's father to intervene. He'd never cared for Stefano, but at the time of the engagement, Vincenzo had been prepared to try to get along with him. The fact that he'd come in person to surprise him rather than phone him first indicated the depth of his desperation.

"Show him in, Fadri."

In a minute Valentina's father stormed in and shut the door. Vincenzo stood up. "Stefano? Come all the way in and sit down. I'll have coffee brought in for you."

"I won't be here long enough," came the wintry response. "You can't duck your responsibilities, Vincenzo. You may no longer be the Crown Prince, but we'll overlook that setback and arrange the wedding for two weeks from today."

Stefano didn't even try to hide the reason for the engagement being called off.

"I hope you mean with the man who impregnated your daughter. I wish her and your family the very best."

Anger brought red patches to the other man's cheeks. "We both know the name of that man."

"I'm afraid *I* don't. But as I told Valentina—whom I've learned is two months along—she can have a test done to prove paternity. That should still give you time to plan a wedding for her and the man she loves."

Stefano's body stiffened. "Your insolence is unconscionable. I've already given the news to the media about the wedding date for you and Valentina. By tomorrow morning it will be all over Europe."

Vincenzo sat back in his chair. "Then the Visconti

family will have another sensational story on its hands you'll have to live down."

"Another?" he asked in an acid tone.

"Have you forgotten the incident with your brother? If you recall, he left Milano and got married. You have a niece, Francesca Giordano Visconti, who happens to be Valentina's first cousin, albeit they've never met. Francesca and I met at the veterinary clinic in Zernez where she introduced herself as Dr. Linard to avoid name recognition. We've fallen in love and are seeing each other exclusively."

"I believe you've lost your mind."

"No. Talk to the owner. Dr. Zoller will verify what I've just told you. The news about me and Francesca will give the media endless joy as they exploit the ongoing saga from the illustrious Houses of Visconti and Baldasseri."

Stefano's eyes darkened in fury. "What piece of fiction is this?" he hissed.

"Ask my mother. She knows all about it. If that doesn't satisfy you, ask your brother and his wife. They'll answer any of your questions."

"I don't believe one word coming out of your mouth."

"You will if you give a false story to the newspapers about your daughter and me. It will cause another media frenzy that will rebound on you. If I were in your place, I'd go home and insist Valentina get that test done before you announce your daughter's intended marriage to the wrong man."

"Your lies won't get you out of this. Valentina foolishly broke the engagement because you neglected her, but she has since regretted that action due to her pregnancy."

"You mean due to the timber shares you've been

praying to get your hands on no matter the cost? I never neglected her and I have my pilot's logs to prove I flew to Milano for every single date made. Don't keep trying to turn this around, Stefano."

He wheeled around and opened the door. Before leaving, he yelled, "You're lying!"

"Then I suggest you phone Niccolo. What's it been? Close to thirty years without contact? He'll put you straight before it's too late."

"It's over for you! I'll take you to court and sue you for breach of contract to marry."

"I don't think so. Valentina broke our engagement."

"You broke her heart," Stefano raged.

Vincenzo shook his head. "I think you've been doing a good job of that yourself."

Stefano shook his fist at him. "You'll be sorry when I get you in court."

"It will never happen."

Valentina's father had a reputation for a white-hot temper, but he was in such a hurry to leave, he disappeared without slamming the door behind him. It would be no surprise to Vincenzo if word of his forthcoming marriage to Valentina made the evening news. By tomorrow anything could happen. He sent a text to the woman he adored.

Francesca was in the middle of an operation when she heard the ding on her phone. Half an hour later she read his text.

Bellissima? Stefano just left my office. He's on the warpath. Warn your father. I'll meet you at your apartment after work. We'll take Artur and drive to the palace to talk to my mother. I have the best news that will change everything for her and us.

Francesca jumped for joy and texted him back.

I'll let Dad know about the visit and be home by five fifteen waiting for you.

Vincenzo arrived five minutes after she got home. The second she opened the door, he swept her in his arms. Artur's barking went ignored while they kissed as if it were their last. She pressed her forehead against his. "Your news made it impossible for me to get any more work done today. I thought I would die until I was in your arms like this."

"When I got your text, I wanted to drive straight to your office," he cried, covering her with kisses, unable to stop.

"I love you so much, Vincenzo. You have no idea. We'd better go inside before everyone sees us."

"Do we really care?" One more kiss before he let her go so they could be private. She settled the dog. "Now tell me everything that happened with Valentina," she begged as he pulled her down on the couch.

"When I told her we both knew it wasn't my child, she admitted it, but she refused to get a DNA test and insists we marry. At that point I realized Stefano is driving all this. I knew there was nothing else to talk about and left. Later in the day he burst in my office."

She kissed his chin. "Valentina's father is scary. He just charged in?"

"That's his way. He said an announcement of my wedding plans to Valentina will be in the news by morning. I warned him not to do it because I wasn't the father of Valentina's child. He called me a liar. I told him to call your father for the facts. In his rage, he charged right out again."

She straightened and gazed into his incredibly blue eyes. "I doubt he's ever been challenged like this in his whole life. Poor Valentina."

"She's terrified, but after Stefano confronts your father, things will change."

"Maybe. Years ago, Dad told me Stefano was more impossible than their father and that's saying a lot."

"Let's not worry about it right now. We need to leave for the palace. I told my mother to expect us this evening. When I tell her that Valentina lied to her, it will turn things around. She'll realize I've been speaking the truth all along. It won't be long before she's crazy about you and Artur."

He started kissing her. Like déjà vu her phone rang, interrupting them. The ringing stopped, then began again. "I'd better let you get it." He stood up and helped her to her feet.

She reached for the phone on the counter. Her eyes flew to his. "It's my father." Francesca put her phone on Speaker so he could hear their conversation and greeted him. "I take it you heard from Stefano."

"After talking to my brother, it's clear he's not about to let this go and has already gone to the newspapers to spread another lie. We both know he wants to get his hands on Vincenzo's timber assets. It's clear he doesn't care whose baby it is as long as Vincenzo's mother is convinced it's his. I fear it will be a fight to the finish. I'm afraid this is up to the two of you, Francie. Be assured your mother and I will back you in anything."

"You're wonderful! But Dad—I don't want you hurt."

"Our good friends will always be our good friends no matter what happens. Need I say more?"

Francesca had broken out in tears. "I don't deserve you."

"Nonsense. If I have a concern, it's for Vincenzo's mother. Does she know the truth?"

She glanced at Vincenzo. "Yes, but she doesn't believe it yet. He and I are visiting her in a little while and will explain everything. We're committed. Vincenzo isn't anxious, Dad."

"Then all should be well in the end. Let us know what we can do to help."

"You already have. I'll call you later."

She hung up and whirled around. "What are we going to do?"

"I'm not worried."

"My concern is your mother."

He hugged her. "When she learns that Valentina told me the truth herself, she'll realize Valentina lied to her. Everything will be all right."

"I hope so. I'll take a quick shower and get dressed."

Francesca was glad she'd bought a new small-print sundress with a jacket the other day. The aqua-and-blue flowers on white had caught her eye. On impulse she bought a pair of heeled sandals in aqua.

"While you do that, I'll get Artur ready to go with us and bring his crate."

"Mamma will love him."

She smiled to herself. Maybe her dog would be the miraculous clay that won over Vincenzo's mother.

"We'll stop for some pasta in Scuol before we reach the palace."

"Perfect."

Francesca hurried to her bedroom. Once she was dressed, she brushed out her freshly shampooed hair and put on some mascara and frosted coral lipstick. As a final touch, she replaced the gold stud earrings with aqua-colored starbursts. Now she was ready to go.

When she entered the living room, Vincenzo took one look at her and let out a whistle that sent the dog scrambling around. "Sorry, Artur. Your mistress is so dazzling, I forgot where I was and what I was doing."

"Thank you. Though I don't believe a word of it, you're very good for my ego."

His eyes danced. "Remember the board meeting? The men were so smitten, they would have kept you there half the night if I hadn't been around to claim you."

"Do you hear all this nonsense, Artur?" She reached down to pick him up. "Come on. You're coming to the royal palace with us and need to be on your best behavior, especially around Vincenzo's mother. She's the one we *have* to win over. Mothers are important. I love mine. Vincenzo loves his. The trick is for her to love all three of us."

CHAPTER TEN

A FEELING OF RELIEF washed over Vincenzo when they reached the palace. For the first time as an adult male, he knew joy. The woman he loved heart and soul clung to his arm as they climbed the stairs to the second floor. The palace guards stared in wonder.

Using his other hand, he carried the crate with Artur inside it, loving this experience like no other. His euphoria was so deep, he didn't realize Bella was already hurrying toward them.

"You have to be the famous Dr. Linard."

Francesca smiled. "You're Bella who along with your brother used to catch fish in the stream with nets."

His sister chuckled. "We had to be resourceful so no one knew what we were up to." She knelt down to look at the dog. "Artur! You're adorable." She looked up at Francesca. "He reminds me so much of Karl, it hurts." She got to her feet. "I'm so happy to meet you."

"I've been excited to meet Vincenzo's young partner in crime."

"Hey, you two," Vincenzo muttered. "*I'm* here too."

Both women burst into laughter. It thrilled him they were already acting like friends with secrets.

"I've been in Chur all day doing a fundraiser and

just flew back. Mother has been trying to reach me and asked me to come to the drawing room. I didn't know you would be here, brother dear. This is exciting."

"Let's hope it stays that way. I told Mother that Francesca and I were coming to talk to her again."

"I see." She patted Francesca's arm. "No matter what, you two have my vote." He could always count on her.

"Let's go in and we'll get the dog settled."

Bella opened the doors and the three of them entered the drawing room. No one was there yet. He put the crate by the love seat and reached inside. Francesca took the dog from him and put Artur on her lap. Bella knelt down in front of her to play with him. He wiggled and licked her.

As they were laughing at his antics, their mother came in with a large brown envelope in her hand. Vincenzo got up from the love seat and walked over to give her a hug.

"I see you've brought her and her dog."

Her unhappy mood hadn't changed. "He looks so much like Karl, we thought you'd like to meet him."

"I don't appreciate it, not when we have very serious things to talk about." She walked over to her favorite chair near the love seat and sat down. Then his grandparents came in the room. He got up to help his grandmother before pushing his grandfather's wheelchair over by the couch.

Vincenzo smiled at Francesca. "I'm glad we're all here because I have important news that is going to change all our lives. The other day I flew to Milano and met with Valentina. I learned from her own lips that she's pregnant with another man's child."

"That's not true!" his mother cried out.

"I'm afraid it is, Mamma."

"But that's impossible. Stefano—"

"Stefano refuses to face the truth," Vincenzo broke in. "What he needs to do is help Valentina deal with her life. Surely my own family knows me well enough that if the baby were mine, I would have insisted on marrying Valentina immediately."

"We know that!" Bella jumped up to hug him. "You're the most honest, decent person I've ever known in my life and I couldn't be happier for you and Francesca."

Her words meant the world to Vincenzo who gave her a big hug.

"Then what's this?" his mother blurted. "It was delivered to me a short time ago." She opened the envelope and took out the front page of Milano's *Corriere della Sera*. Stefano had done the deed, all right.

Francesca exchanged glances with him as his mother read the headlines. *"Bells from the Duomo di Milano will ring out on September eighteenth for the wedding of Princess Valentina Visconti to Prince Vincenzo Baldasseri..."*

Bella looked concerned and sat down next to Francesca and the dog. She had a heart of gold.

"Stefano had that printed to put pressure on me and Valentina, but it won't work. He's been like a runaway train that couldn't be stopped."

His mother looked stricken. "Valentina wouldn't have lied to me, Vincenzo. She's a decent, wonderful girl."

"I agree—however, she didn't have any choice. Stefano has a stranglehold on her. He came to my office this afternoon to intimidate me with this fake head-line announcement. He threatened me with a lawsuit for breach of contract to marry."

"Lawsuit?"

"Yes, Mamma. I told him it was the other way around. She broke *our* engagement. That's when he said it was because I'd neglected her. I told him that was an untrue statement because my visits to the pal-ace were recorded by my pilot and I never missed one. I could submit them and photos in evidence to the court."

His mother put a hand to her throat. "I—I don't be-lieve what I'm hearing."

"That's because you're a good woman, Mamma. But he has a history of having done bad things, espe-cially to Francesca's father. He's hoping the Visconti family can finally lay claim to our timber business by my marrying Valentina. He's out of control. It's tragic that he can't love his daughter and help her during her pregnancy."

"I just can't comprehend this." She'd gone a little pale. "Your wedding has been planned. Every detail. Valentina loves our family and wants to be a part of us. We love her. She's the perfect princess. This sim-ply couldn't be happening. I've wanted her to be my daughter-in-law. Marcello and I talked about it a year ago."

"I know, but those were your dreams, not mine or Valentina's. She's having another man's child which means she's in love with someone else. Not me."

Tears continued to pour down his mother's cheeks.

"I'm sorry you're so distressed. Why don't I walk you to your room so you can lie down?"

"No. No—"

"Bella? Mother probably needs a doctor. Would you find Elsa?" His grandfather's caregiver could take her vital signs.

"I'm on my way. She'll know what to do."

Suddenly Francesca got to her feet holding the dog, and approached his mother. "Princess Baldasseri? I'm so sorry you're in this much pain and I'm going to leave. You've received a terrible shock and both of you need to talk things out." She looked at Vincenzo. "Maybe one of your security men could drive me home? Please?" The pleading in those compassionate brown eyes left him with no alternative.

This had to be Francesca's finest moment. He thought he'd loved her before tonight. But this sacrifice on her part sealed her to him forever.

Just then Elsa came hurrying in the drawing room with a stethoscope around her neck. Bella ran over to Vincenzo while Elsa checked out their mother. She checked her vital signs and gave a nod that she was all right.

Relieved by that news, he put a hand on his sister's arm. "Francesca wants to go home," he whispered.

"Can't say I blame her."

No. Tonight had turned into a disaster. "Would you walk her outside the palace and ask one of the security men to drive her back to Zernez?"

"Of course. *I'd* take her, but I'd better not leave Mother."

"Agreed."

Vincenzo kissed her cheek, then walked over to Francesca. "Bella will see you out. I'll phone you in a little while. I love you so much." He kissed the side of her neck before picking up the dog and opening the crate door. "In you go, Artur."

"Thank you." Francesca avoided his eyes as she carried it out of the room with Bella at her side. Vincenzo followed them.

When he'd said he would endure anything to be with Francesca, he'd meant it. But they were already paying a high price for their happiness at the expense of his mother's health. He pulled her to him one more time.

"I know you're blaming yourself," she whispered against his neck. "But we made our decision together and we'll get through this."

"With you holding on to me, we already are." He pressed a kiss to her temple. As the women went down the staircase, he returned to the drawing room.

His mother was wiping her eyes. "I'm sorry, Vincenzo."

"So am I," his voice grated. The love of his life had put his mother's needs ahead of everything else. What an angelic woman.

"I hadn't intended to cause all this trouble, *mi figlio*."

"I know you didn't. It's going to take time for you to get over your disappointment about Valentina. Do you think you're ready for bed? We can talk in your room."

"I do think I need to lie down. We'll talk tomorrow." He helped her up. "Good night," she murmured to his grandparents who'd sat there the whole time without a word.

"Don't go away," he said to them in an aside. It was time he got to the bottom of their strange behavior. What was going on in their minds?

The housekeeper was there to help their mother get

ready for bed. He kissed her good-night and went back to the drawing room only to discover that his grandmother had left the room.

"Nonno? Why didn't Nonna stay?"

"She wasn't feeling well. I rang for Elsa to take her to our room and examine her. From there she was taken to the hospital in an ambulance."

"What?"

"Thank heaven you came back so I could tell you," the older man called out. "It's her heart."

"What do you mean her heart?"

"She's had a heart condition for about a year." His grandfather had been weeping. It brought tears to Vincenzo's eyes.

"Why didn't you tell me a long time ago? I don't understand."

"Because you had enough on your plate with your father's death and the arranged engagement to Valentina. With the added burden of taking on Rini's duties, she felt you'd suffered enough and didn't need to know her health problems. She swore everyone to secrecy, especially the doctor and Elsa."

"Poor Nonna. I wish I had realized so I could have done more for her."

"No, no."

"Please don't keep anything more from me, Nonno. I need the whole truth. How is she really?"

"The doctor will let us know if this episode is serious. So far she has recovered from various incidences and most likely she'll recover from this one without problem. Thanks to Elsa—she got her to the hospital fast. My son—" He pulled on Vincenzo's arm. "We have another secret, but she insists on being the one to tell you."

"What do you mean?"

"We've kept it for a long time, but now it's necessary that you know all about it. As soon as the doctor says you can visit, she'll be waiting to unburden herself to you. I urged her to tell you much sooner, but she was hoping for a different outcome."

Another outcome? Vincenzo couldn't imagine. "About what?"

"About you and Valentina."

"Why didn't you tell me?"

"Because I didn't know about this secret until after I discovered what your *nonna* had been doing. She swore me to secrecy. I love her and told her I wouldn't say anything, but after tonight, I know she's ready to tell all."

Vincenzo couldn't imagine. "I'm leaving for the hospital now and will stay all night if I have to. Bella will stay with Mamma. Will you be all right?"

"Of course. I have Elsa."

"Francesca and I will be back."

"You really love that girl, don't you?"

"With all my heart and soul."

"I know how that feels." He patted Vincenzo's arm.

"Take care, Nonno. See you later."

Vincenzo rushed out of the palace and drove to the hospital. He knew the way to the area reserved for their family on the top floor. A cluster of staff nodded to him. The attending physician walked over. "Your grandmother had a little upset, but is responding well to treatment and will be able to go home tomorrow."

"That's wonderful. Can I go in and talk to her?"

"Of course. She'll love seeing you."

Relieved to hear the good news, Vincenzo entered her private room and walked over to the hospital bed. "Nonna?"

"Vincenzo—I'm so glad you're here."

"Thank heaven you're going to be all right."

"I am now that you've come. It pains me that after you brought Francesca to the palace so we could get to know her, chaos ensued because of Stefano. Now you've had to drive here because of my emergency, but I'm fine."

"The doctor said as much. Nonno told me about your bad heart. You never breathed a word of it."

"Because I've never wanted to be a fuss to anyone."

"You're a saint."

"Hardly." She chuckled. "Think about it. Your mother has suffered so much from losing your father, I didn't want to add to her anxiety. She's missed him so terribly, I believe that's why she has counted on you and Valentina to fill part of that void. Hopefully tonight's revelations have opened her eyes a little, but it will take time."

"No one knows that more than I do. But now I want to know about the secret you're hiding with Nonno. What's going on?" He pulled a chair over to the bed and sat down.

"You're going to be shocked."

Vincenzo took a deep breath. "I'm listening."

"What I'm about to tell you could end up in a tragedy."

"For whom?"

"Valentina and you."

"What?"

"Just hear me out. That girl is in the most serious trouble of her life and has been confiding in me ever since your engagement."

He was incredulous. "You've been her friend all this time?"

"Yes. She couldn't go to her mother who's terrified of Stefano. So is Valentina. Absolutely terrified. The bottom line is this—she's been in love with one of the security guards at the palace for a year and a half, named Alessandro Piero. When Stefano caught them together in the garden kissing one day, he was dismissed on the spot and served a six months' jail sentence."

"You're kidding!"

"He's made it impossible for Alessandro to get a decent job and has treated her abominably."

Vincenzo shook his head. "I know from Francesca's father that Stefano was always difficult, but to imprison a young man and ruin his life..."

"It's irrational. The next day Stefano phoned your parents to arrange the engagement and plan your first meeting. He chose the right moment to get in touch with them. Since your father and mother felt it was time for you to choose a bride, they were amenable to the idea. After I met Valentina, I could see how lovely and charming she was. I encouraged her to come for visits.

"Most of the time you weren't here. Before long I realized neither of you were in love, but both of you were prepared to do your duty. In time she lowered her guard and told me the truth about her wretched life. When Alessandro was released, Valentina sneaked out of the palace to see him. He was staying with a friend. Of course, he knew she was engaged to you, but he knew why. They managed to meet in secret and then she became pregnant."

"So *that's* why the engagement was broken." It was all making so much sense.

"Yes. Valentina couldn't marry you when she was in love with Alessandro and carrying his baby. She went to Stefano with the excuse that you had lost interest in her and that's the reason why she didn't want to be engaged. Secretly she and Alessandro planned to run away and get married. Stefano became enraged and insisted that she do whatever was necessary to win you around."

He got to his feet. "By then I was totally involved with Francesca whom I adore."

"Anyone can see that." She smiled. "So Stefano went to the media to create a scandal. According to Valentina he wanted to force both of you into court. When she found that out, she ran away before her father could find her and called your grandfather who told me what happened.

"I—" her voice faltered, "I told Elsa to hide and protect her until you were told the truth. One of the maids is Elsa's relative and she's been bringing her food. I'm afraid your mother is going to be shocked when she learns what we've done."

He smiled. "You and Nonno, plotting together."

"Yes, he's used to my ways. We've done it for years."

"Well, don't worry. Mother won't know a thing because I'll get Valentina out of the palace to a safe place. Stefano would never dream you've been helping his daughter and he'll never think to look for her here. Please get better and come home soon."

"I knew we could count on you."

"As I have counted on you all these years. We're in this together."

"We knew you'd fix this when you heard the truth. That's because you're honorable like your grandfather and I know you care for Valentina."

"I do, and I want to help. Nonna? There's no one in the entire universe kinder than you. But you've done enough and need to rest so your heart can heal. I'll take care of everything once I get back to the palace."

"But what about Francesca? That poor dear girl. She saw your mother's suffering. The look on her face when she told you she wanted to leave the palace—I'll never forget the love I saw in her eyes for you. How sad for this to happen when you've fallen in love... She must be beside herself."

"She and I are solid like you and Nonno. When she hears this story, she'll do anything to help. Valentina is her blood cousin. Remember that Francesca's own father was in the same situation with Stefano before he and her mother left Milano. Francesca is a saint as you're going to find out. One day soon I'll tell you all the wonderful things about her."

"Tonight I found out how unselfish she is. I can't wait to get to know her! Unfortunately it might take a little more time for your mother to remove the blinders and be convinced."

"It's going to happen, Nonna. I love you, and I'll see you at the palace tomorrow."

He kissed her cheek and dashed out of the hospital.

With his head spinning, he rushed to the car. Forget phoning Francesca. He needed to see her, even if it meant she had to call in sick at work tomorrow. He sent her a text to say that he'd be at her apartment in twenty minutes.

Francesca had gone to bed in tears. After she read Vincenzo's text, she could breathe again and put on a robe over her nightgown. When she opened the door, their gazes met for a heart-stopping moment before he crushed her in his arms. "I can't believe our evening ended the way it did, Francesca."

"I know." She moaned. "I love you so much I've been in agony. But seeing your mother's unhappiness made me realize it's not going to work."

"Oh, yes, it is," Vincenzo murmured before kissing her nonstop. "I couldn't get to your apartment fast enough to tell you what I've learned since you left. Come and sit with me." He reached for her hand and pulled her down on the couch with him. "Where's Artur?"

"In my bedroom asleep in his crate."

"For once that's good. After you left, I took my mother to her room. She needed to go to bed. When I returned to the drawing room I found my grandfather alone. When I asked about my grandmother, he said she hadn't been feeling well. Elsa sent for an ambulance to take her to the hospital."

"Oh, no—that means our relationship must have upset her too."

"No, my love. Listen to me. Nonno explained she has a heart condition, but has kept it quiet for the last year."

"Are you serious?"

"Afraid so. Tonight it acted up, but when I went over to the hospital, the doctor said the treatment was working and she'll come home tomorrow."

"You've been to see her already?"

"Yes, and I found out she's keeping another secret as well." He smiled. "This one will astound you."

She studied him. "You sound different. Happy. What's this news I'm not going to believe?"

"You'll have to be patient. This story goes back to the first part of July a year ago when my parents announced the news I'd been dreading all my adult life."

"I'm afraid I know what's coming."

"You guessed it, but just stay with me for a few minutes. It's important."

This was a new Vincenzo. She smiled. "Go on. I'm dying of curiosity."

He kissed her features. "I'd just come in from a day of hiking with Luca and some females we'd met."

"Females, huh."

He grinned. "My father called me into the study. Out of the blue he said it was time for me to settle down. My spirits plunged to new depths. He announced that he and Mother had finally found the right woman for me and wanted us to meet officially."

Francesca swallowed hard. "You mean Valentina."

"Exactly. Her parents had approached mine. They said they could search the world over and not find a better husband for their daughter than Prince Vincenzo of the House of Baldasseri. According to her mother, Princess Valentina spoke more highly of me than any other eligible prince in Europe and wanted to meet me. I couldn't imagine what had prompted Valentina to say those things."

"You're not a woman, Vincenzo. I fantasized about you over those videos before I ever met you in person," came her honest confession.

"*Francesca...*"

"It's true. Keep talking."

"I concluded that her family had picked my family for underlying financial reasons."

A groan came out of Francesca. "That I can also believe."

"So our first meeting was arranged by both sets of parents, but it was through my grandmother I've found out why. Within a few days of their phone call, we attended a regatta held on Lake Garda where we joined with the Visconti family.

"I already knew what Valentina looked like. She was attractive and we got along well enough. Though she acted like she was happy, I knew it couldn't be true. But like me, she was trying to honor her parents, so I gave her the benefit of the doubt. A few days later we went through the formal engagement that sealed our fate."

Francesca's heart thudded painfully during the silence that followed. "And?"

"This is where the tale gets interesting. Once engaged, Valentina came to the palace to get to know my family. I knew mother liked her, but last night when I talked to my grandmother, I found out Nonna and Valentina had developed an attachment they kept secret from everyone including my mother."

"Your grandmother?"

"Yes. It led to many future confidences. My grandfather knew all about it and kept quiet while he supported her completely."

"He's a wonderful man to be that loyal to his wife."

"Agreed. Over the last year Valentina came to the palace many times no one knew about, especially me. Nonna asked for Elsa's help to let Valentina in without my mother, Bella or myself knowing what was happening. Valentina told her parents she was visiting me, so she was never prevented from coming. My grandmother took her under her wing and they became the closest of friends."

"Friends?" Francesca cried. "And you knew nothing about it?"

"Not a clue, but what Nonna told me a little while ago has rearranged my entire universe."

"Darling—" Francesca felt she would burst if he didn't explain. "Please don't keep me in suspense any longer."

"All right. The bottom line is, Valentina has been in love with one of the guards at the Visconti Palace for a year and a half."

"You're kidding!" As Vincenzo continued to explain, Francesca couldn't believe what she was hearing.

"When Stefano saw them kissing in the garden, that's when he contacted my parents to force a meeting and engagement. Not only that—he fired the guard and put him in jail for six months. He froze his bank account too."

She cringed and clung to him. "What a ghastly man. When I think how he treated my father… It's horrifying that a royal like Stefano believes he can destroy people's lives that way with enough money and power."

"Nonna said Valentina and her mother have lived in fear of him for years. Now we know why. Valentina had to make up the lie about my being uninterested in her so she could break our engagement. To her shock, Stefano forced her into trying to get engaged again by threatening to go to the media with a scandal she'd never live down."

"Oh, Vincenzo. More than ever, I understand what my own father had to go through to escape his brother. Now Valentina is going through the same terrifying experience."

"It's tragic all right. Once released from prison, Alessandro Piero had no hope of getting a decent job with his prison record. All doors are closed to him. He's been living with a friend. Valentina and he have been meeting in secret. Now she's pregnant with his child."

Their baby—

To think Francesca's cousin had fled to the Baldasseri Palace, fighting for her life. It was incredible.

Hearing Valentina's story had touched Francesca's heart. How terrible to be afraid of your own father. "I'm sick for her. Stefano has tried to ruin many lives. It has to stop. Those poor things." Her voice shook.

"I knew that would be your reaction, Francesca. Your tender heart is one of the reasons I love you so much. After I left Milano the other day, she ran away and came straight to the palace to see my grandmother. Valentina needs help. Elsa is hiding her in her own apartment until Nonna gets home from the hospital. She's safe for now. My grandfather is making sure of it."

"But this is so awful for her, Vincenzo. I would help any woman in this kind of jeopardy, but she's my cousin who has been kept from our family because of

Stefano. We have to do what we can for her. It's important to me."

"And *me*," Vincenzo emphasized. "She tried to do the decent thing and get out of our engagement the only way she knew how. I admire her for that more than I can tell you. It's criminal that she and Alessandro have nothing to fall back on. Stefano has seen to that and smeared all our names in his desire for revenge, but starting tonight the fight is on and he won't win."

"*Mio amore?* Let's drive Valentina to your chalet where she can be totally private and work things out with Alessandro."

"We could do that, but I have an even better idea. Do you think your parents would be willing to let Valentina stay with them for a short time? They're family and I wouldn't be at all surprised if your father hired Alessandro to work in his packaging business in Bern. For that matter I'd be happy to hire him to work for the timber company."

"I *know* they'd come to Valentina's rescue. That's the kind of people they are, wonderful like you. I'm the luckiest woman alive."

"Now you know how I feel since meeting you."

A wave of heat poured through her.

"The point is, we know Stefano will cut off all money to her. Valentina and Alessandro will be destitute. But what no one knows is, when the engagement was broken, I held back some timber money our family would have given Stefano once we were married as part of the marital agreement.

"That money can now go to the two of them for a wedding present. I assured my grandmother it's all going to work out. Alessandro and Valentina can buy a villa anywhere they want and have enough to raise the child they're expecting. Stefano won't be able to touch either of them or their money."

Tears gushed from her eyes. "You're a man so much greater than other men, I'm speechless."

"Say that to me when we're old and maybe I'll half believe you."

"When are you going to tell your mother?"

"As soon as possible. When she sees Valentina with Alessandro, all will become clear and she'll learn to love you."

Francesca looked away. "Of course she'll understand everything, but that doesn't mean she'll want me to be with you."

"She will in time. Listen to me."

CHAPTER ELEVEN

VINCENZO HAD KNOWN Francesca would put up this kind of resistance, but he had news for her and would speak what was in his heart. He let go of her long enough to get down on one knee and grasped her left hand.

"I've been wanting to do this since the moment we met. I hope you realize your apartment is our home now. No more hypotheticals. Francesca Giordano Visconti? I'm asking you to marry me right this minute, and I won't take no for an answer." He pulled a gold ring with a solitaire diamond out of his shirt pocket and slid it on her ring finger.

"I never dreamed of being able to do what ordinary men do. I never had hope of loving the woman I would have to marry. When I took Karl into the clinic, I was in a very dark place for many reasons, unable to imagine happiness. To make matters worse, Daniel wasn't available to take care of my best friend.

"I looked up to see who had spoken and my eyes fell on you, Francesca, the most adorable female imaginable, shining like a star. You seemed to have come straight from heaven to delight poor earthly men like myself. My heart actually quaked."

She slid down and put her arms around his neck.

"Mine leaped to see the Prince I'd fantasized over suddenly appear in front of me. It's leaping now. I want to be your wife more than anything in this world."

"Francesca—" He rolled her to him and kissed the daylights out of her. "Swear to me nothing will change for you."

"Nothing will, *il mio cuore.* Your mother has to be a wonderful woman to have raised a prince of a man like you. I believe it will all work out."

"When Nonna comes home tomorrow and tells Mamma everything she'll welcome you with open arms, Francesca."

"I pray that will happen. My parents already adore you. They're as crazy about you as I am."

"Why don't we call them and let them know our news."

"I bet when we tell them about Valentina and Alessandro, they'll come up with a solution. Being that she's their niece, I know they'll want to help. But first things first." She covered his handsome features with kisses. They were so engrossed, it took a long time before they came up for air and made the call.

The whole conversation was like music to Vincenzo's ears. By the time they'd talked everything through, it was decided he was marrying Francesca at the church of Saint Peter and Saint Paul in Bern. It was the church where her parents had been married. All they had to do was wait for his mother's blessing before they put their plans into action.

They hung up and Vincenzo pulled her into his arms. "I'm going to leave so you can get a little sleep before you have to be at the clinic in the morning." He kissed her once more. "I'll phone you with any news tomorrow. Stay safe and well for me. You're the most precious person in my existence."

A feeling of elation over the plans for their coming marriage filled his being so completely, he didn't remember the drive back to the palace. He sent a text for Fadri that he wouldn't be going into work. Instead, he would stay home with his family. He wanted to be there for all of them.

Just as Vincenzo expected, the morning news announced the imminent marriage of him and Valentina. Bella rolled her eyes and shut off the TV. By noon, his grandmother had come back from the hospital. The whole family sat around her in his grandparents' suite.

"You need to rest," his mother cautioned her.

"Stop worrying about me," she insisted. "I feel fine and there's something of vital importance Alfredo and I have to tell all of you. In a way it's a confession."

"Confession?" Vincenzo's mother frowned. He could tell she hadn't slept well.

She gripped her husband's hand. "It's about Valentina."

Vincenzo had never loved his *nonna* more than he did at this moment while she told her amazing story. His grandfather added more information. When they'd finished, his mother got up from the chair and clung to the backing. Tears streamed down her cheeks.

"Thank you for this. I wish Valentina had felt she could confide in me, but I understand her fear of Stefano. To think he gave that false news story to the media…" Her eyes fastened on Vincenzo. "My poor dear son. He not only abused his daughter to get hold of our family money, he abused you relentlessly. Can you ever forgive me for not believing you?"

He walked over and reached for her hands. "There's nothing to forgive, Mamma. I love you with all my heart, and we're going to help Valentina and the father of her baby. Do you know Francesca wanted to drive back to the palace last night and take her cousin to safety at the chalet?"

She shook her head. "Francesca sounds wonderful. I've been so heartless where your true feelings have been concerned."

"Only because of Valentina. I promise you're going to love Francesca just as much. I also have news on that score. Francesca's parents are going to let Valentina and Alessandro live with them and give him a job. I'm giving them the money I held back from Stefano." He smiled. "You're going to end up with three daughters to love as soon as you give Francesca and me your blessing so we can marry ASAP."

"Oh, Vincenzo—" She threw her arms around him. "You have it with all my heart. I know if Marcello were here, he'd be overjoyed too."

Bella's tear-filled eyes met his. So did the watery eyes of his grandparents. Miracles *did* happen.

He hugged his mother for a long time before letting her go. Now it was time to phone the love of his life with the glorious news. With another hug to his grandparents, he left their bedroom and hurried to his own suite to make the call.

"Francesca? How are things going at work?"

"I called in sick. Poor Daniel. Artur is keeping me busy, but it doesn't stop me from thinking about your mother and her affection for Valentina. Even when the truth comes out, that doesn't mean she'll be able to let go of her feelings."

"Guess what? My grandmother got home from the hospital this morning. While we were all gathered round her, she and Nonno told us their secret. My mother stood there with tears dripping down her face and begged my forgiveness for not believing me. She wants to love you. Everything has been settled, and she has given us her blessing."

Francesca's cry of joy was so startling, the dog started to bark. Laughing, Vincenzo held the cell away from his ear. "Amen, my darling. I'm leaving for your apartment right now and we'll phone your parents to make detailed plans. Let's plan the ceremony for next Saturday. I'll tell the family before I leave here."

"That's only three days away."

"It's not soon enough for me."

"I need to tell Daniel and make arrangements for kenneling Artur."

"There's a lot to do. We need the name of the bishop at the church in Bern. The ceremony needs to be arranged."

"What about a special dispensation?"

"It won't be a problem. I'll phone Rini. He and Luna will want to see us married."

"So will my brother and his girlfriend, Gina."

Two hours later their plans were made. Tomorrow morning they'd fly in the Baldasseri jet to Bern from Innsbruck and stay with Francesca's family. Her mom would take her shopping for a wedding dress.

Their marriage ceremony had been arranged for ten in the morning. After a reception at the Visconti villa, they'd fly back to Zernez and enjoy a two-day honeymoon. A longer one would come later.

They moved to the door. "As soon as I get back to the palace, I'll ask my friend Luca to be a witness."

"Call me tonight, no matter how late."

He cupped her face in his hands. "I promise. Take care of yourself, *tesoro mio*. I couldn't live without you now."

In three days' time he'd be Francesca's husband. They'd raise a family. Over time more Karls and Arturs would come along too. No man could be this happy.

Three days later

"Honey? Are you awake?"

Francesca sat up in bed. "I've been up for hours, too excited to sleep."

"I don't blame you. It *is* your wedding day."

"Oh, Mom, I love Vincenzo so much, I can't believe I'm going to be marrying my heart's desire."

Her mother swept in the room. "I can relate."

She got out of bed. "I know. Vincenzo makes me happy the way Dad makes you."

"All four of us are very, very lucky. Now come on. You need some breakfast and we've got to get you dressed so you're not late for your own nuptials."

"Never." Francesca grinned and hurried into the bathroom to start her day.

Rain had descended on Bern this amazing Wednesday morning of late August, but the inclement weather didn't bother Francesca. Nothing mattered because she was getting married to the man who'd haunted her dreams from that first day he'd brought Karl into the vet clinic. She wanted to look gorgeous for him and had bought a white Alençon lace and silk gown that both mothers and Bella said looked made for her.

The four of them had enjoyed each other immensely while out shopping. When morning came, they helped her get dressed. The lace hem of the graceful slender A-line gown swept the floor. Her mother placed an Alençon shoulder-length mantilla over her hair.

Vincenzo's mother gave her a Baldasseri family treasure which consisted of tiny pearls, diamonds and rubies. She fastened it around her neck and gave her a kiss on the cheek. "This belonged to my husband's mother." Francesca loved her already.

Holding umbrellas, her parents helped her into the limo waiting in the courtyard of the Visconti two-story Swiss villa. Through the rain they drove to the lovely church in the old part of Bern. Built in the mid-eighteen hundreds, it was renowned for its painted ceiling and windows.

Francesca's heart jumped around thinking about Vincenzo waiting for her as they escorted her inside the foyer of the edifice. They brushed her off as sounds of the organ and choir permeated the church. Her father reached for her left hand and pressed an object into the palm.

When she looked down, she saw it was a gold band with a blue diamond her dad had produced for her to give Vincenzo. He and her mother wanted Francesca to know how much they approved of her choice of husband.

Francesca felt overcome as she reached out to hug him. "No one ever had a better father than you, Papa. I love you." She put the ring on her least finger until the time came in the ceremony to exchange rings.

Her mother handed her a bouquet of white roses. "The next time we see each other, you'll be Vincenzo's wife. Nothing could make me happier."

"Oh, Mom—I love you both so much." They hugged before her mother slipped inside the doors. That left Francesca standing there with her father.

They looked at each other as the "Wedding March" started. He reached for her hand. With a smile he said, "I don't need to ask if you're ready."

No. She was practically floating with happiness. Since meeting Vincenzo she'd been an open book.

A church worker opened the doors into the nave filled to the brim with wedding guests and flowers near the altar. Her parents had made many friends over the years. Vincenzo's grandparents sat in front. To Francesca's joy, she saw Daniel and his wife! He beamed at her.

She and her father continued down the center aisle, but her eyes had centered on Vincenzo wearing formal ceremonial Baldasseri dress blue with gold braid. Her Prince was so handsome she would have fainted right there if her father weren't holding her up.

Next to him looking splendid stood the Crown Prince of San Vitano, Rinieri Baldasseri, Vincenzo's cousin. On his other side stood Francesca's darling brother, Rolf. He looked tall and princely in his own right. The last man standing up for him was his attractive childhood friend Luca.

The priest marrying them waited at the altar in ceremonial robes. On his other side stood Vincenzo's lovely mother in purple chiffon. Francesca's mother was gorgeous in lavender. Next to her stood stunning Bella gowned in light blue. At her side stood Princess Luna in pink. The magnificent sight would dazzle anyone, but it was Vincenzo who took Francesca's breath.

The priest smiled at them. "Dear friends and family of the bride and groom, we welcome and thank you for being part of this sacred occasion. We're gathered here to witness the marriage of Francesca Giordano Visconti and Prince Vincenzo Rodicchio Baldasseri. Every human has the desire to love and be loved. Today we celebrate their love.

"If the couple will clasp hands, please come before me while the others take their seats and we'll begin with a prayer."

Francesca's mother took the flowers from her and sat down with her father. Vincenzo's mother followed. Rini claimed Luna. Rolf and Luca sat on another pew. During that whole time, Vincenzo squeezed Francesca's hand, enthralling her.

The priest gave a beautiful prayer, then nodded to the two of them. "Francesca, Vincenzo? Have you come here to enter into marriage freely and with whole hearts?"

"Yes," they said at the same time.

"Are you prepared to love and honor each other for as long as you both shall live?"

"Yes," she declared.

"*And* after," Vincenzo added. It reminded her of their conversation in the meadow after Karl had died when she'd said Vincenzo would see his beloved dog again. It brought tears to her eyes.

"Are you prepared to receive children from God and raise them according to the law of Jesus Christ and His church?"

"Yes," they both responded firmly. Vincenzo gave

her hand another squeeze she felt through her entire body. The priest eyed both of them.

"Because it's your intention to join each other in Holy Matrimony, you will now declare your consent before God." He nodded to Vincenzo who said, "I, Vincenzo Baldasseri, take you, Francesca Visconti, to be my wife. I promise to stay true to you in good times and bad, through sickness and health. I'll love, honor and cherish you all the days of my life."

The priest turned to Francesca who made the same vow. She finished with, "I'll love and honor you through life and throughout all eternity."

Vincenzo flashed her a smile meant for her alone before they kissed without the priest having to say anything. She couldn't believe this was really happening. This magnificent man had just married her. Her joy was almost too much to contain. She didn't want their kiss to end.

"What God has joined together, let no man put asunder. I now pronounce you man and wife. You may exchange rings."

With trembling hands Francesca pulled the ring off her little finger and reached for Vincenzo's left hand. The blue of his eyes intensified as she slid the wedding band on his ring finger. The fire in those orbs rivaled the heart of the blue diamond.

She heard an unexpected intake of breath before he produced a wedding ring and put it on the ring finger of her left hand. Further examination showed it to be a Baldasseri family heirloom with a ruby and diamonds. "My great-grandmother's ring," he whispered as he slid his arm around her waist. "It matches the necklace around your neck. You're my wife, Francesca. No man can put us asunder now."

There was steel in his tone as glorious choral music accompanied by the organ filled the interior. It was a surreal moment for Francesca as they walked slowly down the aisle with Vincenzo's arm around her waist. Once they reached the foyer, they embraced their loved ones before walking out to the waiting limo.

Francesca saw news reporters taking pictures and videos. It wouldn't be long before people watching the news would wonder what was going on. Everyone would ask how Prince Vincenzo could be engaged to one Visconti woman, yet married to another within a matter of days.

But she couldn't worry about that right now. Before Vincenzo helped her in the limo, he folded her in his arms. When he lowered his head to give her a husband's kiss, she was so on fire for him, she forgot everything else. That kiss would be splashed all over the news, but it didn't matter because she'd become Vincenzo's wife.

The rain had turned to drizzle. An indoor reception at the Visconti villa awaited them. Francesca's father stood at the table where she and Vincenzo sat with her mother, Rolf and Gina. Vincenzo's grandparents and mother sat with Prince Rinieri and Princess Luna. Valentina and her fiancé Alessandro had been put at another table also looking blissfully happy. All their friends had gathered round at other tables laden with flowers.

"Welcome everyone on this joyous day of days. There'll be time for all the toasts you want after we eat, but right now I want to make one to my new son-in-law. I've learned things about him that you don't know and never will. But they make me humbled and proud that he has become a member of our family." He raised his champagne glass to Vincenzo.

"Here's to the groom, a man better than other men, who kept his head even while he lost his heart to my precious daughter. These two were meant for each other. To that I can attest and give my blessing. May your joy last through the eternities."

Francesca knew her father's heartfelt words had touched Vincenzo so deeply, he grasped her hand beneath the table and clung to it. She knew the tribute acted like a healing balm after what Stefano had put them all through.

The rest of the party passed in a kind of heavenly blur as they ate and laughed and enjoyed all the many tributes. Perhaps her favorite toast at the end of the reception came from Vincenzo's best friend Luca.

He got to his feet and raised a glass to him. "Dante once wrote that a great flame follows a little spark. Apparently there was more than a little spark the day Vince took his sick dog Karl to the vet. One look at the gorgeous Dr. Linard and he was lit by the brightest light in the firmament. May your happiness last forever."

Vincenzo squeezed her hand tighter.

"Thank you, Luca," she mouthed the words to him.

Francesca's mother smiled at her. "It's time for you to change and get you to the airport for your honeymoon."

Honeymoon—

She shivered in excitement. Francesca had never gone to bed with a man. Now she was a married woman and couldn't wait to be loved by her husband who kissed her cheek. "Hurry," he whispered. "I'll be waiting for you in the foyer."

A thrill of desire darted through her as he helped her up from the table. She left the room with her mother and went upstairs to change into a new summer suit in spring green.

Her mom helped her out of her wedding dress. After they hugged she went down to the foyer where Vincenzo was waiting for her. Everyone had gathered round while she got ready to throw the bouquet.

She knew where she wanted it to land, but it accidentally ended up in Bella's hands rather than Gina's. Vincenzo's sister turned crimson.

He put his arm around Francesca's shoulders. Nuzzling her neck, he said, "I'm glad your aim was off. Gina has already found her happiness with your brother. Now it's Bella's turn. Shall we go, Signora Baldasseri? Our chariot is waiting."

It was late afternoon. There were more photographers outside the villa, but she ignored them. The limo drove them to the airport where they boarded the helicopter. They'd fly to the major airport in Innsbruck, then home. "It's been a perfect day," she murmured against his lips after they climbed inside.

"That's true, but it's only the beginning. I've arranged for my security staff to have my car waiting for us at the airport in Zernez."

"Am I horrible to be this impatient to get back to the apartment?"

"You mean *our* apartment, and yes. It thrills me that you're as horrible as I am to want to go to bed. I'm not sure I'll ever let you go again, so be warned."

Their flight lasted too long, but finally they landed and hurriedly got in his car and he drove them to the apartment.

He shut off the engine and turned to her. "As of this moment everything is under control and we are now on our honeymoon. Nothing or no one is going to interfere with what I've been looking forward to since the moment I laid eyes on my Christmas angel."

"What do you mean?"

"That's what you looked like to me. One of those adorable angels hanging on the Christmas tree full of light and sparkle and so damn beautiful I wanted to steal you away immediately. It took all my self-control not to kidnap you from the clinic and hide you where no one could find you but me."

"Vincenzo—" She laughed.

"It's the truth, my love. In case you haven't noticed, we're here, *mio amore*."

Her apartment was a sight for sore eyes. It was a glorious evening, warm and beautiful. "Stay in the car. I want to take everything inside first, then come back for you. I'll need your key."

Francesca handed it to him. He hurried up the stairs with the food they stopped for plus their bags. Her heart pounded wildly while she waited for his return. Little could she have guessed that when she'd picked this apartment on the internet in July, Prince Vincenzo would become her husband and race up the stairs into their new home. A fairy tale beyond fairy tales, one she'd cherish forever.

The interior felt like heaven to Vincenzo. He took the bags to her bedroom. *Their* bedroom now. After returning to the kitchen to put away the groceries in the fridge, he went back out, leaving the door open.

Francesca had gotten out of her car and lounged against it. Their gazes locked as he came closer and picked her up in his arms like the bride she was. Miraculously she fit there like she'd been made for him. Without effort he carried her slowly along the walk and up the stairs. His eyes studied every feature, still trying to believe this remarkable woman now bore his last name.

"You have no idea how long I've been waiting for you to carry me over the threshold. I'd harbored an irrational jealousy knowing the cousin I'd never met was your fiancée. It seemed cruel that I was being tempted like this when I knew you were as far from me as the planets and forbidden to me in every way. That's what made my longing for you harder to bear. That first night I cried my eyes out."

"Francesca..." He kissed her fervently. "I didn't know that. The beautiful Dr. Linard kept her secrets. The last thing I wanted to do was leave the clinic."

She traced the line of his mouth with her finger. "I never intended for you to know how attracted I was. You can't imagine my shock when you told me your engagement had been broken off. I was so happy I was giddy."

"You never let on, *squisita*!"

He closed the door with his foot and carried her through the apartment to the bedroom. Following her down on the bed, he began kissing her. This was different than all the other times they'd been together. They were man and wife and alone for the first time since the wedding.

"When I took those wedding vows, I promised to worship you with my body, and that's exactly what I'm going to do."

"I love you," she cried from her soul, "more than life itself!"

"Amore." He helped remove her suit, then took off his trousers and shirt. Before long they lay entwined on the bed, enraptured as they poured out their love for each other. To Vincenzo it seemed like after meeting Francesca, he'd been waiting years for this moment.

She was the personification of his every dream, loving and giving. His desire had reached its zenith. For hours they were swept away by needs and longings that no longer had to be held back. Francesca had taken him to a place of pure enchantment.

At one point they both slept with his arm around her hips. When he awakened, he discovered her leaning over him while she smoothed some hair off his forehead. "Do you know you're the most beautiful man I ever saw in my life?"

"I'll take that as a compliment."

"I can't wait until we have children. Everyone will rave that they look like you."

"Our girls will inherit your beauty and I'll have to beat off the suitors."

She chuckled.

Vincenzo found certain places to kiss her that he knew drove her crazy with longing. "Do you want a baby right away?"

"The mention of Valentina's pregnancy has made me think hard about us. Are you anxious to start a family? Tell me the truth."

"I can't imagine anything more wonderful."

"Neither can I."

"I'm glad you said that because I'm afraid I didn't take precautions."

She gave him that fetching smile. "I noticed, and I'm ecstatic because I'm hoping we're pregnant right now. Artur needs competition so he won't get too spoiled."

Deep male laughter poured out of Vincenzo. "He's already hopeless in that department. So am I. Love me again, *mia moglie*." He rolled her gorgeous body against him. "I need you more than I need food right now."

"That tells me more than you know. Kiss me again, and again, and again."

EPILOGUE

The Baldasseri Palace, two and a half months later

VINCENZO HELPED FRANCESCA out of his car. She clung to him.

"What's wrong, darling?"

"I was just remembering the first time you brought me to the palace so I could meet your mother."

He hugged her waist. "Since then a lot of water has passed under that bridge, and now we're *her* guests. Mamma has been dying to have a party. She's back to her old self which pleases me more than you will ever know. It's a good sign she's gotten past that grieving stage for my father. Our marriage has brought new joy to her life."

"You're right. The person I'm concerned about now is Bella. She's marvelous, but I sense she's unhappy. You never talk about it."

"Heartache came to Bella's life in high school."

"I presume you're talking a boyfriend."

"Afraid so."

"Is it a secret?"

"It has been. When we get home tonight, I'll tell you what happened."

They walked past the guards and up the back stairway of the palace to the drawing room.

Francesca almost fainted at the room full of people. Gorgeous Bella sat with her mother on one of the love seats. The older woman got up immediately and walked toward Francesca, holding out her arms. "I'm so excited my newest daughter is here."

Vincenzo let go of her hand so she could run to her. "We're thrilled to be here, Princess Baldasseri."

"Call me Maria, please." Her tear-filled voice got to Francesca's heart. They hugged for a long time. "Can you forgive a foolish woman who refused to let go of her selfish dreams when we first met?"

Francesca stared into blue eyes so much like Vincenzo's. "There's nothing to forgive. The son you brought into this world and raised is the love of my life. I'm so thankful you're his mother. No man can match him, and that has everything to do with you."

She patted Francesca's cheek. "I'm the one who's grateful my son had the wisdom to choose an angel from heaven to be his wife. That's what he calls you. I've learned a great deal about you over the last few months. Words can't express my sorrow that it took me so long to come to my senses. If Vincenzo's father were alive, he'd sing your praises. Welcome home. It's *your* home."

"Thank you so much, Maria."

"Francesca?"

She turned to see her parents over on another love seat. Her brother and Gina sat in chairs next to them. She ran over to hug them. "This really *is* a celebration."

Everyone was smiling. Near them sat Vincenzo's grandfather in his wheelchair with his wife at his side. She hurried over to kiss them. "You two look wonderful."

"So do *you*!"

That was the moment when she spotted Valentina and Alessandro who'd recently been married. Her cousin was a knockout and looked so happy. Why not? Her pregnancy was starting to show.

They hugged each other. "Valentina? Did you ever imagine the two of us meeting, let alone under these circumstances?"

"Never." Her blue eyes glistened with tears. "I can't believe what you and Vincenzo have done for us." She hugged her hard. "I love your parents so much, Francesca. Uncle Niccolo and Aunt Greta are saints, and my cousin Rolf is fabulous."

"I agree. He says the same thing about you. To think we're cousins, and it has taken this long. How are you feeling by now? I know you had a hard beginning with your pregnancy. I feel bad that you had to hide out here when you didn't feel well."

"Vincenzo's grandparents are angelic as you know. All of their family is. So are you and your family. Your goodness has turned my life and Alessandro's around. When I learned how kind you've been through all this, I wept because my father has kept us apart all these years. Having you in my life is like having a sibling. I can't thank you enough for all you've done for us."

"You went through a horrible time."

"So did you. My father was horrible to Vincenzo and ultimately to you."

"I'm just thankful that's all behind us and that you're happily married now."

"We are."

Alessandro broke in. "There are no words to express my gratitude for all you and your family have done for us. It's incredible."

Francesca gave a big hug to the handsome man who'd dared to love Valentina despite all odds. "I'm thrilled the two of you are together."

"We'll never be able to thank Prince Vincenzo enough for his wedding gift and all the help he has been."

Francesca took Alessandro aside. "Before we knew the truth of everything, I wonder if it was as hard for you to think of Valentina's engagement to Vincenzo as it was for me?"

He shook his dark blond head. "I don't want to even think about it now. Those were dark days."

"But neither of us ever lost hope, and now they're over."

"Yes. Valentina's mother is coming to live with us in Bern."

"She told me."

"Vincenzo is a miracle worker, Francesca. Maybe your husband hasn't even told you yet, but his attorney Marko Fetzer is helping my mother with her divorce."

"Valentina said as much. Vincenzo says he never loses a case."

"That's wonderful to hear. Thanks to your husband, we now own a fantastic villa and are decorating a baby nursery. You'll have to come and stay with us."

"We'd love it," Vincenzo interjected.

While Francesca stood there loving every second of this, he slid his arm around her shoulders and pulled her close. "It's fantastic that everyone we love is here," he exclaimed, looking around. "We came with news, Mamma."

His mother got to her feet. "What is it?"

"In about six and a half months, you're going to be a grandmother."

"That means *we're* going to be great-grandparents!" Vincenzo's *nonna* proclaimed. "Happy day!"

Everyone else in the room got up and gathered round to congratulate them. She got hug after hug from her own family and Bella, then she turned to Valentina who smiled at her through tears. "Partners in crime."

They both laughed. "I want us to become good friends, Valentina. When our children are born, I want them to get to know each other. It's taken way too long for you and me to get acquainted."

"We'll never let it happen again."

Vincenzo came up just then and put his arm around her waist. "We're due in the dining room for a celebratory feast." After such a difficult beginning, Francesca was incredulous this day had come. "Will you be able to eat?" he whispered in her ear.

"Yes."

"Thank heaven." He turned to Alessandro. "Speaking as the men in the family, morning sickness needs to be eradicated."

"You can say that again," Alessandro came back, "especially when she says she wants at least three children. She doesn't want ours to grow up alone."

"That I can understand."

Francesca laughed as they walked through to the dining room. Her brother came over and sat down on her other side. "Hey, sis. You look so happy, I think you're going to burst."

"You know you're right?" She kissed his cheek. "How are wedding plans going for you and Gina?"

"We're set for the twenty-first of December. That will give us the vacation to enjoy our honeymoon."

"Where are you going, or is that a secret?"

"A secret."

"So that means you're going to go to Chamonix. She'll love it."

"Don't tell Gina," he whispered. "She's never been there. Dad's renting a small chalet for us."

"Lucky you. If it weren't your honeymoon, Vincenzo and I would join you."

His brows lifted. "Have you two decided where to take a real honeymoon?"

"As someone once said—that train has left the station. We'll wait until our baby is born. Then we'll leave Artur and our child with the family and fly to somewhere exotic for a week."

"Only a week?"

"Any longer would be too hard on us and our children."

He chuckled. "Artur thinks he's your child."

"He *is* in his own way and has taken up residence in Vincenzo's heart."

"What about my heart?" Vincenzo poked his dark handsome head between them.

She looked up into his eyes. "It's as big as the great outdoors. Everyone here adores you and praises you for all you've done. It's disgusting how much I love you."

"Wait till I get you home and you can prove it to me."

Rolf burst into laughter as her face turned crimson.

"Hey, Francesca? Do you want to hear something really funny?" he asked in a quiet voice.

"I'm not sure." She was still trying to recover from Vincenzo's private message.

"I heard your mother-in-law talking to Bella before you and Vincenzo got here. She had no idea I happened to be passing in the hall and had picked up on their conversation.

"Vincenzo's mother said, and I quote, 'After the engagement was broken, Vincenzo told me no more princesses for him. In his emphatic way, he claimed he was going to find the woman he wanted. Period! I think he's forgotten Francesca *is* a princess with a defunct title. I got my way after all!'"

"He got something much better, Mamma," Bella murmured. "A woman who will love him to the ends of the earth and beyond."

* * * * *

A PROPOSAL
IN PROVENCE

DONNA ALWARD

MILLS & BOON

To all the writers who kept writing during this pandemic.
The world is brighter because of you.

PROLOGUE

February

STEPHEN PEMBERTON, EARL OF CHATSWORTH, paced in front of the antique mahogany desk in his office at Chatsworth Manor.

"What are you telling me, George?" He stopped pacing and squared up to face the accountant he'd hired to audit the estate financials. "Where did it go?"

The "it" he was referring to was a sum of money that had been withdrawn biannually from the estate funds for twenty-six years. Not a huge amount compared with the equity in the estate; it amounted to about thirty thousand pounds annually. But over twenty-six years it was more than three-quarters of a million pounds.

"I can try to trace it if you want. Honestly, Lord Pemberton, it's the only anomaly I've found in the audit. That's good news."

Stephen supposed he should be grateful for that. Inheriting the title and the estate at such an early age had been a shock. And the family certainly wasn't hurting for money; Aurora Inc. was massively successful. But Stephen alone was responsible for the estate and his father's legacy. It had been a few years now and the ground seemed to have settled within the family. Performing an audit was, in his opinion, the responsible thing to do.

"Call me Stephen," he said quietly. "It still feels strange having the title."

"You'll have to get used to it." George Campbell gave Stephen a nod. "You are the earl now, sir."

As if he needed reminding.

"Yes, George, you have my authority to trace whatever you need to. If you need papers signed for access, let me know."

"Will do, sir. And whatever the payments were, they weren't automatic withdrawals. The last one was a few months before your father died."

"So he was making them manually."

"It appears that way, for the moment, anyway."

Stephen nodded. "Do what you have to do. For over twenty-five years, someone was getting a piece of my father's money. I want to know who, and why."

George gave a nod and said his farewells. After he was gone, Stephen went back to his desk and sat heavily.

One thing he knew for sure. With his mother's recent health scare, he wasn't about to bring this to her attention unless he needed to. And certainly not until he got to the bottom of the…anomaly, as George put it. There was no need to alarm the family. It could be something entirely benign. His gut was telling him otherwise, but he wasn't so sure he trusted his gut these days.

He sighed and leaned back in the leather chair, closing his eyes. He'd never expected the earldom to weigh this heavily upon him.

Had his father felt the same when he'd inherited?

CHAPTER ONE

April

"ANEMONE, DO YOU have the data I was looking for this morning?"

Anemone looked up over her glasses and stared at her boss, Phillipe Leroux. She'd been seconded to his department a month ago, working as a liaison between Public Relations and his office in preparation for the launch of Aurora Inc.'s new fragrance. The launch was her baby, the first real project entrusted to her at the company, and she wasn't leaving any detail to chance.

Working at Aurora Inc. was a dream come true. The multinational company was a top name in fashion, cosmetics and jewelry. It was also run by the Pemberton family, including the new Earl of Chatsworth, Stephen Pemberton. Who also happened to be Anemone's half-brother.

Except Stephen didn't know that. None of the family knew that she was Cedric Pemberton's illegitimate daughter, and for the time being, she planned to keep it that way.

She reached for the file folder and handed it over. "All printed out for you, including pie charts and graphs with the latest results. Marketing sent it up straight away. The focus groups went well. I think you'll be pleased."

The launch of Aurora's new fragrance, Nectar, was scheduled for just over a week from now, and she knew that it was a particularly important moment for Phillipe, who was himself new to his position. His official title was Executive Manager of Fragrance, one step down from Director of Cosmetics and Fashion, who happened to be Will Pemberton. But Phillipe's education was in chemistry and his background in perfume. He'd been honest and said as much to her during their initial meeting and had expressed how he needed a strong assistant on his team. *No pressure, then*, she'd thought at the time, but she'd also been pleased that he thought she was that person—and that her former boss had recommended her for the temporary position.

Phillipe flipped through the file, giving the pages a quick glance. He looked up, his gray-blue eyes meeting hers. Her tummy always seemed to take a jolt when he did that. For the next two weeks, she reported to him directly, but that didn't stop her from noticing he was insanely attractive, with thick dark hair swept away from his face and a subtle smile that hinted at mischief. He was definitely more the intellectual type, but she'd always had a thing for brainy men. He looked down again and flipped through a few more pages, and she stared at his hands. Nice, big hands with long, graceful fingers.

She should not be having thoughts like this about her boss, no matter how temporary. Not if she wanted to keep this job and move up within the company. And she did want to keep it, she realized. She was relatively sure that if she showed up on the Pemberton doorstep and announced she was Cedric's daughter, she'd be thrown out on her ear. And that was the problem. She wanted to know her family, but she also genuinely loved working at Aurora. She was fairly certain she couldn't have both. So her secret would remain...her secret.

"Thank you, Anemone."

"Please call me Annie," she said, pushing her thoughts aside and smiling brightly at him. "Everyone calls me Annie." Over the years, she'd gotten used to having to spell her name immediately after giving it. She'd been working with Phillipe long enough now they could be on slightly more familiar terms, couldn't they?

"Annie," he said, and offered one of his small smiles. "This is great." He gestured with the file folder. "How am I set for the rest of the day?"

She brought up his schedule. "A meeting with William in an hour, then your afternoon is free from outside commitments." She looked up at him again. "I'm meeting with PR and Marketing later to iron out a few details, and then tweaking the catering menu for the launch."

"Fantastic." He leaned forward, resting his elbows on the counter in front of her desk. "I really appreciate how you've taken this event in hand."

She was determined not to blush at the praise.

He stepped back. "So, are you up for a field trip later today?"

She looked up, perplexed. "A field trip, Monsieur Leroux?"

He put the file down on the counter in front of her

desk. "If I must call you Annie, then you must call me Phillipe." He leaned forward a little. "To be honest, I'm not sure I'll ever get used to this 'Monsieur Leroux' thing." He held her gaze. "I'm almost as new at my job as you are to yours. I like first names. And I think you and I are past being so formal, don't you?"

"All right… Phillipe."

Oh, my. It sounded so personal coming from her lips, perhaps because even after weeks on the job, she was still a little struck by him. He might be the brainy type, but he wore his suits incredibly well and she had yet to see him with a tie; he always left his shirt collar open at the throat. There was an understated sexiness beneath the surface that was incredibly attractive. "Where are we going?"

He grinned then, a much brighter smile than she was used to seeing. It was absolutely dazzling.

"I thought I'd take you to where we store our product and give you a crash course, seeing as the new fragrance is so close to launch."

Annie gave a quick nod. "That would be fine. Shall I book us a taxi for a specific time?"

"Let's leave it until I'm sure I can get away."

"Whatever you like. Just let me know when you're ready." She mentally raced through her tasks and wondered how many she could get through before lunch. She'd probably end up working through her break, but she didn't mind. Not really.

With a parting smile, Phillipe headed back toward his office.

Annie let out a long breath and put her forehead in her hands. This was not good. The best job she'd ever had included proximity to her secret family, and now she had to go and develop a crush on her boss. It wouldn't do at all. This had never been an issue before, and she'd been working in the clerical field for the past six years. But then, she'd never had a boss like Phillipe.

She wished she could go home, call her mum, and have a good chat about it, but that wasn't possible. Not anymore. Losing her mum had broken her heart. And even if it hadn't, finding out the truth about her father's identity would have. Two years too late to even meet him…

Which was why she had this job. Learning she was Cedric Pemberton's daughter had been a shock, and she knew his wife and children wouldn't take the news well. She wasn't even sure she was ever going to tell them. They were all the family she had in the world, but she didn't want to be *that person* who came in and dropped a massive bombshell. She knew how much that hurt. Her longing for family constantly warred with compassion for her father's wife and children— she certainly bore them no resentment. Perhaps she had to deal with never having known her father, but they were dealing with losing him. The situation wasn't their fault, after all. That was squarely on two people who couldn't be held accountable anymore: her mother, and Cedric Pemberton. Besides, telling the family wouldn't change anything, so what was the point?

If only Mum had told her earlier, she might have had an ally in all this. Instead, she'd found out in her mother's will.

Anemone was twenty-nine years old and an orphan. Her best friend, Rachael, lived in Norwich and Anemone had no partner to share this with. But if her mum could raise her alone, Anemone could do this. No decisions had been made about if and when she'd reveal her true identity. In the meantime, she was enjoying her job immensely and was discovering that the Pembertons were not the spoiled, entitled rich she'd expected. She liked them.

The phone rang, disturbing her thoughts, and she rolled her shoulders. She was being paid to do a job, not sit here angsting over a past that couldn't be changed. She touched her headset to answer the call and put the thoughts of the past behind her.

Phillipe ran a finger around his collar and scowled. This was damned inconvenient, wasn't it? He'd needed someone to take over the launch and Annie had come highly recommended from her boss in PR. Her steady temperament seemed to fit his own vibe and they worked well together. But in the weeks they'd been working together, he'd started to notice a lot more.

Like the way her hair curled over her shoulder when she left it down, the light brown flickering with auburn tints in the light. Or how blue her eyes were, even when she wore her cute glasses when she was working. She was amazingly efficient and often anticipated what he needed, which was utterly brilliant. And she was also surprisingly sweet, like when she'd said to call her Annie. Though he somehow preferred the name Anemone. It suited her—bright and cheerful and yet dainty and sweet.

He rolled his eyes. *Mon Dieu*, what was wrong with him? What a sappy thing to think.

He had much more important things to do, like make sure everything was set for the launch next week. This was his first one as a member of the senior manage-

ment team, and he didn't want to let William down…
or Bella, either. The Pemberton family had put a lot of
trust in him when they'd promoted him to the executive team. He'd actually designed this particular scent
two years ago. It was an odd bit of symmetry that had
him in charge of its launch now.

Funny how much life could change in two short
years.

He pushed those memories aside and focused on
his day's itinerary instead. Today's trip to Montparnasse would expose Annie to the wide variety of scents
Aurora had to offer. If the lab were closer, he'd love
to show her how scents were blended, but Grasse was
too far a trip for a day. Instead, he'd show her the end
product and try to explain the steps. If she were going
to work in fragrance, she should understand it. While
they were there, he'd look at the quality control reports
and ensure everything was ready to ship next week.
Nectar would initially only be available online or in
Aurora stores. In six months, they'd expand distribu-
tion to an exclusive number of retailers worldwide.

So many details. There were times he seriously
missed the lab. But getting out of Grasse had been a
priority after his divorce, and when the opportunity
had presented itself, he'd jumped at it.

A knock on the door pulled him out of his thoughts.
"You ready for our meeting, Phillipe?"

He spun to find William leaning against the doorframe. "*Oui, bien sûr.* Sorry. Got lost in my thoughts
for a moment there."

William chuckled. "I hope they were good thoughts.
How are you finding things? I know we threw you into
the deep end in the job."

"Slightly overwhelming," he admitted, putting his hands in his pockets. "But I'm managing. It's a learning curve, that's all." More than a learning curve. Throwing him into the "deep end," as William put it, had been a blessing, because his divorce had nearly drowned him and with the new position, he'd had to start swimming. The less time he had to think about Madelyn, the better. It was also why he shouldn't notice so much about Anemone. She worked for him, and he was still a wreck from the breakdown of his marriage. Two very good reasons to keep his distance.

"We're here to help," William said, sitting down across from Phillipe's desk. He opened up a folio. "Did you get the marketing reports this morning? They just sent copies to my office."

"Yes, Annie had them all printed out for me. The focus groups did very well. It's encouraging."

"It certainly is. The demographic data is quite illuminating…"

The meeting got underway, but Phillipe couldn't seem to erase the image of Anemone's blue eyes, looking at him through her spectacles.

He was in so much trouble.

Annie had never been to the storage facility in Montparnasse before. The building itself was rather nondescript, with a heavy double door that could be used as a loading dock. It certainly didn't have the polished glamour of the Aurora shops or offices, but as Phillipe entered his security code for the front entrance, Annie felt a frisson of excitement. She was still awestruck by the magnitude of the business, and it seemed she learned something more every day. This building was just one in the massive Aurora empire. And clearly, it was a favorite of Phillipe's. There was no hiding the excitement on his face.

"After you," he said, as the panel beeped, and the door unlocked.

There was a reception area just inside, and he signed them both in and accepted key cards. "*Merci*," he said to the receptionist, and then handed the ID over to Annie. "We keep tight security here. There's a lot of inventory."

"Are the perfumes made here?"

"No," he answered. "We have a facility in Grasse that manufactures and bottles the perfume. We use this as a shipping base. Would you like to test some?"

She nodded, trying to keep her head from swiveling to and fro as they made their way further inside. There were no windows into any of the rooms, only steel doors that required a swipe of a card to enter. No marble counters or floors, just unforgiving concrete as their shoes clicked down a long hall. "Is there only perfume here?" she asked, hurrying to keep up.

"We keep our cosmetics here as well, the skin lines and the makeup. I'm still learning a lot of that part of the division. Scent is my wheelhouse." With his slight accent, the *h* was subtly dropped, and Annie was charmed.

He swiped his card and led her into another room. It was plain, but better than the gray, industrial-looking halls. The walls were white and held glass shelves. But the plainness was erased by the vast array of colorful bottles lining the shelves. Glass every shade of the rainbow glittered around them, and she stopped in her tracks.

"Oh. Oh, my."

He sent her one of those big smiles again. "It's beautiful, isn't it?"

Recessed lighting cast a golden hue over the bottles. "Stunning. These are all of Aurora's perfumes?"

"Indeed." He went to a nearby shelf and plucked off a dark blue bottle. "Indigo," he said, "released three years ago. For men *and* women. I used bergamot, cardamom, and sandalwood."

"You made this?"

"Yes. And several others here. Before I came to Paris, I led the team in Grasse."

"Which is the perfume capital of the world."

"Indeed." He smiled at her again. "You haven't been?"

"No, never," she replied, feeling rather provincial.

"We'll have to rectify that someday soon," he said. He put the bottle back on the shelf and gave her a tour of the room, explaining about the three "notes" to a scent—top, heart and base, and how the concentration of oil to alcohol and water made a scent a perfume, eau de toilette, or cologne.

There was a long counter on one side of the room and he led her there, then opened the cupboards beneath. "The bottles on the shelves are empty," he explained. "Light, heat… It can all change the life span of a scent. Humidity, too. Did you know that the worst place to store your perfume products is in your bathroom? Yet that is precisely where most people keep them." He shook his head as he pulled out a few bottles from the cupboard. "These are kept inside, where it is dark and cool. Let me choose a few for you to try."

He let her smell a few samples, setting them on the

counter and spraying a strip of paper with the perfume and letting it dry before holding it close to her nose. "Not too many," he advised, "and you need to give your nose a break in between, or you'll get nose fatigue."

The term made her laugh, but she took in all he told her about the design of the bottles by superior glassmakers. Finally, he took out a stunning amber bottle with bubbles in the glass that made it appear effervescent. "That's the new one," she said, admiring the rich design. "The glass is even more beautiful in person."

"Exactly. It was created by a glassmaker in Biot, famous for their bubbled glass." He removed the top and sprayed another strip. "Tell me what you smell."

She took a slow sniff and let the scent envelop her. She closed her eyes. "Citrus, I think. And maybe… It's warm and sweet, like honey, with some sort of flower."

"You have a great nose," he pronounced. "The base notes aren't revealing themselves to you yet. But yes, blood orange at the top, and honey and jasmine in the heart notes. The base is patchouli and beeswax."

"Which is why it's called Nectar," she reasoned.

"Exactly. Though naming it certainly isn't my department. Hold out your wrist."

She did, and he misted it with the fragrance. "Your top notes will be immediately apparent. But as the day goes on, you'll be able to see how the scent changes with your own body chemistry."

She lifted her wrist and inhaled the warm, soft scent. "This is lovely, Phillipe."

"It is one of my favorites."

"You designed this, too?"

"I did, two years ago. I'm delighted it's finally going to market." He sighed. "It was the last one I mixed.

After that, I moved up to running the entire facility and was more hands-off." His eyes took on a faraway quality, and to her surprise, she thought she detected a flash of pain on his face.

"You miss it."

He smiled at her. "Very much. Don't get me wrong, I like the new job and it's a fabulous opportunity. But my heart will always be in the lab with the oils."

He clapped his hands together then, dispelling the mood. "Come. There's more for you to see."

By the time they finished the tour, it was after five and Annie's stomach was growling. She'd only packed some fruit for her lunch, as her fridge was nearly bare and she was trying to economize, and she'd eaten at her desk, trying to plow through her tasks. She'd never thought she'd live the starving-student diet at this point in her life, but the rent on her studio flat ate up most of her earnings. Thankfully, the seconded position came with a premium added to her regular salary. There was only so much ramen a girl could eat.

"Well, this is where we part, I guess," Phillipe said, as they stepped outside into the spring air. "Shall I get you a taxi to take you home?"

They weren't going back to the office, then. And Annie's budget wouldn't strain to cover a cab, not if she wanted to eat at all in the next few days. Walking was out of the question; she was in her heels, and it was a good three miles back to her flat. "Oh, no need," she said, making her voice breezy. "I'll catch the train."

He frowned. "But it is rush hour. How far away are you?"

Nerves bubbled in her belly. She'd managed to keep her situation private during her few months in Paris.

Once she'd got the job—a miraculous feat in itself—she'd had to sort out logistics. "Only in the third arrondissement," she said lightly. "I really only have to change once. I'll be fine, truly."

"But surely a taxi is much quicker and easier." He lifted his hand to hail one, and Annie reached to pull down his arm.

"Truly, I'm just as happy taking transit."

He stared at her for a long moment as a cab drove by, not slowing. She saw the second he understood because his eyes softened. "We don't pay you enough," he said softly. "I'm sorry, Annie. I never thought."

"It's fine. I'm no different than a million other working women in the city. I have a budget and a cozy place to live, and I can afford transit easier than cab fare. It's real life, that's all." She thought of her mum, struggling to put food on the table with her meager salary. If Annie had understood, she would have insisted on fewer treats and nice things. It was no surprise that there'd been nothing left at the end.

There was no point in thinking about it now. As she was fond of saying, "It is what it is." She just had to work with what she had.

"It was inconsiderate of me. Especially because I seem to be taking my newfound status for granted. Please, take a cab, and expense it. You were here for work."

But it hadn't felt like work. It had felt like a lovely afternoon exploring something new with an incredibly alluring companion. She tucked a loose strand of hair behind her ear. "All right." She relented, because she could tell he honestly felt bad about it. And he was right about one thing—it was rush hour, and the trains would be packed. She'd be home in less than half an hour this way.

Since the initial cab had passed, they'd not seen another, so they walked toward the metro station, where they would be sure to find a cabstand. The air was mild with the promise of spring, and sunny. Annie was finding spring in Paris to be every bit as lovely as she'd heard, and it wasn't a hardship walking next to Phillipe, either.

"When did you first move to Paris?" he asked, making conversation.

She tucked her hair again; the light breeze kept ruffling it in front of her face. "Last October when I took the job in the PR department. I was in Guildford before that...outside of London. I lived with my mum and commuted into the city for work."

"Your mother must miss you," he mused.

She swallowed against a lump in her throat. "My mum died nearly a year ago. She had a brain aneurysm. Nothing we could do, no warning."

He stopped, then took her hand in his. "Oh, Anemone. I'm so sorry. What a horrible thing. Do you have any other family?"

"I never had any brothers or sisters, and my grandparents passed on when I was a teenager." She smiled up at him. "It's okay, truly. I wanted a fresh start and here I am. My story tends to be a bit of a downer. How about you? Are you liking being in Paris?"

He accepted her change of subject and shrugged. "It's not quite home for me yet. I grew up in Grasse, and I miss it."

"You left people behind?"

His jaw tightened. Not a lot, but just enough that

she noticed, and she wished she could take back the question. "My parents. But no one else who would miss me."

Her curiosity spiked. There was a lot in what he wasn't saying, and she figured a relationship had gone wrong. By her best guess, Phillipe had to be in his midthirties. She'd noticed right off that he didn't wear a wedding ring. But that didn't mean much in the over-all scheme of things. One didn't have to have a ring to have their heart trampled on.

"I'm sure that's not true." She couldn't imagine someone not loving Phillipe. He was kind, smart, handsome…the total package, really, when all was said and done. And he was successful. He had a lot to offer someone. "And anyway, her loss."

He turned his head sharply to look at her. "Who said there was a woman?"

"Your face did." She lifted an eyebrow. "Unless I'm completely wrong."

He sighed. "You're not wrong. My divorce was fi-nalized, oh, a year and a half ago now. I'm afraid I haven't quite left all my bitterness behind."

She thought for a moment as they made their way along the sidewalk that was growing more crowded the closer they got to the station. "I think we all have wounds that take longer to heal than we'd like," she finally said. "Don't be too tough on yourself."

They reached the cabstand and stood in the short line. "I find that hard to believe of you." He shoved his hands in his pockets again and met her gaze. "You don't strike me as the bitter type. Or someone who in-dulges in self-pity."

"You'd be surprised."

"What are you bitter about, Anemone Jones?"

She looked up at him and took a breath. There was a lot, and while she tried to keep positive, some days resentments did sneak in. She was human, after all. "I never knew my father," she admitted. "Never even knew who he was until my mother died. And then I found out he'd died before her, so now I'll never know him at all."

Phillipe's gaze softened. "I'm sorry," he said quietly. "That's rough."

"I try not to let it get me down, but there are times when I can't help but think what if." She shrugged. "So I get it. Moving on is hard."

The couple ahead of them got in their cab and Phillipe and Annie stepped ahead, waiting for the next car. It took no time at all for one to arrive, and they slid into the back seat. "Let's drop you at yours, and then I can go on to my place and pay for the entire trip with the company card."

"Thank you," she said quietly, but then realized her boss was going to notice that she lived in a very plain walk-up apartment. Then again, what did it matter? He already knew she was finding it very tight financially. She had to let her pride go sometime.

She gave her address, and the car began zipping its way through traffic. "So," Phillipe said, "on a lighter topic, the launch party next week. You are coming, yes?"

Her eyes widened. The launch of Nectar was a posh event in a ballroom with catered food and champagne and beautiful people. She should know; she was organizing it. She certainly didn't belong there.

"Oh, I don't think so. I'm pretty sure assistants don't usually attend these things."

"But I think you should. You're part of the team and you dived right in with the planning and details. This wouldn't be happening at all if not for you."

She looked him dead in the eye. "Do I look like I would fit in there?"

He stared back. "Do I?"

She imagined him in a tuxedo and bit down on her lip. "Actually, yes."

"Well, I don't feel it. I'll make a confession—half the time I feel like an imposter, and one day William and Bella and the other Pembertons are going to figure out that I'm not management material."

She shook her head. "Nonsense. They wouldn't have trusted you with the position if they didn't think you could do it. Besides, you probably already have a tuxedo and shiny shoes."

He laughed and rested his head against the back of the seat. "Well, yes, I do." He turned his head. "So come with me. We can go as a work team. It's much better than trying to find a plus-one. If we get bored, we can have an impromptu staff meeting." He grinned and she couldn't help but smile back. "Consider it moral support."

"I'll think about it," she replied, because what woman in her right mind could say no to Phillipe Leroux?

"Excellent."

A little curl of excitement took up residence in her belly. She imagined the ballroom, and the glittering lights and crystal glasses of champagne, hors d'oeuvres that she'd ordered but couldn't pronounce, and beautiful dresses and shoes. But just like that, her excitement dissipated, and she came to earth with a thud.

How could she attend an Aurora Inc. function in nothing but a little black dress she'd bought on the high street? And there were no funds to buy something new and appropriate—it would cost her an entire month's rent.

The truth settled in, harsh and deep. She might have a place at Aurora Inc., but she would never be a Pemberton. She might as well face up to that now.

CHAPTER TWO

IT WAS JUST as well that Annie didn't let her fantasies
run away with her, because the next day she was called
to the fifth floor and the executive offices for a meeting. When she'd asked if it was for her to attend with
Phillipe, Stephen Pemberton's assistant said that, no,
only she was required and to please go to the small
boardroom.

She couldn't imagine what it could be about, so she
grabbed her phone and shoved her laptop into her bag
in case she needed to take notes or bring up any files.
Then she made her way up to the executive offices.

She wasn't a stranger to the floor; she dealt with
William's and Bella's assistants often enough. But to
meet with Stephen—he was COO and head of acqui-
sitions. It all felt very strange, and she knocked on the
boardroom door before opening it a little.

"Miss Jones. Come in."

Stephen Pemberton was intimidating at the best of
times, with his tall frame, strong jaw and dark features.
He wasn't smiling as she opened the door and stepped
inside, and then discovered the whole of the Pemberton family seated at the table, looking at her strangely.

Her gaze settled on Aurora, the matriarch of the

family. Her normally placid features looked shaken,
her face pale, and her eyes uncertain.

They know.

Somehow they knew. She could feel it in the slow,
sickening twist of her stomach, the way they stared at
her with barely veiled hostility. How had they found
out? She'd said nothing. As far as she was aware, not
a soul knew she was Cedric's daughter. But to appear
before the entire Pemberton family? There was only
one possible reason.

She wanted to turn and run, but where would she
run to? Nowhere. So she swallowed against the fear in
her throat and stood in the doorway, unmoving, feeling rather like a trapped animal.

"Miss Jones," Stephen began, his voice steady.
"Anemone Jones, daughter of Catherine Jones?"

"Ye—" She tried to speak, and the word caught.
She cleared her throat and tried again, determined to
be strong. "Yes." Better.

"You were born in Guildford?"

She nodded. "Yes." She made herself look directly
at him because she couldn't bear to see the expressions
on everyone else's faces. She'd walked right into an
ambush, hadn't she?

"And you're twenty-nine."

"Just turned."

"It's not true." Charlotte stood, and Annie looked
over at her. Hatred flew like sparks from Charlotte's
eyes. "You're six months younger than I am, and you
are not Cedric Pemberton's daughter!"

"Sit down, Charlotte," Stephen said sharply.

To Annie's surprise, Charlotte sat, but the hostility
in the room rose substantially.

"Please shut the door, Miss Jones," Stephen said, though despite the word *please*, it wasn't exactly polite.

She had to explain, but she didn't know where to start. Panic threaded like ice through her veins. How this had happened was a thought for another time. Right now, she had to keep her focus on answering questions as best she could. She had done absolutely nothing wrong. The thought grounded her. As she was trying to find the words to respond, Aurora spoke from the end of the table with quiet authority.

"How much do you want?"

Annie's gaze shifted to look at the older woman. "Oh, no, it's not like that. I don't want anything."

Aurora scoffed. "Please, Miss Jones. It's always like that."

How sad that the Pemberton automatic default was that everyone must want something from them.

"Do you plan to contest the will?" This from Bella, who seemed the least antagonistic of anyone in the room, her posture attentive but not on edge, her words measured.

"What? No," Annie said, looking at her, hoping to find a partial ally in this ambush. "Of course not. Not at all. I didn't even know myself until after Cedric had passed. I never knew who my father was growing up. Mum refused to say." It had been the thing she'd resented most. Her mum had said it was to protect her and to protect her father, but it had always felt as if a piece was missing. And to find out after his death had been cruelly harsh. Her gaze darted from face to face. "How did you find out? I never intended—"

"Never intended what?" Charlotte demanded. "This

was calculated. You're working here. You have access to any number of things. Just what were you planning?"

"Yes, why are you here, at Aurora?" William took a turn to speak. "You've been working here since October. To what end? Make money selling our secrets to the tabloids, perhaps?"

She swallowed against the tightening in her throat, suddenly angry at the unjust accusations. What kind of world did they live in where everyone was suspected of horrible motives? "I wanted…" She took a moment for a breath, to consider her words. "I just wanted to know more about you. I did not intend to create any problems with the family. Exactly the opposite, actually." She took a breath and looked at Bella. "You're all assigning motives that don't exist. I only wanted to get to know who you were. I never wanted to turn anyone's world upside down."

She took a moment, considered that perhaps the truth would work best, even if it made her vulnerable. "I just… I don't have anyone. My mum died last year."

"Yes, we know."

The blunt, emotionless reply was from Stephen, and she swiveled around. "You know?"

"Of course we do. When I discovered who you really were, I did some digging. And whatever you say about not wanting anything, you're lying. The money stopped flowing when our father died. You must miss that biannual deposit." He dropped his gaze to her simple skirt and blouse, assessing. "Whatever did you do with the money, anyway?"

Annie stared as her lips fell open. "What money?"

"Come, come, Miss Jones. Let's not play dumb." Aurora's smooth voice cut through the heavy silence.

Annie's mind spun. She'd never seen any money. She supposed it had all gone to her mum, really. And what had Mum done with it? There certainly wasn't any left now. Oh, goodness…the little trips, the treats and tickets to concerts, little shopping days… Had that all been Cedric's money?

"I don't understand," she said. "When Mum died, I was her sole beneficiary. Believe me, there was nothing left, not by the time I paid the funeral costs. We rented a little house in Guildford, certainly nothing extravagant."

But there'd miraculously been money for her to go to school in London for a year. And they had never been hungry or cold—their lifestyle had been modest but not poor. She'd gone to a decent school. She'd taken piano lessons. She'd always thought her mum had been a whiz at budgeting on her small salary, but now she wondered if Cedric had indeed been topping up the coffers.

She looked at Aurora. "I swear to you, Mrs. Pemberton, I never knew anything about your husband until Mum died. I just wanted…" She cleared her throat of any emotion and tried again. "I applied for a job here because I wanted to know a little more about him. Not for any nefarious reasons. Not to extort you."

No, she thought to herself. *To feel as if I'm not so very alone in the world.*

She pushed back the thought before it could unravel her any further. "I thought if I could meet his family, I might be able to…"

She stopped. The next words sitting on the tip of

her tongue would make her sound utterly foolish. "I'm sorry," she finished.

Stephen took a step closer. "You thought you might be able to what, Miss Jones?"

"It doesn't matter." It was over now, wasn't it? She'd had her glimpse of her father's family and had a great job for six whole months. She didn't want to start over again, but she didn't have much of a choice.

"I think it matters very much," said Bella. "What did you want to be able to do?"

Being held to account by the very intimidating Pemberton clan was tough; deliberately making herself even more vulnerable was excruciating. Her heart pounded painfully as she stood silently before them, being judged.

Maybe her methods had been flawed, but her motives were pure. Not that they'd believe her, but she knew it in her heart. "I thought I might get to know him a little by knowing you. And I knew if I came to you claiming to be his daughter, I would never get the chance. Was that a mistake? Possibly. But what would have happened if I'd come out of the woodwork, making this claim? What would you have done?"

Stephen raised an eyebrow. "Exactly what I did when the discrepancy showed up in the accounts. Investigated. And shown you the door."

"Stephen," Bella said quietly.

"Yes, exactly," Annie agreed. She turned to Aurora. The woman was powerful and intimidating with all her calm strength, but Annie detected a crack in the facade, a flash of uncertainty in the set of her lips. "I'm sorry, Mrs. Pemberton. I know this must be hurting you terribly. Part of the reason I kept this secret was because I truly did not want to hurt anyone, you most of all. He was your husband and—"

"I knew," she interrupted, her voice like steel covered in velvet.

A hush fell over the room.

"Maman," Stephen said, staring at her. Every eye in the room focused on the woman who maintained such a stoic posture.

"What, Stephen?" Aurora turned cold, gray eyes on her son. "I did not know the details. But I knew about the affair. I knew there'd been a child. And I knew he'd sent money. If you had come to me with your concerns, I could have helped you. But you kept me in the dark."

"But today…" He ran his hand through his hair. "When I told you about this, and asked to set up the meeting…"

Her lips thinned. "I wanted to see for myself. I wanted to see Anemone and I wanted to hear her answers. And now I have."

Charlotte stood again. "I want a paternity test."

"Agreed," said William.

Aurora sighed. Annie desperately wanted to sit down; the adrenaline was still coursing through her system and she was feeling quite wobbly, but she knew she couldn't sit so she took even breaths as she stood before what felt like her jury.

"I agree to take a test," she said clearly, lifting her chin.

"Good," said Aurora, nodding at her with what could be considered a touch of approval. "Though you have his eyes. And you're wearing his mother's locket."

Her hand went to her neck where the silver pendant lay warm against her skin.

"Give it back."

Annie turned startled eyes toward Charlotte, whose hostility was plain in the angry flash of her eyes and flush of her skin. "That was my grandmother's. Give it back."

"Charlotte," Aurora snapped.

Tears finally stung Annie's eyes. The locket was all she had of her father. But he was also a father she had never known. Charlotte, William, Bella and Stephen had grown up with him. They had memories to cherish. What claim did she have, other than blood? Her lip quivered and she reached for the clasp at her neck. She didn't deserve a family heirloom.

She held it for one last moment in her palm, then put it down on the boardroom table.

"It would be best for you to clean out your desk today," Stephen suggested, firmly, but not harshly. "And I would advise you not to go to the press."

As if she would. If she'd wanted to, she could have sold her story ages ago and had plenty of money. Everyone in the room knew that she could have asked for anything and had asked for nothing.

So she lifted her chin a little more. "You know, your actions today are exactly why I never told you in the first place. I knew this would happen. And perhaps you're not wrong. It's a horrible thing, a family secret like this." She thought of Phillipe and his animated face just yesterday, showing her the different fragrances in Montparnasse. The launch of Nectar meant so much to him. Right now she wasn't feeling any particular loyalty toward the Pembertons, but she didn't want to let him down. She made a snap decision and chose to focus on Bella as she spoke.

"But I should remind you that you have a major launch next week, and I'm the only one who knows all the details. It would be unfair to the other staff for me to abandon them now, and utterly unfair to Phillipe, who has so much at stake. I'll make you a deal. I'll take your paternity test and I keep my job until the launch. After that I'll pack up my desk and be gone."

There was silence in the room, then Stephen spoke up. "I don't think you're in any position to call the shots here, Miss Jones."

She kept her gaze on Bella. "Am I not?"

Everyone present knew that she was carrying a PR grenade and all she had to do to pull the pin was go to the press.

"I agree to your terms." Bella gave a short nod.

"Bella!" That outburst was from Charlotte, who seemed particularly distressed about Annie's existence. But who could blame her? Aurora had been pregnant with her while Cedric had been having an affair with Annie's mother. She was entitled to her feelings. Annie reminded herself again that none of this had been her fault.

"Next Friday, then," Stephen said, his voice slightly hoarse. "Next Friday you'll be gone."

"Agreed. Now if there's nothing else, I need to get back to work."

Annie was greeted with silence, so she turned on her heel and left the boardroom.

All the way down the hall she kept her composure. Down a floor and back to her desk, she never wavered. But when Phillipe came around the corner and took one look at her face, he stopped short.

"Annie?" he said, his eyes wide with concern.

And then her tightly maintained composure crumpled, the first sob came out, and she found herself wrapped in his arms.

Phillipe had no idea what had just happened. One moment he was coming out to ask Annie a question, and the next he was holding her as she cried against his shoulder. What on earth could have happened?

"Come into my office where it's more private," he murmured in her ear, stepping back a bit but keeping a steadying hand beneath her elbow. "Come, Annie. It's all right."

She gave a shaky nod and followed him. Once inside his office, he shut the door and guided her toward a chair. "What can I get you? Water? Tea?"

"Nothing, thank you. I'm so sorry. I can't believe I started to cry." The reply was punctuated with sniffs, so he retrieved a box of tissues from the little bathroom off his office and handed it to her.

She took three and dabbed her eyes, then blew her nose.

Phillipe pulled up another chair so he was sitting near her, rather than behind his desk. "When you're ready, tell me what happened."

It took a few moments, and another blow of her nose, before she seemed to trust herself enough to speak.

"It's such a long story," she said softly. "I'll be fine. But you should know… I'm leaving Aurora after the launch."

"What?" Phillipe ran a hand over his face. "Why?" She was sitting in his office, her face red from crying, looking absolutely defeated. What on earth could have happened? This morning everything was fine.

"I expected it would happen if…" She paused.

"If what?"

When she stayed firmly silent, he moved his chair a little closer. "Annie, please tell me what's happened. You can trust me."

"I know I can." She lifted her chin and met his gaze. She looked utterly miserable. "But you're going to look at me differently, and I'm not going to like that."

"Let me be the judge of that," he said, but a flicker of unease went through him. Keeping secrets was high on his list of disliked behaviors. Right up there with betrayal and lying. They all seemed to go together, somehow.

"Don't say I didn't warn you." She twisted her fingers in her lap, then met his gaze. "They—the Pembertons—found out who my father is."

He drew his brows together. "So what? What does your father have to do with anything?"

"My father," she said slowly, "was Cedric Pemberton."

Phillipe sat back in his chair. Of anything Annie could have told him this morning, this wouldn't even have made the top one hundred. Her, Cedric Pemberton's daughter? "I don't understand."

"My mother had an affair with him. I am the product of that affair."

"And you work here, but they never knew about you?"

She shook her head. "Apparently Aurora knew I existed but didn't know it was me. And I wasn't going to say anything, either. I just wanted to know who they are. I don't have any other family, you see. But I knew if I told them, I'd never get a chance to know them at all."

"So you lied to them."

"Yes," she whispered. "Because I didn't want to hurt anyone."

Phillipe got up from his chair and paced to the other side of the room. *I lied because I didn't want to hurt you.* Those words had been Madelyn's and he still hated them. As if she'd somehow spared his delicate feelings. He balled his fingers into tense fists, then let them go again.

"How did they find out?" He should just let her go. He loathed the idea of someone pretending to be who they weren't. She'd got the job under false pretenses, then. Now she was key staff to a major launch. What an unholy mess. "Did they fire you?"

She blew her nose once more and her face took on a stubborn set. "No. I agreed to leave after the launch. As far as how they found out, apparently my father paid my mother money for years, though I didn't know about that. Stephen tracked the money and discovered me."

"I see."

She stood and folded her hands in front of her. "Do you? Really? Because if it was money I wanted I could have gone to them and contested the will. I could have asked them for money to go away. I could have sold my story to the papers. I didn't do any of those things, Phillipe. I just wanted to get to know them. I discovered a job I really loved and one that I'm good at. And as of next Friday, that's all over."

He thought for a moment. She was right about one

thing. If she'd wanted money, she could have gone after it in a variety of ways. He'd seen where she lived. *Modest* was a generous descriptor of her building and one would assume the flats within. She took transit to save money. And while he was no expert in fashion—fragrance was his thing—he knew that despite her tidy and professional appearance, she didn't have a high-end wardrobe.

Money had not been her objective, then. Was she telling him the truth about wanting to know her family? Or was she playing on his sympathies?

"Charlotte insisted on a paternity test. I agreed to it." She wiped her hands over her face. "I'm so sorry I broke down in front of you. It was just delayed emotion from being ambushed. I had no idea what was coming until I stepped into the boardroom this morning and they were all there."

"You're really Cedric Pemberton's daughter."

"I am. Stephen wanted me out of here today, but I'm staying until after the event." She met his gaze and he saw steel under the sweetness. "When I take something on, I see it through. Now, speaking of, I have a lot of work to get through this afternoon. I should get back to it."

She was almost to his door when he called out. "Annie, wait."

She turned around, but her lips were set, and he noticed her hand shaking on the doorknob. She was putting on a good show of strength, but he could tell she was barely holding it together.

"They can't fire you. I don't think they'd risk the chance of a wrongful dismissal suit."

She shrugged. "Technically I did nothing wrong,

but I wasn't honest, either. And I won't stay where I'm not wanted or valued."

She lifted her chin and then stepped out of his office.

He let her go.

CHAPTER THREE

PHILLIPE SAT AT his desk for nearly an hour, trying to sort through what Annie had told him. She was Cedric Pemberton's illegitimate daughter. She'd started a job here under false pretenses. She'd lied.

He tapped his pen on the file cover in front of him and frowned. She'd also said that she didn't want to hurt anyone. Was it true? What did it say about him that he wanted to believe her? Was he truly that gullible? Taken in by a pretty face and some tears? It wasn't like he hadn't done that before. Only Madelyn had had the power to stomp all over his heart. Anemone Jones did not.

It also wouldn't be fair for him to judge her based on his ex-wife's behavior. The truth was, she was a damned good employee, and she was going to be out of a job. Simply because of who her father was.

Who she claims he is, Phillipe reminded himself, but seeing her tears, remembering their conversations... He believed her. Granted, being secretive about it was probably not the best decision. That one point made him more uneasy than anything.

He tossed the pen on his desk, shrugged on his suit jacket, and made his way upstairs to William's office.

William was one of the fairest men Phillipe had ever met. Phillipe wanted to get the Pemberton perspective before forming a definitive opinion.

William was seated at his desk, staring at a computer monitor, when Phillipe knocked on the doorframe. Will looked up and gave a grim smile. "I wondered when you'd be to see me. I'm actually surprised it took this long."

"I found myself comforting a distraught employee," Phillipe said, stepping inside. "I thought it would be good to get a full picture of what happened."

"It's a hell of a business, Phillipe. How much do you know?"

"Her side…or rather, her perspective. I'm not fond of choosing sides."

Will looked at him for a long moment, until Phillipe grew uncomfortable with the scrutiny. Talking about personal lives wasn't something they did. Will knew that Phillipe was divorced but nothing else. Certainly none of the sordid details, and he'd like to keep it that way.

"You know, then, that she claims to be my half-sister."

"Indeed." Phillipe gestured toward a chair and Will nodded in an unspoken invitation to take a seat.

"She can't work here, Phillipe. You know that. She got this job—"

"Under false pretenses. I know." Phillipe finished Will's sentence. "She didn't disclose who she was."

"Who she claims to be," Will corrected.

The family was taking a hard line on this, it seemed. Will was a fairly easygoing guy, but Phillipe got the sense that he wasn't going to budge an inch where Miss Jones was concerned.

"She said she agreed to a paternity test. She must be confident that the results will show she's Cedric's daughter."

"What else is she going to say?" Will asked.

Phillipe sat back in the chair and studied his boss. It was no secret that when something went awry with the family, Will tended to step up and do damage control. As far as Phillipe was aware, that was how he'd come to marry his wife, Gabi Baresi—by keeping her out of the eyes of the press after a major scandal.

"Has she asked for anything? Money to keep quiet, that sort of thing?"

Will shook his head. "No. Which makes me nervous. She said something about wanting to be close to us because she has no family." He angled a wry glance at Phillipe. "I'm sorry, but I'm distrustful of a sob story."

"Maybe it's true," Phillipe replied, surprising himself by coming to her defense. Still, he'd been the one holding her in his arms earlier. She would have to be a very good actress to fake that kind of emotion. He simply couldn't believe it of her.

"Perhaps you don't understand." Will's jaw tightened. "It's difficult to give anyone the benefit of the doubt in our position. There are always those who want something from us. Who are just looking for a juicy detail to sell to the press. Trust is a rare commodity."

"If she is Cedric's daughter—"

"Then we'll deal with that. As a family."

The message was clear: this was none of his business. The dismissal grated on him.

"You should let her keep her job."

"Stephen will never agree."

"With due respect, Will, it's not up to only Stephen."

Will sat back. "The family has to agree, however." He tapped his fingers on the desk, a little wrinkle forming between his brows as he thought. "You know, though, maybe it would be better to have her here. Certainly easier to keep an eye on her."

Phillipe knew coming upstairs had been a long shot. He decided to remain silent, rather than push his case, and let Will's brain take over.

After several long seconds, Will nodded. "Let me talk to Bella. Stephen's a hothead about this and Bella's the CEO." He tapped his fingers on the desk. "We should have the paternity results by the launch. But if the results are negative—"

"Then she lied, and I won't stand in your way." Phillipe knew there was no guarantee Bella would agree, and even if she did, there was no way of knowing if Annie would want to work here after today's debacle. "I'm just asking you to put yourself in her shoes, if she is Cedric's daughter, and treat her fairly."

"I'm always fair."

Phillipe knew that to be true, at least in his interactions with Will. And he didn't want to push his case too far. She'd negotiated a way to stay until the launch and he didn't want to jeopardize that. But there was part of him that could relate to Annie being the underdog here. He'd felt much the same way when he'd entered Madelyn's family sphere—a very different class from his upbringing. Always feeling *less*, and at a disadvantage. No matter how much he tried to make it otherwise.

"Thank you for hearing me out," he offered, standing and holding out his hand.

Will shook it. "You're doing a great job, Phillipe. I know it's been a steep learning curve, moving from mixing to running the lab and now corporate. Don't minimize all you've accomplished. No matter what happens, the launch will go forward, and your department will have the support it needs."

"Thanks," Phillipe answered, and shook Will's hand. But after he left and headed back to his own office, he wondered why he'd felt so compelled to fight for Annie. Was it just because she'd cried on his shoulder? Was he that vulnerable to a crying woman? He rather suspected it was something more. Like making sure she didn't go through this by herself, the way he'd had to. If nothing else, Annie would not be alone. Not if he could help it.

Annie sat in her flat and stared out the window. She couldn't seem to get up the gumption to do anything this afternoon. Normally, she'd be at work, at her desk and working her way through her sizable to-do list. Instead, she was sitting at home—such as it was—and unable to focus on anything. She could read a book or perhaps take a walk along the river, but instead she was staring at the street below wondering what her next steps should be. Nothing, she supposed, until the paternity results came back. Just thirty minutes ago she'd given a swab to a nurse, officially witnessed by a member of the Aurora legal team. What did they think? That she'd fake the sample?

The family's treatment of her hadn't exactly been a surprise, but it had been more acrimonious than she'd hoped. For months she'd worked at Aurora and the Pemberton family had only ever been pleasant and fair. This was a different circumstance, she acknowledged to herself. Especially for her half-siblings. It wasn't just her existence but what it meant that had to hurt them. That their father—the man they'd idolized—had fathered a child while Aurora had already been pregnant. What a devastating blow. She had always been sensitive to that. It wasn't that she didn't understand. She did. She just wasn't the one to blame and didn't like being treated as the enemy.

So what now? Did she leave Paris? To do so would also mean leaving the Pembertons behind. Aurora Inc. was headquartered here, even though they had the manor house back in England and Charlotte lived in Richmond most of the time. Annie had no place to go if she went home; she'd given up the lease on her mother's house and put their belongings in storage. She couldn't go back without a job.

Or should she find another position here, in Paris? It meant staying in this cramped flat, and she'd never land as great a position as she had at Aurora. And it wasn't as if the Pembertons would give her a glowing reference. Phillipe might, she realized, and her cheeks heated.

Yesterday she'd utterly humiliated herself by bursting into tears. She'd always been like that...holding her emotions in and simply dealing with stress until a breaking point where the dam of overwhelm broke and came out her eyes. To do so in front of Phillipe was mortifying, both because he was her boss and because he was...well... She bit down on her lip. Phillipe Leroux was an incredibly attractive, successful man.

She'd have to be blind not to notice and respond. And his hug yesterday had been so reassuring, so gentle, and yet strong and sure.

She was going to miss the job. She was also going to miss working for Phillipe. Oh, it had only been a temporary assignment to his department, but still.

Annie went to the stove and put on the kettle, then cleaned out the coffee press and added fresh grounds. Learning how to make proper coffee had been life changing, and when the kettle whistled, she poured in the boiling water. In three minutes she'd push down the plunger and have it just the way she liked—hot and strong.

She had just gotten her mug out of the cupboard when the buzzer to her apartment rang. She hadn't placed any orders so it couldn't be a delivery. The DNA test had already been completed. Had they forgotten something?

"Bonjour," she said into the intercom.

"Bonjour, Annie. *C'est* Phillipe.*"*

Phillipe! What was he doing here? She bit on her lower lip in consternation. She was in ratty yoga pants and a T-shirt from the last concert she'd gone to with Rachael. "Come up," she said, not knowing what else to do.

She grabbed the elastic holding back her ratty ponytail and quickly pulled her hair back neatly, twisting it deftly and hoping it looked marginally better. There was no time to change.

Why was he here?

The knock came too quickly, and she let out a breath and smoothed her hands over her face. She opened the door and put on a smile, then hoped her tongue didn't roll out of her mouth.

He had on jeans, a shirt unbuttoned at the collar, and a blue sport coat. He looked delicious.

He glanced at her T-shirt and a slow grin crawled up his cheek. "Nice," he offered, meeting her eyes, his own warm with humor. "But not suitable for the office."

Heat rushed to her face. She stepped back and opened the door wider, inviting him in. "I just made coffee. Would you like some?"

"That would be lovely, thank you."

She left him standing there and went to the tiny kitchen to pour the coffee into two cups. Weeks of working with him had taught her he took his black, like hers, so in mere moments she was back, handing him a cup, and gesturing to the tiny sofa—the only piece of living room furniture that fit in the studio apartment.

"You're rather cozy here," he said, a smile turning up one corner of his mouth.

"*Cozy* is a nice word for it," she replied, and took a seat on the sofa. He sat next to her; the sofa was so small that only a few inches separated them. Everything felt...confined.

He chuckled. "I had a studio flat when I was studying. A bed, a couple of chairs, and that was it."

"I bet you don't now," she said, then could have bitten her tongue. She didn't mean to get snippy about his success.

His dark eyes held hers for a few moments. "No," he said quietly, "I don't. And you wouldn't, either, if you'd made any claim on Cedric's estate."

"You're not suggesting that I—"

"No, not at all!" He held up a hand. "I just mean that I believe what you told me yesterday. You don't have to live like this. If you'd wanted money, you could have leveraged this in many ways. But you didn't."

Relief rushed through her, taking away some of the heavy weight on her shoulders. "Thank you," she breathed, cradling her cup. "That means a lot, Phillipe."

"But you can understand the Pembertons' skepticism."

"Of course! I expected nothing less, to be honest. I mean, if I put myself in their shoes, I would have done exactly the same thing. Maybe more." She hesitated, then looked at him over her mug. "I hope this isn't rude, but why are you here?"

"I was worried. You booked this afternoon as a sick day, but you looked fine this morning. I was worried something had happened."

"Oh! No, not at all." She smiled at him. "Actually, the Pembertons don't waste any time. I came home and had my swab this afternoon. Now we wait."

"You're still leaving after the launch?"

She raised an eyebrow. "Yes. I'm lucky that they agreed to let me stay until the end of next week."

Phillipe took a sip of his coffee, then shifted on the sofa and met her gaze again. "Actually, about that. I spoke to Will yesterday. You're very good at your job. I suggested they should let you stay on. If—"

The cup shook in her hand. "If my test is positive."

"Yes." He gave a brisk nod. "But even if you leave next week, I'll make sure you have a glowing reference to help you get another job."

"I don't know what to say." Or feel, she realized. It

was incredible to think that he'd gone to Will Pemberton to plead her case. She'd been right in her assess-
ment from the beginning: Phillipe Leroux was a good
man, and fair. More than fair. For someone who felt
unsure in his own position, it said a lot that he'd been
willing to vouch for her. "Why would you risk your
own position for me? Not that I think they would fire
you, I mean," she said, starting to stutter a little. "I just
mean... Well, Will is your boss. You put yourself in an
awkward position just talking to him on my behalf."

"Because it's what's fair," he said simply. "If you
are Cedric's daughter, they can't just turn you out in
the cold. And to be honest, I don't think they would.
That's not the family I know. They just need time to
come to grips with it."

Now Phillipe was looking at her with what appeared
to be hope, which also seemed unreal. She was nobody.
Nobody! But somehow Phillipe Leroux had made her
out to be someone important. Someone valuable. That
was a very new feeling.

Aurora's words echoed in her head, and she sighed.
"Aurora did say I have his eyes."

Phillipe was quiet for a bit and sipped his coffee.
It was one of the things she'd noticed about him over
the past weeks. He said what he needed to, but then
often sat back and waited for others to speak, and then
he listened.

Phillipe was a difficult man to resist. Smart, charming, but also kind. Slightly intimidating—he was
educated and held a big position at a billion-dollar
company. And yet today he'd smiled as he remembered his own student days in tiny lodgings. He hadn't

been born rich. He'd come to see her to make sure she was all right.

And he'd fought for her—something no one had done before. Ever. A warm feeling expanded through her chest. "I don't know what to say. Thank you for the support. It means a lot."

Phillipe's shoulders relaxed and he took another drink of coffee. "I'm glad you're not really sick. You'll be back tomorrow?"

"You're sure this is okay? I have no desire to put you in a bad position with your boss."

"No worries about that. I promise."

She finished her coffee and put the cup down on a tiny table. "I appreciate you stopping by. I really do." She was even more glad he'd spoken of giving her a reference if—no, when—she left. She had to start looking toward her future. One that didn't include a position at Aurora Inc. Because even when the DNA test proved that she was Cedric's daughter, it was clear the family wanted nothing to do with her. Phillipe seemed to think differently, but she wouldn't get her hopes up. Phillipe hadn't seen the anger in Charlotte's eyes.

Which just meant her initial reasons for keeping the secret were completely valid. And it wasn't like she even blamed them for their response. She just felt… alone. Though a little less now, with Phillipe on her side.

"You all right, Annie?" Phillipe's concerned voice broke through her thoughts, and she looked up to find his startling blue eyes gazing into hers. Her stomach did that little flip again and she told it to go away. Phillipe had put his neck out for her. The last thing she needed to do was act like a ninny with a crush, even if it was true. She'd be lying if she didn't admit that one of the reasons she'd hated to leave her job was because she'd miss seeing him every day.

"I'm okay," she said softly. "This week has been a lot. Lots of drama. I'm not used to that."

He smiled a little and nodded. "This business, and this family? Drama happens. I try to ignore it and keep my part of the ship steady."

"And I appreciate that," Annie replied, giving a light laugh. "I promise, Phillipe, that I'll do whatever I can to make sure this situation doesn't affect my work or the launch. I know how important it is to you."

The light in his eyes dimmed for a moment, but then it was back again, and Annie wondered if she'd only been imagining it. He looked at her over the rim of his cup as he finished his coffee, then put his cup on the table next to hers. "Well, good. I should be going now. Thank you for the coffee. I'm so glad you're not really sick. I don't think we could do this launch without you."

He really shouldn't say things like that. He couldn't know how much someone like her took it to heart. Annie was self-aware enough to know that she needed to be needed, and right now, other than Phillipe, there wasn't a soul in the world who needed her one bit.

She got up and so did he, and she held out her hand, determined to keep things businesslike. "I'll see you tomorrow, eight sharp," she said briskly, smiling her best employee smile.

He took her hand and shook it but held it just a smidge too long, and his long fingers seemed to cling to hers just a little bit as he withdrew. *"À demain,"* he said quietly, and she resolved not to get all swoony, though it was difficult when he spoke French. He made everything sound so soft and lyrical.

Heavens, she really was a prize idiot for letting him get to her like this.

She walked him to the door and said goodbye, then shut the door behind him and rested her forehead against it. One week. She had one week left of pretending she didn't think her boss was sex on a stick. One week to come up with a new plan.

She turned away from the door and went to find her tiny laptop. It was time to polish up her résumé and start sending it out. As she sat on the little sofa again, she looked around the cramped flat and felt a wave of sadness wash over her. It was tiny with no closet space and a miniscule kitchen, but it was hers, and it was in Paris, and she was going to miss it all horribly.

Then she rolled her shoulders and lifted her chin. There was no point in feeling sorry for herself.

CHAPTER FOUR

ANNIE WALKED BACK into the office carrying her favorite travel mug full of coffee, as she planned to keep it replenished. She'd missed a whole afternoon of work, and time was of the essence with the details of the launch.

There were some odd looks cast her way, but she just offered a smile and a greeting and nothing else as she took her position behind her desk and clipped the earpiece for the phone to her ear. With a relieved sigh—it was so good to be back—she booted up her computer and went to log in.

"It's not even eight."

She looked up to see Phillipe smiling down on her, his eyes warm. "I'm a few minutes early. I figure my situation is already tenuous without adding tardiness to my list of faults."

"When will you have the results?" he asked.

"I don't know. A few days? A week, maybe?" She shrugged. "When you're Aurora Pemberton, you can pay to have these things expedited." She sat back in her chair a bit. "Right now, I have a more pressing problem. The catering menu is to be finalized by ten this morning and I have a list of tasks a mile long. Who knew that missing an afternoon would create such a backlog?"

Phillipe frowned. "Do you need a coffee?"

She lifted her travel mug. "Already on it."

His smile was a sexy curve of his lips and flash of teeth, and it lit his face. Goodness, she liked that she'd put that grin there. There wasn't much about him she didn't like.

One week.

"Let me know if you need anything. I can loan you Lisette for the day if that would help." Lisette was his executive assistant, pretty and quiet and efficient. And she had her own workload.

"Thank you. I'll let you know, but if I start now, I should be able to get caught up."

"Anything you need," he replied, his gaze touching hers.

You, she thought, but she wouldn't say it in a million years. Her crush was rapidly turning into more after the consideration he'd shown the past few days.

He disappeared into his office. She looked up to realize that a few curious stares were turned in her direction. It really was strange being in more of an open concept for admin in the department. She was sure her coworkers were wondering why she'd been gone yesterday, and why Phillipe had gone straight to her desk this morning.

Rather than engage—what could she say, after all— she logged in and brought up her project management software.

She'd only been logged in for five minutes when an urgent email notification popped up from a coworker in the PR department who was helping with the launch details. An issue had come up with on-site security and she couldn't find the guest list to confirm attendance.

Annie sighed. She responded asking if they could have a quick meeting to go over particulars and make sure nothing had slipped through the cracks. Ten minutes later she was on a different floor, walking into Claudine's small office.

"You are a sight for sore eyes," Claudine said, grinning up at her. "I got worried when you went out sick yesterday. You're feeling all right now?"

"I'm fine." Annie pulled out a chair and prepared to get to work. She wished she could talk about what was going on with someone other than Phillipe. She'd considered calling Rachael in Norwich, just as a sounding board, but something had held her back. Rachael was the only other person in her world who knew she was Cedric's daughter. She'd also warned Annie against the scheme of working in Paris, worried it would backfire. Now that it had, Annie figured she just wasn't up for a conversation of *I told you so.* She liked Claudine very much, but this was too big, too incendiary. So she kept her mouth shut.

They spent the next ninety minutes going through the guest list and then coming up with a contingency plan for security, since so many VIPs were going to be attending. Claudine was overseeing press releases and then official coverage of the event for Aurora; together they arranged for the press passes that would be needed for the night. Annie didn't recognize many of the names, but she certainly knew the magazines and media outlets they represented. It was hard not to be a little starstruck about it all. It was also a lot of pressure to get things right. She wasn't used to being a cog in a wheel this big.

"Is catering set?" Claudine asked, finally sitting back in her chair.

"I sent the approved lists back this morning, so we should be good there." Thank God she didn't have to organize every detail; mostly it was coordinating and arranging approvals. "I'm nervous about this, Claudine. I've never done something this big before."

Claudine flapped a hand. "You've done fine."

"But I'm out of my comfort zone—"

"Don't be silly," Claudine interrupted. "Maybe this is bigger, grander than you're used to. But what the position needed was someone with great organizational skills, and you've got those in abundance."

Annie appreciated the vote of confidence, but her mind slipped back to Bella and the rest of the family. Would they think the same? Did they care about her organizational skills? And what about Phillipe? He'd put himself smack in the middle. If things didn't end well, how would his career be affected because he'd championed her?

The days passed all too quickly in a haze of planning and preparation. Annie had just solved the security issue when there was a problem with the main display that was to be center stage. Five names were added to the guest list and the press list finalized. Annie was both exhausted and energized. The event promised to be a who's who of entertainment and fashion, and she was the one putting it together. Did she feel out of her league? Definitely. Was she pulling it off anyway? Yes. Because she was smart and capable. For the first time, she'd been given the opportunity to show just how much. And the stakes were high, too. The last thing she wanted to do was fail in front of the Pembertons—or worse, let Phillipe down.

She was in a meeting with him in his office when his phone buzzed. He looked down and frowned. "It's William," he said, and picked it up.

"Yes...yes, of course. Right away."

He hung up and met her gaze.

"What's wrong?" she asked. He'd gone still, and there was a look of sympathy in his eyes that put her on edge.

"William was looking for you. The family wants to see you upstairs. In Bella's office."

Her fingers started to tremble. She'd known this moment was coming. She was confident in the results. Her mum wouldn't have lied. So why was she so nervous? Why was she afraid to hear the results? What difference could it possibly make to her?

"I'm going with you," Phillipe said, rising from his chair once again. "You're not going into this alone."

She nodded dumbly and stood, feeling a bit shaky. "I should say no, but I'd be glad of the moral support."

"You're no good to me if you faint," he replied, his tone dry, and she started to laugh. She could always rely on his subtle sarcasm and dry wit. It was quite charming, really. He seemed to know just how to ease the tension in situations with a little quip. How could he not see that in himself? The jest helped her settle her nerves, too. She was going to walk into Bella's office with her head held high.

"Let's leave that here," he said, taking the file folder from her hands and putting it on the desk. "Ready?"

"No," she said, "but I have to face this head-on. It's the only way I'll be able to move forward, whatever that looks like."

They went together to the elevators and up to the fifth floor. Annie's heart pounded against her ribs, anxiety ratcheting up her pulse and making her slightly light-headed, though she was determined not to show it. Phillipe was steady and solid beside her, and she was so grateful for his presence. He tapped on Bella's door—the expansive office for the CEO that had windows overlooking the Seine—and they stepped inside.

The Paris-based members of the family were already present: Bella, Stephen, William, Christophe. Annie took a breath and faced them head-on. "Will Aurora and Charlotte be joining us?"

Stephen shook his head. "No. We spoke to them already this morning."

She couldn't read his expression. Stephen, she realized, had a heck of a poker face.

"Phillipe," William said, his tone low and serious. "This is a family matter."

"I asked him to join me," Annie said quickly, quite willing to take the blame rather than put Phillipe in the middle any more than he already was. "To…to be a witness."

"For heaven's sake," Bella said, and she came around her desk. "Stephen, you don't have to look so intimidating. And Annie, you are fully within your rights to want to have someone with you. Everyone calm down."

Stephen's expression tightened, but he said nothing, letting Bella take the lead.

Bella smiled a little, though it wasn't exactly warm.

It wasn't hostile, either. It was…sad, if Annie had to hazard a guess. Her presence here was not good news, no matter what the outcome. She'd caused this family pain, and she didn't like that one bit.

"Anemone, we asked you up here today because the test results are in. Your sample was tested against mine. And it seems we are, indeed, half-sisters."

CHAPTER FIVE

ANNIE WASN'T QUITE prepared for the relief that rushed through her at the official confirmation. She stared at Bella for a stunned moment and became aware of Phillipe's strong hand on her shoulder. "All right?" he asked, his voice low.

She gave a quick nod. William and Stephen looked grim, Christophe seemed intrigued with the whole thing, and Bella was looking at her with something like sympathy etched on her features. "I'm sorry," Annie said quietly. "I never wanted any of this. Never wanted to hurt you or your family."

"That's already done," Stephen said. "But if you mean that you don't want to harm our family any further, we're having papers prepared by legal for you to sign."

She frowned. "What sort of papers?"

William spoke up. "A deal that will ensure this information won't get out. Basically, you'll be paid for your silence."

Anger began to flicker in Annie's gut, tiny flames of resentment that the people she'd come to know and even like over the past months were not above simply paying someone off to be quiet. "How much?" she asked.

Fire flashed in Stephen's eyes. "Ah. Now we get to it."

Bella was the one who spoke. "Five million euros."

Annie's mouth dropped open. Phillipe's hand slid off her shoulder. Five million euros... What would she ever do with that much money? Hush money. Money to be someone other than who she really was. She shook her head. "I don't want it. I don't want any money."

Stephen snorted, then looked her dead in the eye. "How much will it take?"

They didn't believe her. It suddenly dawned on her that this was the life they led, wasn't it? People always wanting something, whether it was riding on coattails or money to keep a secret. Everyone's motives were suspect. How sad. At times, Annie had hated their small flat and modest car compared with so many other schoolmates. Now she wouldn't trade it for this type of existence for anything in the world.

"I understand you completely," she said, cold certainty settling over her. "I even understand why. I'm your father's dirty little secret and you don't want it to get out. But I don't want money. I don't want anything. I'll finish up my work tomorrow and you won't have to worry about seeing me again."

Silence dropped over the room. Even Stephen's face had softened with surprise. She turned to leave.

"Anemone," Bella whispered, a note of entreaty in her voice.

"Leave her be," Stephen said, but his voice had gentled the tiniest bit. Perhaps she'd finally gotten through to the implacable earl that she was not a gold digger.

William and Christophe said nothing.

"Go downstairs." Phillipe's soft voice was kind and reassuring. "I'll meet you there in a moment."

She nodded dumbly and left the room. She walked to the stairs, needing to keep moving rather than waiting for the elevator. She got to her floor and went directly to Phillipe's office, and then started to pace as she worked through what had just happened.

She was Cedric's daughter for sure. His family hated her. They wanted to pay her off.

She could take the money and then she'd never have to worry again. Of course, there would be the small matter of her pride and self-respect. At this point, it was all she had left. And she would rather make her own way than do it by denying her own existence. Oh, she'd never sell the story or anything like that, but neither would she profit off her silence. She'd give it with her chin up and head held high.

Two more days. Two more and the launch would be over, and she would no longer work for Aurora Inc.

And she'd no longer have a reason to see Phillipe each day.

Phillipe stood in the doorway to Bella's office. In all the months he'd been at Aurora's head office, he'd never been this nervous. But maybe that was because what he wanted to say had nothing to do with fragrance or business but everything to do with the woman who'd just walked away, looking as if the world had just dropped out from beneath her feet.

He looked at William, the family member he was most familiar with. "You might have been a little gentler with her," he said, his voice tight.

"Why?" Stephen answered ahead of William, and it annoyed Phillipe. Stephen was the Earl of Chatsworth, and he could be a good sort, but he could also be a bit cold and unfeeling. Phillipe understood that he was the oldest and that he was just trying to protect his family, but Annie *was* his family now. And he'd treated her contemptuously.

Phillipe had known boys like Stephen his whole life: entitled, powerful, never questioning their place in the world. It had angered him then, and it angered him now. He looked the earl right in the eye. "Because she is your half-sister. Because she has not once shown any desire to hurt you or your family. Because you grew up with your father and she will never know him. And because it is never a bad thing to show a little compassion."

Stephen's eyes widened, and he had the grace to look a bit embarrassed.

To Phillipe's surprise, it was Christophe who spoke up.

"Leroux is right, or at least partly right. I am not as closely related to you as Anemone is, yet I was brought up in your house and given every advantage, including that of a big family of siblings. It is not her fault she was conceived, nor is it her fault she was kept a secret."

Stephen cut in. "But if news of this got out…"

"Then what?" Bella stepped forward, twisting her hands together. "Then the world would know that our father was not the paragon we made him out to be. And Maman would be the woman who'd been cheated on. Yes, there'd be scandal. But it wouldn't be the first time this family was embroiled in one." She looked at Stephen and William. "It wasn't that long ago that you both brought scandal to the door, and we didn't disown you."

Phillipe had remained quiet because it seemed the siblings had some differing opinions that were worth hearing. But he stepped in again, calling himself a fool for getting involved, but knowing Anemone deserved better.

"She has not asked for any money. And believe me, she could use it. She lives in a tiny little flat and takes transit everywhere... The woman is on a tight budget. You offered her money to go away just now, rather than offering her a place in your family. I honestly thought this family was more generous, but perhaps I was wrong."

"Now, Phillipe," William began.

"I'm sorry. I know I've overstepped, and this is a family matter, but Anemone has been nothing but mature and composed throughout this whole launch project. She's far stronger than people realize, actually." He shoved his hands in his pockets. "I'll be going now, but I needed to stand up for her. Someone has to. I'm not sure anyone has in her whole life."

He left the office with his heart pounding. If he felt like an imposter in his job position, he'd certainly overstepped the mark insinuating himself into a Pemberton family situation. But he felt what he'd said strongly: the more he got to know Annie, the more he realized that no one had stood up for her. As Cedric Pemberton's daughter, she should have had access to opportunities. Instead she'd been hidden away as if she wasn't worth knowing.

Well, she was. He hadn't been able to stop thinking about her, for example.

He found her in his office, pacing the floor, eyes dry now but her lips set in a firm line. She was still angry. Good. She should be.

"They wanted to pay me off. Give me money to go away! I mean, I didn't expect them to greet me with outstretched arms of welcome or anything, but this... Oh, I'm so insulted."

She was beautiful all fired up like this. Her eyes were like blue sparks and her cheeks had a pink flush to them. The more he got to know her, the more he realized how strong she was.

"What would you like me to do? How can I help?" he found himself asking.

She halted her pacing and stared at him. "Oh." For a moment, she looked nonplussed, as if his question was such a surprise that she'd forgotten what she was about. "Phillipe, you've already done too much. You fought for me to keep my job last week, and listened to me, and went with me today. You went far and above what a boss would normally do."

"I'd like to think that by now I'm not just your boss." At her continued confusion, he added, "I'd like to think we're friends."

Friends. That sounded so mundane and didn't reflect his feelings at all. It was, however, the safest and easiest descriptor. For she couldn't be anything more, could she?

"I...um...well..." She seemed flustered as she looked at him.

Phillipe momentarily felt foolish. "Are we not?"

"I just... Well, I didn't expect it, is all. You've been very supportive. And I could use a friend." She started blinking rapidly and then gave her shoulders a shake and cleared her throat. "I'm not going to cry about this. I'm not. It won't help anything."

"You're disappointed."

"Very. I don't know what I expected, but it wasn't Stephen's coldness. It was so calculating."

Phillipe weighed what to say next, finally deciding on: "We talked briefly after you left. Not everyone feels as strongly as Stephen, you know. You might find you have a few allies in the bunch. If you give them time—"

She scoffed. "I doubt it. When push comes to shove, they'll stick together against me, the outsider. I was foolish to even come here." She looked into Phillipe's eyes. "I wish I'd never found out Cedric was my father. I could have just carried on with my life."

He understood the wishing thing. He'd often had the same thoughts about his marriage, wishing he'd never married Madelyn, wondering where he'd be if he hadn't. But that wasn't the reality they lived in, was it? And he said so.

"Well, you can't change it now. All you can do is decide how you want to move forward." He went to her and picked up her hands. "You would have wondered who your father was forever. And if you hadn't come here, you always would have wondered about the family. Now you know. Now you can put those questions behind you and move forward." The truth struck him as he said the words. "The same way I must. I'll be honest, Annie. I haven't been able to move past my divorce, but the truth is I have my answers and I'm still stuck. I'd like to stop being that way somehow."

A small smile flickered on Annie's lips. "What a sad pair we are, Phillipe."

He smiled back, and suddenly the room was warm again and to his surprise Annie was in his arms, giving him a hug.

His arms came around her and tightened. She felt so good, so right. The scent of her hair was slightly floral and soft tendrils tickled his jaw where she was tucked against him. It would take very little to shift, to put his finger beneath her chin and have her look up at him, to focus on her berry-ripe lips before kissing her…

"What is this for?" he asked softly, rubbing a hand over her back. He didn't want to let her go. He didn't even care that he was technically still her boss. She had less than two days left of work. All too soon he wouldn't be her boss and he wouldn't see her at all. The thought made him feel hollow and lonely. He was going to miss her smile, her energy, her everything.

"Because you've stood up for me through all of this. And because that's the first time you've really opened up about yourself."

"I won't let it happen again."

She pulled back a little and treated him to a teasing smile. "Are you sure?"

He nodded. "Actually, yes, because we have a launch to finalize and attend. Both of us."

She slid out of his embrace and the smile on her face fell away. "Me, there? Oh, the family isn't going to want me there, Phillipe. They want me gone and invisible as soon as possible. My presence at the launch is a no-go."

"You did promise," he said. And he truly had meant what he'd said days ago about the moral support. Not in any romantic sense, but having an ally in the room so he didn't have to go through the evening alone. He wasn't good at the mingling thing.

"Well, that was before. You can't hold me to it now." She started pacing again. "When Friday afternoon arrives, and the day's work is done, I'm no longer an Aurora Inc. employee."

"Then go as my plus-one. I am allowed one, you know."

He wasn't sure where the invitation came from. To ask her not as a colleague but as a date. But he'd done it now and he liked the idea. "You've put in so much work. This way you get to admire the fruits of your labors. Drink champagne. Nibble on whatever delicacies are being circulated."

"And feel daggers in my back every time one of the Pembertons sees me? No thanks."

"Please, don't paint them all with Stephen's brush. Christophe understands. And I think Bella likes you. Please, Annie."

But she shook her head. "I can't, Phillipe. I'm sorry. I know I owe you for all your support, but I can't go to the launch. Not after today. I'll be home, making decisions about where my life is to go next."

"You'll stay in Paris," he said, as if it were a foregone conclusion.

"Maybe, but not necessarily. There's nothing holding me here. And nothing waiting for me back home, either. The world is my oyster, as they say. Which makes my decision harder rather than easier."

Nothing holding her here. Of course not.

"Thank you for going with me earlier. I truly appreciate it." She tucked a wayward strand of hair behind her ear. "But now I should get back to work. There's very little time left and still work to be done."

He let her go because he didn't know what else to say. He cared for her, didn't want her to go, but he couldn't identify what it was he wanted from her. Friendship? Perhaps. He had few friends in Paris. And at times he wanted more, but was he ready to give more? Did he want to see her socially, as in dating? To what end? He wasn't looking to get married ever again. Having his heart stomped on once was bad enough. And he certainly didn't want to have a fling. She didn't seem like the fling type. More like the get-attached type, and that just resulted in people being hurt.

No, it was better to let her go. He'd become far too involved as it was. In two days she'd be gone, the launch would be over, and life would go back to what it used to be around here.

It sounded positively horrible.

Annie grabbed her purse from a desk drawer and once more looked around the office. For the second time in a week, she was leaving, only this time she wouldn't be returning. She was leaving more than a job behind. She was leaving the only blood family she had in the world, and they wanted nothing to do with her. It felt like an ending in so many ways, and not the happy ending she'd always dreamed.

Time to find a job. Start over. It sounded like such a huge undertaking.

She was halfway to the elevators when she heard her name being called. "Anemone? Annie!"

She spun around and saw Lisette rushing toward

her. "Oh, good," Lisette said, reaching her. "I caught you before you left. Come with me."

"I'm sorry?" Annie asked, confused. Could she not just leave with a minimum of fuss and put this all behind her?

"We don't have much time. Come with me." She put her hand on Annie's arm, but when Annie resisted, Lisette halted, looked into Annie's face and smiled. "He said you would resist."

"Who did?"

"Phillipe. The launch is in under four hours. We have to find you a dress and shoes and get your hair done."

Annie shook her head. "I'm not going to the launch. I've just finished my last day and I'm going home." And she was going to order in some dinner and drink an obscene amount of wine and feel sorry for herself, and tomorrow she would get up and call her best friend and then start making plans.

"He said you would say that, too. I was shocked to hear you are leaving. When he asked me to see to this, I agreed right away. Come on. There's no time to waste."

Annie trotted after her, not because she had changed her mind about going to the launch, but because Lisette was a lovely woman and Phillipe's executive assistant…and she was already walking away.

"Where are we going?" she asked, hurrying to catch up.

Lisette turned her head and flashed a smile. "Heaven," she replied. They went down two flights of stairs and then Lisette swiped a key card and led her through a set of glass doors into what looked like a miniature Aurora boutique, right here in the head office building.

Annie halted. "Okay, so I knew this was here… in theory."

"There aren't many offices on the second floor. No need for most of the staff to be here. But it does mean we can pluck an item from the season's designs at a moment's notice if needed for an event or publicity opportunity."

As Annie looked around, she realized that it wasn't quite like a shop; the racks were organized in a far more utilitarian fashion and there were no flashy decorations. Just racks of clothes, shelves of accessories, and great lighting.

"All right. You need a gown."

"Lisette, I appreciate this, but I can't go. Besides, what will the Pembertons do when I show up in an Aurora design?"

Lisette grinned. "Hopefully realize how good it looks on you. Listen, Phillipe is a wonderful man. We both know this. And I can tell he cares for you. I don't know why you're leaving, but if he wants you at this event—an event you planned, by the way—I'm going to get you there." She played her last card. "Neither of us wants to disappoint Phillipe Leroux."

Lisette had her there. She was terrified of facing the Pembertons but the idea of walking in there tonight and seeing Phillipe in his tuxedo, meeting him dressed in couture… It was so very tempting.

"I don't even know what would look good," she said weakly.

"Hmm." Lisette looked her up and down. "I think

I have just the dress. It's last year's line, but I think it'd be perfect."

Annie sighed in frustration. "Did you not hear me say I am not going?"

"I heard you." Lisette came over and took her hands, a gesture that was shocking and lovely all at once. "Look, Annie. I've spent over ten years working for Aurora and the last eighteen months for Phillipe. He is the best boss I have ever had. When he first came here, he was in over his head and there was this... I don't know. Sadness about him. But lately... He smiles more. I think you have something to do with that. If this is really your last day, why not take a chance and show up at the hotel and knock his eyeballs out? He's right. You've worked so hard, and you should be there. And it means so much to him that he planned this whole surprise for you. You should be there to support each other. Don't let him down."

Heat rushed to Annie's cheeks. The one sure way to get to her was through Phillipe. Though, supporting each other...the tone of that was slightly different from that of boss and employee. *Friends*, he'd said. Oh, she was so confused. She didn't know how to define their relationship. Even the word *relationship* seemed presumptuous.

She wasn't actually thinking of going along with this, was she?

Lisette went to a rack, sorted through a few items and pulled out a stunning black-and-white gown. "This is the one. Try it on. I think it'll suit your figure perfectly."

Annie reached out and touched a single finger to the fine fabric. The trouble was she wanted to accept. She wanted to go and see the results of her hard work. She wanted to walk in the door and find Phillipe and see his eyes widen when he saw her in an Aurora original. It was probably the wrong motivation, but it was there just the same, tempting her.

"There's a changing area back here." Lisette took her hand and led her toward the back of the room where a few curtained areas were set up. "I'll be back in a moment."

The dress was fancier than anything Annie had ever laid eyes on before. The white bodice was strapless but had a halter overlay of chiffon. The high waist gave way to a long, slender fall of black silk under more chiffon. She shimmied out of her clothes and slid into the dress. The built-in bra cupped her breasts perfectly, and the zipper was a tiny bit snug, but she could still get it to the top.

She looked down. The dress was at least an inch, maybe two, too long.

Disappointment washed over her. Lisette had picked the perfect dress in the perfect size, a testament to her experience and keen eye. But Annie couldn't do anything about her height.

"How is it?" Lisette asked.

"Too long."

"Come out and let me see."

Annie shifted the curtain and stepped out. Directly across from the changeroom was a mirrored wall, and she caught her breath when she saw the dress. Oh, goodness. Was this really her?

"It's perfect. What size are your feet? A good pair of heels and that length will be just right."

Annie gathered up the skirt and followed Lisette

into what appeared to be a huge closet. Inside, the walls were covered with racks of shoes. "Do you like closed heel or open? A sandal or a platform pump?"

"I have narrow heels. I actually like sandals or slingbacks. The strap keeps my heel secure instead of sliding out of the back of a pump."

"I know just the one. There's a pair of Louboutins in here that you'll love."

Louboutins. She could pay rent for a few months for the cost of a pair of those. Was this even real?

Lisette ran her finger along a shelf until she found the shoes she wanted. "Here, try these." The slingbacks had an open toe with a pretty curve pattern bordered by glittering rhinestones. The heel strap was also adorned by the rhinestones, adding some serious bling to the classic design.

"Step into these," Lisette said, kneeling before her.

The fit was lovely, and Annie turned her foot this way and that, watching the stones sparkle. "This is too much. I can't do this."

Lisette looked up at her. "You can." She stood and looked Annie in the eye. "Anemone, I want to tell you something. Please, sit here for a moment." She led her to a soft settee, where they both perched on the stuffed cushions.

"When Phillipe first came here from Grasse, it wasn't all... How is it you say it? Smooth sailing." She smiled. "There was definitely an adjustment for him in his role with the company, but more than that, he was miserable. It took a while for him to be comfortable with me. Oh, we got along fine working together, but there was nothing personal. Until I put through a call one day and afterward I could tell he was upset. He shared with me then that it had been his ex-wife."

Annie nodded as Lisette patted her hand. "I am divorced as well, and I told him so, and while Phillipe never shared very much, I certainly understood why he was struggling. After a while he relaxed, smiled more, grew more confident. But I have never seen him smile as much as he does when you're around. He's…lighter somehow. And maybe there is absolutely nothing between you, and I certainly don't want to suggest there's anything inappropriate. But he wants this for you, and I think you should put on this dress and shoes and get your hair done and go to the launch. He needs you."

The speech was making a lump form in Annie's throat. It was difficult to think of Phillipe being less than his charming self, to be in so much pain that the cheeky smile and dancing eyes she knew didn't exist.

"I don't know what to say."

"Say you'll go. And don't tell him I told you any of this." She laughed a little. "He's a private man, and a good one." Lisette put her hands together. "All right. There's no time to waste. The dress and shoes are sorted. Now you just need jewelry." She reached into her bag and took out a small rectangular box embossed with the Aurora logo.

"I can't. It's too much."

"You can. Open it."

Annie shook her head and let out a breath, feeling far too much like Cinderella with Lisette as her fairy godmother, even if it was at Phillipe's instruction. She took the box and slid off the lid. Inside was couched a delicate gold necklace, with a gossamer fine chain and a pendant in the shape of a bee sipping from a flower. "Nectar," she said softly, taking the necklace out of the box.

"Most appropriate, don't you think?" Lisette took the chain and hooked it at the nape of Annie's neck. "There. In exactly ten minutes, a car is going to take you to an appointment for a mani-pedi, plus makeup and hair. It's going to be a tight squeeze, so the car will wait for you. The driver will deliver you to the hotel. Okay?"

"You're officially my fairy godmother," Annie remarked, and offered Lisette a genuine smile. "I feel like everything will disappear at the stroke of midnight."

"Don't let it." Lisette squeezed her hand. "When you find something worth holding on to, don't let it go. Now, let's get this dress into a garment bag for you and get you to your car."

She changed quickly and before long she was at the front entrance just as the car service pulled up. Lisette pulled her in for a quick hug. "Good luck," she said, smiling.

Annie slid into the car and perched on the soft leather seat. Nerves settled low in her belly. Phillipe had gone to all the bother to arrange all of this—for her. She was going to the launch. And her entire family was going to be there.

As the car made its way to whatever appointment she had next, Annie made a decision. Tonight she would hold her head high. She was a Pemberton, too, and she'd act like it. Maybe she was leaving Aurora

Inc., but she was leaving with her pride and self-respect intact.

And tonight she would live up to Phillipe's faith in her.

CHAPTER SIX

THE DOORWAY TO the ballroom was less than fifty feet away, but Annie couldn't seem to go any farther. Nerves were making her nearly ill, and she ran a hand over the soft fabric at her waist. She'd spent two hours having her hair, makeup and nails done, and the results had blown her away. Her eyes seemed bigger, lips plumper, and her sandy-blond hair was piled on top of her head in an oversize topknot anchored with a braid. She was horribly afraid something would let go and her hair would come cascading down in a poufy mess, even though the stylist had assured her that would not happen.

The hall was quiet, while the sounds of music and voices were muffled through the ornate doors to the venue.

"Bonsoir, mademoiselle," a voice said, and she realized it was a member of staff waiting to open the ballroom doors.

"Bonsoir," she replied breathlessly, her chest cramping. She hadn't thought before about the anxiety that came from entering a room alone—a room in which she knew barely anyone. This dress, her entire appearance—it wasn't her. She was the kind of woman

who was normally found behind the bar or behind the
scenes holding some sort of clipboard. Not tonight.
All because Phillipe and Lisette had decided she was
Cinderella.

A deep breath. *I am a Pemberton*, she reminded
herself. She stopped fussing with her skirt and gave a
nod. It was now or never.

The door was opened, and she stepped through.

The voices and music were much louder once the
doors were open. The ballroom was simply stunning,
just as she'd imagined it, like a spring garden brought
inside. White linens graced the tables, and arrangements of spring flowers were everywhere: pink ra-
nunculus, grape hyacinth, creamy-white rosebuds;
rainbows of tulips, delicate orchids, fragrant peonies
and, of course, irises. The delicate profusion of color
made the room a veritable bower, while a platform
at the front—an empty beehive—showcased the new
fragrance, Nectar.

And about ten feet away from the dais was Phillipe.

It was as if he could sense her gaze on him, as his
eyes flicked up and saw her standing there. There was
a moment of confusion, then recognition, then a smile
so wide that her heart started fluttering. She had to
move. She couldn't stand in one spot for the whole
night. So she let out a breath, prayed she didn't trip on
the mile-high heels and made her way across the room.

Without breaking eye contact, he excused himself
from his companion and gave her his full attention, so
that when she finally stopped in front of him, it was as
if they were the only two people in the world.

"I didn't think you'd come." His voice was low and
smooth, sliding along her nerve endings. *Oh, dear.*

"I wasn't going to," she admitted. "Not after what happened." She smiled and plucked at her dress a little self-consciously. "But you had Lisette play fairy godmother. I couldn't refuse."

His eyes shone. "You look... My word, Anemone. Nothing I can come up with is adequate. Ravishing."

She hoped she wasn't blushing. She clasped her fingers together and licked her lips. "I have never worn a dress like this in my life, Phillipe. It's an Aurora original. How did you... I mean..." It occurred to her that Phillipe had gone to a lot of trouble and expense to make this happen. She would never be able to pay him back.

"You deserve a night of glamour. You planned the event. It wouldn't be right if you weren't here to enjoy it." He offered his arm. "Come. Let's get some champagne and celebrate our victory tonight. All your hard work has paid off. This whole event is amazing."

She linked her arm with his, liking the feeling of the fine thread of his tuxedo sleeve beneath her hand. *Our victory*, he'd said, linking the two of them together. Her heart tripped at the thought before she reminded herself to keep her feet firmly on the ground. "I kind of wanted to have real bees in that hive, you know," she said.

He chuckled. "Of course you did."

"Phillipe... I don't know how I can ever repay you."

"No repayment necessary. I wanted to do this for you, Annie." He stopped and turned her to face him. "You belong here. Your family should have seen to it. You're a Pemberton and you made this whole event happen."

Still, nothing to do with him wanting her here, or anything...intimate, as Lisette had suggested.

"But this puts you in an awkward position at Aurora," she reminded him. "I don't want you to risk yourself just to prove a point or something. It's not worth it."

"Is it not?" His gaze delved into hers. "Perhaps I think it is."

One of the wait staff approached and offered them champagne. Once the flutes were in their hands, Phillipe offered a toast. "To Nectar," he said, touching his rim to hers. "And to you, for pulling this evening together."

"Just doing my job. Or at least, what was my job."

His smile faded a little as she sipped from her glass. "You're really done at Aurora, then? You're not going to fight for your position?"

She nodded. "I'm done. I won't beg, either for my job or for acceptance. I'm better off alone than scrounging for scraps. Thanks to you, I'm leaving with a good reference, and once the clock strikes midnight tonight, I'll be searching the help-wanted ads." She fought to keep her voice cheerful. "A whole new beginning."

He took a drink of his champagne. "You don't sound that sorry. Is this a good thing?"

She reached out and touched his arm. "Phillipe, I have loved working at Aurora and the last few months. It's been amazing. But on a personal level, with the family, it's too complicated. It was a foolish plan from the start."

"I'll miss you."

Her pulse fluttered as his eyes were steady on hers. "I will miss you, too. More than I can say."

Someone laughed nearby and diverted their attention for a few moments; when they looked back at each other, there was something new in Phillipe's expression. "You know," he said, "this does mean I'm not your boss anymore."

"Oh." She took a quick drink of champagne, finishing the glass. Many of her feelings and thoughts where he was concerned had been inappropriate. Not so much anymore, if he wasn't her boss.

"Maybe we could go for coffee sometime. Or dinner. I don't have many friends in Paris, you know." His eyebrow did a slight shift, and she thought she caught a glimpse of a little dimple. He really was too charming.

"That might be nice," she murmured, and when another server came near, she swapped out her empty glass for a full one. Across the room, she saw William and Gabi talking to Charlotte and her husband, Jacob. William looked up and saw her and his eyebrows lifted in shock. Charlotte followed his gaze and her expression darkened.

"I've been spotted," she murmured.

"Ah yes. But don't worry, there won't be a scene," he said. "They wouldn't chance it. Don't get me wrong, I'm so very glad you're here. But I expect it might feel a little like walking into the lion's den, *oui*?"

She gave a shaky laugh. *"Exactement,"* she replied, then forced a smile.

"You are dressed for battle, though," he replied. "My trust in Lisette was not misplaced."

"She was very persistent. She's a good assistant, Phillipe. You're lucky to have her."

He nodded. "She is. After my divorce I'm afraid I was not very fun to work for. But Lisette had been through it after her first marriage, and she was steady as a rock."

"You don't talk about that much," Annie observed.

"For a long time, I stewed in my anger. Lately, though, I've been thinking about what happened. Madelyn had an affair, and there's no question that was wrong. But she was also married to a man who was a workaholic. I put everything I had into the lab. It was my passion. Coupled with my need to prove myself, I think I spent more time trying to be what I thought she wanted rather than who she needed."

"And she found that somewhere else."

He nodded. "It's hard to forgive. I'm not sure I ever will. Anyway, it's over and done, and now I'm in Paris, at this amazing event, with the most beautiful woman in the room on my arm."

"Phillipe," she murmured, her cheeks heating.

"You *are* beautiful," he assured her. "And since I'm no longer your boss, perhaps it is all right for me to say so?"

She nodded, flustered but enjoying his compliments.

Phillipe stopped and introduced Annie to a colleague from another department, and as they were chatting, Annie glanced around and saw Bella staring at her. There wasn't exactly disapproval in her expression, but confusion, perhaps. Stephen joined his sister and when he glanced over, Annie felt the jolt of the eye contact to her toes. She felt like such an imposter.

They were moving on when Annie leaned over. "Bella and Stephen have seen me."

"Are you all right?"

"I'm not going to worry about it right now. I'm just going to stay out of their way."

"I will stay by your side," he promised.

"But you have obligations. Have you met with the press already?"

He led her closer to the perimeter of the room, away from the loudest of the conversations. "I've met with most of them. And completed my VIP obligations during the private cocktail hour before the event."

"You should circulate as the man of the hour," Annie insisted, pleased that he'd offered to remain with her, but knowing deep down she could not hide behind him all evening. "Go. I'll be fine. We'll catch up in a while."

"You're sure?"

"I'm sure."

With a squeeze of his hand on her arm and a reassuring smile, he moved away, taking some of Annie's confidence with him.

She circulated a little, mostly speaking to staff she recognized and a few guests, but she was too starstruck to approach many in attendance. She recognized probably half a dozen models, a few actors, and even a few reality TV stars. She was so out of her element here. The food looked amazing, but she was too nervous to eat and afraid she'd get something on the gorgeous dress, particularly the white bodice. Her feet hurt from the heels—she was unused to wearing ones this high and they were brand-new—and every time her attention was diverted, it seemed she turned back to find her champagne glass full again. That was dangerous, especially on an empty stomach. She put down her full glass and made her way to the powder room, stopping to grab a glass of club soda instead on her way back into the ballroom.

When she turned around, Bella was there.

The two women stared at each other for a prolonged moment, and then Annie spoke first. "Good evening, Bella."

"I'm surprised to see you here," Bella replied, not unkindly, but her tone wasn't overly warm, either.

"Phillipe insisted, since much of the planning for the event crossed my desk. It's going well, I think?"

"It is," Bella admitted. "You did do a good job, Anemone. Despite current…issues, I can't deny that."

"Thank you. I appreciate that."

Bella nodded at the dress as she accepted a drink from the bartender. "Last year's spring line, I think."

"That's what I was told. It's lovely. Beautiful and surprisingly comfortable."

"Phillipe again?"

Annie did not want to get Phillipe in any sort of trouble, but she could hardly lie and say she'd paid for it. Everyone knew she could not afford such a dress. "I couldn't attend wearing a little black dress off the rack," she finally said, giving a little shrug.

"Indeed not." Bella looked at her again until Annie felt rather like a bug in a jar. "Perhaps we should have seen to it. But you were so determined to not take any money."

"I truly don't want it." Annie stared at the wedge of lime floating in her glass. "This is my last Aurora event. After tonight I'll be out of your hair for good. You won't have to see me again. I came tonight as a favor to Phillipe, nothing more."

"He means a lot to you."

"He has been a wonderful boss and a good friend."

Bella turned to walk away but Annie called her back. "Bella?"

When Bella turned back around, Annie swallowed against the tightness in her throat before speaking. "Please, tell the others? Tell them that I never wanted to cause trouble, that I won't be bothering you again. And that I'm sorry for any hurt I caused."

Was it just the light, or were Bella's eyes suspiciously shiny? "I'll pass along your message."

Then her half-sister was gone, disappeared into the crowd of beautiful people, leaving Annie on the periphery of the room.

She heard her name and turned her head too quickly. Her vision was a little fuzzy until she focused on Phillipe again. But the blurry vision made her glad she'd switched to club soda. "The party is going well, don't you think?" She made her voice deceptively perky.

He nodded. "It seems so." He looked at her closely. "You were talking to Bella. How did it go?"

She squared her shoulders. "I think we made our peace, actually, and now I can move on. I was living in a fantasy where I got to work at Aurora and hope that someday I'd be welcomed into the family fold because they already knew and liked me. It was silly and immature of me. I'm leaving on my own terms with my pride and self-respect intact." She gave a little snort and angled a glance at him. "Look at me, still growing up at twenty-nine."

He put his hand on her arm, his fingers strong and warm, and the contact sent a shiver down her body. "I'm older than that, and I feel like I grew up tonight, too. Talking about Madelyn got me thinking about some of my decisions over the last few years with a clearer head. Maybe we never stop growing up. It's kind of a lovely thought, actually. There's always something new to learn, some new wisdom."

She sighed. "Why do we cling so hard to the past, anyway?"

She thought he was going to answer, but they were interrupted by Bella taking the stage. "Ladies and gentlemen, welcome to the Aurora launch of our new, fabulous scent, Nectar." Clapping erupted for a few moments before she continued. "I simply couldn't let the evening slip away without mentioning a few key people in Nectar's development. As you are all aware, it's been a year of change at Aurora. My brothers, sister, cousin and I have all taken on increased roles at Aurora and have brought new and fresh ideas to the table, but there's also been a large learning curve for all of us. Thankfully we had the best of teachers—our mother, the wonderful Aurora Germain." More clapping. Aurora was back in London tonight, and not at the launch. Somehow Annie was glad of that. The last time they'd met, Aurora had revealed that she'd known about Anemone's existence for all these years. Annie had very mixed feelings about that.

"My brother William has taken over much of the cosmetics division, including the fragrance department, and he's done such a brilliant job. Expect more great things to come from him in the months to come." She offered a warm smile. "But most of all, I'd like to thank our executive manager of fragrance, Phillipe Leroux." She swept a hand in his direction, and all eyes in the room turned their way.

Phillipe gave a small smile and nod.

"Phillipe has been intimately involved with Nectar, not only as the manager of this department but because he was a designer in our Grasse lab before coming to corporate. Phillipe actually designed this scent himself—it was his last one before he moved up to managing the facility in Grasse, where he oversaw the next steps in production. And then he came to Paris, working with us at our headquarters, making William's job a little easier by bringing his expertise and intelligence to the role. Phillipe, I know this night is incredibly special to you, so congratulations on such a triumph. We're so very happy you're part of the Aurora team."

It was high praise from Bella, and Phillipe's cheeks flushed a little as the applause filled the room. But Bella wasn't done yet.

"I want to thank one more person tonight before we all go off to enjoy the music and food and drink again. The planning of tonight fell to one person, and she did an amazing job pulling it all together. Thank you, Anemone, for your hard work to make this event a success."

Anemone fought to school her features. Never had she expected any sort of thanks, let alone public gratitude. Her gaze darted to William, Charlotte and Stephen, and saw they were smiling faintly in what she recognized was a public polite face. Christophe was watching her with what looked like sympathy in his eyes, though she couldn't imagine why. Then she looked back at Bella and attempted to respond with the same polite smile. The recognition was nice, but she didn't trust it, no matter how well their last interaction had gone.

And that was it, wasn't it? She didn't trust any of this. She needed to get away from it, from this world, from the torment she felt every time she thought of her blood family—half, anyway. She was here because she didn't want to be alone. But she quickly came to realize that a person could be utterly alone while surrounded by family. Family was not blood. At least not always.

"Now, everyone, enjoy the party!"

Bella stepped off the dais. Annie stepped aside as more people came to speak with Phillipe now that he'd been singled out. It was only half past ten and she was ready to leave the fairy tale behind. She didn't belong here. The acknowledgment had been nice and all, but even Phillipe was more in his element than she was. He looked so comfortable and debonair in his tux, one hand casually resting in his pocket as he chatted to a man who seemed vaguely familiar to her, though she couldn't quite place him.

Her stomach growled. She hadn't eaten since this morning. As gorgeous and amazing as this event was—she'd planned it, after all—she was exhausted from the long day and the emotional energy that had gone into her transformation and appearance at the launch. All she wanted to do now was go home and crawl under a blanket and eat takeaway Chinese food. Maybe with a movie on in the background.

Phillipe paused by her shoulder and leaned in. "I'm nearly ready to get out of here. Wait for me in the lobby?"

She nodded automatically, then felt a whole new surge of butterflies as she realized this meant they were leaving together—and before the evening was officially over. What did it mean? Perhaps nothing.

But she remembered how he'd said she wasn't his employee anymore and how beautiful she was… The line that they'd never crossed before suddenly didn't exist.

She subtly made her way toward the door, pausing occasionally if someone offered a greeting. At the door she was handed a small, beautiful bag of Aurora swag, which she automatically took before sliding out into the hallway. The air was cooler here and she took a deep, fortifying breath before walking down the hall toward the elevator that would take her down to the lobby. The hotel was the fanciest she'd ever been in. Soaring ceilings, rich fabrics, floors so shiny she could see her reflection. And flowers…always fresh flowers everywhere. Staff in livery waiting to open a door or press a button. The luxury, the wide-open spaces and unobtrusive assistance had a surprising claustrophobic effect on her. She needed to get out. Get somewhere where she could breathe again.

A doorman held open the door for her and she prepared to step through when she heard her name being called. She made a half turn and saw Phillipe striding toward her, his brows pulled together. "Annie."

"Sorry," she said as soon as he arrived at her side. "I suddenly needed some air."

"It's all right."

"You're sure you want to leave already? This is your party, after all."

"I'm sure. I've had enough schmoozing and networking for a year." He led her out through the door into the soft Paris evening. "Annie, what Bella said…"

"It was generous of her, but the longer I was in the room, the smaller it seemed to become. Maybe I've been Cinderella for the night, but it's not real. The

Pembertons do not want me as part of their family."
Tears clogged her throat. "I have to move on. I have
to. For my own mental health. I was so wrong to come
to Paris in the first place."

"But if you hadn't, I never would have met you. And
that would have been a shame."

He had to stop saying these sweet things. "I'm ready
to go home and put on my pajamas and get back to
real life."

He watched her for a long moment, then reached
for her hand. "But it's not even midnight."

She smiled a little smile. Every time he touched her
it sent little sparks firing off in her body and in her
heart. "I'm not going to dash off and leave a glass slip-
per, if that's what you're thinking. Truly, I thought I'd
order in a late dinner and just…" Her voice trailed off.
And do what? Feel sorry for herself? Wish she wasn't
alone? Start thinking about what came next? She had
no job, no home to go to. Leaving the party tonight
truly put a period at the end of her time at Aurora Inc.

"That sounds wonderful. Are you up for some company? Nectar has been launched. There's been champagne and speeches and swag and mingling and Nectar
is on its own now. I haven't eaten, either. But I understand if you'd rather not. If you'd rather be alone."

She wanted to be with him so much she ached with
it. Would it make things worse, spending time with him
tonight? Or could she look at it as one last evening to
enjoy his company?

"You're sure you don't want to stay?"

He squeezed her fingers. "I'm sure. It was a great
evening. You truly put together a wonderful event, but

I've had enough. We can order in, my treat. My way of saying thank you for all your hard work."

Her hard work. Just employer to employee, platonic and all about work. It was appropriate but disappointing. And yet he'd gone to the trouble to ensure she attended, to make her feel pampered and cared for. The mixed signals kept ping-ponging around. She should just go home, but she found herself not ready to say goodbye just yet. She gave a nod. "That might be nice. Apparently I have a car service." She smiled at him, teasing. "Looks like we have a ride."

She called for the car and as they waited, she took a deep breath, imprinting the moment on her memory. The city glittered around them, and she realized that she was going to miss Paris. She had loved living here, but unless she found another well-paying job, she couldn't afford to live here alone. She would have to say goodbye to it, and to the man on her arm. But not yet. Not tonight.

The car came to a stop in front of them. She slid into the back seat and then shifted so that Phillipe could climb in after her. After giving the driver directions to her flat, she leaned back against the buttery leather and turned her head to face Phillipe.

"Hello," he said, his voice mellow and lazy.

"Hi yourself," she replied, and smiled. "Are we crazy? We just left an exclusive party at one of the poshest hotels in Paris to hang out at my poky flat with questionable takeaway."

"Maybe a little crazy." His eyes gleamed at her in the dark light of the car. "But that's not necessarily a bad thing. Can I tell you a secret?"

She nodded, loving the little bit of intimacy they were sharing.

"Every time I meet a celebrity, I am horribly afraid I'm going to say something stupid."

She laughed. "I don't think you're alone in that." She mused for a moment. "And you're not tongue-tied around Aurora or my—that is, the Pembertons."

"Because we have a working relationship. But to-night? Charlotte in her silk and diamonds, Stephen in his tux—which, by the way, is a lot more expensive than mine—the differences become clearer."

"Well, you're an executive manager at a multina-tional company known worldwide by a single name—Aurora. That still puts you miles ahead of a girl like me from Guildford, with an office administration cer-tificate and currently unemployed."

His grin slid from his face. "Don't do that. Don't put yourself down like that. You are smart and beautiful. Do you think anyone could have organized tonight's launch like you did?" He reached for her hand. "I went through those details with you. You delegated like a champ. You oversaw the press, the guest list, worked within the budget for the event—"

"I had a massive budget," she reminded him quickly, with a quirk of her eyebrow.

He grinned. "Okay, granted. You did have a signif-icant budget, but you did not have carte blanche and you also reconfigured the internal security at the last minute. Those are massively important skills that not everyone has." His jaw tightened. "In my opinion, you leaving is the company's loss. And the Pembertons not welcoming you in is *their* loss."

His confidence in her was a boon to her bruised

ego. She reminded herself that the agreement was she'd leave with a good reference. Surely there was another company out there who could use her talents.

Phillipe wouldn't be there, though.

They whizzed through Paris, Annie looking out the window at the city she'd come to love almost as much as home. It seemed they were back to her flat in no time, and the driver was opening the door.

Phillipe got out, and then he held out his hand for her. She took it and slid out of the car, trying desperately to be graceful and not get tangled up in her long dress. With one hand in his and her other hand gripping her tiny clutch and bag of swag, she finally had both feet on the ground.

Now she had three floors to climb, and her feet, now that she'd been off them for several minutes, were screaming at her.

"Second thoughts?" he asked, his voice soft by her ear.

She shivered. "No," she breathed. "But I'm suddenly sad that there is no elevator in my building." She held out a foot and wiggled it. The little stones glittered as she lamented the heels and the number of staircases to her floor.

Phillipe took one look at her, then lifted her into his arms and headed for the door of the building.

CHAPTER SEVEN

"PHILLIPE! PUT ME DOWN!"

He only laughed as she fumbled in her purse for keys to the door. They managed to get inside and then he headed for the stairs.

Six flights of stairs, two for each floor. He got up the first one and a half before he was regretting his impulsive gallantry.

She was giggling, though, and he liked the sound. She'd been so tense tonight, so on edge. He knew the feeling. In his heart and his head, he knew he belonged in the Aurora Inc. world. That he could fit in with the Pembertons, carry on an intelligent conversation, even be a bit witty. But it had taken him a long time to be comfortable in the setting. Annie wasn't. Maybe no one else could tell, but he could. Because he knew what one of her unfettered smiles looked like. He knew because she was treating him to one right now.

"I can't believe you picked me up. I can walk, you know."

"Your feet are killing you." He glanced down at her shoes. "Though those are some fabulous shoes."

She rotated her ankle. "Oh, you like?"

He met her gaze. "I like. I also like your arms around my neck."

"Phillipe…"

"Phillipe," he mocked, then grinned. "I am not your boss any longer. But I will put you down and keep a polite distance if that is what you wish."

He hesitated, nearly to the top of the third flight.

Her arms tightened around his neck and his pulse leaped. He'd been bracing himself for disappointment. "All right, then," he said, looking up at the three more flights. She wasn't heavy, not really, but this many stairs was a challenge.

"Am I too heavy for you?" she asked.

"Non." He kept up a steady pace. "We are nearly there."

They reached the top of the steps and he carried her to her door, then let her slide out of his arms. She was standing there, one hand holding her clutch and swag and the other fumbling with her keys, when he dipped his head and kissed her.

The bag dropped to the floor as she lifted her hands and threaded her fingers through his hair.

Mon Dieu, she was sweet. He'd been thinking about doing this for days but hadn't because of their awkward position. He would never, ever step over a line as her boss, even though the chemistry between them had been at a low simmer for weeks. It was one thing to be supportive when an employee—a friend—was struggling. It was another entirely to add a physical component to that relationship. The closest they'd gotten was the hug after she met with the family in Bella's office. Now, though… Her time at Aurora Inc. was officially over. She was in his arms and responding to his touch with such enthusiasm that it was clear his attraction was far from one-sided.

Her lips were soft, and her mouth tasted like champagne. He pulled away slightly and murmured in her ear, "Open the damned door, Anemone."

She shivered beneath his touch. "I dropped the keys," she whispered, and then gave a gasping kind of giggle that made him smile. She was so very lovely, so artless. She'd handled herself professionally earlier, but there was something about her that was less... practiced, perhaps, than the Pemberton women and, for that matter, the women he seemed to meet within this industry. She made him feel...

He reached down and picked up the keys, then slowly put them in her hand, meeting her gaze as he did so. She bit down on her bottom lip, her teeth pressing the soft flesh, and his chest cramped. She made him feel at home. It was at once a huge relief and utterly terrifying.

She spun to the door, inserting the key, while the scent of her—not Nectar, he realized—wrapped around him. A different *parfum*, with notes of jasmine, musk, cashmere. It was pretty and soft, like her.

The door opened and she stepped inside, then half turned and held the door for him to enter.

"Annie, I—"

"Kiss me again, Phillipe."

He didn't need to be asked twice. Without breaking eye contact, he slid his foot against the door and pushed it shut, then stepped forward and curled his hand around the base of her neck. She let out a sigh as his mouth came down on hers again and he stopped thinking. Now it was all about sensation—the way she moaned softly into his mouth, the vibration of the low, sexy sound, and how her body felt in his arms again. The chiffon of her dress was wispy as a fairy tale, and her skin... He ran his fingers over her shoulder and down her arm. Her skin was cool silk.

Her hands fumbled with the button of his jacket, and he moved back just a bit so she could undo it from the buttonhole. The moment it was free, she pushed it off his shoulders and she reached for his tie.

This was going to escalate very quickly if they weren't careful. His body was clearly on board with taking her to bed, but his brain wasn't quite sure. This was Annie. She didn't need one night of passion. She needed care, consideration... Love. Something he was sure he couldn't give her.

He pulled her closer for one more moment, to memorize the shape and feel of her against his body. Then he reluctantly broke the kiss, putting his hands on the smooth skin of her arms and holding her back from him just a little.

"Annie, we need to stop." She didn't answer for a moment, and when he lifted his gaze to hers, he saw confusion in her irises. "Please, don't think I don't want to, because I do. But I can't let myself be careless with you, you see?"

A tiny wrinkle formed between her brows. They were both still breathing heavily from the impassioned kisses, and it tested him sorely to hold her arms and not pull her against him again.

"Careless? Phillipe, you are the least careless man I know."

Her words reached in and touched something in his heart, something he hadn't known he needed. Perhaps because he'd been told so often that he was so focused on his studies and then his work that he failed to notice others around him—that the lack of notice was indicative of lack of caring. For Annie to see past that... Or was he making too much of her words? He gave his head a little shake.

"You are a beautiful woman, Annie. And it's not that I don't..." He ran his hand through his hair. "Having a one-night stand would be wrong. You deserve better. And I'm... I'm not able to give you more than that. So it's better if we cool off."

She stepped back, away from his hands, and smoothed her palms over her dress. "You're probably right," she agreed.

"You're also not easy to walk away from," he added, needing to be truthful, needing her to know that she was, indeed, desirable. So much so he could really use a cold shower right about now. Watching her move around the room tonight, so full of class and elegance and restrained sensuality, had sparked something in him. Something he'd ruthlessly pushed aside when she had been his employee. Without that barrier between them now... Well, it changed everything.

Her eyes shimmered for a moment, but then she blinked and they cleared. "What is it?" he asked. "Did I say something wrong?"

She shook her head. "People have been walking away from me my whole life. It's nice to know that perhaps it isn't as easy as it seems."

"Oh, Annie." Against his better judgment, he drew her into his arms again, holding her close. He felt her words so very deeply. He closed his eyes. "I know it hurts to feel... I don't know, disposable, I guess."

She nodded against his shoulder, and then pulled back and looked up. "Thank you for understanding." She gave a short laugh. "How did we go from kissing to this?"

"Because we're friends, perhaps?"

Her eyes glowed. "I like that. And it takes the sting out a little bit. Of backing away from..." Her cheeks turned an adorable shade of pink. "Well. I should stop talking."

He laughed. The truth was, it would only take a word, a touch, and he'd be on fire for her again. The sensation had washed over him so quickly the moment he'd first touched his lips to hers. She had no idea how alluring she was, how sharp the attraction running through his veins.

Kissing her had unleashed something within him that had lain dormant for a very long time, and he was hungry for more.

"Are you still hungry?" he asked, needing to move the conversation back to something normal.

"Yes!" Her smile brightened the room. "I'm starving."

"Why don't I order in, then?"

"I'd like that." She looked down at her dress. "And I should change out of this. I would die if I got anything on it."

He was sorry to hear it; the gown was spectacular. "It is yours. You can do with it what you wish," he said, reaching for his tux jacket on the floor. He needed his phone to find a place to order from.

"Oh!" Her face flatted with alarm. "I thought it was just a loan."

Phillipe shook his head. "No, Annie. I got it for you. Having it on loan would be like saying you don't deserve to have something so beautiful, and nothing could be further from the truth. The dress, the shoes..."

"The necklace?"

He nodded.

She smiled and gave a laugh. "It's a heck of a severance package."

He laughed in response; how did she make him do that so easily? If he wasn't careful, he could fall for her. Tonight had been magical and, yes, he'd wanted that for her because he cared. It was a big step to go from there to falling in love. A step he was certain he wasn't capable of.

Unaware of the direction of his thoughts, Annie opened a few drawers and retrieved some clothes, then disappeared into the bathroom. He sat on the small sofa and scrolled through nearby takeaways, trying to ignore the path his mind was taking, envisioning her behind the closed door. "Is there anything you don't like?" he called out, looking at an online menu. Food. She'd invited him back here for food, nothing more.

"Squid and octopus!" came the automatic reply, and he grinned. Easy enough. By the time she emerged in a pair of leggings and a light sweater, he'd placed the order.

"It should be here in thirty minutes," he said, smiling up at her.

"I'm out of wine, but I have some sparkling water. Would you like a glass while we wait?" She'd taken her hair down and now tucked it behind her ear, as if somehow nervous.

"That would be nice," he replied.

"Okay. Good."

She disappeared into the tiny kitchen and came back a few minutes later with two glasses. She handed one to him and then sat next to him, tucking her legs underneath her. If she thought changing and being more casual made her any less alluring, she was dead wrong. She was pretty and soft, and the way she smiled, a little bashfully, he thought, only made him like her more.

"So, a toast," he offered, lifting his glass. "To a successful launch, and to whatever wonderful adventures are next for Anemone Jones."

"To a successful launch," she echoed. "And to moving forward for both of us."

He touched the rim of his glass to hers, then took a sip. "Moving forward for both of us? I don't think I'm going anywhere."

"Professionally I think you're set for a while," she offered. "But what you said earlier, about Madelyn... it sounds as if you're leaving some of your...resentments behind."

"Or the proverbial chip on my shoulder?"

She laughed a little. "Maybe that's a better phrase. It's hard to move past old hurts and totally understandable."

"I don't think I've moved past it, exactly." He thought back to all the ways he'd tried to make it work. He'd met Madelyn in college and had been immediately taken with her. She'd insisted that it didn't matter that she came from money and he didn't, but he'd felt the difference from the start. He'd worked to deserve her, or so he'd thought. After the wedding, he'd promised to keep her in the lifestyle she wanted, so he'd worked long hours. But the fights had started even then. He'd taken the management job, along with the prestige and the raise, to try to save their marriage. But by that time Madelyn had found someone else. When the opportunity came up to relocate to Paris, he'd jumped at it. Getting away from her had been his top priority. But perhaps he'd been lying to himself to say that the reason their marriage had failed was because of her infidelity. It wasn't so simple.

Annie took a long drink of water and then hesitated, as if pondering. "You know, I think it's okay if you don't totally move past what happened with your ex-wife. The things that hurt us most shape us. They become part of us. It wouldn't make sense for them to just disappear. The trouble comes if they keep us from moving forward."

She was very wise. "Like you finding out about your father."

She nodded. "He knew I existed. And he gave my mother money each year, and I guess that was his way of taking responsibility. But financial responsibility is the cold, bare minimum to expect from one's parent, I think. He never made an effort to know me. He didn't even want me to know his identity. And that will always sting."

"I'm so sorry," Phillipe said softly, wishing he could hold her, offer comfort. But doing so would make it far too easy to take it further. One moment he'd be touching her, holding her, and the next they'd be kissing again. The attraction still hummed between them like a tangible thing.

"How can I blame his family when he didn't even care enough to see me, even once? And what kind of person would I be if I let this one thing dictate the rest of my life?"

He had nothing to say in reply.

Annie squared her shoulders, though, and sent him a smile. "Well, I'm done now. I came here, I met them, they know I exist. Deep down I truly didn't expect them to welcome me with open arms. It's time to move on with my life."

"Here's to that," he said firmly, admiring her resolve and resilience. "Though the office is going to be remarkably dull without you there each day."

"I did like the job an awful lot," she admitted.

"Do you have any idea what is next?"

She shrugged. "I've applied to a few positions, but truthfully, Paris is expensive. It needs to be an excellent job for me to be able to afford to keep my flat."

So she really was serious about leaving Paris.

His phone buzzed and he reached for it, then glanced at the screen. "Our food is here. I'll be right back."

"I'll get plates," she offered, hopping up from the sofa.

He let himself out of the flat and went down the stairs to meet the delivery person, but he was oddly deflated.

He'd meant what he'd said about being friends. He also was insanely attracted to her. After only a few short months, and only a few weeks of really getting to know her, he realized he was going to miss her terribly when she was gone.

Anemone pressed a hand to her stomach when Phillipe left the flat, leaving the door slightly ajar for his return. Tonight had been such a whirlwind. First the transformation, then the party, which had been a lot to take in and every moment fearing she'd do something gauche or embarrassing. But more than either of those things had been kissing Phillipe, touching him, having him touch her. It had been simply splendid. It was probably foolish of her to set him on such a pedestal, but he was so smart and sexy and charming and kind. What she hadn't expected was the intensity and heat. The way he'd kicked the door shut had fired her desire so sharply she'd worried she might combust. And his reasons for backing away were totally legitimate, if disappointing.

If he hadn't, she would have gone to bed with him. Maybe it was better they didn't, and down the road perhaps she'd be thankful, but right now she was just sorry they'd stopped.

Now he was grabbing takeaway and she reminded herself to be thankful she had a friend. Even if it was only for tonight. She'd worry about tomorrow when the sun rose, and she needed to start over...again.

He came back in the flat carrying a paper bag. The scent of Chinese food hit her immediately, making her stomach growl. She carried the plates and cutlery to the small table and put them down, then went back and got the half-empty bottle of water. With a sideways grin, Phillipe unpacked the bag, setting the containers in the middle of the table. "I haven't done this in ages," he remarked, taking out two sets of chopsticks. "It's the perfect way to end the evening, I think."

She could think of one better way, but they'd agreed not to, so she topped up their glasses and handed Phillipe a paper napkin...nothing fancy here. To her surprise, he held out her chair, and then seated himself across from her. "We have noodles, and some kind of chicken, and vegetables in black bean sauce, which just happens to be a favorite of mine."

"I love spicy food, so this sounds perfect." They opened the containers and fragrant steam erupted from inside. Annie wielded her chopsticks and scooped food onto her plate. The noodles especially smelled amazing, and before long they were happily slurping noodles and munching on spicy veg and tender, gingery chicken.

"This was just what I needed," Annie said, looking over at him. He had a little sauce at the corner of his mouth, so she took her napkin and dabbed it away. "Noodles are messy, but I swear they're my favorite. I'm such a carb girl."

"I'm glad," he replied, deftly grabbing some bean sprouts in his chopsticks. "You know, normally if someone moves on at the office, we do treat them to lunch. I'm sorry we didn't arrange that for you."

"It was a hectic week and a unique situation." She looked over, feeling a little shy but determined to say what was on her mind, since she might not get another chance. "I think I prefer this, anyway. Takeaway at midnight with a handsome man wins."

Did he actually blush when she said that?

"Phillipe, about what happened before..." She hesitated, then made herself look him in the eyes. "I liked it. I like you. I know it can't go anywhere because I'm leaving, but…" She swallowed tightly. "You should know, if things were different, I might not give up so easily."

He put down his chopsticks and took a sip of his water, then dabbed at his mouth with the napkin, all while her pulse was hammering, wondering what he was going to say.

"Annie…" He reached over and took her hand. "You tempt me."

Three words. That's all it took for her body to heat, for anticipation to ripple over her skin.

"But I can't," he said honestly. "I'm not… Well, I'm not a one-night kind of man. Call me old-fashioned, I suppose. I got carried away earlier—you're very easy to get carried away with." The hint of a smile popped his dimple just the smallest bit. "And I wouldn't hurt you for the world. That is the only reason I'm backing off. I hope you know that."

She did. He was easily the best man, the most honorable man, she'd ever met. She'd had relationships in the past—nothing ever very serious—but none of those men had taken the care with her that Phillipe had over the past two weeks.

Annie found herself rather sorry that was the case. Perhaps if she could find a way to stay in Paris… But how? She had no savings to tide her over until she found a new job. And there was no way in hell she'd ask the Pembertons for money. They already thought she was an opportunist. Which was ironic considering she hadn't asked them for anything.

"I do know that," she assured him, pushing her plate aside. "I'm just sorry. I wish… Well, it doesn't matter. If wishes were horses and all that. But thank you. For tonight. For being a friend. For being so supportive through all of this."

"I wish I could do more. It doesn't seem fair that you're left with nothing but a reference." He frowned. "That's cold."

"It's fine," she assured him. "I don't want their money. I'm realizing now that what I wanted was something I was never going to get anyway, so it's back to reality for me. On the plus side, I worked an incredible job, got to live in Paris for the better part of a year, and I met you."

Their gazes clung for a few moments, the air filled with what she'd said and what she wasn't saying, with the knowledge of what had happened between them and what was not going to happen. She would not regret one moment of it. Not one.

"I should go," Phillipe said, clearing his throat. He put his napkin on the table and rose. "It's getting late."

She didn't want him to leave but he had to sometime, so she got up as well and gathered up their now-empty plates and took them to the kitchen, placing them carefully in the sink. While she was tidying, Phillipe retrieved his jacket and shrugged it on, stuffing his tie in the pocket.

She walked him to the door, feeling a little bit emptier with each step. For the past six months she'd got on well with her coworkers like Claudine and Lisette, had gone out for drinks on the odd evening, made what she considered casual friends. But none of them knew as much about her as Phillipe. None had seen past the face she showed the world to what was beneath. She was going to miss him. More than he likely realized.

"Thank you for bringing me home, and for dinner," she murmured, opening the door quietly. "It really was a great evening."

"If it was a success, it was because of you."

She chuckled and looked up at him. "We both know that's not true."

Instead of disagreeing, he stepped forward and kissed her again, a soft, simple kiss by physical standards but one that seemed to say oh-so much in the brief contact. His lips left hers, but for the smallest moment his forehead rested against hers in a gesture so tender the backs of her eyes stung.

"Please take care of yourself, Annie. And if you need anything…"

You, she thought instantly. But of course she didn't say it.

"Goodbye, Phillipe."

He nodded and left, and she shut the door behind him, half wishing he would turn around in the hallway and come back, sweep through the door and take her in his arms and say the heck with no one-night stands, let's have an unforgettable night of passion.

But that wasn't who he was, and the seconds ticked by silently until she let go of the doorknob, flicked the lock, and stepped back.

She went into the tiny kitchen and looked at the

clock on the microwave. It flipped from 11:59 to twelve o'clock as she watched.

Midnight. And with the ticking of the clock, Annie knew exactly how Cinderella felt after the ball. Like she had been touched by magic and left disappointed.

CHAPTER EIGHT

THE CHIME OF her text notification woke Annie from a sound sleep. She squinted, frowned, and grappled for her phone on the tiny stand next to the bed. She was just pressing her thumb to the volume button, turning it down so she could go back to sleep, when it chimed again. And again.

Who the heck was texting her so early on a Saturday morning? Annoyed, she looked at the home screen and saw that it was already past eight...not quite as early as she'd thought.

The phone dinged again, and the message flashed on the screen.

Answer or I'm coming to Paris to find you.

Rachael. Annie flipped onto her back and unlocked the phone, shocked to see so many unread messages. What was going on?

She touched the latest message from Rachael and gave a hurried reply.

Just woke up. Give me fifteen. Don't call.

She added the last bit because she wanted to see what the fuss was about before being bombarded with questions from Rach.

There was one from Bella, just a single message, but the three short words hit Annie right in the gut, leaving her with a horrible, sinking feeling.

How could you?

What could she have possibly done? Everything last night had gone so well. And she and Phillipe had been discreet leaving together. No PDAs, nothing that would cause a fuss.

She went back to her conversation with Rachael and scrolled to the top. Once there, everything became crystal clear.

When did that secret come out?????

After the line of question marks, there was a link to a well-known gossip site. Annie held her breath as she clicked on it.

Ooh, la-la! Secret Pemberton heir at A-list party

Panic hit her right in the solar plexus as she stared at the page. There was a photo of her in that gorgeous dress, her lips smiling as she stood with Phillipe. She remembered the moment; it had been taken when Bella was making her speech. She was shoulder to shoulder with him—heavens, he was handsome. Beneath the photo was a caption.

The late Earl of Chatsworth's love child, Anem-
one Jones, at the Aurora Inc. launch for its new
fragrance at a Paris hotel.

This was not happening. How did anyone know?
How had this leaked to the press? She'd told Phillipe,
no one else. The immediate family knew, but she
couldn't imagine one of them would have leaked it,
especially considering Bella's message this morning.

Bella's message.

She went back to her messaging app and replied
quickly.

It wasn't me. I don't know who leaked it.

Of course it was highly unlikely that Bella would
believe her. She wouldn't if she were in Bella's shoes.
Especially since she now had nothing to lose. Her job
was done. The money was gone. Of course they'd think
selling her story was her ticket. And they'd think that
because they didn't know her. Didn't know that she
had too much integrity to do such a thing. She would
rather leave Paris and start over than make money
by selling a sensational story and causing her father's
family harm.

Her father's family. Not hers. She needed to remember that more often, didn't she?

Her phone buzzed and she expected it was Rach
again, but Phillipe's name popped up on the screen.
She was fully awake now, sitting up in bed and trying to keep up with the messages and information.
She clicked on his name and his message popped up.

Are you awake? I'll be there in an hour. Pack a bag.

She furrowed her brow and moved her thumbs at lightning speed.

What? Why? I'm just trying to figure out what happened.

Three dots appeared immediately: he was typing.

The news is everywhere. There will be paps at your door before you know it. I'm getting you out of Paris.

Phillipe was coming here. To whisk her out of Paris because of a scandal.

A lot of things had happened since she'd discovered Cedric Pemberton was her father, but this was by far the most surreal and jolting.

She shouldn't leave. She should stay and face her half-siblings and try to explain. She'd never been one to run away from anything. She got out of bed and went to the window, though why she walked on tiptoe, she had no idea. There were a few cars parked out front, but nothing that looked different or conspicuous. A couple sat on a bench nearby, sipping coffee, with canvas bags beside them…canvas bags, maybe big enough for a camera?

She stepped back from the window. This was ridiculous. It was one story on a gossip site. Who would be interested in her?

Apparently someone, since Bella was angry and Phillipe was concerned.

Another text came through from Phillipe.

If anyone buzzes your flat, do not answer. I'll text when I arrive. Take the back exit so you can avoid having your photo taken.

Okay, so this was clearly an overreaction. At least she thought so until her phone actually rang in her hand, startling her.

"Rachael—" she started, but her best friend cut her off.

"It's been fifteen minutes, I swear. Are you okay? Is it true? What the hell happened, and where did you get that dress?"

She really should have phoned Rachael sometime over the last few weeks, but she hadn't known where to start. "It's a long story. To sum up, the only people who knew I was Cedric Pemberton's daughter were the family, me, you, and my boss. And the doctor, I suppose, who took my DNA test."

"And you've been working at Aurora. I told you this was a mistake…"

"I know you did. It doesn't matter. I don't work there anymore. Yesterday was my last day. That was the agreement. I leave, I get a good reference. Carry on with my life."

"Hopefully with a truckload of money for your trouble."

Annie let out a slow breath, trying to get her bearings. "No money. I never wanted the money, you know that," she insisted. "And to be honest, without a job here in Paris, I was thinking of giving you a ring and seeing if I could couch surf for a few days. I thought I might come home, find a job there. Be closer to you." Her voice caught on the last bit. Rach was the only "family" she had left. In hindsight, keeping her out of the loop had been a little foolish. Rachael had every right to be mad at her, but she wasn't.

"Of course you can! But no money... Are you sure? I mean—"

"Rach, I love you, but can we table the money chat for another time? Bella has already messaged, quite upset about this being splashed on the internet. I need to figure some things out. But I promise I'll fill you in. Soon."

"Forget all that," Rachael said forcefully. "The most important thing is are you okay? Are you going to be okay today? Do you need anything? What can I do?"

"Nothing right now. I guess I'm leaving the city for a few days until this dies down. A friend is coming to pick me up in..." She glanced at her watch. "Oh, crap. In thirty minutes. I need to shower and pack a bag. I'll message when I get to where I'm going, though. Promise."

"I'm worried about you, Annie."

The concern sent warmth through Annie's chest. "I promise I'm in safe hands. You have nothing to worry about there. I'll fill you in more later, but I need to get ready."

"Message me later today to let me know you're okay."

"I will. And Rach?" Annie's throat tightened. "Thank you. For worrying. For being my friend."

"Always," Rachael answered.

They hung up and Annie darted for the shower, then pulled on a casual dress and a pair of flats. She had no idea where she was going, but she couldn't imagine it was far, so she took her carry-on bag and put in underwear, jeans, light tops, a few dresses, and a couple of pairs of shoes. It still felt like a panic over nothing, but when she went to the window again, there were more cars out front, and the people milling about definitely looked like journos.

Interested in her. What insanity. This was exactly what she'd wanted to spare the Pembertons, not that they'd ever believe her.

Her phone buzzed and she looked down.

Go out the back and turn left down the street above your building. I'm about a hundred meters down in a black Peugeot.

Surreal. Perhaps unnecessary. But the last thing she wanted to do was make things worse, so she typed back.

On my way.

She trusted Phillipe. Right now, he might be the only person she trusted.

She shouldered her bag and, at the last minute, grabbed her phone charger. Then she locked the door behind her, hurried down the stairs, and went out the back as quickly as she could before the paparazzi figured out there was a back entrance to her building to stake out.

Phillipe tapped his fingers on the steering wheel as nerves churned in his stomach. He just hoped the back exit was free from reporters and she made it to the car without being seen.

The call from William this morning had been particularly disconcerting.

The family was angry. He got that, but he also knew without a doubt that Annie hadn't contacted the press and he'd told William so. Hell, he'd been with her until nearly midnight, and she had no desire to cause any problems for the family. This had to have come from someone else, but they could think about that later. Right now he was getting her out of Paris and away from the press. That was his only concern.

A glimpse in his rearview mirror showed her hurrying toward his car. He flipped the locks and got out, reaching for her bag as she drew near. "Get in. I'll put this in the back."

She did what he said, not questioning anything. He put the bag in the back seat next to his own while she slipped into the passenger seat. He got back in and they fastened their seat belts, and then he wordlessly pulled away from the curb.

A few minutes later they had cleared the area and he let out a breath, looked over at her, and smiled. "So. Good morning."

She started to laugh, which told him she was either stressed or she appreciated the absurdity in the morning's events. He hoped it was the latter.

"Just another quiet Saturday." She shrugged, then leaned her head back against the seat. "I don't know what happened. I woke up this morning and my phone had blown up."

"I woke to a rather irate call from William," Phillipe admitted. There was no use sugarcoating anything. "The family is furious. The general consensus is that you waited until the launch to make as big a splash as possible."

"That's ridiculous! I wasn't even going to go to the launch!" Annie shook her head. "I can't imagine who could have leaked it."

"I believe you, and I told William so," Phillipe assured her. "However, the list of people who know is very small, so I understand why they automatically suspect you leaked the story even if I know it's impossible. I don't care about that. I care about you being in the line of fire from the press." He made a gesture at the interior of his car. "It was the best I could do on short notice."

Annie was silent for a few minutes as he navigated his way toward the A6. They were in for a day of driving, but he couldn't think of anywhere better to take her than home. Not because he had any burning urge to visit, though seeing his parents was long overdue, but he remembered her saying she had never been to the south of France. It was too beautiful for her to miss, and if she really meant to go back to England...

A strange emptiness filled him at the very thought. But of course she must, unless...

Unless he could help her find a reason to stay. As soon as the thought flitted through his mind, he dismissed it. To what end? As he'd told her last night, he wasn't a one-night kind of man, and he certainly wasn't interested in a relationship. His marriage crashing and burning had meant that once was enough.

He looked over at her. Her face was drawn, her lips unsmiling. As if sensing his regard, she turned her head and glanced over at him. "Where are we going?" she asked.

"Grasse," he answered. "I'm overdue to see Maman and Papa, and you did say you've never been." He tried a smile.

"Grasse? That's…" She frowned. "A long drive."

"We'll get there just before dinner," he assured her. "And I've already called ahead. Maman is making up the spare room for you and will have a lovely meal for us when we arrive."

As he said the words, he realized how unappealing it must sound. He was taking her to his family home. It was not glamorous or glitzy, just a regular home. His family was not rich. Even putting him through school had been a strain on their budget. "I'm sorry, Annie. I should have asked you first, shouldn't I? My family… Well, I grew up solidly middle class."

Her eyes flashed. "Why in the world would you apologize for that?" Her fingers twisted together. "Good heavens, Phillipe, have I given the impression that I…that is to say…" She stopped, took a breath. "Phillipe, I grew up in a very modest two-bedroom row house with a single mother who worked hard for what we had. When I look back, now I wonder how we would have made it if Cedric hadn't given Mum money. I was never hungry or cold. I had clothes to wear and went to an okay school, but there were times…" She sighed. "My flat in Paris is poky and cramped, but it suits me. Last night, with the dress and the champagne and everything… That was nice, but it's not really me. So please, don't apologize. I do not expect to be whisked away to some five-star hideaway overlooking the Mediterranean. I didn't expect to be whisked away at all. You've been a friend to me, and I appreciate that more than you know."

A friend, ha. If she knew how much time he spent reminding himself of all the reasons he shouldn't take her hand or kiss her, she'd question the friend part. And last night… Last night he would have taken her to bed, tangled with her in the sheets, listened to her soft sighs…

This was the problem. With just the slightest provocation, his mind betrayed him. It was a good thing they were staying at his parents' home. It would keep him from getting into trouble where she was concerned.

"I know you didn't do this, and I don't want to see you hounded by the press." A bubble of anger rose in his chest. "Aurora has a whole staff to deal with this kind of thing. You don't." Nor had they offered. That only added to his annoyance.

She snorted. "Phillipe, I started in the PR department, remember? I know exactly how this works."

"I suppose you do." He glanced over again as they sped along, leaving Paris behind. "Annie, we don't have to go to Grasse. I didn't ask you. I just took over the situation to get you away. I don't apologize for that, but I do apologize for acting like you had no choice in the matter. If you would like to do something else, go somewhere else, please say so."

Her face softened and she reached over and took his hand. "Grasse is fine. Staying with your family is fine, too. I'm honored." She squeezed his fingers. "But Phillipe, I'll make you a similar offer. If you would like to extricate yourself from this mess right now, there are no hard feelings. You're putting yourself in a horrible position with work."

He was. He knew it, but his sense of fairness had won out. Oh, who was he kidding… It was more than that. It was also because it was Annie. He wasn't totally sensible where she was concerned, especially after last night. She deserved better than she was getting.

"I'm owed some vacation, and the launch is done. I can take a few days." He hadn't planned to, but things changed. The company wouldn't collapse if he were absent for a day or two. "I've already emailed William about it."

And had ignored his in-box afterward. For all his glib assurances, William was going to be upset with him.

"I'm afraid I'm getting you into horrible trouble." She bit down on her lip. "Oh, what a mess."

They were still holding hands and he squeezed hers. "Don't worry about it, Annie. All will be well. This gets you out of the line of fire for a few days so things can settle. And you'll be able to decide what *you* want to do next."

A future that didn't have him in it, he was sure. The idea niggled at him, but he didn't dwell on it. He'd made his choices, and his life was in Paris now. He'd done well for himself, proving his doubters wrong.

If he could give Annie a hand to do the same, he'd be contented with that.

No matter how much he wanted more.

Annie glanced at her phone again to check the time. It was after six; they'd stopped for lunch at a café in Lyon and went for a short walk to stretch their legs and get some air before getting back in the car for the rest of the drive. Last night she had figured she would not see Phillipe again, but today they had spent over eight hours in a car together and soon she would meet his parents.

She was a little anxious about that, actually. She hadn't really "met the parents" of the men she'd dated over the years. And even though she and Phillipe weren't dating, it still felt like a big thing. What would they think of her, the English girl running from a scandal?

Certainly, they would not think her good enough for their son. He was so very smart, so successful.

"What's bothering you?" Phillipe asked, looking over at her.

"I'm just nervous," she answered, putting down her phone. "About meeting your parents. About all of it."

"Don't worry about that. Maman will likely have a lovely meal for us, and you will be most welcome." He smiled at her. "It's what she does. And she'll say that it has been too long since I was home."

"How long has it been?"

He went quiet for a moment, then said, "Almost two years," in a low voice.

Ah. "Since your divorce?"

"Oui."

It was interesting that the farther away from Paris they got, the more French words and phrases snuck into his sentences. She turned in her seat. "Why did you not come back, if they love you so much?" She figured she knew the answer but thought it might be good for him to admit it out loud.

"Because Madelyn is nearby, and I didn't want the reminders."

She smiled, the first genuine smile she could remember from the entire day. It felt good. "Oh, well done. I didn't think you'd admit that."

He shrugged. "It was too raw. But I've been thinking about a visit for a while. Truthfully, this situation just prompted me to make that decision a little more quickly." He smiled, too. "And I'm not sorry to have company."

"So you don't have to do it alone."

"Right again."

"Progress." She smiled at him before looking at the phone on her lap. She sighed. "So, I heard from Bella a while ago."

"Oh?" Phillipe's eyebrows rose as he glanced over, then turned to the road again.

"I told her this morning that it wasn't me. She messaged me back an hour ago saying that considering how few people knew, she didn't understand how this could have got out unless I'd either told someone or gone to the press myself. I don't know how to prove it wasn't me."

Phillipe turned on his directional and made a left-hand turn. "You shouldn't have to. I would expect they've been in meetings all day to do damage control."

"Charlotte must really be loving me right now."

Phillipe laughed. "Charlotte is distressingly good at her job. She'll come up with a way to spin this."

She sat up straighter. She was less worried about the spin and more concerned with who went to the paparazzi. Who stood to gain anything by sharing such a story? Maybe if she could figure that out, she could work her way back to who might have discovered her true identity.

She was still working through a mental list when

Phillipe turned up a hillside street, slowing as he drove through a residential neighborhood. The homes here were nice—stone houses with tile roofs, olive and palm trees, little gardens. Annie had never seen a palm tree in person in her life. And here she was, in the south of France, so close to the Mediterranean. Sitting in a car with the handsomest man she'd ever known.

Was it wrong that a day that was so very horrible also kind of felt like a dream come true?

"Nous sommes ici," Phillipe said, and Annie nodded as he turned up a short drive to a welcoming-looking two-story house with wood shutters the color of whiskey barrels.

He turned off the car and let out a big breath.

"Phillipe? Before we go in, I just want to say… thank you. Thank you for caring enough to want to help me. You could have just sent me a warning, but you're a true friend."

He took off his seat belt and turned in his seat to face her better. "If I overstep, please tell me. I can be… bossy. Single-minded."

That didn't sound like the man she knew, today's activities excepted. "I will, though I won't have to. I just want you to know that I appreciate you so much. You have always—" Her throat tightened and she took a moment to swallow, ease the knot that had formed. "You have always treated me with caring and respect." She gave a small, secretive smile. "Maybe more than I wanted. You're a good man, Phillipe."

His gaze held hers and the air in the car filled with the same delicious tension that had shimmered between them last night. But then they both sat back, knowing it would only complicate matters further if they gave in to the attraction they'd done so well ignoring all day.

"Come," he said softly, giving her the smile she found so devastating. "Meet my parents. Be at home."

He retrieved their bags from the back seat and then they walked up the stone path together. Phillipe lifted his hand to knock but before he could, the door swung open and a woman stood there, her smile wide, the joy in her eyes unmistakable.

"Vous êtes ici!"

He laughed, put down the bags, and pulled her into his arms.

"Maman," he said, finally letting her go, "this is my friend, Annie."

"Bonjour, Annie. You are very welcome here."

The woman's English was good but heavily accented and utterly charming. *"Je suis heureuse de faire votre connaissance,* Madame Leroux. Thank you so much for having me," Annie replied, holding out her hand.

"Come in, come in! We will have dinner. Your father is in the back, grilling chicken."

"Papa? Grilling?" asked Phillipe, picking up the bags again.

"It is his new thing since he retired," she said, shaking her head. "Annie, if we forget our English, you must remind us. We do not want you to feel…left out."

"My French is getting better," Annie admitted. "Sometimes I just have a hard time keeping up."

"Come," Phillipe said. "I'll show you to your room."

He led her up the stairs to the upper level, which housed two bedrooms and a shared bathroom. "This is yours," he said, leading her to an open door. It was a sweet room, simple but welcoming, with white walls and pale blue sheer curtains that looked out over the back garden and fluttered in the breeze. A double bed and a dresser made up the only furniture in the spacious room, but there was something about it that seemed to take all the stress of the past two weeks and melt it away.

"I love it. It's so perfect."

"I'm in the other room. We'll share the bath."

"What about your parents?"

"Their bedroom is on the bottom floor. They did that a few years ago when Papa started having trouble with his knees. The doctors say he should wait a while longer for a replacement."

"This is where you grew up?"

"Yes."

She looked up at him. He'd put her bag down by the foot of the bed and suddenly everything about him seemed to fit. His workday suit was gone, and he was in jeans and a button-down, very casual and relaxed, and the lines in his face had eased even more since entering the house. "You have good memories here," she said, smiling a little. "A happy childhood."

"Yes." He looked around the room. "I shared this room with my two brothers as well. I think Maman and Papa are lonely now that none of us are local. Etienne is an engineer and lives in Dubai with his wife. Luc studied business and is with a company in Switzerland. He's married with two children. We don't see each other often."

"I didn't realize you had brothers," she said, wondering at the three of them filling up this one bedroom. How much fun they must have had. She'd always longed for a sibling...

"I am the youngest," he answered, followed by a quick smile. "And so I am the spoiled one."

"I don't believe it," she replied, and smiled back.

The moment drew out for a bit and then Phillipe stepped back. "I'll let you get settled. Meet us downstairs when you're ready. We can have a glass of wine before dinner."

She nodded, and after he was gone, she sat on the bed and texted Rachael to let her know she'd reached her destination and was safe.

Staying with a friend and their family for a few days to lie low. I'm definitely okay. I'll message soon. Xx

She went to the bathroom to freshen up a bit and when she returned Rach had messaged back. There was nothing from Bella, though. Nothing from the family at all, and that worried her. The silence was more troubling than anger.

Annie made her way downstairs and found Phillipe and his parents out on the patio, seated at a table with a bottle of wine in the middle. She took a deep breath and then went out to meet them, putting on a smile even though she was suddenly exhausted. Phillipe rose as she approached. "You're all settled?"

"Yes, thank you." She looked at his parents. "Thank you both so much for having me."

"Papa, this is Annie. Annie, my father, Georges."

Georges smiled widely. "Phillipe, get the girl a glass of wine. Where are your manners?"

Annie laughed, instantly liking the older man. Phillipe had inherited his good looks, it seemed, in the gray-blue eyes and impish smile.

Madame Leroux gestured to the empty chair. "Please, call me Paulette. Phillipe has been telling us a little of your trouble."

"Only that you needed to get away from the press," he assured her, his eyes meeting hers as she sat. "It is your story to tell, Annie."

So he hadn't told them the details. She was glad of that. It was out anyway, but she appreciated that he had deferred that conversation until she was there. Phillipe handed her a glass of wine and she took a revivifying sip, closed her eyes, and let out a slow breath.

When she opened them, she reminded herself that she was here, in the south of France, sipping wine on a patio with friendly faces. She was safe. And oddly enough, it had been a very long time since she'd felt that way.

"My father was Cedric Pemberton," she said softly. "It is confirmed but was not public knowledge until the news broke this morning. We do not know who leaked the information, but the family thinks I sold my story. I did not. Phillipe has been a wonderful friend. He suggested getting me out of Paris to avoid the press while everything gets sorted out." She smiled over at him. "Even though it means he's in an awkward position."

"Doing what is right should never be an awkward position," he said to her, and reached over to squeeze her fingers. She longed to hold his hand, but his parents were there, and they'd promised to be only friends. The squeeze was reassuring but brief.

"It is right he brought you here. Of course you may stay as long as you like." Paulette smiled at her. "He has not been home for a visit in far too long. Maybe I should thank you for making this happen?"

"Maman…" Phillipe chided, but Annie laughed.

"Sometimes men do need a nudge before they do what's right for them," she replied, sending Phillipe a small wink.

Paulette laughed and Georges picked up his glass. "I do not know what you are talking about."

Then everyone laughed. How was it that she could feel so at home so quickly?

Before long the grilled chicken was presented with a simple mesclun salad, some sort of flatbread and oil, and cheese. Simple and oh-so delicious. Annie let the good food and fine wine do its work, as well as the lovely, warm breeze. She could understand Phillipe loving it here. Paris was, well, Paris. But this… This was like a little slice of heaven.

She wiped her lips with her napkin and leaned back in her chair. "Last night we were at a five-star hotel with champagne and hors d'oeuvres and in our finest clothes, and I can tell you that it doesn't hold a candle to the past hour."

Paulette frowned. "Hold a candle?"

Annie smiled. "Sorry. I mean there is no comparison. This has been so very lovely. A soft spring evening with wonderful food and company is a blessing."

Georges and Phillipe shared a look, but Annie couldn't say what it meant. Just that father and son were having a silent conversation.

"Maman, Papa, Annie and I will do the washing up."

"Nonsense! It will only take a moment."

Paulette went to get up, but Phillipe put his hand

on her shoulder. "If it will only take a moment, then it is no big deal."

"Yes, please," Annie said. "It is the least I can do after you made such a delicious meal."

"It was nothing," Paulette protested.

But Annie rose and put her hand on the older woman's other shoulder. "It was everything," she said softly. "You opened your home and made me feel welcome. Thank you." She swallowed around a lump in her throat. It was more than the Pembertons had shown her.

She looked up at Phillipe as they walked inside. "When we're done, I need to send an email. Do your parents have internet?"

He laughed. *"Oui,"* he answered. "How do you think we all keep in touch? Video chats."

They cleaned up the mess and then she disappeared for a few moments to charge up her laptop and to send Bella an email, saying she would be happy to share screenshots of her banking information to prove she did not receive any payments in exchange for a story. Any hopes of a relationship with her siblings had been dashed days ago. She had enough pride to want to prove her innocence, however.

They would either believe her or they wouldn't. The trip to Grasse was a way to escape the paps, but it really changed nothing. She couldn't stay here forever. At some point—soon—she'd have to carry on with her plans. And so far, couch surfing at Rachael's was the best plan she had.

CHAPTER NINE

ANNIE HADN'T EXPECTED to sleep well, but as she stretched in the strange bed, with sunlight streaming through her window, she felt incredibly rested.

There was no sound in the house at the moment, so she quietly got up and checked the time...nearly nine. She'd slept ten hours. When was the last time she'd done that? A quick check of Phillipe's room showed an open door and a made bed beyond. What a sleepyhead she was! She went back to her room and gathered up some clothes for the day, then went to have a quick shower.

She discovered Phillipe sitting in the back garden again, beneath an umbrella and sipping coffee. "Good morning," she said softly, and he looked up at her and smiled.

When he looked at her that way, she knew it didn't matter what either of them said. They would never be "just" friends.

"You slept well?"

"Better than I could have hoped. A comfy bed and a warm breeze...and maybe a full tummy and a little wine. I feel wonderful."

"You look wonderful," he said, putting down his

cup. "Surprisingly relaxed, considering." He had a carafe at his elbow. "Coffee?"

"I'd love some."

He must have been anticipating her company, because another mug was on the tray with the carafe. He poured as she sat. "Where are your parents?"

"Mass," he said. "It's Sunday."

"Oh, right." She gave a little laugh. "Funny how the days suddenly started running together."

"That's not necessarily a bad thing." He handed her the cup and she took it, their fingers brushing. Tension crackled ever so briefly between them, but Annie cleared her throat and took a sip of the strong brew instead.

In the bright light of day, Annie took in the garden. The patio was made of stone and contained the gas grill, the table, chairs and umbrella, and numerous pots of plants that gave off a wonderful fragrance. There were shrubs that Annie couldn't identify, but she did recognize the showy red poppy blossoms, fragrant roses, irises, and what she thought might be valerian. "Your mother likes to garden."

"A little," he said with a nod. "More now that she and Papa have just retired. They are hoping to do some travel. And they have been volunteering at the local hospital."

"That's so lovely."

He nodded. "I had a good childhood, Annie. And their marriage…" His voice dropped off for a few moments. "Well, I wanted to have that. Clearly that's not how it worked out."

She looked at him for a long moment. There was more here than bitterness at Madelyn's affair, but she couldn't quite make out what it was. "They were your role models."

He nodded. "Sometimes I wonder if I wanted what they have so much that I ignored the signs."

"What signs?"

"That we didn't fit, I suppose. And when Madelyn became unhappy, I let my pride get in the way. I thought if I worked harder, if I could give her the life she was used to, it would be fine. But it wasn't." He sipped his coffee, stared out over the valley. "I left the job I loved thinking the promotion would make her happy. Mea culpa." Then he looked back at Annie. "You know, I thought coming back here would be painful, and yes, there are some reminders, but mostly it just feels good to be home."

"I can imagine how you feel. Guildford will always be that place for me. It's familiar, and there were so many good times." She shifted to look out over the small stone wall that gave a bit of privacy. The view was stunning, down over a valley, and she thought she might actually be able to see the sea from here. Surely not, though... It had to just be the sky on the horizon. "I know this is home for you, but this feels like a vacation to me. Isn't that odd?"

He smiled. "Not at all. If this is an impromptu vacation, what would you like to do today?"

"I have no idea. I mean, coffee in the sunshine is a fabulous start." She laughed a little. "What do you want to do?"

"I have an idea for tomorrow, but today... I wondered if you'd like to go for a walk in a garden. Not just any garden, mind you."

"We're in perfume country. I wouldn't expect it to be your average garden. I'd love to."

He smiled. "Fantastic. Let me make a call. I know the estate owners and I'm sure we could forgo the standard group tour for something a little less...structured." He started to get up and then hesitated. "But you haven't had breakfast yet. Am I a bad host for suggesting you help yourself to what is in the kitchen?"

"Absolutely not," she assured him. "I'm far more comfortable with that than being waited on. I'm sure I can find something. Am I dressed okay?" She wasn't sure her jeans and casual top were appropriate. Should she put on a skirt? She mentally went through her limited wardrobe choices.

"You're fine. I am going as I am." He wore gray cargo shorts and a golf shirt.

"All right."

"Let me call to be sure. But you should enjoy the patio as long as you like." He smiled. "There's still coffee in the carafe."

He disappeared into the house while she topped up her coffee. The air here was so different from Paris somehow...softer, and yes, warmer, and so fresh and fragrant. Or maybe it was just her, and how she'd needed to leave her stressful situation behind for a bit. Get out of the city. Breathe again.

Annie thought back over the past few months. She'd done nothing wrong, had she? Well, except maybe lie in the beginning...a lie of omission, but still a lie. But her motivations had all been pure. She was not going to feel guilt or anxiety over something she did not do. She had never been after financial gain, and certainly hadn't wanted to punish anyone. Even if the Pembertons didn't believe her, in her heart she knew the truth.

Energized, she picked up the coffee tray and went back inside, rummaging briefly and grabbing some fruit and a yogurt from the fridge. Today she would not worry about Aurora or the Pembertons. Today she would walk through a garden with a gorgeous man and count her blessings.

Phillipe had always known that Anemone was sweet and lovely, but he had never imagined she'd fit in so well with his parents.

She was walking slightly ahead of him through the Mas de Pivoines gardens, her honey hair glistening in the sun. He'd once thought of her as artless, and that description remained accurate as she strolled, turning her face to the sun, stopping to take a picture with her phone as a bee lit on a flower. The tour group had started out well over an hour earlier, so Phillipe and Annie were able to meander as they pleased.

Before they'd left the house, his parents had arrived back from mass. Seeing Annie speak to them in halting French, watching his mother and father fall under her spell… It highlighted some things he had tried to ignore for years. Madelyn had never had this simple warmth about her. She wouldn't have been caught dead in faded jeans and a simple top, her hair in a ponytail for a walk in the gardens. Nor would she have looked at his backyard like it was some kind of paradise. He wasn't trying to be judgmental. He was just starting to realize that maybe the two of them hadn't quite fit together the way he'd thought they did. Was it any wonder it hadn't worked out?

Annie turned around and smiled at him. "Did you see that butterfly? So pretty." She took a deep breath and sighed. "What a glorious day. What's Paris like in the summer? I moved in October. I'm going to be sorry if I leave, aren't I? I'm going to miss Paris at the best time."

He didn't want to think about it. "Maybe you'll find a job."

"Maybe." She shrugged. "My best friend offered her couch until I find something back home. I mean, in England back home. She's in Norwich."

That was a long way. "You're really thinking of going?"

"Thinking about it." Her gaze met his. "I haven't decided anything yet. I don't want to make a big decision on impulse."

She turned back to the garden. "I love these perennial borders. It must take so much work to keep everything cared for."

"But worth it, yes?"

She nodded. "Very. And the house... It suits perfectly, too, doesn't it, with that peachy exterior and blue shutters."

He didn't answer. He simply reached for her hand and held it as they walked along, something new and tenuous running between them.

"Phillipe..."

She turned to face him. She had sunglasses on, and she slid them up onto her head as she looked up at him. Today she wasn't wearing any makeup, and she had the smallest dusting of freckles across her nose.

"Don't say it," he said hoarsely. "Please don't. I

know all the reasons. They don't stop me from wanting to kiss you."

"I was going to say thank you for bringing me here, but clearly there's more on your mind."

Oh, he was such a fool. While he tried to come up with a response, a smile bloomed on her face that put the roses to shame.

"Are you tongue-tied now?" she asked, her eyes twinkling. "I didn't think it was possible. You always seem to know what to say."

"I don't know what to say with you," he admitted finally. "Everything is at odds. And you're different here, somehow."

"So are you."

He frowned. "I am?"

She nodded. "A part of you is more relaxed, and when I see you here, it's like a lot of things just start to click together and make sense. And then there's another part of you that seems on edge."

"You are probably right on both counts." His fingers were still twined with hers. "This is my home. I have always loved it. And yet…"

She lifted her other hand and touched his face. "And yet, it's like you said this morning. Your failed marriage has ruined a bit of it for you. In coming back you accept the beauty, but it also means you have to accept the pain."

"Yes."

"And probably face some truths you would rather not face."

She was far too astute. "Maybe."

"When I go back to Paris, I have to face things. I have to face that my decisions might have been wrong.

If I go back to England, I have to face that I no longer have a home to go back to. There are possessions in storage for wherever I land, but I don't know where that will be. I can ignore all that here, or at least try to. But in the back of my mind those things are always sitting there, poking me from time to time. Reality intrudes and it sucks."

He gave a small chuckle at her turn of phrase. "How do you know me so well?"

Her thumb traced along his jaw. "Sadly, I think pain recognizes pain. In some way, the people who should have loved us turned us away. It was your wife and my father, but does it really matter? Rejection is rejection. And so we learn to be strong alone."

He reached out and touched her hair, tucking an errant piece behind her ear. It was hot from the sun, fragrant from her shampoo this morning. "He was the one who lost out, Anemone."

"And she was the one who let you get away. She was a fool."

He knew he shouldn't. They kept talking about being friends and supportive. Their paths were going in different directions. But Phillipe could no more resist kissing her than a bee could resist dipping into the sweetness of a flower. He lowered his head and touched her lips with his, and this kiss was different somehow. It wasn't the champagne-induced passion of Friday night, or the temperate *this-is-goodbye* kiss when he left her flat. This was more. More of everything—awareness, gentleness, acceptance. His chest cramped from the sweetness of it.

"I kind of love it when you do that," she whispered against his lips as the kiss eased. "I know it complicates things, but I like kissing you. I could kiss you all day."

Why did she have to say things like that? It made him want to grab her hand, drag her out of the garden, take her to a hotel and spend the afternoon seducing her. He took a step backward and ran his hand through his hair. "I like it, too," he said. "Too much. Why do you think I suggested staying at my parents' instead of a hotel?"

A smile crept up her cheek. "Are you hiding behind your mother and father, Phillipe Leroux?"

He cursed—in French—and shook his head. "Of course I am. I'm trying to do the honorable thing."

She came closer again. A fragrant breeze came along and ruffled more of her hair; some had come loose as they'd been kissing. "You are definitely honorable," she agreed. "But you don't always need to be. You don't have to make that decision for me, you know. I can consent...or not."

He swallowed.

"Unless you don't want to, because you too can consent...or not."

"Annie."

She lifted up one finger. "We both know you are not ready for a relationship." She lifted a second. "We also both know that my future is up in the air and that I probably won't even be staying in the country." She lifted a third. "And I remember that you said you are not a one-night kind of guy, and I respect that. Nor am I a one-night kind of woman. Usually." She lowered her hand. "But none of those things seems able to stop what happens when we're together. I'm just saying, I'm willing to explore this during the time we have. I don't want to look back on this and have regrets either way. You don't have to protect me, Phillipe. Even though I know that sounds a bit crazy since I'm actually here because you are protecting me. But that's from the press. You don't have to protect me from being hurt or…or from myself."

God, he had such admiration for her. "You definitely know your own mind," he said, shaking his head a little in a "what am I going to do with you" kind of way. "And you're an optimist. I never quite got that until just now, but you're always looking forward, aren't you?"

She turned back to the path and started walking again, slowly. He joined her, reached for her hand again. For some reason he needed to feel connected to her in some way. Maybe for some of that optimism to rub off.

"I can't change what is behind me," she said simply. "And if I think about it too much, it gets overwhelming. So I try to live in the moment, think of the good things. And sometimes dream a little for the future. I suppose all that optimism is a little naive." They went deeper into the garden, the flowers and plants and trees affording them a privacy that felt rather intimate. "Maybe that's why my plan to work at Aurora was flawed from the beginning. I was so sure that I could somehow sneak my way past the very obvious barrier of being a secret love child."

"Did your mother and Cedric still… I mean, after you were born."

She shook her head. "As far as I know, Cedric broke off the affair." She looked over at him. "Me coming along cost my mum the only man she ever loved. And you know, it might have saved his marriage in the end because he left her and went back to Aurora. Who knows?"

They dropped the subject for a little while, passing through an arbor where a field lay in front of them. "What is this?" she asked, staring out over the expanse.

"Lavender," he answered. "It's not the right time for it to bloom. Tomorrow I'm going to show you the most famous rose in the region. But for now, I want to show you the peonies. It's over one hundred feet of different varieties and it's splendid this time of year."

He focused on giving her the tour of the garden, including the fragrant and showy peonies that the garden was named for. Afterward, he took her to a café for a light lunch before they headed home. It seemed she was willing to let their previous conversation drop, but it kept playing in the back of his mind. What if they were to take things further? They were both consenting adults. They did not work together any longer. Neither of them was attached to anyone else. And she was right. They both knew what was standing in their way, and what this was and what it wasn't.

But there was no time to talk to her about it again, and definitely no time to act on it, as they ate another evening meal *en famille* and went to their separate beds at night.

He wondered if she was sleeping as soundly as the night before…because he surely wasn't.

He was still trying to figure out if bringing her here had been a big mistake or perhaps the smartest move he'd ever made.

For the second morning in a row, Annie woke long past sunrise and stretched, luxuriating in the soft cotton sheets of the bed.

Today Phillipe was taking her on another adventure.

Not that a walk through the gardens yesterday was really an adventure, per se, but this whole trip felt like a holiday. Grasse was stunningly beautiful. She adored the area—the undulating hills that seemed to roll right into the sea, the terraced buildings that looked like steps climbing the hillside, the warm, fragrant air. She totally understood why he said he loved it here.

It presented an additional complication, however. Because seeing him here, with his family, in the area where he'd grown up and trained... It deepened her regard for him. Her understanding of what made him tick. She was starting to care for him far too much. For all her words yesterday about being consenting adults and regrets, she knew that no matter where she ended up, having Phillipe in her life even for a short time was going to leave an indelible mark.

She wanted to hope. Clearly they liked each other, and there was no question that they were attracted to each other. But she couldn't see a way where they could get past the big things. He still maintained he did not want a relationship, and how could she blame him when he'd been hurt so badly? More than that, she was a major complication for him. His livelihood, his career, was taking off. She would not be the one to negatively affect that trajectory simply because of who she was. How could he possibly be with her and work for them? It would put him in the middle, and she refused to do that to him.

Even though she wished there might be something after this trip.

She got out of bed and tidied the sheets. If she'd

learned anything over the past few years, it was that wishing never achieved anything.

But she was willing to take a risk and not play it safe. If she had to move on, wouldn't it be nice to at least take the memory of being loved by Phillipe with her? If only he could see things the same way...

But if he did, he wouldn't be the Phillipe she'd come to know and love.

The thought stopped her hands as she was tucking the spread around the pillows. There was no *love*. She'd thought the word in a colloquial sense, that was all. A common turn of phrase: *know and love*. It didn't mean she was *in love* with him.

Though when she thought back to the tender kisses in the garden yesterday, she knew it wasn't much of a stretch. She could love him very easily. Madelyn had been a fool to cheat on him and leave him as if he meant nothing. Annie didn't know how anyone could do such a thing to a man so warm, handsome, principled. Certainly he hadn't been perfect, but still.

If he had any flaws at all, she rather thought it might be that he was too cautious. Too bound up in his sense of honor to allow himself any indulgences.

Perhaps she could convince him otherwise.

After a quick shower she dressed. Phillipe had said she should wear trousers, so she took out a pair of bone-colored linen pants, frowned at the wrinkles, and put them on anyway. She chose a pink collarless blouse to go with it, frowning again in the mirror, wondering if the ensemble was too shapeless or casual. But when she walked downstairs and into the kitchen, he turned from the counter and his eyes warmed with approval. "That is perfect. You just need a hat. Maman has said you can borrow one of hers. It will protect from the sun."

"The sun? We're going to be outdoors again?"

"*Oui.* May is the month of the rose here in Grasse. There are fields and fields of them, waiting to be plucked at just the right time to create the essential oil needed for so many perfumes. You will love it. But first, breakfast."

Paulette breezed into the kitchen from the garden. "Oh, *bien*, you are awake! I shall make fresh coffee, and the croissants are still warm."

"I feel so spoiled," Annie replied, smiling at Paulette. "The last few days have been so wonderful."

"I am enjoying it. Usually I only cook for Georges, and it is not exciting." She rolled her eyes and Annie laughed. "Phillipe says you are to go to the roses today." She got out a plate and put several croissants on it, then retrieved butter and preserves and put it all on the kitchen table. "He used to love going to the fields when he was still here in Grasse. Maybe even more than being in the lab."

"I love seeing the process from plant to perfume," he admitted. "It always feels a little bit miraculous to me."

His passion was clearly with the fragrance, so why was he stuck in an office in Paris? Why give it up? Unless it really was about the money, but he didn't strike her as the kind of man who worried about that.

Georges joined them for coffee and once they had breakfasted, they set out for the rose fields.

It took perhaps fifteen minutes for them to reach the fields. There was a large farmhouse with several out-buildings on the right, and he pulled in next to several other cars. "This is the Chabert farm. They've been growing flowers for the industry for four generations now and produce exclusively for Aurora."

"Only for you?"

"Yes." He shut off the engine and looked over at her. "I worked here as a student. When I say I started at the bottom, I really did, Annie. Roses, jasmine, lavender… This was how I fell in love with scent."

"I thought it was through chemistry."

He grinned. "I like to think of it as a marriage of science and senses. The quantifiable and the unquantifiable. Come."

They got out of the car and Phillipe led her away from the house and down over a knoll. The scent of rose filled the air and she breathed deeply. Once they reached the field, though, she stopped and her mouth dropped open.

Rows upon rows, and workers moving among them, harvesting the blossoms as if they were ripe fruit to be plucked. "Amazing, is it not?" he asked, and she nodded, still taking it all in. "Come. Meet Andre."

She was introduced to Andre Chabert, and before long she found herself donning a white apron and putting Paulette's wide-brimmed hat on her head to keep away the sun.

"The blooms are best first thing in the morning, before the heat of the day. They cannot be wilted. Time is of the essence. I'll show you," he said, leading her to the row Andre had assigned them. In no time at all he'd shown her which blossoms were ready, how to pluck them and then tuck them into the soft apron gently to keep them from being crushed. Everyone filled their aprons and then carefully dumped the blossoms in a main bin before returning to the shrubs. She lifted her hands once and took a deep inhale of the flowers cushioned in her palms. Had anything ever smelled sweeter?

"This rose—the Centifolia rose—is so important here that there is a month-long festival happening," Phillipe explained. "It's a huge tourist draw, and we can go if you like, but I thought you'd appreciate more of a behind-the-scenes look at my city."

"This is much better than wading through crowds," she replied, invigorated by the sun, fresh air and heady scent. "I'd far rather experience it than observe."

"I thought you might." They carried on for over an hour, chatting easily, conversing in snippets with other workers who talked and laughed. Annie struggled to keep up with the French, but Phillipe translated some bits to keep her included in the conversations. As the heat from the sun grew, Phillipe drew her aside after they'd emptied their aprons once more. "I have more to show you. Would you like to see?"

She'd had such fun she could have worked all day, but the excited light in Phillipe's eyes had her nodding instantly. "Of course."

Over the course of the next few hours, Phillipe showed her how the blossoms were instantly put into burlap bags—all indelibly stamped with "Aurora"—for transport to the factory.

Then they left the Chaberts behind and he took her to the Aurora facility, where he'd plied his trade before moving to Paris.

She looked over at him as they entered not through the main doors that were there for public access, but the employee entrance. He was buzzed in and immediately a woman came around the front desk and captured him in a hug.

"Phillipe! You are home! Oh, welcome back."

Annie stood back, utterly amused, trying to imagine this sort of welcome at Aurora HQ. It simply wouldn't happen.

"*Bonjour*, Danielle. It is good to be back. I've brought a friend for a tour. I hope that is all right?"

The woman looked over at Annie and her smile widened. "Of course. Hello, I'm Danielle. I've been working this desk for fifteen years, since before Phillipe started with us in the lab."

"Annie," she replied, and held out her hand. "It's lovely to meet you."

"We've just been at Andre's. I took Annie to the morning harvest. It looks good this year."

"Things are going very well, but we miss you around here."

"I'm sure that's not true."

She wagged a finger at him. "Paris's gain is our loss. But you are here now. How long are you home for?"

"Just a few days." He didn't say more, and for that Annie was grateful. It felt a little odd being on Aurora property, if she were being honest, considering how furious the family was with her just now.

"See me before you leave again," she said as the phone rang at the desk. "Sorry. I must answer."

"Of course! *Merci*, Danielle."

He led Annie away as Danielle returned to the desk.

"She likes you a lot."

"Everyone knows each other here. It's like family."

Annie pondered that for a moment. "More so than in Paris?"

"Paris is nice, and the family has been more than welcoming. But corporate just has a different feel to it."

She nodded. "May I say something, Phillipe?"

They halted in front of a set of double doors. "Am I going to like it?" he asked.

She looked up at him. "I don't know, but I feel I must. You belong here. Seeing you at your family home, in the field, here, in this building... The pieces all seem to fit somehow. Why did you ever leave?"

A muscle tightened in his jaw. "You know why."

"Because of Madelyn?" She kept her voice low; the building wasn't exactly private.

"There were too many reminders."

"That's a shame. Because the way I see it, she not only ended your marriage, she took away something that was a part of you. Your..." She scrambled to come up with the right word. "Your essence. That's too big of a cost for any one person to pay."

He led her through the doors and into a larger room filled with what appeared to be copper tubs and pipes. "I do not dislike Paris, and I have a wonderful job," he replied.

"Not disliking something is a far cry from feeling like you are where you belong. Just think about it. Why shouldn't you be happy?"

She let the question settle and decided not to press anymore. Who was she to give life advice, anyway? Hers was in the biggest mess ever.

For the next hour, Phillipe took her on a tour of the facility, explaining the extraction process and how it took between three and five tons of rose blossoms to make a single kilo of essential oil. The sheer thought of it had her mouth dropping open, thinking of how long it had taken her to fill her apron just once this morning.

"Some of our ingredients are synthetic," he continued, taking her on a quick walk through the lab. "That's where chemistry comes in. Take, for instance, lily of the valley. It's beautiful, light, a very desirable scent, but does not produce the oil needed. So it is manufactured to mimic it instead."

She didn't know that. "There's something rather magical about having the oil from the plant, though, don't you think?"

He smiled. "I do, but I appreciate science, too. Especially when it comes to manufacturing elements we would normally source from animals."

"Ethically, I also approve." She smiled up at him.

They moved on past the mixing process and into aging. "You might think that once the oils are blended, the scent is ready, and sometimes it might be, but quite often the result is greatly improved with an aging process."

"Like wine," she offered, and he chuckled.

"Yes, I suppose. It helps the notes to all blend together. So while I blended Nectar over two years ago, it is just now ready for market as it has been aging. One must be meticulous and patient."

"And are you?" she asked, looking up at him again. "Meticulous and patient?"

Their gazes held for a few seconds, and the meaning behind her question shifted. She already knew he was patient. If he weren't, he would have taken her to bed after the launch rather than walk away. But meticulous... She swallowed, her throat tight, as she imagined being the focus of his laser-like attention.

"I try to be," he murmured, and it was as if everything around them disappeared.

The day thus far had been full of activity and new things, but one little bit of innuendo and the delicious tension between them was back. It made her breath catch and her nerve endings tingle to imagine his hands that had so gently plucked the roses this morning touching her skin.

"It's no good, is it?" he asked, his eyes searching hers.

"What isn't?"

"Avoiding this. Between us. We can pretend for a little while, but then I look at you, and I'm right back at your flat on Friday night, wanting you."

She wanted to tell him how she felt. That she was falling for him. That he was perhaps the best man she'd ever known. But that would surely send him running. He didn't want her to be in love with him. He did want her, though, and she wanted him, and it would be enough.

"I told you yesterday that we were adults, and we could consent or not. I'm consenting, Phillipe. I'm sorry you left my flat on Friday night and I've wanted to be with you ever since. I'm not going to pretend otherwise. I've been attracted to you for weeks and sometimes I feel like I might die from wanting you to touch me again."

His nostrils flared slightly as his eyes widened. "You just said that to me in the middle of a perfume factory."

"I did."

"Why the hell did I insist we stay at my parents'?"

She started to laugh, and he did, too, but then he abruptly planted a hot, searing kiss on her lips.

"Oh," she said when he released her.

"I can't offer you—"

"I'm not asking for anything. I have no idea what lies ahead, anyway. But can't we have today? I can't stay here forever, Phillipe, and neither can you. We can't run away from reality and our responsibilities indefinitely. Don't we deserve one day before we have to return to real life and deal with our messes? Or at least my mess. I dragged you into it with me."

"One day," he repeated, lifting his fingers to her cheek. "Yes, Anemone. We can have one day."

CHAPTER TEN

Phillipe had formed a plan in his head on the way back to the villa. If this was going to be their one chance to be together, it would not be a rushed job in his childhood bed hoping his parents didn't arrive home early from their volunteering. He was a fairly wealthy man, when all was said and done. He could afford to give her a better memory to take with her when she left.

He only felt a little guilty that he'd cut their factory tour short.

Now she was in her room, packing her bag, and he was on his phone booking a room in Cannes, which was only a half-hour drive. The first few places he tried were fully booked. But on the third he hit the jackpot: a prestige suite with a king-size bed, a soaker tub, and a balcony looking out over the water. He whipped out his credit card and booked it before he could change his mind, then took his own bag downstairs. Chances were they'd be back tomorrow, but she had been right about one thing earlier: soon they would have to deal with their responsibilities. He couldn't stay away from Paris forever. She would have to come up with a plan for moving forward as well, a plan that included what to say and what not to say to the press. Time was ticking and those decisions would have to be made soon.

But not yet.

She came downstairs as he was writing a note to his parents, explaining that he was taking Annie sightseeing for a day or two and that he would be in touch about their return. "I feel odd leaving this way," she said, standing behind him as he penned the note. "Without saying thank you."

He looked over his shoulder. "You can thank them when we return," he said, and then held his breath as he added, "unless you've changed your mind."

"I haven't," she said, coming forward. She reached a hand up into his hair and drew him down for a kiss.

She was sweet and sultry all at once and he was unnerved by the whole plan to dash away for an illicit rendezvous. It felt irresponsible somehow. The feeling wasn't strong enough to make him change his mind, however. He'd been trying to do the "right" thing for days, but as Annie said, they both knew what they wanted. Each other. There were no false hopes here. For once, Phillipe, who always seemed to plan everything with an eye to the future, was going to try living in the moment and see how it felt.

He broke the kiss and smiled against her lips. "Hold that thought," he murmured.

"For how long?"

"An hour."

She shuddered beneath his hands. "I can do an hour." He stepped back a little, and she added, "Maybe."

The drive to Cannes was blessedly short, except for one quick stop at a *pharmacie*, where he spent five minutes picking up protection for the night ahead. He was thirty-five years old, and he felt about twenty as he stood in line to pay, but he refused to be irresponsible, and it wasn't like he carried a condom all the time since he didn't do hookups. Annie had blushed when he'd pulled into the parking lot, but she hadn't said a word.

Now they were walking through the lobby of the hotel to check in, and Phillipe's body felt like a wire pulled so tight it was ready to break.

What would Annie say if she knew he had not been with a woman since his divorce?

Key card in hand, they made their way to the elevator bank, then inside the car. He swiped the card and pushed the button for the correct floor.

The whole time his pulse hammered at his throat, his chest. The silence between them only amplified the tension, the anticipation, the *Oh-my-God-what-do-I-do-next?* feeling coursing through his veins. Out of the elevator car, down the hall, a green light on the door before he opened it and ushered them inside.

The door closed with a loud click.

Annie put down her bag; he did the same, and they stood looking at each other for a prolonged moment. Her chest rose and fell as if she'd been running, even though they'd just made the short walk from the elevator. Her cheeks were a delightful shade of pink and her eyes... Her eyes were hungry. He thrilled knowing she was hungry for him.

Then she bit down on her lip—did she not know how crazy it made him when she did that?—and began unbuttoning the pink blouse.

He had the brief thought that maybe he was supposed to be undressing, too, but he was too mesmerized by the slow play of her fingers over the covered buttons. Five, six, seven… Finally the last one was undone, and she slipped the blouse off her narrow shoulders.

She wore a blush-colored lace bra that took his breath away.

A few more moments and she had slipped out of her trousers, revealing a matching pair of bikini panties.

The last strand of his frayed restraint popped, and things moved faster after that. He pulled off his shirt and then took her in his arms, thrilling to hold her against his body, feel her skin beneath the pads of his fingers. Her kiss was equally as demanding as his, and she reached for the button of his cargo shorts, releasing it and the zipper and pushing them to the floor, taking his underwear with them. He reached for her again, sweeping her up in his arms and laying her on the bed.

She wriggled out of her panties.

"I meant to take this slow," he said, breathing heavily. "To make it good."

"We can finesse it next time," she said firmly. "Right now, I just need you, Phillipe. I need you to let go and just—" Her voice quavered with anticipation. "God. Just take me. Please."

Urgency took over. He reached into the bag for the box of condoms. In what felt like the next breath, he'd slipped inside her.

They both froze, absorbing the moment, the feeling, the ultimate connection of body to body.

Then she shifted beneath him, turned those liquid blue eyes up to his and whispered once more, "Take me."

What else was a man supposed to do?

Annie lay on her back and stared at the ceiling, her body still humming.

She'd wanted Phillipe to let go of the polite restraint he seemed to wear like armor, and she'd thought she'd been prepared, but nothing could have prepared her for the magnificence of his lovemaking.

She started to laugh—a blissful, satisfied giggle that echoed through the suite that she hadn't even looked at yet. She was in a luxury suite on the French Riviera and all she knew was that the bed was a king and that she and Phillipe could fit on it while lying in any possible direction.

"What's so funny?"

His rich, low voice shivered over her nerve endings.

"Not funny. Happy." She paused and then added with a smile, "Satisfied."

"Mmm... Good to hear."

She let out a contented sigh.

"Just so you know, next time will be better."

She did laugh then. "If it's any better, I might combust."

"I shall make that my goal, then. To set you on fire." He rolled to his side, and she felt his gaze on her face. "Inch by inch. Slowly."

It wouldn't take much. Just his words had her heating up all over again.

She looked over at him. "Hard and fast was what we both needed. For the first time, anyway. I've wanted to do that for weeks."

"Weeks?" His brows lifted in surprise.

"Um… Have you looked in the mirror? You're just so…*gah*! Hot, all right? And you do this thing with your eyebrow and the corner of your mouth when you smile that's so sexy. Working for you every day was sweet torture."

Said brows lifted into his hairline. "This is all news to me."

"I'm glad, because I'd have been mortified had you known."

"So the night of the party—"

"Yeah…you left me…um…" She thought of a slightly crude term normally reserved for men but said instead, "Frustrated."

He gaped at her.

She blushed.

"Well, if it's any consolation, I was feeling much the same but determined not to cross a line as your boss."

She rolled to her side and trailed her fingers over his chest. "Which I appreciate and have the utmost respect for." She smiled a little and let her hand slip over his abdomen. "And I am now ever so glad I am no longer in the employ of Aurora Inc. To think I would have missed all this…"

He laughed, a low chuckle that rumbled in his chest and filled her heart with happiness.

Thoroughly sated and in no hurry to do anything in particular, Annie finally let her gaze take in the room. It was as big as her entire studio apartment, but with much better furniture and doors leading to a balcony. "We have an ocean view, don't we?" She turned her head to study Phillipe's face. It was utterly relaxed and his eyes were closed, but he gave a small nod.

"Yes, we do."

"This place is huge. Gorgeous. It must have cost you a fortune."

He turned his head and opened one eye, squinting at her. "And worth it to have you all to myself. Though there is lots of day left if you want to explore Cannes."

She rose up on her elbow so that she was looking down into his face. Emotions she didn't want to acknowledge filled her heart and soul. He was such an easy man to love. "Cannes will always be here," she whispered, "but my time with you is short. I don't want to waste a single moment."

He opened both his eyes then, and they burned right through to the very heart of her. This was a short-term thing; they both knew it. But it was not without connection or deep feelings for each other. She didn't want to think about it ending when it was just beginning. It would take away all the pleasure in the right now, and hadn't she earned that? She traced her finger over his cheek, along the soft curve of his lips. She'd been so lonely. Not just for the physical, though that was clearly a revelation. But the sense of having an ally. Someone to share things with, even if it was a simple meal or a glass of wine or a smile.

She appreciated him, and so she shut out the world around them and spent the next hour showing him exactly how much.

It was nearly seven when Phillipe finally insisted they dress and have dinner. Annie compromised by putting on the simple dress she'd brought with her and requesting they get room service rather than going out. "I'd like to eat on the terrace, overlooking the water with the sea breeze on my face and no one else but you."

"That sounds perfect," he agreed, so while he looked after ordering, she freshened up and then tried to make some sense of the sheets on the bed. Her cheeks flamed when she thought of how they'd spent the last several hours, but she refused to be ashamed and had no regrets. How could she when she'd felt so desired and cherished? She was self-aware enough to know she'd been starved for love for a long time, and to put what she was feeling in perspective. It didn't stop it from feeling wonderful just the same. Happiness—life, for that matter—was fleeting. It was too short to waste on regrets or perhaps even playing it safe.

She thought briefly of the Pembertons in their ivory tower and knew she wouldn't trade her life for theirs, which gave her a surprising amount of comfort. Even considering the stunning hotel room she was in now, or the glamour of the launch last week. In their world, privacy was a rare commodity and image was everything. There was so much pressure that came with the fame and fortune. As she put a swipe of gloss on her lips, she thought back to her time in the PR department. She'd come on board just after Bella had taken over as CEO and the revelation of her scars was still a news item. While she was there, she'd learned about the sabotage earlier in the spring at New York Fashion Week, which targeted Charlotte, and the scandal surrounding Stephen and Will had been all over the papers before she'd even learned that Cedric was her father.

Having her own photo show up gave her a taste of what that was like. Fame definitely wasn't without its drawbacks. And despite everything, she did think the

Pembertons were good people. All it took was putting herself in their shoes to understand their suspicions and worries.

"Dinner won't be long," Phillipe called.

She opened the bathroom door and smiled. "How do I look? Suitable for dinner *à deux*?"

"Lovely," he responded, holding out his hand. He'd changed, too, into a pair of jeans and a crisp blue shirt that brought out his eyes. "How about champagne on the deck?"

"There's champagne?"

"The ice in the bucket is mostly melted, but yes, there is champagne."

He deftly popped the cork and poured them each a glass, then they went outside to the balcony and sat at the small table and chairs.

"To running away," he offered as a toast, and she laughed and touched the rim of her glass to his before taking a drink.

Bubbles exploded over her tongue. "Rachael isn't going to believe this. Me, sitting on a balcony in Cannes, having postcoital champagne."

His eyes twinkled. "You could send her a selfie."

"I'm not eighteen."

He shrugged. "You still could." He hesitated for a brief moment, and then said, "You do trust her, don't you?"

She nodded. "With my life."

He smiled, looking more relaxed than she'd ever seen him. "I truly don't mind if you want to message her. Friends are important. And you said she'd been very worried."

It did sound fun. And she wouldn't put in any sordid details. She popped inside to get her phone and then back out. "Here," she said, moving in close to him. He held the champagne flute in his hand as she put her head in close to his shoulder, then maneuvered her thumb to take the pic. She looked at it and got a strange swirl in her tummy. They looked so…happy. And wonderful together. She was glad he'd suggested it, because she'd have the photo now as a memory of this crazy week.

"It turned out cute," she said, and forwarded it to him.

Then she sent a copy to Rachael, prefacing it with a FYEO text.

Top secret: hiding away in Cannes with the friend I mentioned. As you can see, everything is fine.

It took less than thirty seconds for the reply to come through.

OMG you have been holding out on me! "Friend"? Right… I need details.

Annie started laughing and turned the phone to show Phillipe, who also grinned. Then she sent one last message.

About to have dinner. Just wanted you to know that I'm fine, and that I miss you. I promise to share everything soon. Xx

Then she put her phone down. She wasn't going to squander another moment of this gorgeous night with her face in a screen.

They supped on foie gras with toasted brioche, seared scallops, and roasted veal entrées, plus a bottle of a dry white that Annie was not familiar with and was most certainly out of her price range. As they ate, they talked…about their childhoods, little anecdotes about their schooling, likes and dislikes. There was laughter and a few sad moments, too, as Annie briefly mentioned losing her mother. Phillipe's strong, reassuring squeeze of her hand felt so good, so right.

"You know what bothers me the most about my father?" she asked, examining a salted caramel profiterole, wondering if she possibly had room for it after the divine meal they'd just consumed. "I thought it would be that I didn't find out until it was too late to know him. But it's not. It's knowing that he sent money. That's what's made me feel like a dirty little secret."

He nodded. "And your mother… Are you mad at her, too?"

"For not telling me? Sometimes. For getting involved with a married man who already had a family? Yes, but then I remind myself not to judge. I wasn't there. I don't know their hearts. That's the thing, though, right? I will never know their hearts, if they loved each other, if they were even happy about me."

"Annie." Phillipe scooted his chair over a little. The sunset softened the light around them, casting them in greater shadow as the sky turned pink, the same soft color as was on the rose… Heavens, had it just been this morning? It felt like a lifetime had passed between then and now.

He put his hands on hers. "I know right now that your mother was happy about you. Perhaps not at first, but from the moment you were put into her arms. How could she not be? You are wonderful. You light up every room. And as far as Cedric, well, not knowing you was his great loss. Trust me, I know this. Because right now I'm so incredibly grateful that I have had the chance to know you."

Her vision blurred as tears sprang into her eyes. "Oh, Phillipe…"

"I mean it. You have changed my life. I do not know where we go from here, but it won't be the same again, and that's a good thing." He gave a soft laugh. "I needed someone to come in and shake things up a bit."

"Oh, Phillipe, I—" She stopped abruptly, then camouflaged her near slip with a sniff. "I'm the lucky one. You could have let me be sacked and lick my wounds all the way back to Britain. Instead you fought for me. No one has ever done that for me before. And today… I'm grateful for you," she finished. And maybe inside she had said the words *I love you*—but she wouldn't ruin this beautiful evening with something that they both knew had an expiration date. It was better this way, anyway. They could go their separate ways and not have the chance for anything to be ruined.

She twined her fingers with his. "It's been a very long time since someone made me feel, I don't know, worth it, I guess. Seen and important. Losing Mum was so hard—she was my only family. And then I discovered I had another family, but I had to deal with the betrayal I felt, the loss of a parent I had never known, and fear that if my half-siblings were to discover who I was, I truly would have no one. I played it so safe, hiding who I was from them. But by doing that, I could never be a part of them, either. I was still alone. So when I say that you standing up for me is a major thing, please believe me. It means so much to me. I can never repay you for this."

"Why on earth would you have to repay anything? Maybe at first it was my sense of fairness, but I also cared about you. What would it say about me if I—"

He halted, looked away and sat back in his chair.

"What is it?" She was alarmed at how quickly he'd gone quiet, midsentence. "What's wrong?"

He turned his head and faced her again, his gaze wide with what appeared to be surprise. "Nothing is wrong, really. I just realized that I was so very quick to stand up for you, but I was never able to stand up for myself, most of all in my marriage. I've been so quick to blame Madelyn for her affair, and it was horribly wrong. There's no denying that. But the truth is we made a mistake. We never should have married in the first place. We wanted different things, even though we never really said so. Or rather, I never said so. I went along, did what I thought would make her happy, fix things, instead of being true to myself."

"Don't be too hard on yourself," she cautioned.

But he shook his head. "It's not really about that. Look, I disagree with what she wanted. She wanted money and status and a certain life and I let her believe it was what I wanted, too. I mean, at least she was honest about it. I wasn't. She was off making her way as a journalist, surrounding herself with beautiful people. She thought my potential was wasted at the lab, so I put in for the management job. I left the lab behind and oversaw all the development here in Grasse. It's an enviable job, with its own prestige, but I really took it to make her happy. But she was already in another's arms by that point."

He sighed. "The funny thing was, I took that job to please her, and I thought maybe it might be a good time to talk about starting a family—the thing I wanted. But she didn't want that, either."

"Then she is the fool," Annie whispered, hating the way he was talking about himself as if he had no value. "And not worthy of you."

He gave a bitter laugh. "It's not even being worthy or not. It's that we were flawed from the beginning. I tried to prove her wrong. When the job came up in corporate, I put in for it right away. Being here—in Grasse, I mean—was just too close. So I went to Paris, and within six months I was promoted. We could have had the life she wanted. Ironic when you think about it."

"But is it the life you want?" Annie asked. "I know you said it's a great job and that Paris is 'okay,' but is it really the life you want to live? Because I've seen you the last few days, Phillipe, and you're lit up. This morning, in the fields, and then in the lab, talking about extraction and distilling and blending... That's your passion. Is Paris where you want to be, or is it here?"

He ran his hand through his hair. "I don't know anymore. But I know I have to figure it out. I've been running for two years. At some point I have to stop."

She nodded. "I want you to be happy. Everyone deserves the chance to be happy."

"And you, Annie? What do you want out of life?"

"I need to figure that out, too."

"Do you think you might be able to figure things out in Paris, at least for a while?"

The implication of his words swirled around her, as warm and seductive as the wind off the ocean. They were seated in near dark now, the sun having dipped below the horizon, with only the lights of the hotels above the beach casting their glow. Even that was muted, blocked by wide palm fronds that afforded little bits of privacy on their balcony.

He reached out and cupped her jaw. "I don't know what's next, but I don't want these few days to be the end. Can't you stay a little longer?"

She wanted to say yes. Wanted it so badly. But she had no job, no money for rent... And she was definitely not going to ask him to support her. If they kept seeing each other, she'd feel like a kept woman. What if they decided to go their separate ways? Then she'd feel indebted. She'd rather be alone than face that kind of rejection again.

It seemed that after everything, she still had some pride left.

As she opened her mouth to answer, her phone buzzed against the table, surprising them both. Annie jumped at the jarring sound and then pressed a hand to her heart. "Oh, my. Hang on."

She lifted the phone and stared at the screen. "It's a message from Bella," she said, tapping it so she could see the entire thing. Then she looked up at Phillipe. "I've been summoned," she said, annoyance bleeding through her voice. "Apparently I'm to meet the family at the château tomorrow at noon. She is sending through the address."

"Does she say anything else?"

"No," Annie answered. "But my gut tells me that whatever happens tomorrow will determine how we all move forward."

And her gut was not giving her a good feeling.

CHAPTER ELEVEN

IT LOOKED LIKE a freaking castle.

Phillipe navigated the drive to the Pemberton château while Annie simply stared. Manicured lawns and precisely trimmed shrubs bordered the lane leading to a magnificent white structure that looked like it belonged in a fairy tale. The Aurora head office was intimidating, but this… This was a whole other level that screamed power and privilege and, she thought, home-court advantage.

"Wow," Phillipe said. "This is something."

"I might faint," Annie replied, and at least he laughed a little. She wasn't entirely joking. Walking into the boardroom with the family in attendance had been intimidating. This, on the other hand, was terrifying.

And perhaps that was exactly their intent. Annie inhaled deeply and rolled her shoulders. She would not be cowed. Not by a house. Not just any house, granted, but that didn't matter. It was still just made of stone and glass. The people inside put their pants on one leg at a time, just like she did. She lifted her chin and kept up the internal pep talk. She would stand up for herself.

Phillipe pulled the car to a stop and reached for his seat belt, but she put her hand on his arm.

"Phillipe, I'd like to do this alone," she said quietly.

His gaze delved into hers. "Are you sure? Because I will walk in there beside you. You don't have to be alone anymore."

She melted just a bit. "I know, and I appreciate that so much. But you have already put yourself in a difficult position and I don't want to make it worse. And more than that, I need to stand up for myself. I was so naive before, and since they found out who I am I have been at the mercy of their decisions. I will not be anymore. This is the last time they will summon me anywhere. I will listen to what they have to say and then I will make my own choices." She let out a breath. "I thought I needed them. I thought I needed their acceptance to not be alone. But that's not true. I've been guided by the wrong ideas all this time, probably from grief and shock. It's time I looked at things clearly."

"All right," he said, giving a nod. "But I will be close by. All you have to do is call and I will be back here to pick you up."

"Thank you. Wish me luck."

"I'll do better than that." He leaned over and kissed her.

Her stomach trembled with anxiety, but it was nearly noon and she needed to get this over with. Without saying anything more, she gathered her handbag and opened the car door, preparing to meet her father's family.

The door was opened by a servant before she could even reach for the knocker. "Mademoiselle Jones," he said. "If you will follow me, please."

Do not let me pass out. Do not let me pass out.

She ignored the opulence around her, knowing it would only intimidate her more. Instead she focused on her footsteps, the confident sound of her heels on the marble floor and her posture. She would walk in as an equal, she determined.

They stopped in front of a double set of doors and the servant opened them, making room for her to enter.

It was a library, and it was stunning. Floor-to-ceiling bookshelves and long windows that gave a glimpse of a garden through the wedges of light let through by the brocade draperies. And in the middle, a strategic grouping of chairs, beyond which sat a glorious fireplace that would surely crackle merrily in the winter.

The Pemberton family had taken their positions. Will and Stephen shared a settee with curved arms and tufted cushions. She was sure it was probably some Louis-whatever-number furniture—she had zero knowledge of antiques—but it looked old and expensive. Bella and Charlotte were both there as well, sitting next to each other on a set of tapestried chairs, each holding a teacup. Christophe was the only one standing, slightly behind a glorious wing chair in which Aurora was ensconced, her gray hair perfectly in place, an ice-blue suit on her slight frame. The matriarch. And, Annie was more than willing to concede, the woman who, other than herself, had been the most wronged in this whole situation. It was Aurora, therefore, who got her undivided attention.

"Lady Pemberton," she offered quietly, choosing to address her formally.

"Anemone," she offered, not unkindly, but not exactly warm, either. "Won't you please sit?" She waved her hand toward an empty chair.

"I think I'd prefer to stand for now," Annie said, trying to ignore the way her stomach twisted and knotted.

"As you wish." Aurora held eye contact. "Thank you for coming to the château. We've found that in most cases it is more private than Paris."

"It was barely an inconvenience. I'm sure you already knew I was in Grasse." Annie saw William shift on his seat out of the corner of her eye. But Aurora was still the one who held her attention.

"We did, yes. Monsieur Leroux has been a good friend to you."

"Indeed he has, ma'am."

There was a flash of something in Aurora's eyes that Annie would almost swear was approval. Maybe faking her bravado was working just a little? But she wasn't sure how long she could sustain it.

"Miss Jones, I called for a family meeting because there are things I should say to you and my children should also hear them."

Annie was quiet and waited, forcing herself not to fidget.

And then Aurora's steely gaze softened. "I am sorry, Anemone, for the part I played in what has happened."

An apology was the last thing Anemone expected, and she could see she was not alone. A quick glance showed surprise in everyone's faces. It also seemed everyone knew now was not the time to interrupt. Annie would give Aurora this: she knew how to command a room.

"I was pregnant with Charlotte and William when I discovered Cedric's affair. It very nearly destroyed our marriage. I won't go into all the reasons why—that was between Cedric and me—but his actions afterward had very much to do with ultimatums I delivered, and they affected your life."

She paused, then leaned forward to take a drink from a glass of water sitting on the table in front of her.

"Anemone, I made Cedric promise to break off the affair. I made him promise to keep your parentage hidden, and it was I who suggested he pay your mother a biannual stipend on the condition you never know your father's identity. I wanted the whole thing to go away, and I knew your mother would struggle greatly financially. If word got out or she told you, the money would stop."

"Maman." Stephen went to her side. "Why did you…? How could you not have said something before?"

It was odd for Annie to hear emotion crackling through Stephen's voice. He was always so composed, almost to the point of being brittle. But not now. Was it possible that Aurora had kept this from all of them, even after Annie's existence had come to light?

"I was ashamed," she admitted softly.

"But…" Charlotte's voice interrupted. "But we… we've been so…" She didn't finish the sentence. Annie looked into her half-sister's face and saw remorse etched on her features.

"I know," Aurora admitted. "I am not proud of it. He did step out and have an affair, but I can't avoid my responsibility for what happened any longer." She looked up at Annie and put her hand to her heart. "Cedric agreed to all these things to save our marriage for the children we already had and the children yet to come, and he spent the rest of his life being the best husband to me. He was a good man who made some big mistakes. When he died, the money stopped. Then I heard your mother died, and that should have been the end of it."

"But she told me at the end. In her will."

"Yes, she did. And as a mother, I do not blame her for doing so. She kept her silence all those years in order to provide you with a better life."

"It paid for my schooling. We were never hungry. It might have been so very different without the money," Anemone admitted. "And I'm sorry, too, ma'am. Because my very existence must be a reminder of a very painful time in your life."

"Your existence is not as painful as knowing I was responsible for depriving you of a father and directing the course of your life."

Tears slid out of the corners of Anemone's eyes and down her cheeks. "Why now?" she asked. "You could have let this be the end and I would be gone. No more reminders."

"Because it would be wrong," she said simply. "And when things are wrong, you must do what you can to make them right."

The words settled through the room.

"I am sorry, Anemone," Aurora said softly. "Sorry for what I did and sorry I let this go on so long. I have too much pride."

"It's all right."

"You seem very forgiving."

"I got it from my mother," she said softly. "She was kind, and compassionate, and she always told me to put myself in someone else's shoes before making a judgment. It was not my fault for being born, but I also am very aware that you were the wronged woman." She lifted her chin. "But I have also tried to not sit in judgment of my mother and Cedric, either. It is not my place to judge anyone."

The room was so silent they might have heard a pin drop.

"So," Aurora continued, her shoulders relaxing a bit, "about Paris."

"Yes, that did turn out to be a bit of a mess, didn't it?" Anemone smiled faintly. "All I can say is that my decisions for moving to Paris and working at Aurora Inc. were made partly out of a misguided hope and partly out of grief. Looking back, I can see how foolish it was to try to get closer to the family in that way, and I certainly understand your mistrust of me. As far as the leak, I can only assert that I had nothing to do with that. As I told Bella—" she spared Bella a glance "—you are free to examine my banking records if that will help. I never sold my story or any part of it to the press. I went to the launch, Phillipe saw me home, and I was in bed shortly after midnight. I knew nothing until the next morning when my phone blew up, and Phillipe said he would be by to get me out of Paris for a few days while we figured out what happened. That's the whole story."

She took another breath. "My employment at Aurora is done. My plans are loose at the moment, but I am likely going to go back to England to stay with a friend while I find a new job and start over. You won't have to worry about me again."

"What about what we want?"

This came from Bella, and Annie turned a little to

face the woman whose text on Saturday morning had
reeked of accusation.

How could you?

"You?"

"I think I recognized from the beginning that you
were not looking for leverage. You were looking for
love. Does that make you naive? Very. But I recognized
the look of someone needing to be loved and terrified
to ask for it. I've been there enough myself, and I've
always had the security of a supportive family."

Annie didn't know what to say. She scanned all the
faces in the room. Charlotte looked abashed, while
Stephen was looking a little shell-shocked. Will was
harder to decipher, but Christophe… His face held the
same softness as Bella's. Christophe had been adopted
by Cedric and Aurora when his own mother hadn't
been able to care for him. He knew, probably more
than any of them, how she might feel.

And then her gaze lit on Aurora again.

"I think," Anemone found herself saying, "that
whatever decision is made with regards to what is public knowledge about my existence must rest with Aurora. He was her husband. She is the one who will be
talked about most."

Stephen spoke up. "Even if it means denying the
story?"

Anemone looked at him and felt certain this was a
test. Even if it weren't, she knew her answer. Maybe
she was Cedric's daughter, but the only one responsible for the person she was or would become was her.

She didn't need some official paternity claim to have her own identity. She was in charge of that.

"Even if it means that. Because at the end of the day, where am I? Back where I was a year ago, no better off but no worse, either. And I go on." She looked at Aurora. "Is that what you want?"

Aurora shook her head. "No."

Anemone had been fully expecting a yes, and she stood in stunned silence for a moment.

"You are Cedric Pemberton's daughter. You deserve better. I'm sorry I deprived you of that and that I also deprived you of him, because while he was not perfect, he was a loving, generous man. The PR team is at this moment polishing a draft statement acknowledging your existence and a welcome to the family."

Annie finally took the seat that she had been offered at the beginning.

Charlotte cleared her throat. "This family is no stranger to scandal. We'll weather this one, too. Take charge of the narrative. It's what we do."

It was positively shocking to hear those words from Charlotte's lips.

Bella nodded in agreement. "You can decide if you want to stay in Paris, or if you want to go back to England. The choice is yours. You are entitled to the biannual allowance that has been missed since our father's death, so you can have the freedom to make the decisions you want. It'll take a bit longer for the lawyers to work out how and if the assets of the will should be reallocated. There is a lot and it's a bit more complicated." Bella looked around at the family. "Agreed?"

"Allowance...inheritance... This isn't why I came to Paris," she said, then covered her mouth with her hand.

"You came for family." This was Christophe. "That, too, might take time. It's complicated. But for now, take what is rightfully yours. I think we all know that it is what Cedric would have wanted."

Her throat was so tight with emotion she didn't know what to say.

"He let you go to make me happy," Aurora said, her throat catching. "But he once told me that it was the hardest thing he'd ever done, walking away from his own child. Christophe is right. He would have wanted this. I should have made things right long ago, but I'm not perfect, either. I was afraid. I hope today we can all start over."

Walking away was the hardest thing he'd ever done.

Those words reached in and wrapped around her little girl's heart, the one that had thought for so long that she was so forgettable. She was fighting tears when Charlotte got up from her chair, came over and knelt before Annie. Charlotte reached out and took one of Annie's hands, opened her fingers and put the locket inside her palm. "I'm sorry, Anemone, for the part I played in this."

And that was the moment that Annie couldn't hold back the tears any longer.

Phillipe had started to get antsy the first hour after leaving Annie at the château. By the time the second hour was up, he'd started pacing outside the pub where he'd stopped and had a soft drink just to give his hands something to do. When his phone finally buzzed, two hours and twenty-six minutes after he'd driven away, he swiped across the screen to read her message.

Please join us for tea at the château.

That was it? Just "join us for tea"? He had no idea what kind of situation he was walking into. Perhaps this was all outlining a way to eject Annie from their lives. Or some cold, calculating plan to deal with the press. Either way, she'd messaged, and he'd be there. He sent a quick response, saying he'd be there in ten minutes, and then reached inside his pocket for the car keys.

He'd had time to think during the time he'd been waiting; think about all the things Annie had said over the past few days that made perfect sense. The truth was, he did not enjoy Paris. Had he been lucky in his opportunities? Yes. Was Paris a fantastic city? Of course. But his heart was in the south, in Grasse, not in a suit in a boardroom. He'd taken that job for all the wrong reasons. And while he wasn't sure what to do now, he did know that staying in his current role wasn't what he wanted to do for the rest of his life.

He needed to go home.

And perhaps this was the best timing of all, because after today Annie would be free, wouldn't she? She wasn't locked into staying anywhere right now. They might be able to make plans...together.

Of course, it would take her a while to get past everything that had happened since her identity had been revealed. But that was fine. He would be there for her. The one thing he was absolutely sure of was that he didn't want to let her go.

For the second time that afternoon, he parked the car in the château drive and this time he got out and made his way to the front door. He rolled his shoulders and told himself to relax… He didn't need to enter like he was spoiling for a fight. He didn't generally think the Pembertons were unfair; on the contrary, he'd come to care for them a lot. But it had taken very little time for his allegiance to fall with Annie. He was already half in love with her. How could he not be? He'd never met anyone with a larger heart.

The door opened. "This way, sir," the man said, and immediately began leading him through the house.

Tea, as it happened, was being served in the gardens, which Phillipe had never seen and which, for a brief moment, made him forget his mission. They were absolutely glorious, and right now the roses were blooming profusely. An arbor with climbing roses led to a fountain, and it was there that he found the Pemberton family enjoying tea and an assortment of cakes.

How very English of them.

"Phillipe, welcome." William came forward with a smile. "Thank you for driving Anemone today." He shook Phillipe's hand. "And for getting her out of Paris to avoid the scandal. Smart move. One I've used in the past as well."

"William," he said cautiously. He still had no idea what he was walking into, though the mood seemed almost…jovial.

"You're here." Anemone was standing with a cup of tea in her hand, but she quickly put it down. "I'm sorry it took so long to text you. Let's go for a walk and I'll explain." She looked over her shoulder. "Excuse us, everyone."

So much for joining them for tea. However, if Annie wanted to fill him in, he was grateful. The last thing he wanted was to say or do the wrong thing and upset whatever fragile truce had been forged.

There was a path that led out of the garden and they headed that way, Annie's arm through his. "I have no idea where I'm going," she whispered, "but there's a path so it must be all right." She laughed a little. "This place, Phillipe. Isn't it amazing?"

He angled a look at her. "Clearly this went better than you planned. You look happy. I confess, I was expecting the worst."

"So was I." She met his gaze and he noticed what he'd missed before… There had indeed been tears. The telltale redness rimming her lashes gave it away.

She squeezed his arm. "I barely know where to start. I guess with Aurora apologizing for forcing Cedric's hand. She told me she demanded he not see me, and that the money was to care for me but also to ensure my mother's silence."

He stopped, dumbfounded. "That's so cold."

"How would you feel if you were pregnant with twins and found out your husband had fathered another child? I can't judge her too harshly, Phillipe. Who's to say I would have done differently? Besides, there's more."

Which he expected. They'd been two hours, after all.

They walked through a stand of Aleppo pines now far enough from the house that the voices of the family were barely discernible. "And what about the rest of the family?"

"I think they realize that none of this is my fault,

and I'm sure they no longer think I alerted the press. Thank you for whisking me away. I'm sure that helped. Moreover, they are immediately restoring my allowance from the estate, including what I missed over the past two years, in order that I can take some time and not worry about cash flow while making decisions."

She sounded so happy about it, but those funds were a drop in the bucket to their overall worth. Did she not understand that?

"And what do they expect in return?"

"That's just it, Phillipe. Nothing. They are not demanding my silence or anything, not like before."

"Not much point, now that the story is out."

She stopped walking and took her arm out of his. "What's wrong? I'm trying to tell you that this is all going to turn out all right and you're... I don't know what you are. You're acting like you're annoyed."

Was he? *Annoyed* wasn't the right word. *Cynical?* More than likely. "I'm just having a hard time wrapping my head around it. They haven't exactly treated you well since the news broke, Annie."

"All right. That's true. But why would I hold that against them?"

He shook his head. "Are you really that nice? Don't you ever get angry?"

She stared at him as if she didn't know him. "Phillipe, if I'm not angry at them, why are you?"

He didn't know how to answer. Maybe it was because he was tired of money and status and how it influenced people. It had certainly played a role in his divorce, and not only from Madelyn's point of view. From his. Annie was the last person he thought would be excited at the prospect of a fat deposit in her account. But maybe he didn't know her as well as he thought.

"You were so determined to not take any money before. What changed?"

She met his gaze, her eyes wide and innocent. "But before, it was to make me go away. This time, there are no conditions. Aurora said it is because it is what Cedric would have wanted, and it's the right thing to do."

"And so you automatically said yes?"

"Well, yes. Don't you see? This gives me choices, Phillipe. When I thought about going back to Paris, I had a flat I could no longer pay rent on, no job, no savings. Everything taken away except really two options—find a job immediately, which is nearly impossible, or leave France altogether and sleep on my best friend's couch. I am no longer forced into one of those scenarios."

She looked away. "That's not all, but I'm not sure I want to tell you now that I see your reaction. Which I don't understand at all, by the way."

He closed his eyes and let out a breath. He was scared. He could admit it to himself but not to anyone else. Annie was the last person on earth he'd ever thought would have her head turned by money, and he was sure that wasn't truly the case. He knew deep down she wasn't that sort of woman. At the same time, he understood why this news was so welcome. He didn't blame her for taking the money and taking some security for herself. He just was afraid that...

Afraid that if she had so many lovely options, she wouldn't need him. And how small of a man did that make him? In his heart he wanted a happy ending for her. But right now, all he could feel was her slipping away.

Yesterday had changed everything. The words hadn't been said, but he'd never felt such an intense connection to a woman before. Being with her had made his heart soar. Hearing her laugh, seeing her with the rose blossoms in her hand, seeing the look in her eyes as she'd said, "Take me." He had left Cannes this morning a different man than yesterday.

In Cannes he had been enough. Now he wasn't so sure.

"Phillipe, I am going back to Paris tonight, and then to London for a few days. The family has decided to start looking at Cedric's will. I have no idea what the outcome will be, but they want me to have a portion of his estate."

His stomach dropped. She was about to become an heiress. Not just any heiress, but daughter of the late Earl of Chatsworth, half-sister to the current Earl…

Gone were her days of poky flats and public transit.

And then the first part of what she'd said sank in.

"You're going back to Paris? Tonight?"

She nodded, and the smile she'd been trying to keep in place slipped away completely. "I'm so sorry. I know it means you have to drive back alone, and I won't get a chance to thank your parents. But I'll be back in Paris by the weekend." She reached down and squeezed his hand. "I would love to see you and fill you in. I'm just still trying to absorb everything right now. Phillipe, I know this sounds too crazy to be true, but it's really not about the inheritance to me. It's what it represents. It's a welcome, don't you see? I might just have…a family."

He was a selfish ass. He realized that now. During

their little "vacation," he'd felt as if maybe he could be her family of sorts. She'd fit in so well, with his parents, too. Would he seriously deprive her of her own family just to make himself feel better? Of course he would not.

An hour ago, he'd been thinking about asking for an actual demotion and going back to Grasse—with her. A simpler life, just the two of them. Now she was going to be a very rich woman and her entire family would be in Paris. How could he ask her to give that up when she'd just found what she'd been longing for all along?

He couldn't. He wouldn't. Instead he pulled her close and kissed her forehead. "I'm so happy for you," he murmured. "You wanted to find your family and you did. I'm not surprised. No one can stand against your sweetness for long."

Her arms snaked around his waist. "So much is going to change. I'm glad you're going to be there."

Phillipe simply held her for a few minutes, trying to cling to the memories of yesterday and wondering if their brief time together was enough to get them through what was to come.

CHAPTER TWELVE

ANNIE WAS STILL trying to wrap her head around everything that was happening.

They'd flown back to Paris in the Aurora private jet. She'd felt ridiculously conspicuous, but Christophe had taken the seat across from her, poured her a glass of wine, and before long had her laughing.

Bella wouldn't hear of Annie returning to her flat and invited her to stay at her apartment she shared with Burke. Burke was working all night at the hospital, and as Charlotte generally stayed there during her Paris trips, the three of them went to Bella's.

Charlotte was the first to break the awkward silence in the car. "Annie, I'm sorry about how I was that first day. Well, more than just the first day. We were all horrid. I was angry but I was unnecessarily cruel."

"You were hurt. I understand, Charlotte."

"You were right, though. We got to know him, and you didn't."

Annie met her half-sister's gaze. There was only a few months' difference in their ages. "I think it's okay if we say goodbye to blame. Especially blaming ourselves. It changes nothing, you know? Everyone did what they felt was best at the time, even your mother. What's important is how we move forward."

They arrived at Bella's home and before long she'd made herself at home in a guest bedroom and had joined her half-sisters—sisters!—for a cocktail. Charlotte had just called home to talk to Jacob and say good-night to their sweet baby daughter, and Bella entered the living room with a tray of cosmopolitans and a big bowl of popcorn.

They each reached for a drink, and Annie still felt a layer of awkwardness between them. "Okay, I'm just going to say it. This feels really strange."

Charlotte nodded. "Yeah, but it'll get better with time."

Bella hesitated before taking a drink. "Annie, something has been bugging me as well. I'm sorry for what I said about trusting you the morning after the launch. I knew it made no sense. If you'd wanted to sell your story, you could have done it a million times."

"Did you ever find out who leaked the news?"

"Not yet. Maybe we never will." Bella's gaze darkened. "But if it was anyone at Aurora, they'd better hope I don't find out."

"I hope it's okay if I say I'm glad." Annie shrugged and gave a small smile. "I mean, this is the end result."

They touched glasses and Annie took a sip of the vodka drink. "If you'd told me a few days ago this was where I would be, I'd have laughed."

"I know. We're really not mean people." Charlotte looked sheepish as she reached for popcorn. "It's just that when we feel threatened, we band together."

"It's how families should be," Annie said. She thought for a moment about Phillipe's parents and how she never thanked them for their hospitality. "Speaking of families, I really need to send something to Phillipe's. His parents were very welcoming."

Bella snorted into her drink. "Wait, you stayed with his parents?"

A crooked smile lifted Charlotte's cheek.

"I know, it sounds… Well, my mum would say it sounds a bit twee." She laughed. "Truly, though, I had no idea what was going on, and they have the loveliest little house. Paulette is a tremendous cook. And Phillipe did take me to the facility yesterday for a tour. I got to pick roses." She drank deeply and then realized the other two women were staring at her.

"You are totally smitten with him," Bella said.

Heat rushed up Annie's neck. "I, uh… He's been very supportive."

"Do not kid a kidder, Anemone. He fought to get your job back. He barely left your side at the launch. And at the first bit of trouble, he rode to your rescue. Even today. The moment you texted he was at the château in mere minutes. You cannot say there is nothing personal between you."

"I didn't say that," she said quietly, then looked up. "Oh, all right. I am totally smitten. He was acting strange today, though, and I'm not quite sure why." She thought back over their time together. He had asked her about staying in Paris and insinuated he wanted her there. But today when she'd told him she would be back in Paris on the weekend, he'd changed. Become very quiet. Had he changed his mind?

"It's all very new," she finally said. "Everything is new. I don't want to rush anything." Which was a lie. If Phillipe said to her this very minute that he wanted a relationship, she'd say yes. What had happened between them wasn't ordinary.

"Speaking of jobs," Charlotte said, finishing off her drink and pouring another from the pitcher, "would you be interested in staying on at Aurora? Your former job in PR hasn't been filled yet. It would give you a place to start, to learn the ropes before moving up. That is…if you even want a career with Aurora Inc."

A job. One she loved and was good at. She could keep her flat. Oh, who was she kidding. She could get a nicer flat with the other money coming her way. And she would be here, in Paris, closer to Phillipe. So they could explore what was between them.

"I would love that," she answered. "To be honest, I seriously considered never telling you who I was because I liked the job so much and I was sure if you knew I would be out of a position. Thank you, Charlotte."

"You're welcome. You start on Monday. Your first job will be working with me on the statement to confirm your identity and your place within the Aurora empire." She smiled sweetly. "Just a minor assignment. But it can wait until you are back from London. Stephen is anxious for the two of you to meet with the solicitors."

Oh, my.

A few more drinks were shared, and the comfort level increased. It was then that Annie asked the question that had been on her mind for months, but she had never dared ask before.

"Bella? Charlotte?"

They looked up.

"Will you tell me about Cedric?"

A smile blossomed on Bella's lips as Charlotte gave a brisk nod. "Well, here's the thing about our father. There was this one time when I was what, maybe five years old, Bel? The time that I…"

Annie held back tears as for the first time ever she was introduced to the man who'd given her life through the eyes of his other daughters. She closed her fingers around the locket. She just wished Phillipe were here with her. He was all she needed to make everything absolutely perfect.

Phillipe prepared to leave his office on Friday with the weekend stretching out before him. It had taken him all day Wednesday to drive back to Paris, and he'd been back in the office bright and early Thursday morning. It was all he knew how to do right now. His thoughts and feelings were still in such a jumble. Work was the one thing that was constant for him right now. Just too bad he couldn't seem to focus on it at all.

Well, now it was the weekend, and he'd had a text from Annie saying she would be back in Paris today and that she'd like to see him this weekend. He hadn't yet answered because he didn't know what to say.

Tuesday morning they'd made love before leaving the hotel. They'd held hands in the car and he had thought he would be there to help her pick up the pieces after her meeting with the family.

Instead she'd been all smiles and light as the Pembertons had opened their circle to include her. And she'd jetted away on their plane without giving him another thought. Without wondering what he might be feeling.

Right now he was trying to figure out exactly who

Anemone Jones really was. He knew who he wanted her to be, but—and this wasn't much of a shock—he didn't trust himself.

He'd just turned the corner out of his office when he halted, surprised to see her standing in the waiting area, in a pretty green dress and heels and a smile on her face.

"You are such a sight for sore eyes," she said, and then she came forward, moving into his embrace, holding him tightly.

He held her close because he honestly didn't know how not to; his heart had taken the lead.

"You're back."

She nodded against his collar. "This afternoon. I've been waiting for you to finish. Your office staff left twenty minutes ago." She pulled back and looked into his face. "You are happy to see me, aren't you?"

The question sent a jolt of pain through his heart, and his doubt was reflected in the concerned expression that dulled her face. "Oh." She stepped back, as if suddenly embarrassed to have hugged him. "Oh."

"I'm sorry, Annie. Yes, I'm happy to see you. I've been dying to see you since Tuesday. But there are things we need to talk about."

She nodded. "Okay. I see. Actually, no I don't. Did I do something wrong?"

Did he want to have this discussion here? Maybe. The other alternative was to go back to his place, and he hesitated to offer. He wasn't quite in the mood to put off the discussion any longer, particularly since it had been brewing for three days already.

"Not wrong. Just…" He sighed and ran his hand through his hair. "I have a lot of thoughts about what happened this week, and every one of them makes me sound like a jealous jerk. I seriously do not know how to do this."

"I can't imagine you being a jerk. You have always shown the greatest kindness and consideration. But this is eating away at you, I can tell. Let's go sit and talk about it."

She led him back into his office and to the pair of chairs set in a corner.

There was something different about her, a confidence, perhaps, that had been missing before. He liked it even though he felt it pulled her further away from him. She tucked her hair behind her ear and smiled gently, then took his hand in hers. "First of all, I need to apologize, Phillipe. So much happened on Tuesday that it wasn't until I was back in the city that night and I realized how I'd just abandoned you. I should have told the family that we would drive back the next day. It was thoughtless of me."

"But you had to go to London."

"It could have waited an extra day. I'm sorry. You went to great lengths to help me and as soon as things shifted, I was gone. Please forgive me for that."

"Of course," he murmured.

"Is that the reason you've closed yourself off to me?" she asked, her voice more hesitant. "Please, tell me what it is. It's been eating away at me. Ever since you found me in the garden at the château, something has been off. Have you changed your mind about… about us?"

His head snapped up. "Have you?"

"What?"

He ran his hand over his face. "Annie, God, I don't

want to hurt you, but I have so much going on inside and I know I'm going to say it all wrong."

"Please, just say it. Not knowing and being confused is worse than having something we can talk about and deal with."

He met her gaze. "When I walked into the garden, you'd transformed. You walked in there a scared young woman with her chin held high in defiance, and the next time I saw you, you were sipping tea and telling me about a cash settlement and how you'd be flying back to Paris. It didn't fit with the Annie I had come to know. With the Annie I cared about so very much. And all I could think of was—"

He looked away.

"Was Madelyn." She finished the sentence for him, her voice barely a whisper. "Because Madelyn wanted all those things, and you did not give them to her. Am I close?"

He nodded. "I know in my head that's unfair. But my heart's been kicked a few times. It doesn't dismiss the feelings so easily."

"You must know that private jets and bags of money are not my motivators, Phillipe. At least tell me you believe that."

"I know that. I do."

She waited a full five seconds before responding. "But I left in pursuit of all those things, including meetings about a further inheritance. And I left you behind."

He nodded. "I like to think I'm a strong man, but that hit me exactly in my soft spot."

She sighed. "I need to be honest with you, too, Phillipe. There is going to be an inheritance of some sort, though it's going to take weeks or months for the legal team to figure out exactly what. In the meantime, I start my old job back here on Monday. I can get a nicer flat in a better neighborhood. Isn't that what you wanted? For me to stay in Paris so we could see where this is going? Are you trying to tell me your feelings have changed?"

"No!" The word exploded out of him, and then he tempered it with a quieter "No. That's not what I'm saying at all."

Silence fell over the office.

Finally, Annie reached out and touched his arm, prompting him to look up into her eyes. The blue depths were swimming with tears. "I'm not her," she said, a little brokenly. "I thought you knew that. I thought you got it. My head can't be turned by status and wealth."

Annie heard the words come out of her mouth and then knew exactly where everything had gone wrong. Dammit. She'd known his biggest fear and she'd unwittingly played right into it by dashing away and leaving him behind. It was more than being inconsiderate. It had been poking at his deepest wound and making it bleed again.

"Oh, Phillipe," she whispered, as a tear slid down her cheek. "I am so, so sorry. That's exactly what I did, isn't it? I was so overwhelmed with it all and the chance to be with the family that I never considered how it must look, or how you would feel."

"I did feel that way, at first. But once I thought about it, I knew you were just following what you really wanted…a family. I want you to have that, so very much."

"I was so insensitive." She slid forward, put her hands on his knees. "Phillipe, you are enough. My God, you are so much more than just enough. I hope you know that."

His chin trembled just the tiniest bit.

"I would never want to begrudge you time with your family," he said firmly. "Not when you've been searching and yearning for so long. And I do know that. Our time together forced me to look at my marriage and realize where both of us had gone wrong. Maybe Madelyn strayed, but I was trying to be something I am not. And that cannot work."

She reached out and took his hands in hers, desperately needing the connection.

He looked into her eyes. "I'm so glad you're no longer alone. And you don't need me. You're strong and resilient. Everything is going to turn out fine for you. And so you don't need me anymore."

Her mouth dropped open. "That's what you think? That I don't need you?" She shook her head, then squeezed his fingers. "Oh, Phillipe. It's not about need. You're right about that. And I never want to have to need anyone again. It sets up all sorts of obligations and expectations. *Need* is very different from *want*. And what I want for you is your happiness. I'm not sure that it's in Paris, though. I think your heart will always be in Grasse."

He slid a hand away from hers and cupped her cheek. "Darling," he said softly, "my heart is where you are. Haven't you figured out by now that I love you?"

The backs of her eyes stung. "You love me?"

He nodded. "I certainly didn't expect to. I think I knew when you walked into the ballroom that night. You looked so beautiful and yet so delightfully out of place. Our eyes met and that was it."

She sniffed. "I thought I was alone in those feelings. I really thought you'd changed your mind, that you'd decided I wasn't the one for you anymore. But love... That's different. That's not something you can just shove aside, now, is it?"

"Never," he said.

"I love you, Phillipe. In all my excitement I forgot to tell you the most important things. It wasn't the money I cared about. It was that I could now do what you wondered was possible—I could stay in Paris. I wouldn't have to go back to England and leave you behind. It would buy me time...us time...and give us a real chance. I should have said all that on Tuesday. We should have said all this on Tuesday. Instead we spent three days agonizing and speculating." She cupped his face in her hands. "I was thrilled to gain a family. But I was ecstatic that it meant I could stay close to you. That I had options for us. I knew when we were in Cannes that I loved you. Only love could have made me feel the way I did in your arms. I've never felt that way before."

He turned his head to the side and kissed the pad of the thumb cupping his cheek. "We need to communicate better," he decreed. "I've been so torn up inside."

"But being open means being vulnerable, and that's the hardest thing of all when you've been hurt. No more, though, okay? Phillipe Leroux, you are and always will be enough. Not because of your bank balance or job title or where you live, but because of the man you are. Tender, kind, funny, hardworking, passionate, honorable. Those are the reasons I love you. The only reasons that matter."

"I know you want to be with your family. And the division is looking at growth. Do you think you could be happy in Paris?"

She frowned and shook her head. "I could never ask you to stay here if you want to be somewhere else."

"It doesn't matter, as long as you're with me." He lifted her hand and kissed her knuckles. "It's different this time. I have nothing to prove. I just want you to be happy."

"I love that you'd do that for me. But I want you to know this—if you want to find a way to return home, to live and work in Grasse, I'm more than okay with it. I fell in love with it when I was there, and your parents are so wonderful. The Pembertons are amazing, and I'm happy to be a part of the family, but I still want my own life. I still want *you*, Phillipe. Whether that's in Paris or Grasse or Timbuktu."

"You mean that."

"I truly do." She leaned forward and brushed her mouth against his. "I love you."

He kissed her back and her heart soared as he murmured, "I love you, too, Annie," against her lips.

CHAPTER THIRTEEN

August

PHILLIPE LOOKED OVER at Anemone in the passenger seat and felt a wave of love wash over him. They had once again made the trip from Grasse to Provence, for a weekend with the family. It was the first real family trip with all the significant others and children—Jacob and Charlotte were bringing their daughter, and Christophe and Sophie had eight-week-old Mathieu now. Add in Will and Gabi and Bella and Burke, still newlyweds, as well as Aurora and Stephen, and it was going to be a full château.

"Happy?" he asked, as they turned up the lane and the château came into view.

"Very." She smiled over at him. "No regrets at all. Plus it'll be good to see everyone."

Good to see them because since the first of July, Phillipe and Annie had relocated to Grasse, where he was managing the department from an office at the Aurora Inc. facility.

They'd spent that weekend after her return from London at his flat, reconnecting, talking, dreaming. For the first time in his life, he'd laid everything out there: what he was passionate about, what meant the most to him, his dreams. Anemone had supported it all without hesitation. Grasse was his home. She'd already seen it for herself. They'd lain in bed and talked about possibilities and plans and it had been the scariest, most wonderful moment of his life.

Until now.

When they arrived, it was Christophe who opened the door to welcome them in. He was holding his son in his arms, and Annie immediately started to coo and fuss while Phillipe got their overnight bag.

She liked children. They'd talked about that, too.

"Phillipe, look at this little nugget! Oh, he's so sweet and he smells like baby."

"That smell can change at a moment's notice," Christophe said. "Trust me."

She carried the baby inside. Their bags were taken upstairs to their room and Christophe ushered them out to the garden, where everyone was having drinks. Phillipe was anxious but willing to be patient. After all, he'd waited a very long time for Annie. The right moment would happen.

That moment came when babies started to fuss and Charlotte and Sophie went to put them down for naps. Will and Gabi decided to take a drive into the village and Aurora went to check on dinner preparations. Stephen, ever the lone wolf, headed for the library. Everyone would reconvene for pre-dinner drinks at six.

"I'd like to stay in the garden a little longer," Annie said, breathing deeply. "It really is a bit of paradise here. And the smell! This time the lavender is blooming and it's glorious." She leaned back in her chair and closed her eyes.

Phillipe took a deep breath and reached into his pocket for the little bottle that had been resting there since their departure from home.

Then he shifted out of his chair and dropped to one knee in front of her.

"Annie," he said softly.

When she opened her eyes and saw him there, her hand flew to her mouth and tears sprang into her eyes. A smile lit him from the inside out, and he spoke around a growing lump in his throat. "Let me say all this, please."

She started to laugh; they both knew she had a thing for interrupting.

"Anemone, you gave me back myself again. You made me smile, you made me love, you made me dream. I'd forgotten how to do that, you see. But you, with your constant optimism and joy and energy... You lit a spark that had been extinguished. I will always love you for that.

"You finally found the family you were searching for, but without thinking twice you left them behind in Paris and encouraged me to follow my dreams, making them yours, too. You have loved me, and my parents, and embraced our new life with an enthusiasm that blows me away. But there is one more dream I have and today I'm asking you to share my dreams one more time by becoming my wife."

She gave a little sob-cough as he said the word *wife*, and he was horribly afraid he was going to cry himself, so he took another big breath and forced himself to carry on through the rest.

He took out the bottle, delicate pink glass with a silver band around the spherical cap. "I designed this for you," he said. "It will never go on the market. It will never be duplicated, just as you are one of a kind. The top notes are sweet and energetic, like you—pear, green apple, citrus. The heart notes… Those are the ones that are your true essence. Rose, to remind us of the day we fell in love. Jasmine, for your beauty and sensuality. And blue anemone, for you, and the excitement and anticipation I feel when I think of our lives together. And the base notes are the ones that will last long into our future. Sandalwood, for trust and unity. And vanilla, for the comfort and warmth you'll bring to our home in the years to come."

He uncapped the bottle, then took her hand in his, turned over her wrist and kissed it before adding a dab of the scent. The perfume filled the air around them with the sweetness of hopes and dreams.

He capped the bottle and put it down. When he looked at Anemone again, she was crying, happy salty tears sliding down her cheeks, and he grinned foolishly, so in love with her it was ridiculous. He reached into his pocket for the one last thing he needed to make the proposal complete. "I didn't forget a ring," he murmured, pulling out the black velvet box.

Sophie had been in on the surprise and had custom designed the ring for Phillipe. He opened the box and the diamonds sparkled in the afternoon light.

"Oh, Phillipe."

He took it out of the box and slid it on her finger. The oval diamond looked perfect, and the smaller pavé cuts made the platinum band twinkle and flash as she moved her hand.

"That's a yes, right?"

"Oh, yes! Of course I'll marry you." She got up and

tugged him to his feet, then launched herself into his arms. "I can't believe you made me my own perfume."

"Of course I did," he murmured, kissing her hair, feeling like the luckiest man on earth. "Until you, I was just going through the motions. And then you came along and all my senses came alive. I love you, Anemone Jones."

"And I love you," she whispered back, before capturing him in a kiss.

When their lips finally parted, she opened her eyes and they were dancing with laughter. "Phillipe?"

"Yes, darling?"

"Let's go tell the others."

And she laughed her way out of his arms, the sound ringing through the garden like a happy benediction.

* * * *

COMING SOON!

We really hope you enjoyed reading this book.
If you're looking for more romance, be sure to
head to the shops when new books are
available on

Thursday 3rd February

MILLS & BOON

Coming next month

BABY SURPRISE FOR THE MILLIONAIRE
Ruby Basu

All the different instruction leaflets scattered on her counter said the same thing—the best time to take a test was first thing in the morning. Saira knew this already. She didn't need to read the instructions to know what to do. But reading them was a good distraction from thinking about why she needed the tests...

She ran her fingers through her hair. She could be worrying about nothing. Probably was. This was a situation she was all too familiar with, and each time she was left disappointed.

Saira picked up one of the boxes. How many times had she bought one of these, full of excitement, full of joy, and then seen Dilip's crestfallen face each time she told him the negative news?

Apart from that one time. Which she didn't let herself think about. Couldn't let herself think about.

She took a couple of deep, centring breaths and focused on the boxes in front of her. After all those times when she'd yearned for a positive result, she couldn't be pregnant from a fling. Could she?

She hadn't even considered it a possibility until that morning. When Dilip died, Saira had put away her ovulation kits and thermometers and trackers, never expecting to need them again.

It was only when she saw her stock of unused sanitary

supplies and put them together with her dizzy episodes and mild morning nausea that she even entertained the thought.

The hope?

The previous times she'd taken these tests she'd been part of a loving, committed couple, for whom a child would have been a much-wanted addition to their family.

This time it couldn't be more different.

She'd returned to England to start again. Get a job. Find her own place. Be independent. Her future plans hadn't included having a child.

But those plans were based on her false assumption she would need to be in a relationship before a child could be part of the picture. Life didn't care about her assumptions. If she were pregnant she could easily adjust those plans, and would happily do so.

Pregnant.

Could it be possible?

She half-laughed, half-cried at the prospect. The fear, the worry, the doubts had already started to creep in.

She needed to be practical. She deliberately turned her thoughts to Nathan. To how he would react. She had no idea how to handle this situation. Was there some etiquette for telling someone you'd had a fling with that you might be pregnant with their baby?

Continue reading
BABY SURPRISE FOR THE MILLIONAIRE
Ruby Basu

Available next month
www.millsandboon.co.uk

MILLS & BOON

THE HEART OF ROMANCE

A ROMANCE FOR EVERY READER

MODERN

Prepare to be swept off your feet by sophisticated, sexy and seductive heroes, in some of the world's most glamourous and romantic locations, where power and passion collide.

HISTORICAL

Escape with historical heroes from time gone by. Whether your passion is for wicked Regency Rakes, muscled Vikings or rugged Highlanders, awaken the romance of the past.

MEDICAL

Set your pulse racing with dedicated, delectable doctors in the high-pressure world of medicine, where emotions run high and passion, comfort and love are the best medicine.

True Love

Celebrate true love with tender stories of heartfelt romance, from the rush of falling in love to the joy a new baby can bring, and a focus on the emotional heart of a relationship.

Desire

Indulge in secrets and scandal, intense drama and plenty of sizzling hot action with powerful and passionate heroes who have it all: wealth, status, good looks…everything but the right woman.

HEROES

Experience all the excitement of a gripping thriller, with an intense romance at its heart. Resourceful, true-to-life women and strong, fearless men face danger and desire - a killer combination!

To see which titles are coming soon, please visit

millsandboon.co.uk/nextmonth